Hexes of the Deadwood Forest

HEXES of the DEADWOOD FOREST

AGNIESZKA SZPILA

Translated from the Polish by Scotia Gilroy

PANTHEON BOOKS NEW YORK

FIRST HARDCOVER EDITION
PUBLISHED BY PANTHEON BOOKS 2026

English translation copyright © 2026 by Scotia Gilroy

Penguin Random House values and supports copyright. Copyright fuels creativity, encourages diverse voices, promotes free speech, and creates a vibrant culture. Thank you for buying an authorized edition of this book and for complying with copyright laws by not reproducing, scanning, or distributing any part of it in any form without permission. You are supporting writers and allowing Penguin Random House to continue to publish books for every reader. Please note that no part of this book may be used or reproduced in any manner for the purpose of training artificial intelligence technologies or systems.

Published by Pantheon Books, a division of Penguin Random House LLC, 1745 Broadway, New York, NY 10019. Originally published in hardcover in Poland by Wydawnictwo W.A.B., a part of Foksal Publishing Group, in 2022. Copyright © 2022 by Agnieszka Szpila. The English translation of this novel by Scotia Gilroy was edited for an American audience by the Pantheon Books team.

Pantheon Books and the colophon are registered trademarks of Penguin Random House LLC.

Library of Congress Cataloging-in-Publication Data
Names: Szpila, Agnieszka author | Gilroy, Scotia translator
Title: Hexes of the deadwood forest / Agnieszka Szpila ; translated from the Polish by Scotia Gilroy.
Other titles: Heksy. English
Description: First U.S. hardcover edition. | New York : Pantheon Books, 2026
Identifiers: LCCN 2025013832 | ISBN 9780593700891 (hardcover) | ISBN 9780593685891 (trade paperback) | ISBN 9780593700907 (ebook)
Subjects: LCSH: Ecofeminism—Fiction | Feminism—Fiction | LCGFT: Fiction | Novels
Classification: LCC PG7219.Z67 H4513 2026
LC record available at https://lccn.loc.gov/2025013832

penguinrandomhouse.com | pantheonbooks.com

Printed in the United States of America
1st Printing

The authorized representative in the EU for product safety and compliance is Penguin Random House Ireland, Morrison Chambers, 32 Nassau Street, Dublin D02 YH68, Ireland, https://eu-contact.penguin.ie.

Hexes of the Deadwood Forest

I

THE STORY OF ANNA FRENZA'S MADNESS

Concerning the Flaming-Fucking-Fury, a Foreshadowing of Something Yet to Come

In a market square with church towers rising high above the roofs of magnificent houses and a huge, ornately decorated town hall, people were strolling about, dressed in old-fashioned clothing—women in wide ankle-length skirts and white embroidered blouses with ruffs at the neck and puffed sleeves stitched with silk thread, and men in long trousers tucked into boots topped with silver buckles or in short breeches revealing stockings that clung tightly to their calves and festive shirts, waistcoats, and long colorful coats, with elegant hats on their heads. Along the winding streets paved with cobblestones, shaded by the wealthy burghers' three-story townhouses that had Dutch-style granaries on the upper floors and beautiful red-tiled roofs on which pigeons and sparrows contentedly perched for hours on end, cats were sauntering lazily, heading toward the market to try to snatch some scraps from the butchers' stalls.

The hustle and bustle in the market square and the constantly flowing waves of people transporting wares of all kinds in wooden carts—squawking fowl, patterned fabrics, dried cuts of meat, and jugs so full of milk that they sloshed around, splashing some of the passersby—gave no indication that, apart from all the activity at the market, there was anything extraordinary happening in the town.

But there was an increased number of guards in the square compared to a typical market day, and this sent a shiver of uneasiness through the crowds.

Suddenly, bells began to ring in all the churches. They tolled unevenly, which caused even more anxiety throughout the town, cutting as it did like a wedge through the safe everyday life of the place.

When the bells started ringing, the crowds, urged by mounted guards, began to part and line the streets. About a dozen women appeared, walking between the rows of onlookers. Despite the warm weather, they were chilled to the bone. They were completely naked, with huge penitential crosses hanging around their necks. With their heads shaved bald and sprinkled with ash, they looked like phantoms. Living corpses returning from war. They dragged their feet, walking very unsteadily because their toes had been crushed and broken. Their fingers looked similar—they were dangling limply, as if connected to their hands by nothing but skin smeared with blood. Some of the women were bleeding from their reproductive organs, while others had blood dripping from slashes on their breasts, their bodies having been lacerated with a sharp instrument.

The women were pelted with insults and horse shit, of which the town square was full, especially on market days. It was mainly men who targeted them because the women in the crowd were raising their eyes to the heavens, as if seeking help there, or casting their gazes toward the ground, whether out of shame, a sense of guilt, or some other reason.

An old woman touting homemade liqueurs made the sign of the cross on her forehead three times, while potters offering their wares—bowls, platters, and large clay spoons for scooping victuals—banged ladles on pots, which, accompanied by the cursing holier-than-thou men, created a charivari-like cacophony. Only the foreigners selling fragrances in richly ornamented silver boxes and exotic birds, such as canaries and parrots, stared at this dismal procession with incredulity and dread.

A group of bishops dressed in robes richly embroidered with gold thread and precious stones walked at the very end of the procession, keeping an eye on the women to make sure none of them tried to escape. The first two women were walking the most confidently, despite their wounds. Their heads were raised proudly.

Next to the Weigh House, a structure suddenly loomed in front of the women whose purpose they weren't yet able to guess. It was eight feet high and built of red brick, with a brass door that one could enter only by bending nearly in half and stooping right to the ground. On top, instead of a roof, there was a layer of bundled straw stretched across it, covered with randomly scattered logs and wooden planks.

After the women had all been forced inside, they saw something that confirmed the rumors that had been spreading through the city for a long time: a grate under the ceiling.

Several of the women pleaded to be beheaded before the fire was lit and were granted this mercy. The executioner signaled for them to lay their heads on stumps. There were exactly as many stumps as there were women being herded into the furnace, but fewer than half took advantage of the privilege. The rest, led by the two women who walked at the front, preferred to be burned alive.

After the door of the structure had been closed and the grate ignited from above, the women, unseen from the outside, lay down on top of each other and created a pyre from their bodies, clinging to each other so tightly that not even a piece of straw could be squeezed between them.

Before the straw burst into flame, they began to move gently, one on top of another, their movements as slight as those of leaves in a spring breeze. And each movement aroused an urge to move in the woman lying above, as if an avalanche of imperceptible but palpable vibrations had been triggered. And from this subtle motion that contained stillness at its core—somewhere inside this dense organism, this single entity—an intense flame burst forth and the women were ignited by rapture.

They seemed to know what they were doing. When the flames began to lick at their feet and hair, the women were at peace, for they no longer belonged to the corporeal realm—they were completely separated from their bodies. Alive though dead in the flesh, turned to ash.

When the guards opened the door after three-quarters of an hour and confirmed that they were all deceased, a wind suddenly picked up, and it was so powerful that all the ashes from the furnace were blown outside.

Most of the witnesses in the town square covered their noses and mouths so as not to inhale the ashes of the women who had been cursed by the Catholic Church, but there were some who stood close to the furnace, inhaling the ash deliberately, as if wanting to absorb the entire event as deep within themselves as possible.

The year 2025.

Anna Frenza wakes up suddenly, suffocating from smoke and spitting ash. She puts a finger inside her mouth to see if any soot has settled in her throat, even though she knows it was just a dream. All day long she'll have that foul taste in her mouth and acrid smoke in her nose. And the stench will haunt her. Of burnt human flesh . . .

In addition to the olfactory and gustatory sensations, her feet have started to feel like they are burning again. She hates these dreams that burn inside her like a torch. As if, for the rest of the day, there were a fire within her, impossible to extinguish. Not with an argument or a blowup. Neither at home nor at work. Nor at the post office, where she'll go just so she can pull off her favorite stunt—namely, raising hell for whatever happened to someone else in her dream. She'll give the bimbo in the customer service window a rough time. A quiet little fucking mouse wearing a synthetic blouse who sits behind the counter hoping to hide from the likes of Frenza. But she won't be able to hide.

Frenza fantasizes about her visit to the post office, scene after scene, with unbridled delight. Whom would she pick first? Who would dance with her today? Would the young lady behind the counter be unable to stand it, once again, and break down in tears? Would she summon the manager for help? Let's hope so! Then Frenza will have a chance to vent the rage building up inside her, because the manager gets on her nerves. With her meekness. With her compliance. By nodding and apologizing. Or as men call it—submission.

This is what Frenza hates the most. It knocks the flare out of her hand. The more submissive the manager is, the more Frenza will rip into her. Then somebody from the line will join in—Frenza knows this script by heart because she's been rehearsing and performing it for years. He'll have hell to pay too. She'll leave, slamming the door, shouting at the top of her voice, "It's the twenty-first century! Shove your nineteenth-century delivery notices up your ass!"

She'll feel better after that. At least temporarily.

Fortunately, Bartek's home. There's an opportunity to rip into someone else that day. When he asks her to wash his ass, she'll do it, in complete silence as usual, swallowing her rage because, after all, she can't pummel a cripple. And then she'll eventually reach for a knife or a fork, or at least a pencil with a very sharp point. And only when some blood has been spilled will she finally feel at home.

The rage flaring up inside her after such a dream is blood-red. It's like a massive ball of fire rolling down a hill and gaining incredible momentum. A voracious fireball devouring all docility and tenderness.

"Yikes, must be that time of the month." She'll overhear remarks like that and wish she could immediately fire whoever said them—if only that were possible. It's not, but she'll get even some other way. After all, she's the one who calls the shots around here. She's always felt it—that all it takes is to touch a lit match inside her and she'll flare up so intensely that the mountains will burn, the forests will burn. And anyone she encounters on her way will burn as well.

She loves this moment. And if it torments people . . . too bad! Dealing with other humans is a torment to her. It's only when she's consumed by this fire, blazing within her from head to toe, that she feels she's not alone. It's as if through this FLAMING-FUCKING-FURY she becomes one with the women in her dream, the women who were burned in the furnace.

Concerning Houndstooth, Hypouresis,
and Various Approaches to the
Cultivation of Plants

You don't stand at the helm of a major national oil company if you have a fluffy animal between your legs, be it a raccoon, a beaver, a weasel, or an owl. Nor do you stand at the helm of a major national oil company with an atavistic pussy, vagina, or cunt as vast as the Ackerman Steppe between your legs.

In order to take the helm of—let us repeat the phrase again—a major national oil company, one with a bird in its logo of the species revered by all the great Roman emperors, Charlemagne, the Holy Roman Empire of the German Nation, and then later by the Hapsburg dynasty, and finally by contemporary Germany, Russia, the United States, and . . . Poland—well, one must have an eagle between one's legs. Preferably a white one.

But let us turn once again *ad vaginam*. These cute, furry animals that represent the female species usually stand no chance at all when competing with the predatory raptors that represent men. The corporate raptors, clad in briefs or boxer shorts, are covered on the outside with an extra layer of carefully pressed, tailored trousers, one pair of which—especially those worn by the wealthiest Poles in the garden cities on the outskirts of Warsaw,

Podkowa Leśna being the most exclusive garden city of them all—can cost as much as a secondhand midrange car or the annual living expenses of twenty families in the Democratic Republic of Congo. Let's take a close look at the patterns on the fabrics used to make these suits and the buttons on the cuffs, also known as "kissing buttons"—a secret attribute of the rich. Patterns like houndstooth or stripes, the patterns most often chosen by the establishment and intellectual elite of the garden cities—places snatched from nature by the rich and for the rich, so that, unlike the poor, they won't have to inhale the by-products of the industrial revolution. Places where a swath of forest has been clear-cut to build cities for the chosen ones, far away from Twatville and Cuntborough—Anna Frenza's nicknames for the neighboring backwater towns inhabited by whores, perverts, thieves, and the mentally ill.

The houndstooth worn by the rabble living in Twatville and Cuntborough isn't true houndstooth but coarse, common houndstooth. The difference is immediately apparent—the checkered pattern on the shoulders of a jacket and on the side seams of trousers is never joined properly, the lines don't merge smoothly the way they do in elite houndstooth, and instead of generating a peaceful sensation in the beholder, the refined joy of finding harmony in a seamless pattern, it brings disillusionment, chaos, and animosity. The wearing of houndstooth only befits the inhabitants of exclusive garden cities.

The same is true of stripes. In Twatville and Cuntborough, you can see at the very first glance that a suit has been cut from a single piece of cloth, whereas in the elite world, represented by big business (with the national oil company at the forefront) as well as by the so-called intelligentsia, five more meters of fabric is used per suit, on average. So that the stripes align with one another. And so that every man wearing such a suit can feel confident and safe. It's as if the smooth connection of these stripes, these gabardine longitudes and latitudes, ensures the secret flow of energy that controls the world.

In addition to exquisitely tailored clothes (including expensive brand-name tracksuits), the aforementioned intelligentsia living in Podkowa Leśna, the crème de la crème of Polish garden cities, boast too of a very unusual demographic status. Namely: an extraordinary number of art and cultural icons per square meter! Not to mention the fact that the Club of Catholic Intelligentsia organizes all of the city's cultural events. With peacocks wandering through the churchyard gardens and trendy masses sung to pop music.

"Please imagine, ladies and gentlemen, a famous writer living right next door to you on the left, and Poland's most brilliant theater director on the right! While loading your dishwasher in the kitchen, you catch a glimpse from your window of two people jogging past your house: a movie star and the politician who left his wife and children for her. Isn't it wonderful? So many outstanding people in such a small space?" It's no wonder that Podkowa Leśna, having been advertised in this way at numerous congresses as well as in ordinary, everyday conversations, is gaining an increasing number of antagonists.

This same town, in addition to the abundance of Catholics, artists, and businessmen, can also boast the highest number of books (often dusty) per cubic centimeter inherited from ancestral bookcases, as well as the highest number of paintings on walls per square centimeter! Paintings passed down from ancestors—real Polish ones, without any foreign blood mixed in, we should add! Ancestors who were true patriots. The paintings in question are often portraits of horses. Horses standing by a mountain spring, horses on a battlefield, horses licking the face of an insurgent, horses at a marketplace, horses at sunset, horses with other horses standing behind them—as if the entire country abounded in powerful steeds instead of fools horsing around and putting their carts before their horses. Sometimes, instead of a horse in a painting, there's a weeping woman sending her son off to war like a horse to slaughter. To fight on horseback and sacrifice his life for the White Eagle. Such history! Such a distinguished member of the intelligentsia! What incredible art he has on his walls! Though when it comes to the business elite, the allure of historical family narratives, for which the portraits of steeds and patriotic mothers serve as a passport, is often replaced by that of modernist furniture. A modernist chair, a modernist villa, a modernist garden, even a pseudo-modernist toilet.

Anna Frenza—suffering from hypouresis and vaginal dryness as well as bipolar disorder—has lived in Podkowa Leśna with her disabled husband for six years, ever since she became CEO. For the first few years, she lived here with her soul torn between portraits of ancestors (not her own, from the town of Mszczonów, but purchased at an auction house) and modernist furniture. But eventually she decided to go all in with design, so she carried the paintings of her non-ancestors and their trinkets and knickknacks (also from the auction house) up to her attic and locked them away, covering them with a century-old shawl from the Kurpie region of Poland that she also passed off as a family heirloom. Thus, instead of wielding an identity derived from ancestors (thanks to the auction house), she staked everything on the Polish myth of the middle class and started playing the role of a modern person, breaking away from a historical context and instead becoming attuned to the "here and now."

Few things trouble Frenza because her life is, one could say, "successful." Her only problems are her husband, who's paralyzed from the waist down and uses his disability to poison her life, and her parents, who come to visit twice a year—at Easter and Christmas—from the small town of Mszczonów, which is geographically close but mentally and culturally as far as can be. The very name of the town (etymologically derived from the Polish word for "revenge") evokes associations that are hard to escape. Imagine coming from there! Frenza's parents dress badly: her mother likes to wear a two-piece dress suit with a houndstooth pattern (the coarse, common kind of houndstooth, of course, without the kissing buttons), and her father's usually dressed in a secondhand sweat suit with a puma on the calf, looking as worn out as if it had been pulled from a puma's throat. The only thing that connects Frenza's parents to Podkowa Leśna is the church, where the same prayers are said and the same beautiful and moving hymns are sung as in Mszczonów.

Frenza always asks them to arrive late in the evening, to avoid the gazes of nosy neighbors, who are unaccustomed to such extravagant fashions. She feels bad about it, and she blames herself for letting the garden city and the large national oil company taint her with superficiality. But by hiding her parents from her neighbors, she is, on the one hand, protecting her so-called image, and on the other, taking revenge on them for not dressing properly despite the hefty monthly sum she sends them for living expenses. As a result, instead of visiting the capital city—to which she commutes via a tolled wind tunnel designed to keep the wealthy from inhaling carbon monoxide, nitrogen oxide, or smog—with her or touring Podkowa Leśna, the pearl of the Mazovia region, they remain invisible, slinking like shadows around the house, which, fortunately, she surrounded with a high wall.

When her parents ask her to take them with her to work, or at least to let them take a commuter train into the city, Frenza flares with irritation and snaps: "Why on earth do you need to go to Warsaw?! It's impossible to breathe there! The purest air in Poland is right here, in Podkowa Leśna! You're inhaling more iodine here than you would at the Baltic Sea! Our iodine is produced exclusively for residents of Podkowa Leśna by a special air ionizer the size of a high school sports field. It's filtered through Finnish moraines!"

"My child, what are you babbling about?" Frenza's father obnoxiously interjects. "Iodine's only in the air at the seaside."

"Not if you have money. Once our company had sufficiently fattened the Catholic Church's bank account with our profits, we started pumping capital into sustainable technologies like these. Personally, I think it's a waste. Why should I care about global warming when it's so pleasant here?"

"But, my child, we're not alone on this planet. This isn't how I raised you," says Frenza's mother, becoming upset. "You really don't care about melting glaciers, wildfires in Brazil, species going extinct, and the torture of walruses, seals, and cute little penguins?"

"Everyone has their own struggles, fears, and problems. You have global warming and the suffering of penguins; I regularly have to eat dinner with the parish priest, because my husband decided to convert. He suddenly became convinced that it did him good to talk about God. So don't bother me or yourself with problems that don't directly concern us."

"Well, if your company has invested funds in saving the planet," her father butts in, "someone there must think these problems concern all of us."

"We just didn't want to piss off the environmentalists. The Greens wouldn't get off our backs. They snitched on us to the European Union. And to Denmark and Sweden. The Germans didn't give a damn, they have their Nord Stream, but the Vikings wanted to rip us to pieces. That's why we're testing out modern solutions in Podkowa Leśna. We've manufactured artificial iodine, which is actually said to be healthier than the iodine at the seaside; we've imported moraines from Finland and freeze-dried them, and they filter our air still more—so please, instead of whining about the death of the planet, just focus on your own health and breathe, because there's nowhere else in Poland with such a microclimate, maybe nowhere else in all of Europe, besides the Black Forest."

"Do you remember that German TV series from the 1980s called *The Black Forest Clinic?*" her father says, changing the topic.

Frenza reaches—very carefully, so as not to attract her parents' attention—for the lithium she takes every night; she knows that if she doesn't take some at that very moment, she'll inflict considerable emotional harm on them. Her father's idiocy has sparked a flame inside her that's about to consume not only the house but also the garden shed and the dog kennels where she keeps her two rottweilers. More than anything else, Frenza can't stand her father's constant references to lousy TV series that her family watched together in the past. No one outside the family understands them, and when her father is asked if he finds any connection to the existing conversation apart from one word in the show's title, he usually sounds like someone who knows nothing more about these shows than their titles, and even these he often garbles up.

In fact, whenever Frenza asks herself why she has cut herself off from her family, this is exactly what comes to mind—the stupidity of her father and the monotonous single-mindedness of her mother, whose thoughts revolve exclusively around her garden and all the preparations that need to be done for the next competition. And for the next season.

One year after Frenza moved to Podkowa Leśna, she invited her parents to the town's largest community event—the Open Gardens Festival—which had been held every single year, without fail, since World War II. During the festival, Frenza's mother jabbered at everyone whose gardens she visited and offered to redesign them to resemble her own, showing them the copy of *Polish Allotment Gardener* she kept in her purse, an issue with an article on her little slice of Eden in Mszczonów. Frenza didn't show her face in town for a whole year after that, did all her shopping online, and never ventured beyond her own garden, which had been thoroughly modernized by a local landscape architect. Every morning she drove her gorgeous car to work and then returned home after nightfall so no one would notice her. That's how much shame she felt. The shame of a small-town girl judged by a garden city with rich cultural traditions.

Now Frenza's mother paces anxiously around her daughter's garden, which she designed herself right after Frenza moved to Podkowa Leśna, before Frenza had a modernist come in and completely redo it. Frenza's mother knew how to landscape, after all—for ten years, from 2009 to 2019, her allotment garden had won first prize in Mszczonów's competition for most beautiful garden.

As a child, Frenza had enjoyed her parents' allotment garden, drowning in perennials, with a neatly planned mini-orchard of plum and cherry trees. But the difference between the allotment plots in Mszczonów and the luxurious gardens in Podkowa Leśna was greater than an abyss. It was like the division of the Roman Empire in the fourth century. When nature was organized according to the tastes of Mszczonów residents, it was dominated by bulging peonies, dahlias, and phlox interspersed here and there with the protruding penises of gladiolus, while the gardens in Podkowa Leśna, which the residents were so eager to share once a year with curious visitors (except the Chechens, who lived in a refugee camp on the outskirts of town), were lorded over by the queens of shade—plantain lilies, in all their spectacular varieties—as well as azaleas and rhododendrons that rivaled in beauty the specimens in the botanical garden at the Polish Academy of Sciences in Powsin. These lilies and rhododendrons were nothing like the ones in the flower beds of Mszczonów. In Podkowa Leśna, the rhododendrons were as huge and fat as elephants! And the queens of shade ranged from the Blue Elf variety to collector specimens, the price of which not infrequently rivaled that of an entire allotment garden in Mszczonów.

The approach to plant cultivation itself was also significant— in Frenza's hometown, plants were grown from seeds or cuttings, and so these herbaceous beings lived out their entire childhood, youth, autumn, and winter of life within a particular family's allotment garden, terrace, or balcony, while in the garden city of Podkowa Leśna they were put into the ground at their most impressive stage of development. After all, to dazzle was more important than to grow—a "big wow" prevailed over the complex secrets of plant cultivation, the gift of a green thumb. What mattered more here was having a green thumb for money, money with which to buy the most beautiful plants in Poland.

"Anna, darling, where are those beautiful strawflowers and King Solomon's seals that I planted for you? I don't see any of our plants here. And the viburnum? Where is it? Has everything died?"

Frenza curls her toes and clenches them so hard they hurt. She's learned this during her years at the oil company: how not to show that your interlocutor, with his innate stupidity, is forcing you against a wall that you're prepared to slam into if that's what it takes not to look at him anymore. You clench your toes until a red mist veils your eyes and thus the sight of that face from which no intelligent thought whatsoever is reflected can no longer torment you. No longer knock you out. Instead of clenching your hands into fists, which would immediately betray your murderous intentions, you clench your toes with all your strength, curling them under your feet. This is difficult to accomplish in tight stilettos, but not impossible (as Frenza knows, for if she didn't, she wouldn't now be the CEO of a national corporation).

"Yeah, everything, Mom, everything. The soil's not the same here... I've told you so many times."

The pain emanating from Frenza's clenched toes is so intense that she eventually begins to breathe more deeply, as if she were about to snort a massive line. This moment of pain-born self-control is interrupted by the mantra of the Blessed Mother of Mszczonów: "We could have brought you soil from Mszczonów. I've offered it so many times..."

Frenza bites her tongue to prevent herself from flaring up and screaming that Mszczonów is Mszczonów, and Podkowa Leśna is a garden city, and that an allotment garden on the edge of town isn't the same as a *real* garden. And that she had to tear it all up by herself one night and dump it on the compost, and then stick in the ground the kinds of plants that are grown by inhabitants of the garden city. Do they think that was easy for her to do? To uproot Mszczonów, her entire childhood—a childhood during which she spent every single summer not on exotic vacations but rather in the allotment garden that belonged to her parents and, before them, her grandparents? She can't say, "It hurt, Mom. It hurt as much as someone banging me suddenly from behind, out of the blue, and mixing up the holes." No, she can't tell her parents the truth, because deep down she knows it would kill them. It would be like taking the portrait of Pope John Paul II down from the wall in their bedroom and pissing on his face.

And so she lies again, for the sixth year in a row, about the very same topic, discerning in herself, as always, an ungrateful bitch who has succeeded in getting where she is solely through this type of self-serving behavior. And calculation. And social observation.

The ability to successfully play the games that those around her are playing is Frenza's strongest quality. She knows a thousand games just like this but only engages in the ones being played at any given time. Moreover, when she wins, she always steps back to let someone else win the next round. She's talented at assessing when to yield and to whom, in order to appease the vanity of her male colleagues and business partners (female colleagues are rare in the oil industry). Women are completely absent at the level of management, even outside Poland, for they've long preferred to gnaw at the branch on which Frenza perches, demanding a total ban on oil drilling and refinery development in their fight to protect the environment and save Mother Earth.

Concerning Strawflowers, King Solomon's Seals, and Composting the Dead

---

Frenza's relationship with Mother Earth is exactly like the relationship she has with her biological mother. She doesn't feel indebted to her for anything apart from life itself. Everything connected to both mothers must be altered and kept under control, because otherwise they would utterly consume her. They would wrap their vines around her and trap her in their roots. Frenza's glad she's capable of not allowing any bonds to develop between them. It's safer that way. And rational. How can you trust someone so unpredictable? Someone who can't control their emotions, who cries while watching soap operas, screams at people over the phone, or—as the Earth does—relentlessly threatens the world with floods, fires, and pandemics? And so she has eradicated both mothers from her life and looks down on them with contempt.

It's precisely because of this inability to accept things that are out of her control that Frenza has renounced her connection to the Earth. She doesn't trust its resources and claims they only exist to be exploited. She responds to environmentalists' accusations arrogantly, quoting her colleagues in saying that, from time to time, the Earth likes to be screwed so hard with a drill it gets a decent borehole—a statement for which she has been condemned many times at press briefings and industry conferences.

"Even if you were to bring me soil, strawflowers and King Solomon's seals would still struggle to grow here," Frenza says, trying hard to suppress the fire engulfing her feet, which is about to ignite everything that stands in its way, beginning with her parents. "Special filters purify the air here in Podkowa Leśna—which is, let me remind you once again, an official *garden city*—and these filters successfully eliminate everything that man-designed nature views as unrefined, noxious, or a weed."

Frenza's mother bursts into tears. Strawflower a weed? King Solomon's seal a weed? A sword lily—also known by the beautiful Latin name gladiolus—a weed? She has changed so much, this daughter of hers, ever since she stopped coming home to Mszczonów and eating the cherries in their allotment garden. This isn't how they raised her to be. Their neighbor was right. Warsaw has transformed her. Into a freak. Into a stranger who came here from God knows where and from God knows whom, because it certainly wasn't from them. And this repulsive town she lives in! The worst place in the world. Instead of being overgrown with moss, it's overgrown with corruption and depravity. A town full of Pharisees in the service of Mammon! Just imagine a church having such a garden! With parrots and peacocks in it! Who has ever seen such a thing? Moreover, what's a garden without phlox? Without dahlias? Just those giant, artificially fertilized azaleas and rhododendrons everywhere.

"What filters, my darling? There's nothing above us! I can't see anything up there!" she finally finds the courage to say, despite the angry thoughts circling in her head.

"They're transparent, Mother! The same color as the sky!

What you see overhead aren't real clouds but 3D clouds superimposed on an aerial mesh as thin as mist. Maybe they're not real, but they're prettier than real ones."

"You're full of shit, kid," says Frenza's father when his daughter presents this argument—rather abstract, in his view. "If you can't see something, it doesn't exist. Don't even say such nonsense." Frenza's father's dismissive approach to the matter empowers her mother to speak up for herself and her values again. "Tell me, darling, where do you bury dead people here? Where is the cemetery?" she asks.

Frenza doesn't say anything. She knew this loaded question would be asked sooner or later, as it is every year. Once again, a showdown is about to begin between her and her parents. A new assault is about to be launched on her life, which she has been carefully building and arranging for so many years.

"And where will you bury Bartek when he decides he's sick of being in that wheelchair, swallows some pills, drinks a bottle of wine, and kicks the bucket?"

Indeed, corpses aren't buried in Podkowa Leśna. The bodies of the dead are transported to Warsaw in a black Lincoln and cremated in a private crematorium with the literary name of Ashes and Diamonds, where, for a special fee, a diamond is made from the ashes of the deceased. This is the posthumous fate that awaits the rich citizens of Podkowa Leśna. A very different postmortem reality awaits the poor people living in towns and villages on the outskirts of Podkowa Leśna, such as Owczarnia and Żółwin. In Twatville and Cuntborough—the nicknames given to the small towns adjacent to Podkowa Leśna but outside the orbit of the gods—different laws are in force. Laws established by the wealthier sector of the garden city. The bodies of the poor aren't cremated but simply tossed onto a huge compost heap between Podkowa Leśna and Żółwin, right behind a statue of Jesus Christ.

Contrary to what automatically comes to mind, this practice is inherently linked to the local way of life, in which the gardens owned by rich people occupy the highest position in the social hierarchy. The decomposed bodies of the deceased are sprinkled onto the beautiful azaleas and rhododendrons in the gardens owned by those who pay a special annual fee. The compost fee.

It's pointless trying to explain this mortal—and simultaneously immortal—philosophy to her backward parents from Mszczonów. Thus, just as Frenza did during their last visit, she pretends they haven't provoked her at all. She leads her parents to the guest rooms upstairs, asking them, as usual, not to remove their shoes, which they do anyway out of concern for the oak floor (which Frenza hires professionals to polish regularly), and this gives them yet another opportunity to look around in her house and criticize everything they see.

On Coprophilia and Corpocareers

T he tap in the downstairs bathroom needs tightening. Water keeps dripping from it. Someday it's gonna flood the whole place."

"And the drawer too," Frenza's father blurts out like a nerdy, four-eyed schoolboy, eager to show off his random knowledge in front of everyone. "This one right here, with your underwear in it. It doesn't move the way it should. It doesn't pop out. And it should, shouldn't it?"

"Your ceiling got a crack in it somehow, darling. Oh, right there—that spot right there, do you see it? Maybe your dad could repaint it while we're here?"

"And it's so dark in here, as dark as a coffin . . . Why is it always so dark in here?"

While brewing some tea for her parents to drink with supper, Frenza struggles to control the anger consuming her from inside, gnawing at her liver and pancreas. And to stop herself from sprinkling rat poison into the tea.

"And is there ever light in the forest? That's why we have these lamps everywhere." Frenza walks over to the wall and presses a button. The light that immediately shines from the ceiling so eerily resembles real sunlight that her parents feel as if they have been suddenly transported to a beach on the shore of the Baltic Sea. "It imitates the sun. Fortunately, without any carcinogenic radiation. I can also turn on the rustle of forest leaves or the sound of the sea. Would you like that?" asks Frenza courteously but through clenched teeth.

Deep down, she fervently wishes they would leave already, close the door behind them, drive back to their backwater town, and devote themselves to their favorite activity—discussing what has happened to her since she left Mszczonów for college. Since she started working for the oil company. Since she stopped eating cherries from her family's garden. Since she became their daughter in name only, which for some incomprehensible reason she chose to keep after she got married instead of taking her husband's.

Thus, once or twice a year, Frenza's parents take a tour of her house room by room, floor after floor, polishing the oak staircase with their discounted slippers brought from Mszczonów. They drink the purest tap water in all of Poland and enjoy molecular gastronomy as well as the world's most expensive ice cream from a local artisanal confectionery, scathingly referred to by Twatvillians as "ice crème de la crème," after which they expel the most organic excrement into modernist-style toilets to be treated with the world's most state-of-the-art biodegrading methods and then used as compost.

It's worth pointing out that Frenza succeeded in getting where she is without any major sacrifices. On a few occasions, at banquets, she let a certain deputy prime minister become more intimately acquainted with her, and as he sensed in her a willingness to experiment and push boundaries, he requested from her something that no woman had ever been willing to give him, even for a large sum of money. All of them, including upscale prostitutes, had rejected his offer with disgust, even though they could've earned a heap of cash. All of them, that is, except Frenza. She did it not in exchange for money, however, but for the position of CEO in the national oil company, for this turned out to be the easiest role to free up for her on short notice . . .

The arrangement with the deputy prime minister was simultaneously sordid and pure. And for Frenza, in a certain sense, it was even healthy, for it allowed her to rid herself of all the frustration and anger she felt toward herself, her parents, her husband, and the world, and thus finally feel at ease. The arrangement would probably have lasted for many years if it hadn't been for the deputy prime minister's unfortunate slipup when he developed some photos from a holiday with his wife and children to the island of Rhodes. Through some strange accident, a particular photograph had gotten mixed in with the holiday snapshots—a most inappropriate one, with such potential to shock that it caused the worker developing them at the photo shop in the underground passage to vomit. She'd never seen anything like it in her entire life. She'd heard of such things, of course, but she didn't think such a deviation really existed. She thought it was merely legend. Fortunately for Anna Frenza, who had taken the photograph at his request during the act of perversion, he was the only one whose face was visible in it: the deputy prime minister, an exemplary husband and father of five children . . .

"Mommy? What's this? What's this? Some lady pooped on Daddy's face!" shouted five-year-old Jadzia, the deputy prime minister's daughter, while she was looking at their holiday photos over lunch.

Not only did the man lose both his wife and the roof over his head in a single hour, but the outraged housewife also took a snapshot of the photo with her phone and sent it to the government fax machine in the Belvedere Palace. He was a goner. All it took was two hours. In the end, he hadn't been destroyed by the Central Bureau of Investigation but rather by an inclination he'd never grown out of because his parents had put him on the potty too soon.

The "shithead"—as Frenza calls him in her thoughts—had, however, managed to plant her in the position of CEO several months earlier, and so to pay tribute to him after his suicide she often thought of him during her own sexual fantasies. After all, he was the only man who had allowed her to realize them fully, creating opportunities for the most extreme transgressions.

A Slice of Ham and How It Led to Oil Wells in the Baltic Sea

Finally, the Easter weekend is coming to an end. The grand finale is the same as always—a crucifixion of all illusions that she and her parents have anything in common beyond a surname.

Why does she hate them so much, and why won't they finally wave a white flag and give up? Hasn't she performed a miracle? Escaping from Mszczonów to Warsaw, becoming the CEO of the national oil company, buying a house in Podkowa Leśna, where just two flower beds in her garden are worth more than her parents' apartment, four-door sedan, and painstakingly squirreled-away life savings in the bank all combined—isn't that enough for them? Can't they finally appreciate what their daughter has achieved? And entirely on her own, for that matter—for what support could she possibly have received from her plebeian family?! Is being a CEO not enough for them? How many have risen out of their cesspool? How many have achieved something? Her mother's sister, Lidka, works in a haberdashery; her father's brothers, Włodek and Edek, run a lamp shop; and her cousins, Lucyna and Robert, who are the same age as Anna, spend most of their time getting hammered on cheap booze and smoking homemade cigarettes, which they also sell to Ukrainians at the local market. And there she is, alongside all of them. The only one of that screwed-up lot who made something of herself. She has achieved so much more than first prize for the prettiest allotment garden in Mszczonów. It took a huge amount of effort: two university degrees, fluency in three foreign languages, and an affair with the deputy prime minister, whose weakness would have made even the marquis de Sade blush with shame.

And so, while pulling the strings at work, she's careful not to jerk any of them too hard. She hasn't made any spectacular slipups so far, which hasn't been easy when she's surrounded by so many government idiots and must interact with them at receptions and banquets. And of course many of them are waiting impatiently for her to stumble in her stiletto heels—indeed, nearly every one of them dreams of having Frenza's job. Seventy thousand złoty a month, mostly in bonuses because it wouldn't be appropriate to categorize it otherwise (the press would tear her to pieces). Frenza is immediately able to justify the payout to herself—the company is thriving. Everything's running smoothly. There hasn't been any outcry over the new contracts that were signed. She prefers to place stakes in Saudi Arabia and cut ties with Moscow. She's got balls—much bigger balls than her predecessors. In fact, Poland has begun drilling extensively in the Baltic Sea, and it's entirely thanks to her. She created a new base. A new platform. And provided jobs for hundreds of unemployed people. The geologists she hired found substantial deposits of domestic shale gas. In a spot that had spoken to her over thirty years ago. One day, while buying some ham at a delicatessen in Podkowa Leśna, she suddenly remembered a pier in Kołobrzeg, on the shore of the Baltic Sea, and a gap between the planks wide enough to see the water crashing against the pilings below. Frenza had gazed down as if enchanted, noticing rainbow reflections shimmering on the waves. Just like on the slices of ham. After catching a glimpse of those rainbow-hued shimmers, Frenza tugged at the hem of her grandmother's skirt. "Go, child, go play with the other kids, give me a bit of peace," her grandmother told her, immersed in knitting a sweater. But no, little five-year-old Frenza had to show her something now! Immediately! Annoyed, Frenza's grandmother put down her knitting needles, knelt beside her on the wooden boards, and saw what Frenza saw. Gasoline! Oil!

While buying the ham, Frenza greedily seized a freshly cut slice and shoved it in her mouth, then tucked the rest into her purse and rushed out of the deli. Wishing to maintain as much consistency with the past as possible, she didn't travel to Kołobrzeg by car but by train, just as she used to with her grandmother. A few hours later, she was lying on the pier in Kołobrzeg, searching for traces of the illumination that she'd seen three decades before. And although this time she couldn't discern the shimmering rainbow-colored "gasoline" on the water's surface, she trusted her own body's reaction—an excitement that immediately made her pussy moist—and decided that drilling must commence in that spot, successfully convincing the minister of industry and prime minister over the phone.

When asked what proof she had that there were oil deposits in this exact spot, she wanted to shout into the phone: "My cunt doesn't lie!" But she lacked the courage. She reduced it to a simple "I know. I just know." And since none of her decisions so far had turned out to be misguided, the minister of industry and prime minister both gave the go-ahead for the drilling, although the latter told Frenza: "The environmentalists are going to rip us to fucking shreds over this."

Concerning Tree Huggers and Fucked-Up Soyheads

What happened two weeks later confirmed Frenza's brilliant intuition. All the headlines, both online and in print, announced just one thing: Poland had become a major player on the oil market! No more bending the knee to Abu Dhabi or Moscow. Poland would be thrashed no more. For decades, it had been declared that there were no oil deposits in Poland—no more than a drop or two, at least—but now that had turned out to be a lie! Or maybe a conspiracy created by environmentalists and NGOs. Just some Avaaz activists fucking with us, Frenza suggested to the prime minister. We're all going to die anyway, so why let the global economy screw us while we're still around? Everyone else can get off on global warming and melting glaciers. She sang the Polish national anthem while puking inside the prime minister's limousine: "Poland has not yet perished, so long as we still live!" Screw the World Wildlife Fund. Screw Greenpeace. Screw the Green Party! Wiping her mouth on the sleeve of her black merino wool jacket, she commanded the prime minister to crack down on every single environmental protest. She shook her finger at him like a stern parent and scolded him for his weakness when, shortly before they struck oil, he had become intimidated by Greenpeace and nearly backed out of the drilling. It seemed to the prime minister that Frenza had lost her mind; she shouldn't have drunk so much at the party. He grabbed her firmly by the wrist, and then he bent her finger back where it belonged.

Frenza perceived this as violence. She was afraid of the prime minister and realized she should stop haranguing him. She had heard about what happened when he lost his temper—and about the bizarre punishments he sometimes inflicted upon his colleagues. It had been said that he made people stare at a wall while kneeling on cat litter, or lick cat piss from a litter box. Or squat like frogs and hop up and down the steps of the monument to the victims of the Smolensk plane crash late at night until their muscles burned. She started to feel hot just at the thought of it—she unfastened the top button of her white silk blouse and took off her three-inch stilettos, which were so frequently mocked by feminists and tree huggers—the Fucked-Up Soyheads, as Frenza calls them.

She knows them all inside and out. She spies on them while they camp outside her house. Whole squadrons of them, day and night. Filthy and dressed in wrinkled, worn-out secondhand clothes: the dregs of society. Sham proponents of democracy with scrambled tofu for brains. They started taking suburban trains straight to her house after an idiotic left-wing journalist leaked her address. They threw eggs and squash at her windows, pickles and homemade kimchi. Stale falafels. And tempeh—more expensive than meat and made by the tiny fingers of starving children in Africa, which absolutely does not stop them from pretending it's fucking "fair trade." They care about fair trade as much as they do about the monkeys rescued by eco-freaks from being transported to the zoo. Or old tigers marked for culling. Frenza can't wrap her head around any of it. What motivates these hypocrites who claim to be the saviors of the planet but would, in reality, do pretty much anything for a Hass avocado and an almond milk latte? Some ecoterrorist bitches started sending her death threats. So she built a wall that was three times their height to keep them away from her, and installed glass noise barriers so that she wouldn't hear them either. She believed this would rid her of those pests once and for all. What has she done that's so terrible, anyway? She's creating jobs for people! Jobs that give them money—which means they'll be able to send their kids to college, so that they can escape their shitty hometowns just like she did. So they can learn foreign languages and sail across waters far beyond the Baltic Sea. She's helping to boost Poland's economy so that it'll last for many years to come. "Culture will be culture, nature will be nature, and civilization will be civilization. There's no escaping it," Frenza often repeats at government banquets, explaining to the attendees that the industrial revolution didn't cause nearly as much harm as is popularly believed. She goes so far as to suggest that its second wave is on the way, and if Poland opposes international environmental policies, it will emerge as a leading economic power. Behind the scenes, however, even the strongest opponents of so-called green solutions whisper that her stance is unnatural. Not just against feminine nature, against nature *en général*. They say that the European Union will eventually make Poland sit by itself in the corner on the dunce's stool, or even kick it out of school altogether and send it back to the cabbage patch from which it managed to crawl by fluke or sheer cunning. And yet, no matter what they say, when top accountants begin to analyze the revenues of Frenza's oil company, they find that not only is the balance sheet for the past six months up to par, but also that the company has earned more than all other industrial sectors combined!

Concerning Somnambulism
and Tree-Mounting

———

By no means a modest person, Frenza has no qualms about giving herself a generous bonus. Her subordinates too. Smaller bonuses for them, though; they already thought she was a bitch, so she may as well prove them right. But how much more money did she need to earn, for fuck's sake, before her small-town parents could start feeling proud of her?!

Unable to wrap her head around it, Frenza reaches for a double dose of lithium, knowing full well she shouldn't increase her prescribed dose after the recent unfortunate incident when she was caught late at night trying to steal chocolate bars, chips, and cookies from one of her company's own gas stations.

Her tendency to sleepwalk (a side effect of taking lithium), exacerbated by stressful family situations and a no-less-stressful job, has already gotten her into trouble more than once. It would have been a complete disaster for her if it weren't for Rair, a young employee at the gas station who, in return for keeping quiet about her unconscious shoplifting, demands just one thing: that she rub against him in the back room late at night, when there are no customers. He remains fully clothed, because only then can he convince himself that he isn't sinning with her. Clinging to storage shelves full of motor oil, windshield washer fluid, and dashboard cleaning wipes, she has no choice but to pay for her unwitting and irrepressible desire to steal cheap nut-flavored chocolate wafers, sesame snaps, and halva with forty-five minutes of petting and stroking, as this is the only sexual act permissible for Rair and his huge puffed-up cock. She does wonder if his wife would feel the same way about it, though.

Fortunately, Frenza's personality has liberated her from any petit bourgeois feelings of shame, and the only disgust she feels in this situation is caused not by the immoral acts themselves but rather by his sperm, in which she can detect a hint of cumin, a spice she detests.

Tonight, to minimize the risk of sleepwalking, she straps her left hand to her bed frame with a belt. Just in case. So she won't have to commit the halal transaction again, which always leaves her with pain in her lower back for several days, thanks to the extremely uncomfortable position in which it's performed.

But sleep eludes her. After another half hour of tossing and turning, unfastening the belt on one hand and fastening it on the other, Frenza gives up and reaches for a nearly full bottle of wine she keeps hidden under the bed, despite the clear warnings she's received about mixing alcohol with the lithium prescribed by her psychiatrist. "Through my fault, through my fault, through my most grievous fault," she thinks, smiling to herself as she washes down a third lithium capsule with a glass of Rhine wine, her favorite. "And God said, 'Let there be lithium,'" Frenza whispers to herself, gazing at her reflection in the mirror with the bottle in her hand, raising a toast to her own intelligence and ironic wit, which are, in her opinion, her most powerful protection against the world.

Happily downing two and a half glasses of the elixir of Dionysus, she forgets to fasten her hand to the bed again. She finally falls asleep at about two o'clock as the silvery light of the moon, as round as a loaf of rustic bread that night, licks her face and tickles her eyelids. At that moment, the mirror reflecting the entire contents of Frenza's mind from the past few days shatters in a kaleidoscope of dreams. A kaleidoscope of freeze-frames—fragments of reality torn from their context and rearranged in a new cause-and-effect order. But though the mirror breaks, Frenza doesn't wake up. She remains, like every sleepwalker, trapped between two worlds.

As she gets out of bed in a somnambulistic trance, her neighbor from two houses down—an important strategic employee of the same oil company, holding the position of chief financial officer, known at work by the nickname "Will" (Will-He-or-Won't-He-Give-Me-a-Raise)—is about to finish banging his daughter's private French tutor while his wife, a TV commercial producer, is on her way home from a shoot in Los Angeles. It's a quarter to three. It's not completely accurate to say that Will is banging the tutor. While banging the tutor, he's actually banging himself banging the tutor, and thus it's Will, himself, who's both the subject and object of the act. For Will is such a fantastic lover that he's self-referential. With whom, by whom, and thanks to whom he's screwing himself is of no significance to him whatsoever at that moment, so it could hardly even be considered infidelity. His wife doesn't need to know anything about it: after all, nothing is even happening here, Will explains to himself while shifting to doggy style—more comfortable, as it eliminates the risk of eye contact. It's in that moment that he happens to glance at the designer clock on the mantelpiece above the faux fireplace. It's 3:33. Three threes in a row don't bode well. He knows he's unlikely to climax; the alignment of three identical digits has always been a terrible omen in his life. Three years ago, on the first of January at precisely 1:11 in the morning, he broke his arm while skiing down a slope in the Alps while highly intoxicated, in defiance of strict rules against exactly that, while attempting to prove to the obsessive-compulsive Austrians that Poles have a zest for life. Seventeen years ago, at 5:55 in the morning, he found his father, a policeman from Pruszków, hanging from the doorknob in the bathroom. And the day before yesterday, right at the stroke of midnight (0:00), the home security alarm went off because someone was trying to break into his garage, once again. And now it's 3:33 and Will is suddenly struck with the realization that there's no point in continuing to screw the young woman; it's a waste of time. Why tire himself out, become completely exhausted and out of breath, crumple up the bedsheets that were changed just a few days ago, get someone else's germs all over himself, and rub off dead skin? And then reek of sweat afterward. Will pulls the plug out of the socket, no longer crackling with a surge of electricity, and apologizes to the cute little *maîtresse*, to whom he pays 120 złoty per hour to give private French lessons to his daughter. "*Excusez-moi, ma chère* mattress," he says in his primitive French, then gets out of bed and walks over to the window. He wants to look the moon straight in the face and feign some degree of metaphysical connection with nature, with its rhythm. Perhaps at least in this way he might impress the pretty teacher.

It is this very moment that, unbeknownst to Frenza, who is running naked in a somnambulistic trance, will be the turning point in her career. Click, click—Will takes a snapshot of her with his phone and immediately sends it to his buddy at the Polsat TV channel. The notification sound of the incoming text message wakes him up.

OMG, the Polsat guy texts back laconically. Seconds later, he's in his car. It takes him no more than fifteen minutes to track down Frenza. He's lucky. Barking dogs have revealed her location. He sees her turn the corner from Larch Street to Beech Street and then run into the woods. Not only naked but barefoot too. The snow behind her is streaked with blood. She must have injured her feet. The Polsat guy parks his car in front of a grocery store. He sneaks along, runs a few feet, then follows her. He watches as she stops in a clearing; he focuses on her, zooms in, and refocuses, all while hiding in the bushes.

With her eyes closed, Frenza straddles a huge felled tree covered in moss. She leans forward with her arms and thighs wrapped tightly around the trunk, as if she were riding a horse bareback. She settles comfortably on it, pressing her breasts and stomach against the mossy bark. As if she and the fallen tree were lovers, locked in a tender embrace. She puts her index and ring finger into her mouth to wet them with saliva, then slides them gently into a tiny hollow she has sensed with her fingertips. Instead of jabbing her fingers straight in, she runs them gently around the edge of the hole before penetrating it. She moves her face closer. She slowly caresses the mossy patches around the crevice with the tip of her nose and tongue, lubricating both herself and the tree. As she licks the drops of resin that are oozing from the slit in the tree's trunk, she shares her own moisture with it. So that she's not just taking but exchanging mutually. Then she becomes completely still, drawing deep tranquility and life-giving strength from this caress. After a time, she shifts her body and changes her angle, pressing even closer, touching her own crevice to the moss growing on the tree's trunk. She rubs back and forth, nuzzling her cheek against the bark. She remains motionless for a moment, then thrusts her hips more and more rhythmically, as if trying to kindle a fire. Her grinding against the moss is as rhythmic as the beat of a metronome. As if the tree were setting the tempo and she were merely following it. At a certain point, Frenza begins to emit a low, monotonous sound with a frequency that resonates with the creaking of the oldest oak branches on Park Avenue. It's as if nature has picked up her monody and has begun adding its own sounds: the glassy, metallic crackle of icicles breaking and hitting the frozen ground, or the howling of the wind in the tangled treetops. At a certain point, Frenza's rocking transcends her hips, seems to come from something greater than her, from her very essence. A bestial howl erupts from her throat and nearly makes the Polsat guy crap his pants: Never in his life has he heard such a harsh, dreadful sound. And he's heard a lot in his life.

At first he just snaps some photos of Frenza straddling the oak, but then he switches his phone to video mode and records. After the horrible, brain-piercing sound fades away, he dares to open his eyes and sees Frenza with her own eyes half open, as if in some kind of a deep trance, still straddling the tree, shifting and squirming as if she were laying a massive egg through her cunt, which is wide open and purple from rubbing against the bark.

The journalist's hands are shaking as if he has advanced Parkinson's, his heart is pounding like crazy, and there's a whooshing sound in his ears as if the rough waves of the Baltic Sea were crashing through them. His penis, terrified by the spectacle, has shrunk as if it will never emerge from his cotton boxers again. He just prays that the battery in his phone will last.

Half an hour later, as he's sitting in Will's kitchen drinking a glass of vodka, which he requested along with some coffee in the hope that it would obliterate what he's just witnessed from his memory, he exclaims, "I'm never going to have an erection again!"

Will pats his friend on the back, encouraging him to try a "baby crocodile"—a pickled delicacy made by his mother-in-law.

"We've got this!" he says, and pours a shot of vodka down his friend's throat.

Concerning the End of a Career

First thing in the morning, the video appears on the internet. The prime minister receives a text from Will with a link and summons his men to the Owl Café.

"The national oil company is run by a fucking sleepwalker! Gentlemen, our ship is sinking and you, instead of rowing, have got your right hand down your trousers and your left hand on a remote control. Meanwhile, Anna Frenza, that bitch, is fucking us in the ass with her razor-sharp red claw!" This is how the prime minister begins his speech, perfectly timed to the arrival of ice cream sundaes at the table.

The prime minister has a habit of eating dessert before the main course because that's what his private nutritionist advised him to do—to speed up his metabolism.

His gaze is drawn to the waitress's firm buttocks, shaped by the sweat of her brow and a hundred squats a day. In fact, they're being shaped more and more all the time, for the process never ends: her buttocks are an *opera aperta*, a work of art that is never completed. Every day, whether in sun or rain, in sickness or in health, sober or drunk, the buttocks are toned, pumped, and squeezed—

either through sumo squats, as if their owner were sitting on the earth while defecating, or by clenching the cheeks together with her legs up in the air, as if their owner were an upside-down caryatid who, instead of holding something on her head, is supporting it with her feet. But what is the waitress supporting? At that point, the prime minister's imagination falls short.

Regardless of the nature of the exercise, the strategically important employee of the major national oil company with the White Eagle in its logo greatly appreciates the results of them and is already fantasizing about sowing his seed in the waitress, although in real life he'd probably be too excited to get it up. Only in his imagination, especially after feeding it with freeze-frames from thousands of pornos, does he come in a flash. Without even touching the organ created for fornication . . .

The prime minister asks the waitress to open her mouth and put a spoonful of ice cream into it—from one of the sundaes served to them at the table—and use her tongue to check it for wiretaps.

At first bewildered by this request, the waitress quickly overcomes her shyness after several fat banknotes are tucked into her cleavage. She does what she's told and even puts some theatrical flair into it, perhaps hoping for more government subsidies. Finally, she confirms that this time, not a single word uttered at the Great White Eagle's table will fly off and nest under the thatched roofs of Poland's respectable citizens, who want nothing more than to peacefully enjoy a good night's sleep, peacefully barbecue sausages from discount stores at family picnics, peacefully fuck their (and other men's) wives, and then peacefully vent their anger on the women in their lives whenever they deserve it— instead of drowning in shit that leaks out into the world from wiretapped conversations in restaurants. It happened once already, back in 2014. The secretly recorded conversation befouled every TV screen in Poland and the speakers of every radio, and even ended up on the front pages of newspapers across Europe—that's how massive the scandal was.

"Well?" asks the prime minister, who has sunk so deeply into a huge, plush armchair that he's nearly fused with it, resulting in a whole new being. Physically materialized and plush, yet illusory. A prime minister who exists and yet does not exist, appearing and disappearing like the Cheshire cat.

"Who's going to take this bitch's place? Let's see a show of hands! Maybe you, Will? Are you up to it? Show us how hard your dick is!"

Will can't hide his excitement. He's finally succeeded, at long last. He'll have to give the Polsat guy his cut. But at least there's some justice in this world, after all! That idiotic experiment of having a female CEO went to shit. The testicle owners are back on board!

At nine thirty, right at the start of the workday, the telephone on Anna Frenza's desk rings. Unaware that overnight she has become a new Polish porn star—in second place right after Teresa Orlowski—Frenza answers the phone. Moments later she's being driven across the city in the prime minister's limousine. She detects a faint fragrance of incense in it. "Does he screw altar boys in here?" she wonders. "Or maybe even the nuncio of the Holy See himself?" She gets out at the Belvedere Palace. The staccato of her stiletto heels on the marble floor gives her entrance just the right amount of drama. The tension rises.

She enters the office of the highest authority in the country as a human being. But by the time she leaves, she's a mere shell of the person she once was. Her body is now encased in a chitinous exoskeleton instead of a high-end trench coat with a houndstooth lining. On her head are antennae instead of eyes, registering every tiny movement around her. She has shrunk to the size of an insect in only seven and a half minutes. That's how long it took for Frenza to be demoted to the position of a rank-and-file employee in the HR department. And even that job will only be available to her after a psychiatrist issues an official report certifying that she has made a complete recovery from her manic episode. Clad in her cockroach shell, Frenza politely declines a ride home from the chauffeur who is waiting for her outside, since, unbeknownst to the driver, she's no longer entitled to one, and then creeps into a subway car.

The faces on the anthropoids occupying the seats across from Frenza are straight out of paintings by Hieronymus Bosch or Pieter Bruegel the Elder, which she's seen on the quick jaunts that she's made into museums while away on her various business trips. She studied the paintings closely, examining the features that reminded her so much of people from her hometown of Mszczonów—Polish facial features that don't exist in Podkowa Leśna at all. That was why she'd decided to move there six years ago, after being promoted to CEO. She wanted to escape as far as possible from those narrow streets, those apartment building doorways reeking of cat and human urine, those faces unmarred by any trace of deep thought. She gloated over the fact that she had managed to achieve it in such a short time, despite the vagina between her legs.

But now, on the subway, even those Bruegel-Boschian faces seem superior to her own. She can feel her bones, joints, and muscles all disintegrating. Her brain crashes, along with all its information-transmitting controllers. Frenza tries to contort her face to scare off the people looking at her, but she fails to make a single grimace—as if the conversation she had with the prime minister completely stripped her of the mask she wore every day, and now it turns out there's not much left underneath. She has the sensation that everyone is staring at her. And checking their smartphones to see if it's her—the famous Anna Frenza, CEO of the national oil company who was caught tree-fucking in the middle of the night. Frenza is on the verge of total collapse. How could she have done such a thing?!

That evening, someone insistently tries to contact Frenza by phone. She rejects the calls. She isn't ready to talk to anyone— despite having been offered fifty grand for an interview with Poland's leading women's magazine. To be accompanied by a photo of her naked, straddling a two-hundred-year-old oak tree. Then a text message sent from the pushy caller's phone number momentarily catches Frenza's attention: *Congratulations! That was the best environmental protest-performance we've ever seen! With respect, the EcoDivas—the women's faction of the Green Party.* Moments later, another notification pops up on her phone. Frenza's blood starts to boil at the mere thought of these women. She still remembers how those maggots pelted her windows with rotten apples, tomatoes, and kimchi. The second message reads: *We believe your act to be a clear expression of your decision to finally join our side. Therefore, as a sign of appreciation for your audacious courage, we would like to offer you a position as head of PR for our organization.*

When Frenza doesn't respond, dismissing the messages as nothing more than a provocation, she receives a third text message: *In four days we plan to occupy the Białowieża Forest—the oldest forest in Europe. We'd like to borrow your idea—and copulate with trees slated for logging.*

Frenza can't believe it. She remembers how, when she discovered shale gas in the Baltic Sea and ordered drilling to begin, this nutcase wanted to shoot her with a crossbow! "You nasty cunt!" she thinks. Then, in one swift movement, she throws her phone—the latest iPhone with a Herkimer screen—against the wall, smashing it to pieces.

Frenza gets very little relief from this act of violence, so she runs downstairs to the garden, forgetting that she didn't put any pajamas on after her bath. Stark naked, she starts up her electric lawn mower, which resembles a mini-Batmobile. It's the best and most expensive lawn mower in the world—unless the salesman in the shop was pulling a fast one on her. She impulsively revs the engine and steps on the gas, eager to wage a battle against nature for mocking her, as punishment for not having eliminated those eco-bitches from the start. She steers the machine with the aim of ravaging as much terrain as possible in one fell swoop. She rams into the rhododendrons, mutilating them with the mower's Pac-Man jaws. The vehicle gets jammed among the branches, but Frenza skillfully maneuvers backward. Now it's time for the azaleas. The battle rages on for hours. Eventually only the trees remain. There's nothing Bartek can do about it, sitting there in his wheelchair. Frenza can't hear him as she sinks deeper into madness—into her well-known self-immolation, the effects of which are quite often felt by her surroundings.

She grabs a branch. And she starts doing what she did throughout her entire childhood—banging the deadwood.

When the psychiatrist she visits a few days later asks her to explain what she means by "banging the deadwood," she tells him about it.

"There aren't any forests like that here anymore. No other forest or grove offers the possibilities that one did . . . I was taken there for the very first time by my cousin, who was a child of the forest, a defender of trees. I trusted him completely as I followed him into the forest, which had never really been a forest. Just a foul-smelling little grove of trees next to a sewage treatment plant, which you could only reach by walking along the train tracks. It was a strange, eerie place. There was nothing but deadwood growing there—trees with dead branches. A thick, dense grove of them. The only hint of greenery was far above our heads, where young shoots were growing out of the dead boughs. There were no paths either, so we had to find our own way through the trees, and once in a while there were sweet-smelling violets peeking through the thin layer of fallen twigs, bark, and pine needles covering the ground. Their fragrance was intoxicating. When it wasn't violet season, the grove was dry, ugly, and stinky, full of mosquitoes and flies buzzing around the snags."

Frenza begins to shift in her chair as if suddenly, having tapped into her memories, she has become erotically aroused. She seems no longer capable of sitting still. Her eyes are glowing in a way that's completely unfamiliar to her psychiatrist. Never before has he seen her so animated.

"Please continue," he says encouragingly, handing her a glass of water because he notices that her mouth has gone dry from excitement.

"Every time I went to the deadwood forest, I left everything behind! We entered that space with love and utter devotion. The sticks in our hands took on a life of their own. Sweat, dirt, mosquitoes—suddenly, none of it mattered. We used sticks to bang most of the deadwood. And rumblerods for the bigger ones—huge, solid, two-handed slabs of wood for those fucking deadwood trolls! For the trees that were completely dead. Those were the ones my cousin went for! The swift movements of his wrist were accompanied by the crunching sound of dry branches, resonant and beautiful, and this set a rhythm for us. To walk through the forest, we had to hack a path for ourselves by banging the deadwood. We plowed right through that deadwood forest at full speed, in a fucking blaze of glory. Wham, smack, swoosh. You don't have a rumblerod? Then you can fuck off. I lost control of myself, banging those trees. I was in a frenzy, or a trance. I was possessed, as if something had entered me and taken over my body and soul."

The psychiatrist asks Frenza if she knows the meaning of the verb "to bang." Could she tell him something about this word? Did she ever have the urge to masturbate after "banging the deadwood"? Or to have sex with her cousin? Or with a stick?

Frenza doesn't know.

The psychiatrist says he's treated people for sleepwalking before but has never encountered a dendrophile. And while he can imagine men inserting their penises into tree hollows, scooped-out pomelo flesh, beef liver, or watermelon, well, he could never . . . No, he just can't fathom it. Really, how could a woman be a dendrophile?!

"How on earth would she do it?" he asks himself out loud, at which Frenza's feeling of consternation is only amplified. "By shoving pine cones into her vagina? Twigs, maybe? Or mushrooms and acorns?!"

Frenza's devastated. This isn't how this was supposed to go. This isn't why she revealed the most intimate secret of her life to him. Feeling misunderstood and scorned, she recedes into herself and sinks lower in her armchair.

"The only thing I can think of recommending right now is to try going off your medication for a month or two. Perhaps your state of hypomania will remain stable for the time being and not turn into mania, until we come up with a long-term solution. You should try prayer too. Talk to your parish priest about your problem. After all, you've got some very wise priests in Podkowa Leśna.

The entire country envies you. Those gorgeous peacocks in the monastery gardens. And the masses held there for the Fatherland are nothing short of legendary. You should turn your eyes and, above all, your debauched cunt toward God. Otherwise, you'll surely fly off into outer space again. And then, the only option we'll have is electroshock therapy . . ."

Concerning the Full Moon, Insomnia, and Salem Cigarettes

After a two-week break from her lithium pills, Frenza begins to notice an improvement. She no longer has trouble sleeping at night. And the absence of the slightest evidence of somnambulism in the bedroom indicates a total victory! The amount of trash scattered across the floor—empty chocolate pudding containers, herring jars, and little Styrofoam trays that used to contain chicory—has been reduced to zero. There are no empty plastic baggies of cashews, which Frenza often snacked on instead of cookies during attacks of hunger. Nor does she spy any blue-and-white packages of homogenized cheese, empty ketchup bottles, or jars that once contained jam sweetened with apple juice, not—heaven forbid!—sugar.

Frenza proclaims to herself the end of the era of nocturnal binge-eating—the sole thing in her life over which she had no control. Until now, things have been like this: during the day she would eat her special diet meals delivered to her in Styrofoam containers printed with the information "1,200 calories," which is only three times more than what concentration camp inmates received, and at night she would attack the freezer. Right down to the icicles growing on its frosty walls. What she would find on the kitchen floor and by her bed when she woke up every morning terrified her more than the prospect of never having oral sex with her husband again, which he could easily have given her, being paralyzed only from the waist down, but didn't, for some unknown reason. Since the accident, he had denied Frenza even this minor pleasure.

It had happened more than once that Frenza had called in sick to work, claiming to have come down with a stomach flu or migraine, after having downed an entire bottle of red wine quite unconsciously during the night, or a bottle of Suze, her beloved aperitif made from gentian root! After several episodes like this, she decided to lock up all the alcohol in the pantry—though occasionally, it's true, she sneaked a bottle into her bedroom—making sure to maintain a steady temperature of sixty-four degrees Fahrenheit inside it. She gave the key to her husband to make it more difficult for her to access the liquor vault at night. And since they've slept in separate bedrooms since the accident, the chance of uncontrollable somnambulistic intoxication has been reduced to zero.

Tonight the silver moon is glowing so brightly that Frenza decides to do something she hasn't done for a long time—put on a wool hat before bed. In the past, before she met Bartek, she used to do this every time the moon was full. Now she does so only when the light is most intense, to insulate her brain so the moonbeams won't fuck it up. To protect it from the reflected light of the sun that causes even the oceans to rise up in stormy waves, not to mention a human being composed of more than 80 percent water! A wool hat she bought during a holiday in the mountain town of Zakopane, plus some wine. A duet that will guarantee sleep.

She sneaks out of her bedroom and tiptoes into her husband's to steal the key to the liquor cellar that lies, at her request, at the bottom of the nightstand drawer next to his bed. What she discovers stuns her, for Bartek's bed is empty, even though his wheelchair is in the middle of the room! Frenza rubs her eyes, thinking she's either gone crazy or is dreaming. But no! She isn't mistaken! The electric wheelchair, which, due to its prohibitive price, is used by few physically disabled people other than injured NBA players, is sitting right there—parked as it is every night, with the brake applied. Frenza shelled out 130,000 złoty for that hot rod a year ago as a Christmas present so that her prince could experience an extension of his manhood, which would now be spending the rest of eternity in a state of rest. And so that she could, at least to a small degree, purge herself of the nasty sensation of guilt that was plaguing her, preventing her from having a normal life and destroying her marriage. Guilt that was making her loathsome to both herself and the world.

Not seeing her husband in the bedroom, Frenza unfurls her cerebral ganglia and activates her gray cells, which is no mean feat while experiencing withdrawal from the medication she's been taking for years! Forcing her brain to make even the slightest effort is like getting blood out of a stone. The brain cells, instead of playing rugby or ice hockey together, are playing a game of foosball. Frenza's mind—a flightless bird—soars to new heights and issues a directive to her body to search the house—bravo, fucking bravo!—and track down that liar!

Ablaze with anger and seething with fire, with a swollen liver, Frenza races around all the upstairs rooms—he's not there! Then the kitchen, living room, bathroom—nothing! Breathless and overwhelmed from head to toe by "aggressive energy," as her acupuncturist used to say (he should go fuck himself), she runs up to the third floor of the house and checks the gym, which is full of exercise equipment: rowing machines, treadmills, stationary bicycles, multigyms, and ellipticals, all doubled—for her and for him—purchased back in the days when he could still get it up. He's not there! Then there's the library—thousands of books of which she's only read the covers, but for fuck's sake, who's going to care about that now? Even back in college she was clever enough that by reading only a title and table of contents, or occasionally two or three pages from the middle, she could figure out exactly what some Barthes or Borges was writing about, which was always just the same old trash, anyway, because later in life it turned out that at parties and banquets, whether at the corporation's headquarters or at the ministry, not only had no one read any of those books, they hadn't even bothered to leaf through their pages as she had, hadn't even creased the corners of their pages for the sake of appearances, so it was easy for her to boldly show off her knowledge of this or that writer of her choosing. Or this or that book. That's how she always ended up seeming like the most educated person in the room—which was never received very positively.

Now, standing here in the library of unread books, Frenza finds it empty too! She sinks into a plush armchair and lights a cigarette from a pack that has probably lain here for a decade. Salems! Who smokes Salem cigarettes these days—who smokes at all these days?! She'll start. She makes this promise to herself. As soon as she finds that imposter!

Frenza's head suddenly clears as the nicotine rushes to it. With the cigarette in her hand, she runs down the stairs to the entrance hallway and reaches the front door. It's locked from the inside with not only the dead bolt but also the chain. This means Bartek couldn't have left the house—he wouldn't have been able to attach the chain from the outside. It occurs to her to take a look at the security cameras, which capture everything. She checks the footage, rewinding it one hour. He must be hiding somewhere. On one of the cameras, she spots him tiptoeing out of his bedroom and down the stairs. Frenza does the same. She runs downstairs again, trying to spot even the faintest source of light in any of the rooms.

The pantry! Frenza's attention is snagged by a thin stream of light trickling from under the door! "Careful on the steep stairs," she warns herself, recalling how often she has hurt herself by tumbling down them during her somnambulistic attempts to sneak some wine. But it's empty. Not a trace of the deceitful rat! There's still the spacious basement adjacent to the pantry, where, following the architect's advice, she set up an extravagant home cinema . . .

The basement door is slightly ajar. Frenza can hear strange noises coming from inside, as if a pack of grunting cavemen were snarling over freshly killed prey. Frenza extinguishes her cigarette against the wall and quietly enters . . .

Why You Should Never Masturbate While Driving

S he remembers that day five years ago in vivid detail. The whole world was gripped by the pandemic, and its dark cloud was hanging over the garden city to which they'd moved a year earlier. Despite that, Podkowa Leśna was awash with colorful azaleas and rhododendrons in full bloom. Richly fertilized by the decomposing bodies of society's poorer class, all the plants were so magnificent that they reached the sky—or at least the rooftops of the luxuriously furnished houses. Panic was spreading throughout the country. All sports facilities, shopping malls, cultural institutions, and restaurants were closed. People wore masks—not carnival masks—and had thus lost their external identity, their image. Humanity had become faceless. A phantom species. Podkowa Leśna was the only place that remained as calm and dignified as it had ever been, for it was equipped with the highest number of respirators per square meter in Europe, with terraces full of the most expensive chaise longues and recliners with bodies stretched out on them—the pride of the country's best plastic surgeons. Unrealistic Podkowa Leśna, soaring on the wings of sweet idleness—where everyone was lounging in the sun, doing minor gardening work, sculpting the rhododendron bushes, throwing sticks to purebred dogs, brushing the lustrous fur of Russian Blue cats, listening to birdsong, making lemonade, and pouring water into mini-pools tiled with genuine labradorite and lapis lazuli. According to the architect who designed Frenza's house, a labradorite mosaic would allow her to have—right here, in this Polish landscape, in this garden in Podkowa Leśna—her own private Atlantis. And she would be enveloped in positive vibrations. For, according to the architect, energy was what mattered most. "Hopefully it'll be Atlantis from the time before it sank to the bottom of the ocean," Frenza thought, after hearing the architect spew this nonsense.

All the televisions and radios were unplugged to avoid hearing anything about the ever-increasing number of deaths. There were no children hollering in the gardens thanks to online education. And when a few kids did venture into the gardens, they played quietly in their tree houses made of ebony wood so as not to disturb their parents' corporate calls, yoga sessions, and Pilates classes. Driven by an excess of money and boredom as well as an excess of sadness stemming from her husband's increasingly painful sexual rejections, Frenza decided to do something crazy. And since her frenzy wasn't a feminine kind of madness— all-consuming and out of control—but rather a simple reaction bringing instant gratification, a weekly automotive magazine inspired her to go to Gdańsk and buy a blue Mercedes CLS 400d advertised by a dealership in the Tri-City area with the slogan "All hail the king of cars!" A Mercedes for which she paid 369,000 złoty in cash, having made a compromise with herself, for she had been dreaming of acquiring a Rolls-Royce Phantom advertised by the same dealership with the slogan "God has come down to earth!" But that cost three million. Faced with the uncertain future of the global pandemic, she said bye-bye to her Phantom dream.

"It's more elegant to say *farewell!*" remarked her husband, who had a degree in English philology.

Bartek enjoyed the purchase even more than she did. He enjoyed the luxury with which his wife surrounded him, especially the fact that, as her husband, he co-owned their house and Mercedes. Just as his mother had instructed him to do when he was young, he protected his own interests. After his marriage, his interests became—of course, only indirectly—his mother's interests as well. The only thing about this situation that didn't sit well with him was the fact that Frenza earned fifteen times more than he did as an English teacher at a local public school.

Their journey home from Gdańsk passed in a pleasant manner, except for one problem: the bathrooms at the rest stops were all closed due to the pandemic. Frenza is incapable of peeing in nature. It's completely beyond her. This is why she's never gone camping. Not being able to urinate and defecate in normal, civilized conditions terrifies her. Sometimes on the team-building trips she has to go on with her colleagues she sees one or two of them popping into the bushes to take a leak and she can't contain her anxiety. It disgusts her so much, she can't bring herself to drink wine or dance with anyone who she knows has urinated outside. It's as if peeing on grass strikes a person off the list of humanity. When it comes to defecation, Frenza only accepts toilet bowls that have no "ledge." This makes it all but impossible for her to take business trips to Germany or Austria—countries where people relish the sight of their own excrement before flushing it down. This is something else Frenza is unable to comprehend—how a nation that has produced so many outstanding composers, writers, poets, and philosophers could have created something as monstrous as toilet bowls in which shit doesn't immediately descend into the abyss but just lies shamelessly on the flat porcelain surface. It simply boggles the mind. Frenza would rather not shit at all. She's even tried nourishing herself intravenously with food from a tube that penetrates her blood while bypassing her stomach and intestines, allowing her to use the toilet as infrequently as possible. She's equally disgusted by hair. A hair in a soup is a nightmare comparable to a toilet bowl caked with feces. And absolutely unbearable is the pubic hair that Bartek leaves behind in the shower. And any unshaved armpits, including Bartek's. In Frenza's world, women with unwaxed pubic hair or thick moss under their arms simply don't exist. She'll meet them later, but even after she does, for a long time she'll think she's hallucinating.

Conversations with Bartek don't go smoothly even when they avoid difficult topics, which of course include their lack of sex. If she ventures into that thorny territory, Bartek shrinks, cringes, winces, coughs, scratches his head, as if he's allergic to the subject. And then Frenza cries again, but the tears are no longer streaming down her face. She cries on the inside, silently.

For a long time now, they haven't looked each other in the eye. As if the tennis game their souls are playing together at Wimbledon were merely a simulation of a real game. There isn't even a ball in it anymore. It bounced off the court and no one bent down to pick it up. Lovers' eyes only communicate with each other for as long as the ball remains in action. Once the connection is broken, it will never again electrify the body or spark arousal. And yet it was different at the beginning. Maybe not very often, but nevertheless there were occasional moments that could be filed away in the "happy" drawer. If there's sex once a month, it means something's happening, at least. Frenza had friends who made love to their husbands less frequently than she did. Daria was the only exception—she had sex twice a week. They all envied her. And she didn't have to ask for it. She even sometimes had to fend off her hypersexual husband.

Frenza had always dreamed of this; she wanted Bartek to come home and grope her. She wanted him to put his hands on her breasts, on her hips. After two glasses of wine, she would begin to fantasize about being molested by her husband at corporate banquets as well, thereby earning the approval of her male colleagues. They would pat her on the back, while mentally slapping her buttocks. She laughed louder than the men at jokes about the stupidity of women. She was sometimes verbally abusive to female drivers. This fired up her male colleagues. They fantasized about anointing her with sperm—only with her face sprinkled with their sacred seed could she belong to the male Order. Only when they objectified her did she feel attractive.

That's how it was until the accident. Then she fell silent. She never again referred to sex in conversation. It was as if overnight she had deleted from her vocabulary all words that might seem suggestive. Fortunately, by that time she had managed to rise to the very top of the company's hierarchy.

The accident happened when they were halfway home from Gdańsk. Bartek had fallen asleep. Frenza pressed hard on the gas pedal. She'd never driven so fast. It excited her. Just like on a roller coaster, when gravity slammed her into the seat and her G-spot was stimulated by an invisible vector. Even though it wasn't at all her style, she slipped her left hand into her panties. She hadn't done this for several months, wanting to remain pure and unspoiled for Bartek, hungry for his touch and receptive solely to his member. So that once the penetration occurred, she could come just like that, without rubbing her clitoris (secretly, of course, so that he wouldn't notice that she was enhancing what he was doing, since he wanted to believe that his member was enough to satisfy her).

She quickly became so wet that her panties were soaked, which, considering what a fossil her vagina had become after marrying Bartek, surprised her and made her feel slightly disgusted. However, she didn't stop touching herself. She moved her finger in a swirling motion on her clitoris, as if drawing an invisible orbit around it. Sometimes she pressed and pinched it gently. And then, just when her vision became filled with a light so intense that her eyes almost hurt from the brightness and a powerful shudder rocked her body, something happened that turned their lives upside down.

Concerning a Disability That Fits Like a Glove

When a man used to have four functional limbs (the upper two of which were used for leafing through pages in books, changing TV channels with the remote control, making a gimlet—his favorite cocktail, straight out of a Raymond Chandler novel—and masturbating until he nearly collapsed from exhaustion while his wife was away accumulating capital, and the lower two were used not only for moving from place to place but also for running marathons, skiing, snowboarding, and kitesurfing, activities funded with the capital that his wife had accumulated), but now only the upper two remain, for after a car accident the entire lower part of the man's body, including his penis, stopped working—life becomes very difficult. He has to learn to live all over again, practically from scratch: for the first few years, he tries to find meaning in his continued existence, then, later, he seeks out minor pleasures to compensate for the disability.

After the accident, Bartek quickly recovered psychologically. Doctors said it was due to post-traumatic stress—an aberration in his reactions caused by extreme shock and an inability to integrate the trauma. Or not so much an inability to integrate as a radical failure to recognize it, as if the accident was not at all the worst thing that could have happened to him. After he woke up from the anesthesia, when the friend operating on him informed him in Frenza's presence that most likely he would never regain control of his lower body, Bartek received this news indifferently, perhaps even with visible relief. It was as if the paralysis of his lower body was something that would liberate him from some aspect of active life that he'd never been very fond of.

However, for Frenza, everything had changed. Not only could she no longer count on Bartek's help in everyday matters, but she also had to get used to the idea that there would never again be any real sexual intimacy between them — something she had pursued at any cost throughout their marriage but that happened very rarely. And when it did, it was always initiated by her. It was as if sex didn't matter to Bartek at all, a fact that had been slowly destroying Frenza throughout their years together. The dynamics of their relationship consisted of silent domestic violence — the more Bartek rejected Frenza, the more she desired him, but the feeling of rejection simultaneously made her want to give him a decent thrashing, most often verbally, though once or twice she really tore into him with her claws and then cried half the night from shame and hopelessness, disappointed at what kind of person she'd become. And what kind of woman. It must be said that through his rejection of Frenza, it was Bartek, not her — the CEO of the national oil company earning fifteen times his salary — who held the power in their relationship, and in response all she could do was cry or burn with the anger that grew inside her day by day, or rather, night by night.

Apart from sex, after the accident, Bartek didn't lose much. He persuaded Frenza to help him continue to pursue his passions — he swapped his snowboard, skis, and kite for the world's most expensive paraglider for disabled people and flew through the air like Daedalus, except in a wheelchair with a parachute attached to a special frame. It was an expensive and dangerous sport, but Bartek, it seemed, didn't feel he had much to lose. If he died, what a beautiful death it would be! Poetic, Icarus-like, the kind of death one could only dream of, unlike the one his mother had orchestrated for herself after his father's death by putting her head in the oven and turning on the gas.

Frenza was happy that Bartek didn't break down, that he'd even developed, according to his doctors, an increased appetite for life, as if ending up in a wheelchair had been his secret dream or calling. Neither the surgeons at the military hospital where Frenza had arranged for Bartek to be operated on in the immediate aftermath of the accident nor the physiotherapists he worked with later had encountered such a reaction in all their years of practice. While working with Bartek, they grew exasperated and eventually concluded that he didn't have the slightest desire to change his condition, literally or figuratively. "It's as if he were born to be disabled," they said, unable to comprehend how such an attitude was possible in a handsome thirty-five-year-old man otherwise at the peak of health.

After two years of fighting for Bartek's recovery, Frenza gave up. It had all taken a toll on her mental health, of course. Until then, she'd continued to believe they might still succeed in climbing that eight-thousander together, the summit of which they hadn't managed to reach—namely, sex. But after numerous strenuous attempts, she abandoned those dreams and instead focused on starting a new phase of married life.

There was an extremely sensitive matter that she couldn't handle: Bartek didn't allow anyone but her to help him with his toilet and hygiene needs. She didn't understand it, but as the years passed, she began to detect in it a desire for revenge. For the fact that she was successful. That, unlike him, she didn't work in a public school trying to teach children a language they could just as easily learn from YouTube or Netflix, and that she wasn't earning the pitiful average national salary. She began to analyze seriously the reasons why Bartek was treating her like a nurse without a trace of shame, quite unlike in bed, where before the accident he'd been embarrassed about everything. He always slept with his back turned to her, wearing pajamas or a sweat suit. Nudity—both his and hers—disgusted him; he found it unbearable. Especially when a little fold of fat appeared on his wife's hips or belly. As if it didn't belong to her. As if something had latched on to her body and wouldn't detach itself. A fatty burr. Disgusting. Bartek tried not to look at Frenza's surplus flesh, but whenever he did, he could barely restrain himself from making a vicious comment.

Because of this, his openness to being touched for personal grooming—cleaning his body after physiological processes, washing and wiping, which suddenly ceased to be a problem for him because they weren't connected to sexuality—surprised Frenza and deeply troubled her.

How to Successfully Gain Weight While on a Diet

Bartek's oppression of Frenza by forcing her to do things for him that any generously paid nurse could have easily done led her to retaliate in her own way. She gained weight at a lethal pace: gram by gram, centimeter by centimeter. She'd always worn size XS clothes, but eventually she expanded to size XL. She was still attractive to her colleagues, however—or perhaps had become even more attractive, since the fat she'd gained accentuated her hips and breasts. As for her waist . . . yes, she still had it, though the former thirty-centimeter difference between her hip and waist circumference had already become irrevocably obliterated. By then Frenza had discovered the pleasure of eating at night—something she'd never indulged in before, even when tipsy. The food she was eating wasn't healthy—not by a long shot. She gorged on greasy potato chips dipped in cream cheese, and when she had bouts of depression, she would cook mashed potatoes at midnight, with nutmeg, heavy cream, and half a cube of butter mixed in. Each spoonful was like a balm for her shattered heart. Unlike Bartek's penis, the carbohydrates gave her instant gratification and pure, undiluted joy. It was an orgasm that lasted from the very first spoonful to the last lick of the bottom of the pan.

She went through various phases. Once, in a delicatessen in Podkowa Leśna, she discovered master-level potato chips: salt-and-vinegar Pringles. The kind she'd eaten during an Erasmus exchange trip to London during her university days. She stood in front of a shelf on which about forty packages of them were arranged in an even row. It was as if she'd run into a lover she hadn't seen in years. To make matters worse, the store owner, whose eye had been caught by Frenza's voluptuous curves, revealed to her that he had a hundred packages in the storeroom that were nearing their expiration date. It was unnecessary honesty. Honesty that nearly finished her off. With a sore pancreas and a liver swollen from Pringles chemicals, she wound up in the internal medicine ward, where her stomach was pumped and she had to endure a weeklong detoxification. Just like when, during her turbulent youth, she'd stuffed herself with motion sickness pills and washed them down with her father's whiskey. While lying in the hospital, she'd had plenty of time to examine her conscience. She calculated that over the course of one month she'd consumed seventy-six packages of chips, while praying to God every night to deprive her of strength in her legs and arms: in her legs so that she wouldn't be able to go down to the basement to get another package, and in her arms so she wouldn't be able to reach for it once she was there.

After the potato chip episode and her stay in the hospital, where she was initially suspected of bulimia but later diagnosed only with compulsive overeating, she decided to reach a compromise with herself. She would continue to binge eat but no longer indulge in food products that would ruin her health. So when she was craving carrots, she would puree a whole kilo of them in the blender, add half a kilo of almond flakes, and toss in half a bottle of pumpkin seed oil. Delicious? Absolutely! Healthy? Definitely! The most fattening healthy salad in the whole world. Three thousand calories. One and a half thousand more than the dietary requirement for the entire day. A salad for a miner heading to work for the night shift. However, when asked by a nutritionist what she was eating, she could always answer, "Carrots with almond flakes and a splash of oil." And that was exactly what she said.

When Frenza discovered German alpine cheese at a health food store in Milanówek, she bought kilos of it, leaving a fortune in the store's cash register. She ate it all day, though it tasted best at night. In the bathtub. With a glass of wine, while watching Ewa Chodakowska, Poland's leading fitness expert, on YouTube. Frenza ate and worked out with her eyes. She listened to the warm-up instructions, then watched the exercises. Stomach, thighs, buttocks—and thirty dekagrams of cheese gone in no time. From the screen, Ewa Chodakowska exclaimed: "Bravo, girls! I'm so proud of you. You're amazing!"

"Yeah, we're fucking awesome!" thought Frenza, shoving another slice of alpine cheese down her deep throat, before, with inevitable pangs of remorse, grabbing the silver showerhead and masturbating furiously until she collapsed from exhaustion. Three or four times, so as to lose at least three hundred of the four thousand calories consumed that day.

Thus Bartek and Frenza continued to exist side by side, serving as each other's executioner and victim. The two roles were deployed interchangeably, bringing to both of them equal amounts of ecstasy, suffering, resentment, anger, contempt, and everything that should have no place whatsoever in a supposedly happy relationship.

But really, what does it mean to have a "happy relationship"?

Frenza began to ask herself this question after the accident, silently taking revenge on her husband and trying to justify to herself the continuation of their toxic bond.

And so the years passed, one after another. Empty, sleepless nights and days filled with a workload so heavy that in the whole fabric of existence there wasn't a single ripped stitch through which the intrusive thought of a living death could creep in. A thought that a once-loved person might not even notice . . .

Now, looking at this body that she had desired for so many years, she feels nothing but resentment. Not toward the owner of the body, but toward herself. How could she have wanted this carcass, which has been leading a second, secret life, not at all in a wheelchair, taking full advantage of her all the while? The body she washed and rubbed with baby oil to prevent bedsores; the body she helped sit on the toilet every day; the body she lifted from the wheelchair to the passenger seat of the car, straining her back; the body whose nooks and crannies she knew by heart but which, it turns out, she hasn't really known at all . . .

A scar on the left knee—a souvenir from his first schoolyard fight; his classmate cut him with a piece of broken glass. She has kissed that spot so many times. A ridge of carelessly stitched skin after his appendectomy. She always found it funny that halfway down his belly it looked as if he'd had a C-section. How many times did she place her hand on that ripple of skin while giving him head? He always pushed it away in a gesture of disgust. She was never quite sure whether this was caused by the pleasure she was giving him or embarrassment about his imperfection. The dimple in his chin, which she loved to touch with the tip of her tongue while they were kissing, causing him to flinch and squirm. His earlobes, which she roamed over with her fingers, lightly bit with her teeth. He hated that most of all.

Frenza didn't know how to touch him in a way that would

make him happy. Everything she did was wrong. The pleasure she wanted to give him seemed unbearable for him from the very beginning, as if her caresses were as unpleasant as hard labor in a Siberian penal colony—instead of leading him to a peak, they led straight into an abyss. It was as if his body were dying at her touch. An agonizing death, moreover.

And now this body, aching and sore from the severe beating that Frenza has just given it, lies face down on the floor in front of her. Next to the head is a bloody computer keyboard and a crystal bowl, from which some potato chips have spilled out. The head is bloodier than other parts of the body—Frenza smashed Bartek's face with the bowl, right across the brow. After a while, he regains consciousness. Whimpering, he struggles to free his hands, which Frenza has tied behind his back with the laptop cable. Well now, look at that! Are legs that have been paralyzed by a car accident able to move so nimbly? Frenza notices the fire extinguisher hanging on the wall behind the door. She grabs it and starts clobbering his sham nonfunctional limbs. He howls in pain. She's just about to stop, but then the flame of rage smoldering inside her flares up again as she glances at the huge screen hanging on the wall.

There's a woman being taken by several men at once. She has huge hips and powerful breasts filled with a substance that makes them remain motionless despite the movements caused by the men's pounding thrusts. Breasts made of silicone. Or bronze. Huge, peach-sized hyaluronic lips. Bartek once told her that such lips weren't attractive to him—he could think of nothing more asexual. Hologram lips. Realizing that he lied about this too, Frenza gives him another kick in the ribs. Her whole life on a diet, just to be attractive to him. He often told her that she was too fat, and it was why she didn't turn him on. She swung back and forth between diets. Low carb, sirtuins, raw food, fasting, Montignac, Dukan, keto, Paleo. And *à rebours:* Normal meals with intervals of extreme overeating, nearly to the point of unconsciousness. To the brink of utter revulsion. The experience of eating not just one centimeter of halva but compulsively shoving half a meter of it down her throat was very familiar to her. In the days before Bartek started acting out that farce in the wheelchair, they'd have sex only once per season, no matter how much weight Frenza lost, and so she started devouring megapacks of potato chips with dip the way others might snort a line of coke. And after the chips, she'd run to the gas station for a coconut-flavored Ritter Sport chocolate bar. If there was nothing green in the fridge, she'd nibble on the oat grass growing in a flowerpot for the cat, an attempt at injecting a bit of fiber into her body so the carbs wouldn't be absorbed and transformed into a tire on her belly. Then some slices of ham, so that her stomach would burn calories while digesting the protein, so her rascal of a stomach wouldn't get too lazy at night. She had, after all, been struggling to speed up her metabolism ever since the machine at the fitness center displayed her metabolic age as sixty-three years old! Twenty years older than her actual age!

She asked her personal trainer if the machine could be wrong.

"No, ma'am," he replied. "Take a look at that sixty-year-old guy over there. It tells him he's twenty-six years old—four percent body fat, and the rest is pure muscle."

That day, Frenza ate more than usual. And she vomited longer than usual too.

What Really Happened That Night

As she remembers all this, Frenza gives Bartek a powerful kick right between his legs. He curls up in a ball and shrieks in pain. Frenza finds pleasure in beating him. It arouses her. Animalistic howls with intervals of silence. And all of it performed according to her own orchestral score—one that she's composing herself, through violence.

And then, although later Frenza will never be certain if it really happened or not, she hears a low, sensual female voice coming from a mouth that was engaged just moments before in performing fellatio on the giant screen of their home cinema:

"Look at me while I'm doing what I do. And what I do is something that only I'm capable of doing—nobody else. I make my tongue vibrate so that it pulsates as fast as a hummingbird's heart. Look into my eyes. In the very depths of my irises you'll see a tiny speck of perfidy. The men never notice it because they don't look into our eyes. They only look into the cleft between our legs, because all they want is to penetrate us. They try to access what's hidden deep within us. And when they penetrate all these secret clefts of ours, pulling hard on our hair while doing so, they think they have power over us. They assume we like it. But, sister—they don't have power over us. We sit on them or receive them into our bodies for one specific purpose. We want to keep them in front of the screen for as long as possible in order to deprive them of their strength. With every orgasm, they consume their fuel, and their store of vital energy gradually becomes depleted. And then they won't have enough energy to create new mechanisms of oppression or laws against us. Or sign new and ecologically harmful economic pacts. Or hunt animals. Or beat their women and children at home. We porn stars are not victims of objectification. Nor symbols of that objectification. We're heroines. Batwomen who whip the asses of idiots who get hard when we give them a good flogging. As if they sense that they deserve severe punishment for the fate they've inflicted on us. Sasha, Tanya, Tamila, Samantha, Tracy, Linda, Jenny, and I, along with hundreds or even thousands of others, are breaking viewing records on porn sites for one reason only: we're doing everything we can to draw men away from other areas of society—culture, science, politics, economy, religion—so that women can finally take over the world."

She can't believe these words are being directed at her—Anna Frenza, who has just discovered that the porn industry and her husband's addiction to masturbation are responsible for the long-term lack of sex in their relationship. And just when she's about to switch off the screen, the mouth starts talking again:

"This is a revolution, sister. The radical demise of all that is stiff, all that is erect. When dicks stop being hard, there will be no more rape, war, or religious conflict. No one will burn us at the stake ever again. And they burned thousands of us—the ones who survived after they tried to drown us in swift rivers with ropes around our necks. Do you know why? For being too intimate with Nature—for our knowledge of plants, for our ability to regulate pregnancies and births with herbs, and for expanding our consciousness with plant-based psychoactive substances. But it was in this way, by expanding our consciousness, that we regained a connection with the universe that had been lost."

Anna Frenza's head is beginning to spin. It's too much information for her to digest. With some sort of eco-friendly blather thrown in. Why the hell would she care about any of this?! Suddenly, the camera filming the massive mouth pulls away and zooms out, showing the woman speaking to her in a completely different setting. The woman is no longer indoors but in a forest. And she's no longer alone, or in an orgy with several men. The forest is full of naked women. Some are old, some are young; some are slim with firm, tiny breasts, others are massive with round hips and large breasts sagging toward the ground. All the women, including the one who spoke to Frenza, are either crouching or kneeling, trying to bring their genitals down so low that they aren't only touching the green, carpetlike layer of moss on the ground beneath the trees but actually adhering to it somehow, latching on to it. After a while, all of them, right before Frenza's rapt gaze, begin to move their hips, rubbing their vulvas against the moss. They rock back and forth, and sometimes passionately move their pelvises in a circular motion so that the soft, moist vegetation will give them as much pleasure as possible. Some of them plunge their fingers deep into the soil and, in an act of unbridled ecstasy, rub themselves with it, as if immersing their faces in its subcutaneous fluids, its moisture. Others who are closer to trees rub up against them, pull off strips of bark, and lick the trees' resin as it oozes out. Some lie down on the moss, press their bellies tightly onto it, and begin to rub their clefts against it more rhythmically and urgently, eager to absorb every single subterranean current—to accept the moisture into themselves and blend it with their own, so that they can finally pulsate with the Earth in one rhythm. And when the inner pulse of the Earth begins to throb inside their clefts, the women emit strange sounds: whimpers and murmurs, something between the cry of hatching chicks, the yowl of mating cats, the squeak of Styrofoam rubbing against a pane of glass, and the dying roar of an ox being slaughtered. All of these sounds, interwoven into a fugue with the rustling of leaves stirred up by the wind, sound like the primordial song of humanity blended with the chirping of birds, the chords of thunder, and the staccato of rain drumming against the thatched roofs on the huts of a tribe that died out long ago or transformed into another one, somewhere in the antipodes of Papua New Guinea or Old Mexico.

Frenza isn't sure if the scene in front of her eyes is real or just a random fabrication of her sick mind, which—as a result of a doctor's disastrous decision—is highly unstable.

She grabs Bartek by his battered legs and drags him to the elevator. She ascends with him to the third floor, where there's a gym, a library, and two terraces—one for each of them, facing east and west. She's an early bird, preferring to get up at the crack of dawn to exercise, eat a healthy breakfast, drink some coffee, and then meditate on the powerful and beautiful energy of money while sitting in a lotus position with a banknote in her hand. She learned this from a business coach. "The hologram on banknotes," she said, "is a gateway to the world of fulfillment and abundance. Smell money, taste money, lick money, make yourself a dildo from a roll of banknotes, and you'll earn so much cash, you'll be drowning in it!" Bartek's the opposite: a night owl, rotting away in bed until noon whenever he has the opportunity.

Frenza yanks at him, dragging him by the legs down the long corridor. She passes the gym and the library. She stops at his terrace. She had it built for him so that he'd have a special place where he could sit in his wheelchair and sip wine, leaf through newspapers, and admire the stars. "What was the point?" Furious thoughts mixed with bitterness flash through Frenza's agitated mind. "I could have built him a bunker for jerking off. He probably would've been happier."

She's exhausted but doesn't feel it yet. Nevertheless, she stumbles now and then: over Bartek's legs, then the threshold, then the giant pots of monstera plants that line the sides of the terrace. Suddenly she notices that her husband's toes are starting to move. Frenza knows she needs to act quickly.

She takes the elevator down to Bartek's bedroom to get the wheelchair. When she returns to the terrace, she uses all her remaining strength to lift her husband and place him in it. Then she positions it to face the railing. She sits down next to him, leaning back against the cool wall of the house.

She takes some Salems out of her pajama pocket. She inhales deeply, trying to prolong the icy, numbing blast of menthol in her lungs. Salems from Salem. Will the coolness of the menthol bring relief to her body, which feels as if it were being burned alive? She starts playing with matches, arranging them into a little pyre between Bartek's thighs, close to his testicles.

While doing so, she glances at her husband's battered face. Her husband—with whom she was just sitting at the same table, having dinner, a few hours ago! And with whom she later watched a TV series that provided their only moment of closeness, during which they held hands like in the old days. She snuggled up to him. With a sense of guilt, as usual, but also with a desire for more. This body still aroused her. A body that was eternally independent of her. A body disobedient to her. A body never wanting or desiring her. Now this body was completely disintegrating. It was slumping inertly forward with its head soaked in blood. And the hands that, less than an hour ago, were so lively and nimble that they were able to resurrect what had seemed impossible to resurrect, making vertical something that had existed (officially) only horizontally—hands with short, stubby fingers that had looked suspiciously lewd and sneaky from the very beginning—no longer struggled against the cable with which she'd tied them together like a butcher curing ham. Taking a drag on her cigarette, Frenza recalls how once, not long after their wedding, while they were still living in a rented apartment, she came home from work one day, exhausted, to find Bartek standing naked on a stool in the living room with a leather belt wrapped around his neck and his hands tied behind his back with a pair of her pantyhose. At first, she burst out laughing; it looked absurd, especially since his lazy member had completely surrendered to the law of gravity, which, instead of adding some spice to the scene, stirred in Frenza a genuine childlike joy, comparable to what she'd felt when witnessing a kindergarten classmate spit into another's juice. After activating her powers of critical judgment—that is, foreseeing what might have happened if she'd returned two or three hours later—she marched up to him and slapped him on the cheek as punishment, followed immediately by a hard spank. The lazybones immediately came to life and changed coordinates, shifting from south to north—from the Tropic of Capricorn to the Tropic of Cancer. "How stupid of me," thinks Frenza, "to make him feel good then! I should've left the idiot like that!"

Once, while they were on vacation in Croatia, Bartek had chosen to stay in the hotel room tied to the radiator with the iron's electrical cord instead of going to the beach and floating in the delightfully warm sea. Then, on the island of Krk, she'd left him tied up for several hours, even though he'd asked her to untie him immediately after intercourse, which they'd had—at his request—in a threesome with the radiator in the starring role. Bartek was in a sitting position, leaning back against the radiator, while Frenza sat on Bartek with her back to him because, from the very beginning, he'd made it clear to her that he never wanted to make eye contact during sex. Later, he added to his repertoire of (what some might call "strange") sexual behavior by collecting wooden hairbrushes and spatulas. By the end of their first year of marriage, there were 116 cooking utensils in one of their kitchen drawers, of which Frenza used only three or four. And in Bartek's nightstand in the bedroom that they still shared at that time, there were at least a dozen hairbrushes—ranging from wooden ones, including mahogany and ebony brushes that Bartek had asked his friends to bring back when they went on exotic vacations ("Why the fuck does he need another brush when he's been shaving his head completely bald for years?"), to cheaper ones made of metal or glossy black plastic. In addition to the visual aesthetics of each hairbrush, the surface texture and weight were important to him. Frenza needed to be able to give his ass a hard whack when she administered the spankings he yearned for. The ones that left purple welts on his butt, bruising several hours later, were the most desirable. Brushes had an advantage over spatulas and wooden spoons because they left bruises on his body, while kitchen utensils whistled through the air like forty-pound catfish tails hitting the surface of a lake, giving them the acoustic advantage.

Frenza was exhausted by all of it. By playing the role of dominatrix. By being caught up in this fantasy of power, in which she de facto was being held hostage by his imagination. She supposedly held the power—after all, she was the one wielding the brushes, spatulas, and spoons—but she didn't really, since she was merely fulfilling his twisted desires. She was tired of never having ordinary, traditional sex, the kind to which God would've given a little nod of approval. She dreamed of tantra. Intercourse while gazing into each other's eyes. She wanted it to matter that she was with him and not somebody else, not some porno fucktoy.

Instead of flogging him with a pancake spatula until he ejaculated between her thighs as he lay draped like a naughty schoolboy across her knees, she craved sex that involved a mindful connection, built on intimacy—but Bartek reacted as if someone were puking in his face at the mere sound of the word "intimacy." He confessed to her on their third date that it was even worse than getting germs in his ear from her saliva. She was surprised to hear him describe her habit of kissing his earlobes in this way. She enjoyed doing it so much. She thought it gave him pleasure.

As she now weighs her husband's life in her hands, Frenza has a belated revelation that they've always been playing two different games. But at the same table and on the same game board, which is very confusing! The same thing happened in bed. Before the accident, of course, because afterward they no longer shared a bed. Instead, there were two separate pieces of furniture in two different bedrooms that weren't even next to each other. And on top of them, two bodies that were no longer connected by intimacy of any kind. However, before all this happened, sexuality didn't seem to Frenza like Pandora's box lined with dark velvet or a foul, nasty source of suffering. She perceived sexuality as something bright, luminous, and pleasant, like a white Persian cat rather than a fat, slimy earthworm. Frenza understands that she has fallen victim to a massive deception. The intimacy she longed for so desperately was replaced for Bartek by porn-site whores projected on the screen in the world's most expensive home theater, purchased with her money. Lighting a pile of matches between his legs isn't all she plans to do. The traitor must die. It flashes through her mind that this time she can't botch the job. There will be no more fake surgeries allegedly performed by a surgeon who was obviously in cahoots with her fraudulent husband! She grabs the wheelchair and pulls it away from the railing, for she knows she needs to do this with enough momentum to destroy the iron bars. She delivers the first blow, crushing his shins. The railing doesn't budge. She tries a second time, then a third—each time slamming his legs against the metal.

The impostor is still wheezing and gasping for air when she finally manages to ram through the railing and launch him off the balcony.

On the Splitting of the Soul

Anna Frenza doesn't even notice when the police arrive. They were called by a neighbor—a yoga enthusiast who had been greeting the sunrise on a rooftop terrace. Frenza's consciousness is elsewhere. It's drifting toward those who have been calling her since the very beginning. In almost every dream. In fits of frenzy. During full moons. During solstices. Toward those who have been longing for her, who have been hungry for her. Those who lack what Frenza carries within her, the ability to form a hologram of frenzied madness, the sacred cat's-eye of an enraged deity, contoured with ash. From thousands of pyres. From the hair and bones of women who have been tortured and burned.

Immediately after killing Bartek, Anna Frenza walks across the elegant Spanish tiles of her terrace, though in fact she isn't treading them at all—rather she's walking on cool, damp moss and fallen leaves, in a landscape full of overturned tents and uprooted trees. The setting is familiar to her; she has just seen it under slightly different circumstances. Except that now nothing remains of the women making love to the forest's foliage and undergrowth, crouching with their clefts pressed to the Earth.

There are only tents, dishes, and clothes drying in the sun. It's difficult for Frenza to believe this, for this place was just teeming with life, and with intense bliss resulting from the ecstasy that the women were experiencing all at once, as if they were synchronized with each other. Nothing about the scene foreshadowed misfortune of any kind. But now, something is looming in the air over the forest glade—something Frenza is unable to define, having only just begun to perceive it in the ominous silence. It's as if all the animals, even the birds, even the women, have left the forest . . .

Amidst this silence, which has wound itself around the tree trunks like ivy, Frenza hears a child whimpering. She looks for it, but it's not easy among the remains of the camp. Something terrible must have happened here. The voice, however, is coming from somewhere farther away. Frenza leaves the glade and enters a denser part of the forest. It's full of trees with withered branches. Similar to the forest she used to plow through as a child. Led by instinct, she glances into a pit beneath a huge fallen oak tree and finds that it leads to a cave. Perhaps it once belonged to a fox, but now it's empty. This is where the whimpering sound is coming from.

Frenza crawls into the pit.

The child is here. Hidden at the very back of the cave. Frenza reaches for it, and although it shies away from her, she manages to pick it up and hold it in her arms. The child turns out to be a frail girl with skinny, crooked legs and a small hump on her back. And with hair as golden as rye plaited in a thin braid. The girl is clothed so meagerly that she's almost naked, and she must be hungry, for she starts pecking at Frenza's breast. She's surprised when the girl's hand reaches for her nipple, and at first shudders at the thought of what this ungodly creature might want, but after a while she lets her suckle. The baby whimpers, working her mouth and tongue urgently because no milk is flowing. But just when Frenza is about to pull her away, some milk, to her great surprise, begins to flow.

How could this be possible? She's never been pregnant. She's never given birth. And yet the hungry baby nuzzles for several minutes, greedily drinking. And she gazes at Frenza in a way that no one has ever looked at her before. It's as if this small creature has a magnet in her pupils that attracts Frenza so powerfully, she can't break eye contact, even for a moment. The communication between them, or rather between their eyes, occurs without any words, facial expressions, or gestures. For Frenza, it's the most intense encounter with another human being she's ever experienced. It's pure love.

The girl, having drunk her fill, makes clear that she no longer wishes to be held. So Frenza puts her down on the moss and starts following her. Clumsily setting down her crooked feet, the girl walks ahead of Frenza, turning frequently as if checking to make sure she's following her. They walk through the forest. The child limps, every now and then losing her balance and falling over. After walking a long time, they come to a river.

On the riverbank lie calves with their bellies ripped open. Frenza instinctively covers the child's eyes, but the girl pulls her hand away. She approaches the bodies, all still steaming, and lies next to them. She snuggles up to them as if they were her long-lost relatives.

The strangest thing, however, is that the calves' bellies are devoid of entrails, as if they were disemboweled at their hour of death. A few meters away, Frenza sees a huge cauldron over a tiny fire. She looks inside. A white liquid is just beginning to curdle in the fire's heat. The women must have put the cows out to pasture here and made cheese from their milk. Maybe it was their livelihood. As Frenza tries to comprehend what has happened, the gaunt, sickly girl hobbles over and tugs at her hand, leading her to the river and pointing at something on the bank. Frenza sees a word there, formed from the calves' entrails, in which the letter X is replaced with a cross.

"*Hexen,*" she reads, and a wave of fear grips her. She enters the river, stepping carefully on the stones. The water is swift, and in some places she notices erosion along the bank—the river must have flooded not long ago. And then, in the thickets of calamus growing along the river's edge, Frenza notices something that confirms what she was beginning to fear a few moments before.

The body of a woman, clad in a plain, coarse dress without the petticoats typically worn by the townswomen of Neisse, is bobbing on the surface of the water, as if deeply asleep. The face is aimed downward, rather than toward the sky. The body drifts half a meter forward, then half a meter back, caught by its hair on the stems of the calamus reeds, entrapped.

Frenza doesn't know why she decides to walk toward the body—after all, its soul has long since left it. She feels something underfoot: something that's definitely not the muddy river bottom, full of algae and stones. It's something oval, warm in places, and Frenza keeps slipping off it, only to feel the pleasant warmth and texture under her feet again a moment later. As she walks against the current like this, holding on to the weeds and rushes on the riverbank, trying to keep her head above the surface, she does something that frightens her but which she must do to keep from drowning. She submerges her head to see what she's walking on.

There they are. The mothers of the slaughtered calves—dozens of cows. A whole herd. And between them lie the drowned women. With ropes around their necks. When she raises her head above the surface, she sees some women walking toward her, against the current. They're staggering with fatigue. And lamenting. "Some of them survived," she thinks. At the front of the group, leading them, walks the woman whose face Frenza has always known. She's seen her in shop windows, in mirrors, in the surface of the pond in Podkowa Leśna. Whenever she happens to glance at a reflective surface. When she hasn't managed to prepare herself to meet the reflection. On the streets. In photos of herself. Only in the moments when it happens without any scrutiny and by surprise. In hallucinations. In illuminations. In delirious reveries. In the recurring nightmare she's had about women being burned alive in a furnace.

Mathilde Spalt and the twelve women with her managed to survive only because they knew how to swim and weren't afraid to let the current carry them downstream, even though they were unsure whether the deadly whirlpools that abounded there might sweep them away. Mathilde knew there was no point in running; the hounds would track them down by their scent. The river was their only hope.

They approach Frenza now as if they've known her forever. As if they've been waiting for her. Just as they do in the dream that Frenza often has, the dream that kindles anger within her, in which the women just barely catch a glimpse of her as she inhales the ash from their burning bodies.

"Mathilde Spalt. Granddaughter of the founder of the Earthen Ones, Helene Spalt," says the woman. Then she cuts off Frenza's attempt to introduce herself with the following words: "You need not say anything. I know who you are and how you've come to be here. I have waited for you for many a spring. We have all been waiting, calling out to you. Summoning you."

Suddenly, one of the trees rustles more loudly, and the little girl jumps down from it and lands on all fours, like a cat, prowling. Shaking with fear, whimpering and sobbing, she begins to describe what has happened in that spot.

While hiding in a tree, high enough so that Harold and Bremen, the bishop's vicious hounds, couldn't catch her scent, the girl witnessed Bishop Johann Balthasar Liesch von Hornau and his retinue surround the Earthen Ones while their cows were grazing. She watched them chase the women into the river. Anyone who fought back, either with feet or hooves, was shot in the limbs or belly, even if they were pregnant or nursing calves. Women and cows, panic-stricken, fell into the water, trampling each other, and died in agony. Anyone who managed to rise to the surface was beaten with spears by the torturers.

With every death, she too died — the little Earthen One hiding in the tree. In the moment in which each of the women and cows took their last breath, her breathing ceased too, for her breath was aligned with theirs, in keeping with the teachings of the Primeval Virgin. She saw the men put ropes around the necks of the Earthen Ones to subject them to trial by water, which Bishop Johann Balthasar Liesch von Hornau referred to as "witch-bathing," and then stab to death any who survived. They seized the calves and butchered them one by one, then disemboweled them, cut off their tails, and spelled out a word on the riverbank with the entrails — the word with which they had "christened" the Earthen Ones from the very first days of the community, heedless of the fact that not only did the Earthen Ones not sleep with the Devil, they didn't sleep with anything that was hard or rigid.

When the little Earthen One's words catch in her throat, Mathilde gestures for her to be silent and holds her tightly to her chest. After their breath gradually synchronizes again, Mathilde commands them all to return to the forest glade. It's only once she's there, in the glade, that Frenza recovers from her fear. She watches as Mathilde bustles around the newly lit campfire, places a cauldron over the flames, and sprinkles some twigs and herbs into it. Then Mathilde tells everyone, including Frenza, to find a comfortable place by the fire. She takes the cauldron and pours the liquid from it into a clay pot, then passes it around for everyone to share. The women all drink.

They feel a new strength enter them, and don't protest when Mathilde tells them to return to the river and pull the bodies of the Earthen Ones out from the water. Their strength is so great, it's as if it has flowed into them from the most powerful animals or the ancient oak trees growing all around them. It's a nonhuman force—that's certain. Only with a force so strong could they carry out such an extraordinary task, since the bodies of those who drowned number nearly four dozen. By the time they're done and the Earthen Ones are laid out in even rows on the riverbank, dawn has begun to break. Mathilde stokes the fire and, looking deeply into Frenza's eyes, begins to tell her tale.

From the first words, Frenza has the impression that the little girl whom she took from the uprooted tree and nursed at her own breast is sitting between them. However, after a while, she realizes that this figure isn't the girl but a toothless old woman—someone Frenza hadn't previously noticed. And then, to Frenza's great surprise, as she looks at this toothless old woman in the flickering light of the fire, she sees her gradually merge with Mathilde to become one, as Mathilde tells her extraordinary story.

II

MATHILDE'S TALE OF HOW THE WORLD BEGAN

In the beginning there was lightning. A bright flash that created the world. The lightning split the darkness with its sharp tip and Heaven and Earth emerged. Two different worlds that immediately aligned themselves, one on top of the other, so perfectly that not even the tiniest sliver of Earth protruded from beneath Heaven. As far as the eye could see, Heaven and Earth were joined as one. And they remained so, sometimes motionless, sometimes rocking back and forth and sideways, penetrating still further into one another.

But the union with Heaven began to make Earth squirm in discomfort; the penetration had become unbearable for Her. Heaven punished Her by sending down torrents of rain so abundant that the Earth could barely drink it up. And that which She received unto Herself allowed bodies of water, land, and creatures of every kind to emerge out of fear and love for both Heaven and Earth, Father and Mother.

Heaven soon revealed Himself to be more capricious than Earth. And jealous of the love for Earth that sparked in every living creature. Driven by jealousy, He scorched Earth with a sun so hot that all the plants withered, and unleashed still more torrents of rain so abundant that everything green rotted, bringing disaster, famine, and suffering to all animals and people.

It came to pass that the immense love between Heaven and Earth transformed into a feud so great that it gave rise to mutual hostility. No matter what, Heaven insisted on His dominion over Earth by reason of His physical position over Her, which allowed Him to lie on Her whenever He wished, no matter the suffering it brought to Earth.

And when it so happened that Heaven lay on Earth by force, striving to cling to Her as tightly as He had at the very beginning, Earth began to suffocate, and responded with a convulsion so great that volcanoes erupted with liquid fire across Her surface, for She was unable to contain Her rage.

From such violent tension and struggle, beneath a tree as immense and sprawling as one hundred oaks, the Primeval Virgin was born. A child of Heaven and Earth as old as the world but young as a newborn just emerged from its mother's womb. An infant with hair woven in a thin braid like an ear of rye, crawling unsteadily but already in possession of incredible intellect. An intellect that spanned all that had been and all that would be, probing deeply into all of creation and perceiving everything in the world, even from its farthest corners. And as the infant grew, it became apparent that its thin braid and the clumsiness of its movements were not imperfections but rather a remembrance of the movement of the first creatures that had emerged from the water onto land to transcend their erstwhile state and begin life anew, in a different form. As if in the frail, imperfect, and nearly translucent body of the Primeval Virgin there was a record of every living being that had ever been created in either Heaven or Earth. Thus, slithering like a snake or moving on all fours like an ape was as suitable for the wee child as walking upright on both legs. It was able to rejoice in all things by employing the skills it had accumulated over two hundred thousand years, simultaneously making use of knowledge from the present and the past. Over time, the infant began to hunch even more beneath a heavy bundle it carried on its back, its appearance becoming still stranger. But it never complained. It accepted ever more tasks and kept moving forward, sometimes tumbling along the road, sometimes helping itself move with a front limb or two, sometimes creeping like a lizard, and sometimes flying slightly above the ground or even somersaulting.

Heaven was mightily displeased by all of this. He made His child stoop even more toward Earth, taking revenge on disobedient Mother Earth with plagues, pestilence, and calamities of sundry kinds.

Nevertheless, the frail, bowlegged child continued to grow, slowly transforming into a beautiful girl. The hump on her back shrank, her strides became more confident, and her braid, which had been very thin until then, came undone, delighting all living things, for her hair covered Earth like a cloak, each strand connected to the life of a living creature. When it fell out or was broken, the soul was extinguished.

One day, the long-haired girl sat down on the ground. She noticed blood flowing from the cleft between her legs onto the dark green moss and it was then that she became a woman. A woman who enjoyed sitting on anything that gave her pleasure, be it tree stumps, plant rhizomes, or moss. She would spread her legs, sit back, shift ever so slightly, and rock back and forth, just as she had in her cradle at the dawn of time, when she was a mere newborn suckling. As she rocked, she felt sparks inside her, then flames would rise and a conflagration would sweep through her body. When this happened, she laughed so melodiously that the cliffs carried her voice into the world as an echo. The blood in her body throbbed so intensely that every female creature on Earth felt the pulsation in the pit of her stomach and throbbed with it. The monthly blood simmered and boiled in them at once. And when the Primeval Virgin, in her long-haired, more mature form, discovered how much distress and suffering was caused by the male creatures of the world, her body heaved with peals of thunder, and lightning bolts streaked out of her into all forms of female life—old and young, thin and fat, with long hair and short—causing explosions of fury as powerful as earthquakes. It was in these bursts of anger, these peals of thunder, and the fury that enveloped their bodies that they were finally united as one. Without any divisions. Without differences. All connected by the unity of the cleft. Forming a community of clefts aroused by pleasure and rage, each one in communion with all the rest on Earth, sharing pleasure and sending lightning down into Earth's inner depths.

And then the long-haired girl transformed into an old woman. She wove her hair, which was loose and tangled from the wild winds, into a thin braid once more. A braid that looked like an ear of rye or wheat. And she hunched again, leaning toward her beloved Earth. Her eternal mother. Toward the cavernous clefts from which she had emerged or slithered with serpents thousands of years earlier. Lower and lower, to the moist cave from which she'd been born.

But no matter her age, the pleasure she found in rocking back and forth never dwindled. She knew how to settle her cleft onto the moss or a fallen tree and rub, as if striking rocks to make fire. This allowed her to remain constantly connected to Earth, spreading immense, uninterrupted delight among all living beings. She absorbed life through her cleft from the soil on which she sat and clenched herself shut to contain that life inside her so its energy would be restored to everything that sprouts from Earth and pierces the soil toward Heaven, carried through the vast currents and channels of subterranean waters. She accomplished all this with a toothless smile on her face—the smile of neither an old woman nor a child. Constantly life-giving and life-taking. Receiving her entire harvest in her viscera once again. With a face distorted by old age, but also with a gleam in her eye, as if it were the frolicsome Beginning.

III

HELENE SPALT
AND
HER GOSPEL

Concerning the Very Beginnings of Belief in the Primeval Virgin

None of the women saw which man had done it. Which one had slit open the calves' bellies, disemboweled them, and arranged the entrails to spell out the word on the riverbank. A word that was appearing more and more often on the walls of houses, market stalls, and workshops in the Duchy of Neisse. It occurred to them that it might have been Bishop Johann Balthasar Liesch von Hornau himself, although they doubted His Excellency would want his hands to become smeared with the blood of a cow, not a ram. Perchance, then, it had been Heinrich Babel, who was old but exceedingly skilled in his vile trade. He had been eager to take revenge on Mathilde Spalt—the granddaughter of the Earthen One whom he'd never been able to capture but whom he'd long sought to destroy. She was the chaff produced by the woman who had robbed him of his childhood, the one on account of whom he'd always been known as a "nasty little teat-sucker," forever inferior to everyone else. It was because of her that he'd been rejected by Brother Albert at the monastery as well as Kunegunde Kreppel, whom he'd loved as if she'd been his own mother—and even more than that. Other men also took part in the hunt for the Hexen—as the women were called—such as Chapter Councilor Petrus Gerbauer and the prosecutors Franz Zacher and Martin Lorenz, although the idea hadn't been theirs. To instill in themselves enough courage to participate in this secret project of the Catholic Church, which had been planned for one whole month, they had drunk as much strong liquor at the Golden Crab Tavern as their bellies could hold. But Bishop Balthasar, who was suffering from a stomach ulcer, and Inquisitor Heinrich Babel, who never consumed a drop of liquor due to his advanced age, were both of exceedingly sober mind. This time the roundup had to succeed, for the previous efforts, undertaken for more than a decade, had failed to produce a satisfactory result. Hence, it could have been the bishop and the inquisitor together, or each one on his own, who had come up with this terrifying idea.

Babel wouldn't have denied it to anyone. Indeed, he swelled with pride at finally having rid the world of these jezebels, even though he'd failed to capture the one he wanted most of all. Maybe she'd been swept away by the whirlpools and perished in the river, like all the others.

He had seen it. He was the only one. But he'd been preparing something much greater for the women—a kind of death that no one in the duchy had ever experienced before. "It's only a matter of weeks now, even days," he'd reassured himself, rubbing his hands together at the thought of the fate that awaited them.

But it had turned out not to be so easy to catch the Earthen Ones, to lay charges against them, and to drown them in the river according to protocol, in a way that wouldn't lead to Gerbauer or Zacher later being implicated. He wanted to destroy their encampment and kill any who survived the drowning test, their survival serving as proof of their guilt. He sweated like a hog from the exertion, despite how experienced he was in trials and executions of all kinds. Torturing women was one of his daily duties, and he was truly the best at it in all of Silesia.

Verily, what had been done to those cows (may their diabolical udders never produce another drop of milk again!) seemed like something that would have been dreamed up by both Inquisitor Babel and Bishop Johann Balthasar Liesch von Hornau, who ruled over the entire ecclesiastical duchy of Neisse—a duo to whom schemes and intrigues of various kinds had long been attributed.

The truth of the matter was that neither Bishop Johann Balthasar Liesch von Hornau nor his two predecessors, Balthasar von Promnitz and Johannes von Sitsch, who had sparred with the founder of the community herself—Helene Spalt, Mathilde's grandmother—had known what to do with the Earthen Ones. Before the roundup, the council of church canons had convened in the bishop's palace in Neisse, where, at a table lavishly laden with food and drink, the bishop had uttered words that could not be retracted. Words that set a powerful machine in motion, and which were preceded by a pause and a dramatic banging of his fist on the table. Never before had the assembled members of the chapter heard the bishop utter such harsh, vulgar words.

That day, when Bishop Johann Balthasar Liesch von Hornau ordered a hunt to begin, a hunt not for wild game but for the Earthen Ones living on the bank of the river east of Neisse, thunder erupted in the heavens.

The bishop swept his gaze over the faces, all full of disbelief, and, wishing to add weight to the decision he'd made, reminded the assembled men that the accursed founder of the Earthen Ones, Helene Spalt—the "heretic," "wild woman," "swamp demon" (oh, what was not said about her in the canonry!)—had caused them grief for many a year. How many clergymen had she destroyed with her blasphemy and false belief in that abomination she called the "Primeval Virgin"? How much misfortune had befallen the town of Neisse, whose population had dropped by reason of the evil potions she'd created to prevent the procreation of Christians?

And now her granddaughter, Mathilde Spalt—even more brazen a reprobate and sinner than the old woman—was still, so many years after the death of her accursed grandmother, engaged in that sinful practice in the forest with other harlots that had caused so many husbands to lose their wives and children to lose their mothers! How many families had been broken! Destroyed! Led down a path of evil!

The bishop continued his passionate disquisition, reminding those who were nodding in agreement with him—the richest merchants, lawyers, and doctors in town—that several years before, the newly wed Mathilde Spalt had tried to poison one of their own! Some cheese made from the milk of the cows that she held under her power with her diabolical enchantments was intended to rob her husband of life.

The bishop was blazing with a rage as fiery as Moses's bush. He burned until his testicles became sweaty and overheated because, after all, he had no way to air them under his cassock.

"This time these whores won't escape us! They're done for!" he exclaimed in an emphatic tone, eradicating even the slightest hint of doubt. The guilt of Mathilde and the other Earthen Ones was now indisputable, and their death had been decreed.

Concerning Plague, Filth, and Evil Shit

It had all begun seventy years earlier, Anno Domini 1569, when Helene Spalt—Mathilde's grandmother—was born in the ecclesiastical duchy of Neisse. The event that took place in Mathilde's lifetime on the banks of the river, an event without precedent if one considers the cruelty with which the women and cows were murdered—living beings who had not only nourished many with their milk but also had brought splendor to the entire duchy—could trace its genesis back to the birth of old Spalt.

The calendar used by the Earthen Ones indicated a completely different date, one that had nothing to do with the Year of Our Lord. It began with the start of winter, when life first froze and descended beneath the Earth to await the spring in its most immortal, albeit necrotic, form. One might wonder when—counting the Years of Our Lord, hence those connected not with the Primeval Virgin but with Jesus Christ—this first winter occurred in the history of the world. It could be calculated by simply locating the world's oldest tree and studying the number of rings in its cross section, though even that would probably make the Earth a good thousand years younger than it truly is. But what's a thousand years compared to all the dawns and dusks that have brightened and darkened the heavens? Perhaps, then, we should try to establish the date of Helene Spalt's birth in a different, more conventional manner . . .

When attempting to pinpoint this moment on the map of world events, it could be claimed that the birth of the Catholic Church's greatest enemy in the history of these lands, Helene Spalt, occurred three years before the triumphant return of the bubonic plague, which nearly fifty years earlier had wiped out precisely half the population of the archdiocese, and had taken only seven of the longest nights and days in the town's history to do so.

As her doting parents mentioned at every possible occasion, Helene was born into the world like Jesus Christ—on a pile of hay in a barn where her mother, Gertrude Spalt, was delivering a calving heifer. It was not an easy birth, as the heifer's cleft refused to unclench, wouldn't open even a crack under the pressure of the calf's hooves and head, and Gertrude had, at that point, been alone on the farm with her children for several days because her husband, a free-spirited drunkard, hadn't come home, despite knowing that both she and the heifer were imminently due. Gertrude knocked back a whole jug of beer to dull the pain and ease the nausea, for as she walked around the house, she couldn't keep from vomiting either on the children scampering about her or on herself. She headed for the barn as soon as she heard the animal's roar shattering the evening silence. And when she investigated the matter, she came to the conclusion that the heifer's cleft was too narrow to let the calf through, so she shoved her arm in, right up to the elbow, and tried to pull the calf from the uterus. But the calf was hell-bent on remaining inside its mother, so Gertrude twisted a loop out of rope and wrapped it around the baby's head to guide it out. As a result of the intense strain of her exertions, a sudden splash of liquid wet her shoes as her own child pushed its way into the world. As it was her sixth one, it happened quickly: at exactly the moment the calf entered the world, so too did a wee babe slip out of Gertrude. It landed on the ground, its tiny behind covered in blood, piss (both human and cow), and cow manure. But instead of letting out a wail, it opened its mouth in a smile.

The baby girl was given the name Helene, such a lovely name that at its mere mention, whoever said it smiled too. The name fit the lass like a glove, for she was so radiant and joyful that everyone's spirits grew lighter just looking at her, as if she filled any gap within them through which darkness might enter.

Nevertheless, darkness still found a way to infiltrate Helene Spalt's joyful existence. The Black Death once again knocked at the gates of the duchy, bringing a new wave of suffering to its population. It was a plague that couldn't be halted even by the world's best doctors—only by thieves who sneaked onto ships arriving in the ports to steal vinegar, spices, and oranges to brew into an elixir. They smeared themselves with it from head to toe and then prowled among the corpses of those who had fallen victim to the plague, looting their pockets and even their mouths, which were contorted into silent screams of pain, and in which sometimes a gold tooth flashed. Those who possessed this cure, which came to be known as "four thieves' vinegar," had less chance of perishing. But it was difficult to get hold of the concoction in the Duchy of Neisse, as distant as it was from the harbors. Whoever had some savings forced their kreutzers into the hands of any merchants they came upon who were traveling to the coastal regions so that they would bring the four thieves' vinegar back for them from major trade outposts of Northern Europe.

Although the bubonic plague had afflicted them many times before, this time it struck the town and the surrounding countryside particularly severely, sending two thousand citizens of Neisse to the Pearly Gates over the course of just ten days, to face the majesty of the One who, according to the faithful, had sent the plague for the specific purpose of scaring the heretics and infidels so that they'd wake up and stop sinning. Catholics regarded the epidemic as the finger of God being shaken at them threateningly, as if He were a stern father out to annihilate the most disobedient among them.

Many surnames disappeared that week, for entire families were wiped out, unable to rescue any descendants from the clutches of the Black Death. Helene was the sole survivor of the Spalt family, and she'd only been alive for three springs. The little girl, who had still been suckling at her mother's breast, witnessed her loved ones perishing one by one—first her siblings and then her parents, who had instructed her with their last breath to lie down in the doghouse and wait for someone to find her. They knew that every evening, civil servants appointed to count corpses passed through the town and the neighborhoods outside its walls, such as the one where the Spalts' house stood, and designated them to be burned to prevent the plague from spreading.

The plague inspector didn't come that same day, however, but three days later, when the corpses had begun to take on the pale blue hue that occurs nowhere else in nature but on the body of a person from whom the divine spark has been extinguished, in whom the blood has solidified, like candle wax on a catafalque. The bodies were all lying in the room as if in their usual resting places—except that they were exceedingly disfigured by disease. The worms that had infested them were feasting to their hearts' content, leaving behind in the eroded areas a large quantity of excrement. Johannes Klage, exhausted from his work, wouldn't have found little Helene had the Spalts' dog not caught a whiff of the lard his beloved wife had slipped into his satchel first thing that morning. When the Spalts' bitch, more ravenous than she'd ever been in her life but too weak to chase a hare through the fields or woods, smelled the pork fat, similar to what her mistress had often fried in the evening, she barked with delight, waking up Helene, who was starving and thirsty. Then, for the first time in her three years of life, the little girl cried. And once she started, she couldn't stop. She wailed, unable to say a word to the stranger on horseback—first because she couldn't speak well yet, and second because even if she could've expressed herself clearly, she wouldn't have been able to describe what she'd witnessed because she didn't understand what had happened. But the images from those seven days of death's reign would be engraved in her memory forever; there's nothing on earth that could erase such horror and pain from a child's mind and heart.

Johannes Klage, who was acutely sensitive to the suffering of children, for although he'd brought three of his own offspring into the world, they all had died, immediately jumped off his horse and, mindful not to touch anything on the plague-stricken farm, crawled into the kennel where the little girl was cowering like a puppy, crying uncontrollably.

When Johannes's wife, Barbara Klage, saw Helene sound asleep on her husband's saddle, she knelt on the ground and crossed herself at the heart-wrenching sight. The child was so small and frail that even a chicken would've weighed more than her, and so dirty she looked like a small swamp demon, even with the golden ringlets encircling her head like a halo. Barbara crossed herself three times, then she spat once over her left shoulder to ward off the plague, just in case, for she didn't believe that such a scourge could have been sent by God, especially here in Neisse—the "Little Rome," as visitors called the town, due to the number of churches within its limits. Barbara picked up the wee foundling, as filthy as the Devil himself. It was how she imagined Hell: awash with foul-smelling mud mixed with shit. Human, bird, cattle—every kind of shit, and everyone wallowing in it up to their ears, falling over every time they tried to stand up, as if sticks were tied to their shoes with string and they were going down a slide, all praying for the slide not to collapse beneath them, dragging them beneath the surface to Hell's dungeon, where the devils boiled people alive in cauldrons and served them to others as food in such a way as to ensure that everyone ended up eating someone they knew and liked in their lifetime.

With wee Helene in her arms, Barbara went into the house, lit a fire in the stove, and heated water for a bath, and although the girl was crying, Barbara didn't let go of her until she'd scraped off the thick layer of dirt and revealed her tiny pink body. And when she saw the girl's ruddy little earlobes emerging from under the filth, Barbara gently rubbed them with her fingers, as she did with her cows, and with the cats that prowled around her house, and with her dogs, and the piglets in the pigsty, believing as she did that when ears are well rubbed, squeezed, and stroked, life immediately returns to all of God's creatures, without exception. Well, except her own children, who were taken by the plague one by one, no matter how they'd been rubbed and cuddled. With those horrible images once again before her eyes, she held this poor little creature, who was still crying uncontrollably, and cuddled her so long and hard that finally, exhausted by her weeping, the girl fell silent. And since Barbara had just lost her last child a short time before, pressing the girl against her breasts made the milk flow into them again, which Helene sensed immediately, reaching for a nipple, forming her mouth into a little pout, and suckling like a stray kitten or puppy.

They would have lived together for a long time to come — Barbara Klage; her husband, Johannes, a civil servant appointed by Bishop Kaspar von Logau to count plague victims; and Helene, who slowly, day by day, opened up more and more to the love of her new family and even began to reciprocate it with affection — if

Barbara hadn't suddenly fallen ill. Death snatched her away from the little one after four wonderful years full of loving care and support, which all the citizens of Neisse had begun to express toward each other after the plague left the town.

Johannes completely lost his mind after Barbara's death and turned into an animal, committing an act of heresy during her funeral by shouting, in the presence of all the mourners, that he no longer believed in God; everything he loved had been mercilessly taken away from him and he'd rather rot in Hell after he died than stand before the heavenly throne. After his outburst, Bishop Kaspar von Logau himself seized Johannes's adopted daughter from him and sent her that very day to the Franciscan monastery, with a letter in which he asked the friars to care for her and educate her at the discretion of the father general. And if the little girl turned out to be clever, then she should stay in the monastery forever, so as not to shock or offend the townsfolk of Neisse. For nobody, after all, believed that girls should study in those days, but rather that they should live simple, pious lives.

Concerning Kunegunde Kreppel and Helene's First Years of Life Under Her Wing

Little Helene's life at the Franciscan monastery was quite pleasant. She was placed under the care of Kunegunde Kreppel—the woman who served as the monastery's cook, housekeeper, and "duenna," as the father general, Bernard von Hinterling, affectionately called her, thus elevating her status. At first Kunegunde wasn't very pleased about this situation, as she already had her hands full washing the friars' clothes, cooking their food, and mothering an unbearable boy named Heinrich Babel, whose father, the mayor of Edelstadt, had dropped him off at the monastery after his wife had died in childbirth. But soon, like all the other residents of the monastery, Kunegunde fell head over heels for Helene.

Kunegunde's surname, Kreppel, happened to be the name of a popular type of jam-filled doughnut, a coincidence befitting her person—her build was round and stocky, with curves that would have made the Venus of Willendorf proud. She was so preoccupied with cooking oats and spelt—in keeping with the precept she'd formulated for herself that "there's nothing above oats and spelt but Heaven itself!"—and breastfeeding the boy, who no longer needed to drink breast milk due to his age (the rascal had already lived for nine springs) but refused to give it up, as well as her passion for embroidery, that she was barely able to find time for her new ward. Her penchant for oats and spelt stemmed from her belief that they acted as an antidote to the heat that surged from time to time in the friars' balls, capable of subduing their boundless, soul-destroying lust. Lust that she herself, quite obliviously, aroused in them.

However, despite giving the friars her special elixir to drink every day—liters of water left over after cooking the miracle grains—their balls were still boiling with a passionate heat, only slightly subdued. It was no wonder, considering plump Kunegunde's alluring appearance. And every time she pulled a huge tit, twice the size of her head, out of her blouse to give milk to little Heini—as she called Heinrich Babel before she later baptized him as "the nasty little teat-sucker"—there wasn't a single friar whose halberd didn't rise at the sight of it.

Whether she was kneading yeast dough for the midafternoon meal or preparing poppy-seed dumplings, she seemed to each of the friars, without exception, the most beautiful woman on earth, many times more beautiful, forsooth, than the Virgin Mary, who was both a dried-up old nag and a mere child at once; none of them would even have glanced at her in real life. The sight of Kunegunde, meanwhile, brought forth a repressed gluttony within the friars, not only for food but for everything—an appetite for life—igniting desires in them that she was unable to satiate. She had strong arms capable of embracing half a dozen of them at a time, and legs as plump as the cured hams and pork loins from the butcher shops in the market square or Rudolf Jaeger's sausage stall; she could take the other half dozen between them and crush them while they were reaching the pinnacle of pleasure. Many of the friars admired Kunegunde Kreppel's sweet ham hocks from hidden spots in the grove of trees where she liked to squat down and shoot streams of urine boldly in front of her—so boldly, in fact, that the golden rain fell a meter away and then, swirling in a golden rivulet, soaked into the ground. At the mere thought of Kunegunde's fat knees and even fatter thighs, many of the friars' peckers hardened, which caused them quite a bit of trouble but also gave them so much pleasure that they felt it was worth sneaking a peek at her while she released her torrential stream.

Peeing in nature, whether under a raspberry bush or a fruit tree, or sometimes directly into a bed of carrots, turnips, or parsley, was an experience so wonderful and beautiful for Kunegunde that even when the father general shook his fist at her angrily, she was simply unable to swear on the cross that she would never do it again. She knew she would succumb to the temptation. Pissing into a bucket in her chamber or in the latrine outside, which reeked of the friars' excrement, was for Kunegunde completely devoid of the poetry she found in urinating with a powerful burst directly into the soil she loved and cultivated. It felt to Kunegunde as if she were pouring herself into the ground to water it. To give it a drink. And it made her feel, for a brief moment, at one with the Earth.

The breeze that wafted over her vulva during this act was as delightful as the caresses she experienced while cooking for a townswoman from Ferrara. When Kunegunde and the lady caressed one another (and only then, for this had never happened with her husband, who had drunk himself to death after Kunegunde had borne him a dead offspring), when the lady from Ferrara squeezed one particular spot of which Kunegunde had previously been unaware, having never managed to reach it on her own, she shot out a waterfall so great that no stream of piss, even one held back for hours, could match it with its violent force. This waterfall was accompanied by a pleasure so immense that Kunegunde, as if there were not enough moisture already, added a little more, bringing herself greater relief than the world had ever known before the invention of the female orgasm.

In addition to releasing powerful streams of urine—which the lady of Ferrara referred to as golden rain—and other liquids too, Kunegunde took great pleasure in several other activities that the friars knew nothing about, such as plucking feathers from fowl after they'd been shot, and milking cows and then drinking the fresh milk and washing herself with it so that, as she often repeated to Helene (for with whom else could she speak about such things at the monastery?), her vulva would never suffer from sores or itching. Her only sanctioned hobby was embroidery, and she spent hours embroidering liturgical vestments and altar cloths with colorful thread.

While little Helene wasn't fond of plucking shot fowl—the smell of the entrails nauseated her to such an extent that she sometimes fainted and fell to the ground while doing it—milking cows and being in their company was one of her favorite activities. And Kunegunde liked to milk in the presence of Helene too, for she had the impression that the cows yielded more then. Milking with Helene was often twice as bountiful as without her, so Kunegunde insisted that the girl accompany her every day. And the cheese always came out best in Helene's presence as well, even if she was just nearby; the milk curdled faster and took on a firmer form, allowing Kunegunde to supply the friars with cheese and still have some extra to sell every Thursday at the market in Neisse, on the side, so as to earn a bit of money for herself. She divided the earnings fairly, putting aside half for the girl's future. Helene knew about this and was grateful for it, even though she understood very little of the outside world. Kunegunde explained to her that it was important for women to have their own material assets that they'd earned themselves, no matter how modest they were, which no one, not even their own husbands, could take away from them.

After the girl had lived for eight springs, Kunegunde started taking her to the forest and teaching her how to survive in the event of war, plague, or famine with nothing else at hand but what God had created. She showed her how to prune trees in the spring so that as much sap as possible would flow into the vessels she set on the ground below them. She taught Helene how to identify edible mushrooms, revealed where the best blueberries and blackberries grew, and showed her how to preserve them so as to have food to eat during the winter. She also taught her how to catch a fish, gut it, and cook it over a fire, how to wash clothes in the river and remove stains with sand and stones, as well as how to rinse the clothes in such a way that the water smoothed out all the wrinkles made by one's hands while washing them.

Thus it can be said that by the time Helene Spalt had reached the age of eight, she knew things that most other girls didn't learn until they were old enough to be married, and that many never learned during their lives at all.

Over time, Helene gradually began to occupy the place in Kunegunde Kreppel's heart that had hitherto been held by Heini. Kunegunde's heart opened more and more every day to the girl, thereby closing, unfortunately, to the boy, who remained insufficient for her and who, furthermore, never lifted a finger to help; he merely demanded attention and love, as if he'd sprung from her womb and weren't—like little Helene—a fosterling.

But since there were considerable sums of money flowing from Edelstadt every month, sent to the Franciscan friars by Heini's not entirely conscienceless parent, the father general ordered Kunegunde to keep her big mouth shut and continue suckling the boy, even though it seemed inappropriate to all the friars on account of Heini's age. They were also jealous of him, since they all dreamed of latching on to Kunegunde's massive breasts themselves and sucking them all night long like that "nasty little teat-sucker," that "snot-nosed bastard," as everyone called him, including Kunegunde, though she did so only when the boy was out of earshot.

Concerning Heinrich Babel, the Nasty Little Teat-Sucker

Helene was a sweet, cheerful, and pleasant child, and the more disagreeable Heinrich Babel, who was nearly three years older than her, became, the more affection Helene received from everyone around her. Heini became increasingly jealous of Helene, sullen and—unfortunately—vindictive.

Jealous of the attention bestowed upon Helene not only by Kunegunde but also by the friars, who had tried to bond with him in the early years before little Helene arrived at the monastery, the boy found pleasure solely in exacerbating the feeling of failure he held within himself. A stain appeared on his heart that grew larger and darker each day. When he injured his knee, for example, he would rip off the scab to prevent the wound from healing. He found carnal pleasure in the pain. The blood flowed when he decided it should; he grew accustomed to the sight of it and relished its metallic aftertaste. As time went on, he began to harm himself. At night, when Kunegunde, who still slept in the same bed as him even though he'd turned ten, would sink into a deep sleep, Heini would suckle her milk with delight. Immediately afterward, he'd feel an overwhelming urge to punish himself, for Kunegunde was now refusing to breastfeed him during the day and would drive him away with a wet rag if he tried. After his nocturnal feasts, he'd cut himself with a small knife he'd stolen from the kitchen.

When he pestered the friars, the latter, sensing a strangeness in the boy's disposition that they found difficult to comprehend, turned fully to their own affairs, which suddenly had taken on great importance and urgency. They'd panic because they feared that little Heini would take revenge on them for pretending to be too busy to spend time with him. After all, everyone in the monastery had plenty of free time.

Kunegunde's rejection and the friars' ever more thinly concealed resentment didn't hurt Heini as much as being rejected by Brother Albert, who, before Helene arrived at the monastery, had mattered more to the boy than his own father. For now it was no longer with Heini but with Helene that Brother Albert spent each day from dawn to dusk—with breaks for meals and prayers—taking long, meandering walks, listening to birdsong, feeding deer, and even, it must be admitted, sneaking peeks from time to time at lewd nature. Sometimes they locked themselves together in the monastery's library to look at old books and study the structure of plants and their medicinal properties. It was there, in the southwest tower of the monastery, where the scholarly tomes were kept (which had been donated by a wealthy merchant from Neisse whose ill wife's life had been saved by his prayers to Saint Francis of Assisi), that Heini had experienced his sole moments of happiness, when Brother Albert, upon noticing the boy's pious concentration as he looked at the prints, tenderly touched his head as if in an expression of pride. Heini had never been a source of such pride for his father.

But nothing was ever the same for Heini Babel after Helene arrived at the monastery and almost immediately stole the hearts of all the friars, and Kunegunde Kreppel too. All eyes turned to the pretty, charming little girl who, despite being only seven years old, was far more clever and resourceful than any adult at the monastery, apart from Kunegunde.

This surprised everyone. Both children had been afflicted by hardship, but only one seemed to have been scarred by it. The dark stain on Heini's soul was so vast and immense that it spread to everything around him and seemed unfathomable to the adults. And since the human soul craves light, not darkness, the friars and Kunegunde soon directed their tenderness and love toward Helene, depriving Heini of what he'd been accustomed to since he was born.

One day, there was an incident in the library that was impossible to ignore. Heini, taking advantage of Brother Albert's momentary inattention, picked up little Helene, went up to the bifora, and tried to push her through it. He was severely reprimanded by Brother Albert and locked up in the dark, cramped cellar with nothing to eat but bread and water, and only hungry rats to keep him company. He spent a full day and night there, and when he was released into the world streaked with tears and his own excrement, he turned even more passionately toward evil.

After this event, Brother Albert and Kunegunde Kreppel lost for him all the affection they'd taken such pains to cultivate over the years and began to avoid him like fire, perceiving in the boy a calculated inclination to evil. Suddenly Brother Albert realized that the trampling of a baby blackbird that had fallen out of its nest, which could have survived with some tender care, had not been accidental, as little Heini had assured him while swearing on his father's life. And that the monastery kittens hadn't really drowned in the river on their own but had in fact been thrown into the water by Heini. And that perhaps the beehives hadn't caught fire from a lightning bolt but rather as a result of the ungrateful boy's mischief-making, eager as he was to draw constant attention to himself no matter the cost.

Heini knew that the library was strictly off-limits to everyone except three people: Brother Albert, Brother Hubert, and the father general. He decided to report to the father general that Brother Albert was taking Helene there in secret.

The vengeful act had negative consequences not for Brother Albert but for Heini himself, for the father general found it easier to forgive any sin other than denunciation, of which he himself had been a victim in his youth.

From that day onward, the boy was perceived by everyone at the monastery as a good-for-nothing scoundrel from whom it was best to keep a good distance, for he couldn't be trusted. After Heini's denunciation came to light, Helene also intuitively avoided him, even though she understood very little of what had happened. Instead of "little Heini," Kunegunde now only called him, in her mind and also out loud, a "nasty little teat-sucker" and a "blockhead," having suddenly understood why the mayor of Edelstadt—Franz Gustav Babel—had rejected his own offspring. Heini's father had deemed the birth itself a curse and had tried to forget it, for it had taken his beloved wife from him. And he cursed with all his might the months leading up to Heini's birth as well, months in which a pastor from Freiwaldau, highly skilled in exorcisms, was brought to his wife seven times, visits that created a high risk of their neighbors noticing and spreading rumors that they'd resorted to getting help from Protestants. Hanna thrashed about while the Devil was chased from her soul and her belly, for she had felt—as she told her husband every day—that her state was not a blessed one but cursed, and that the child sitting in her womb was endowed with superhuman strength, for the kicks she felt were too painful to be inflicted by any human being.

When her beloved husband brought the exorcist into the house, she threw herself across the floor, hitting her head against the wall again and again until blood gushed out and she lost consciousness. After the birth, which occurred shortly after the seventh exorcism attempt, she died, barely having placed the newborn to her breast. He received no milk from her, for she took her final breath before it began to flow.

Kunegunde had disliked the nasty little teat-sucker from the very beginning, but she'd striven with all her might to soften her reaction to him so that the child, who'd had such a hard time coming into the world, wouldn't one day leave it with nothing but unpleasant memories. And perchance it was because of this attempt to overcome the instinctive dislike that everyone in the monastery felt toward Heini, though no one would ever say so to his face, that Kunegunde breastfed him for more than eleven springs. It was either fear or a sense of propriety that motivated her to compensate for the wretched hardship Heini had suffered as well as for the rotten character he'd developed despite his life at the monastery, blessed as it was by both Jesus Christ and Saint Francis.

As for Brother Albert, he was denied the privilege of using the library for an indefinite period and forbidden to use herbs to cure ailments. He was replaced by Brother Hubert, who was regarded by the friars as the most learned, having studied theology in Bologna and Padua in his youth.

When Heini's father finally arrived to get him at the behest of the father general, everyone was relieved and said prayers of gratitude that the little shithead would finally be out of their way.

Everyone except the boy himself, who, upon losing sight of Kunegunde, lost the only positive connection he'd had to the world. She'd been the only person he'd truly loved, though he'd been incapable of showing it.

On Fervent Love for All Things Earthly

———

The transfer of responsibility for the monastery's library to Brother Hubert happened at a time when there was an increase of lustful desire among the friars, who were not immune to Kunegunde Kreppel's charms.

They wandered around the monastery's garden with their halberds protruding so stiffly beneath their habits that fear of divine punishment filled their hearts. Thus, when a short, handwritten treatise of fewer than four pages with the provocative title "On Fervent Love for All Things Earthly" appeared in the monastery through means unbeknownst to anyone, the friars could at last find some relief, thanks to the practice described in the work, which was carefully kept secret from the father general.

It should be noted that the treatise in question was passed from hand to hand primarily at night, and so intensively that after only a few days it was difficult to find a spot on the pages that wasn't smeared with sticky secretions and saliva.

The treatise described ways to make love to all things that have risen from the Earth since the creation of the world. The recommendations were accompanied by clumsily executed yet compelling illustrations by the anonymous author that were meant to demonstrate to readers effective ways of dealing with unquenched lust and passion, by shifting the object of desire from humankind to all manner of plant species begotten by Mother Earth, even those that were, at first glance, quite far from inspiring erotic enthusiasm. Hence, just after midnight, when the father general, plunged deeply into a lager-induced stupor, was snoring so thunderously that no one could sleep, moans and whimpers emerged from under the animal hides and blankets with which the friars covered themselves, as did sounds of rubbing, rustling, grunting, and smacking.

When they looked at the illustrations, which depicted examples of copulation with hollowed-out squash, pumpkins, potatoes, apples, and plums, the friars became aroused at the sight of this divine creation in which they could perceive a foretaste of heavenly bliss. Hence, they no longer burned with desire solely at the sight of Kunegunde Kreppel; a fleeting glance at the petals of a pansy was enough to make a gardening hoe immediately stand at attention beneath many a habit. Thanks to the anonymous treatise, all of Mother Nature began to excite them, revealing millions of living things, each of which enticed the friars with beauty. Even in a caterpillar they were able to discern evidence of divine, cosmic harmony by looking at the regularity of its body's segments. Not to mention in the mating of butterflies. This, along with cats in heat and the copulation of dogs, ignited in them a flame so intense that they would insert their protruding rodkins, in the ways depicted by the clumsily etched illustrations in the anonymous treatise, into anything Nature offered: the slightly decayed squash and zucchini tossed by Kunegunde onto the compost heap, hollowed-out apricots into which the tip of a rodkin could be delightfully plunged while the fruit was rotated on its axis, a squirrel's nesting hole in the fallen trunk of an oak tree at the edge of the garden, a fox's tail cut off after the carcass was found in the woods (the softness of which promised thrills of delight), cool cabbage leaves ribbed with veins, and fuzzy dandelion heads that only had to be blown over a burning rodkin so that the soft seeds would land on it, thus teasing, as gently as possible, skin of a smoothness equaled solely by Chinese silk.

However, after several weeks of indulging in carnal lovemaking with native flora (far less often with fauna—although that did happen from time to time, especially with small fluffy ones, like weasels, squirrels, and foxes), their habits became increasingly difficult to maintain. The summer eventually ended, then autumn passed, and a harsh winter was beginning to appear on the horizon, during which fruit, vegetables, and flowers would be scarce.

Stealthily, so as not to catch the eye of Kunegunde, who guarded the supplies, the friars scavenged for potatoes, pears, and apples in the monastery's cellar, all the while dreaming of more exotic lovers, such as the ones in Brother Hubert's botanical books from Padua. Many of them returned to their old practices, making Kunegunde, once again, the object of their sexual desires.

Wishing to relieve their suffering, Brother Hubert, with the approval of Brother Albert, secretly smuggled into the monastery some plant seeds from the Republic of Venice. He brought the seeds of mandarins and Sicilian oranges, peaches and grapes, as well as a wide variety of flowering plants—geraniums, campion, Chinese peonies—plants for which the inhabitants of the Republic of Venice had an excessive—or even unhealthy, one might say—love. There were also some vegetable seeds—tomatoes; viper's grass; Italian cabbages with softer, more wrinkled leaves; and eggplants that were wonderfully smooth, as if they'd been polished—all so it would be possible for the friars to make fervent, passionate love to anything on Earth, instead of indifferently poking their rodkins into potatoes.

On the Passing of the World and a Deep Friendship with Brother Albert

---

Helene was fond of all the friars, but most of all rotund Brother Albert, who had a bald spot right on the top of his head with fuzzy, fur-like hair growing around it, making him look very much like the pauper saint from Assisi himself. Brother Albert unintentionally boasted this hairstyle; mischievous Mother Nature had simply played a trick on him. Indeed, it would be more accurate to call this stirring in Helene's heart love, for while she liked the other friars, toward Brother Albert her feelings went beyond mere affection.

Helene was generally liked in the monastery, and all the friars strove wholeheartedly to please her, for they perceived innocence and purity in her that seemed to come from the Virgin Mary herself. This purity served as a shield for them to combat the lust and impure thoughts aroused both by Kunegunde Kreppel and, ever since the treatise by the anonymous author had begun circulating secretly among them, by Nature herself. The friars would thus summon thoughts of sweet Helene whenever their minds began to roam once again toward Kunegunde. Helene's name, repeated often like a prayer, whistled over their heads like a penitential whip at the slightest thought among any of them of the cook, crouched down, her voluminous skirt pulled up and crotch spread open, a golden stream shooting forth in front of her.

It was with Brother Albert that Helene spent her time "observing the passing of the world," as he called the quiet activity of staring motionlessly at the world around them without speaking. They would sit together and gaze at puddles, hollows in trees, decaying leaves, plant stalks protruding awkwardly from the ground, flower stems, pale yellow butterflies clinging to the buddleia flowers in the garden and the purple echinacea, from which an extract for boosting immunity was made in the monastery with an ancient recipe. As Brother Albert and Helene stared at the natural world, little gasps of delight would burst out of their mouths so intensely that, despite having vowed to each other to remain silent so as not to mar this beauty of the most perfect kind with words, a rapturous but sinful exclamation of "Oh Jesus!" would occasionally erupt from their breasts.

And although Helene was told by Brother Albert and the other friars that no words could ever describe the wonders with which nature abounds, she learned to read and write thanks to Brother Albert's efforts, for he could clearly perceive in the girl an extraordinary connection with nature and felt it necessary to convey to her his knowledge of herbs and herbal remedies in as much detail as possible, in secrecy from the father general, who often said that, for the glory of God, no woman had ever defiled the monastery's manuscripts with the touch of her hand.

Brother Albert contemplated this, and every time feelings of guilt and remorse for lying to his superior troubled him, he consoled himself with the thought that Mother Nature is female and that most certainly when the Heavenly Father created the world, He intentionally included females in it alongside the males so that there would be harmony. And it would be impossible for the world to survive without females among its hoofed, crawling, swimming, and flying creatures, not only by reason of their ability to carry new life within them but also by reason of how they complemented nature with their beauty.

Thus, Brother Albert secretly taught Helene everything he knew. Above all, he strove to instill in her a love of books. He believed that the world contained within the letters of the alphabet would never pass away; it would endure forever, thereby reaching eternity.

"Reading opens the frail, transient human to immortality. In the letters of the alphabet created by God, from alpha onward, thou shalt not die. Jesus is a letter, and this letter brings one closer to eternity," he explained to Helene.

He taught her not only his native German but also Latin and Greek, so that she would be enlightened. He did this in secret from everyone. For the sin of allowing a female into the library, he could have been expelled from the monastery and left destitute, without any means of support. But Helene's enthusiasm and her desire to study books, especially those concerned with botany, kept Brother Albert from abandoning his efforts. Over the years, he had tried to instill a love of knowledge in his fellow friars, but with the exception of Brother Hubert, who had received an excellent education at world-renowned universities, he had always been met with an attitude that was less than lukewarm.

Luckily, Brother Hubert had a vast collection of books in his monastery cell, so he used the library's resources quite rarely. But even so, Brother Albert was cautious—he locked the door to this sanctuary of knowledge from the inside, giving himself just the right amount of time to hide the girl between the bookcases should someone start to tug at the door handle from outside.

The girl thus grew up between Kunegunde Kreppel, who gave her the warm, loving care of a mother, especially after the disappearance of the nasty little teat-sucker, Heini Babel, and

Brother Albert, who was like a father to her. Helene benefited from this arrangement as much as she possibly could, for she had an extremely receptive mind and absorbed nearly everything with which she came into contact.

And since Albert served as a healer in the monastery, taking care of the friars' health with the help of that which had grown from the Earth, Helene gained knowledge of herbs and the various beneficial concoctions that could be made from them. During her years spent in the monastery she learned about many plants and their uses for various health problems—she knew how to cure insomnia with henbane, how to macerate jimsonweed in order to suppress Brother Marcus's hallucinations (which he often had after secretly binge-drinking communion wine in the monastery cellar), how to use Saint John's wort to effectively drive away the intense sadness often afflicting the friars in the early spring, and how to extract milk from spelt and oats and use it to extinguish the fire that was ignited in the friars' loins by spying on Kunegunde Kreppel.

On the Banging of Deadwood

Although Heini Babel's departure from the monastery initially seemed to be welcomed by everyone, after only one month, Kunegunde Kreppel discovered that she nevertheless missed the nasty little teat-sucker. She preferred not to admit it to herself. She could barely stand looking at him, for his character and temperament disturbed her, yet at the same time he was an object upon which she could, without any witnesses, vent her dislike of the entire male species. A dislike that did not arise from unpleasant experiences and disappointments but that Kunegunde had sucked from her mother's breast, and her mother from her grandmother's breast, and so on, as if simultaneously, alongside the love hormone that floods a child in the flow of milk from its mother's breast, a hormone of hatred was also secreted, directed at all that was male. Now Kunegunde had no one to scold, no head at which to flick a wet rag. Helene, who had become Kunegunde's right hand at the monastery, was entirely unsuitable for that. She was a kind, helpful child, bringing joy rather than vexation, and she seemed to lack any traits of bad temperament, which made the entire situation even more difficult for Kunegunde.

With nobody around for her to unleash her negative feelings onto—for she could do so on neither the kindhearted friars nor the "golden child," as she called Helene—Kunegunde became increasingly irritable and volatile as time passed. She was unable to channel the searing heat of her anger outward, and so it blazed fiercely within. Her sole respite from suffering came from applying leeches to her most sensitive parts: her ample breasts, groin, and thighs. Then the fury that blazed inside her was released with her blood, and with it came temporary relief.

But when this method began to fail her, she sought out new ways of venting her pent-up anger. Soon she discovered something that would bring her the greatest relief of all—banging deadwood while overcome by fury.

It began by sheer chance. There is the possibility, however, that all of this—the banging of deadwood and its significance to the rest of the story—was simply preordained for Kunegunde. One morning in the month of May, while lugging a heavy basket to the river with Helene to wash the winter clothes of the not overly hygiene-conscious friars, she stopped to rest beneath an oak tree that had been split in half by a bolt of lightning many years before.

Out of the corner of her eye, Kunegunde Kreppel noticed a deadly nightshade bush growing nearby, also known as *Atropa belladonna*, covered in little black berries. The friars at the monastery called them wolf berries, for they'd been using them for many years to poison wolves. Kunegunde recalled a conversation she'd overheard between Brother Albert and Brother Hubert, from which she'd learned that these shiny black berries caused hallucinations in wolves as they died, allowing them to experience great happiness before perishing in painful convulsions. And she also learned that some women in Franconia—as Brother Hubert divulged—were known to make an ointment from the plant that they rubbed into their clefts to give themselves extreme pleasure. Kunegunde decided to ingest a small quantity of the berries to find out if there was any truth to what Brother Hubert had described, or whether it was merely a tall tale.

The friars had said that an adult would be deprived of life by ten to twenty berries, and a child by only five, so Kunegunde picked ten and carefully counted out seven of them for herself and three for Helene, beseeching the girl never to divulge to anyone that they had done this—if they survived, of course. They were scared, but their curiosity overcame their fear.

They swallowed the berries and drank some water from the goatskin pouch hanging from Kunegunde's belt. They didn't have to wait long for the effects of the poisonous plant to kick in. Suddenly, a forest sprang up from the soil and grew all the way to the sky, so dense as to completely eliminate the gaps between the trunks and branches where previously light had shone through. The darkness intensified and became so concentrated that Kunegunde Kreppel couldn't take even a single step forward, so hindered was she by the sticky black substance from which night and darkness were made. The tree roots sprang to life and, like a swarm of vipers, entwined her legs and entrapped her. Kunegunde didn't scream, for there was something powerful and enchanting in this immobility. She began to grow into the Earth, becoming one with the tree under which she stood. Her own roots became entangled with the roots of the tree, pulling her down beneath the Earth. Suddenly she saw a disheveled little boy lying in front of her, and she realized it was the nasty little teat-sucker—Heini Babel. He was lying on the trunk of a fallen tree, seemingly asleep. He was naked. The cadaverously pale little body was almost glowing against the backdrop of the dense forest and the dark tree trunk that gleamed with spots of jade-green moss.

Out of the darkness, from the thicket of trees, a strange figure emerged. An old woman with a youthful cleft, which Kunegunde Kreppel caught a glimpse of when the woman pulled up her coarse linen robe and straddled the sleeping youngster. And when he woke up and began to wriggle and squirm beneath her like an eel, a horrible peal of laughter burst out of her toothless mouth, terrifying the boy so much that he froze and let the old woman sit on top of him. She covered his eyes with a bunch of weeds and then placed some stones on top of them so that the boy wouldn't see what she was about to do but would feel everything, absolutely everything. She knew that it would be harder for him to open his eyelids under the weight of the plants, and she sat like that, completely motionless, until he stopped wriggling and twitching like a cat's tail when the beast has caught sight of a mouse. Uttering a shriek like the sound of a rooster being slaughtered, the young boy crawled out from under the old woman's robe, now transformed, as Kunegunde Kreppel noticed, deducing this not from his appearance—which hadn't changed at all—but from the confident stride with which he now made his way through the forest.

Meanwhile, the old woman, after sitting heavily on Heini Babel and then climbing off him, looked at Kunegunde and gestured for her to follow. But Kunegunde couldn't; her legs were entwined with tree roots. She was no longer a person but a tree. She grabbed one of the low-growing branches and tore it off the tree, which wasn't easy. She stripped the smaller branches off the large one, turning it into a powerful rod. Then she started wildly bashing the rapacious tree with it, right on the roots, to force it to release her.

When she finally liberated herself and regained the use of her legs, she saw that the old woman was still waiting for her, although greatly changed, as if she'd become half her age after absorbing Heini Babel into her. Not only did she now look like

Kunegunde's peer, but she was as spry and lively as a little girl, equal even to Helene. She dashed through the forest as nimbly as a cat. Kunegunde found it difficult to follow, for she noticed that all the trees around her seemed half dead, with withered branches. She began to force her way through this dense thicket of ailing, desiccated trees, bashing the dead branches with her stick so that they would fall away from the living part of the tree. And so she could pass through. Slam, bam! They snapped and fell! Most of the trees were her beloved birches and alders. The fallen branches were instantly absorbed by the Earth, as if they were feeding it, nourishing the Earth with death. More trees, dozens of trees, yielded to Kunegunde, as if inviting her to smash them. They didn't fight back but willingly exposed the withered parts of themselves to death. The rod in her hands was infallible. She put all her strength into banging the trees, and after the twentieth or thirtieth one, blinded by the sweat that was pouring into her eyes, she began to run out of steam.

 Having hacked all the lifeless parts away from the trees, she felt that she'd also chopped all that was withered from inside herself, all that had drained the life from her, like that unbearable boy Heini Babel, whom she nevertheless missed, though she never would have admitted it to the friars or to Helene. And now that her battle with the half-dead trees was done and a path had been cleared for herself, she suddenly felt an overwhelming urge to slide the wooden rod with which she'd just been banging the trees into her vulva. As if this dance with death could end only in the most life-giving place.

 Hence, she proceeded, and not at all gently; under the influence of the belladonna berries as she was, she didn't notice the blood flowing from between her by-no-means-virginal thighs. And when she felt the stick inside her, it was as if she'd begun to fly, for all of a sudden... she was soaring above the treetops, over the shimmering, silvery river, and sailing through the sky past the clouds and toward the town of Neisse. She peeked through upstairs windows, saw couples making love in attics and merchants weighing grain in their storehouses, floated over the churches—the Church of Saint Barbara and the Basilica of Saint James and Saint Agnes—and nearly bumped her foot on a carillon with a gilded cockerel and the tower from which the bells summoned the town's residents to prayer. And as she flew over the crescent moon, she deliberately lowered her flight and impaled herself on it, thrusting its curved hook into places that she herself could not reach. So that it would touch the spot deep in her cleft from which a waterfall of moisture gushed, thrusting itself so deeply and inflicting a pain on her that was so intensely infused with pleasure, she would never yearn for anything again—she would be replete with everything in the universe, liberated completely from all desire. It would tear into her and pound her so hard that everything inside her that was feverish and perpetually hungry would finally be satiated, and it would pour out of her like a river overflowing its banks, bursting through any dams and barriers in its path.

As she flew, Kunegunde Kreppel suddenly noticed that the moon had slipped out of her completely and was no longer in its new phase but full. And the stars around it were connected by multicolored threads, like strings of sparkling beads.

She landed on the ground as she regained consciousness. Then she turned to look at little Helene Spalt, whose face, in that moment, seemed to resemble the face of the figure whom Kunegunde had seen bent over naked little Heini Babel in a loving embrace—a face that was not that of a child, a young woman, or an old one, but all of these at once. Helene was lying on the ground, unconscious. Pale, as if death had claimed her. Waxy and cold. As if the blood in her veins had frozen and her breath had been stifled forever.

Terrified, Kunegunde began shaking Helene vigorously and rubbing her chest to restore her heartbeat. It took a while, but finally Helene gasped for air and opened her eyes, the sight of which Kunegunde would never forget for the rest of her life. The moonlight was reflected in them, making them shine like stars. They were twice their usual size and brimming with moisture. Then Helene's breath suddenly quickened and her heart began to pound so hard it seemed about to burst from her chest. Kunegunde slapped the girl on the face, poured water on her from the goatskin pouch, and shook her so roughly that she nearly knocked the soul out of her. Helene finally regained consciousness, but Kunegunde was unable to get a single word out of her—almost as if Helene, normally a very talkative little girl, had suddenly lost her tongue.

Kunegunde picked her up and carried her through the forest. It wasn't easy, for her legs were spread wide after her experience with the stick, and torrents of blood were flowing down her thighs.

She never thought again about what had happened that day, for fear gripped her so intensely that she was afraid to delve into the mystery. It was bad enough that she'd torn open her cleft so violently that she now had to wash it with oak bark and rub it with comfrey ointment, trying to repair what she'd destroyed.

Although Kunegunde couldn't remember very much about the experience, from that day forth she avoided the place where it had all happened entirely. She hoped that Helene wouldn't remember it either. She was careful never to mention the incident, quietly hoping it would remain a secret between them for the rest of their lives. Especially since Helene was still unable to speak. No one knew if her silence had been caused by an external event or a vow she'd made. But to whom would she have made such a vow? The friars wondered about this and questioned Kunegunde about the circumstances surrounding Helene's loss of speech, but her lips remained sealed.

What she didn't know, though, was that the girl had embroidered everything she'd seen in the forest with colorful thread on an altar cloth that Kunegunde had started stitching long before but had quickly abandoned due to a lack of inspiration. When Helene finished her handiwork, she laid the cloth on the altar.

As the father general stood before the cloth to pray, his gaze fell upon it. He pretended not to notice, but immediately after the liturgy he summoned Kunegunde and asked her how such very ungodly depictions had appeared on the cloth.

For Helene had embroidered an oak tree with dead, broken branches on which, here and there, a leaf or two were hanging. The tree was very ugly, with withered boughs. But what had chilled the blood in the father general's veins as he'd conducted the mass in Latin was the symbol carved into the tree's bark. A symbol that had been forbidden for centuries, a symbol that Christianity had brought an end to once and for all. "A symbol of the pagan goddess of fertility and her omnipotent cunt, which is, however, utterly powerless when compared to God the Father's cock!" the father general proclaimed, with words as sharp as a knight's spear. Kunegunde cowered, afraid of being struck by them. "You were supposed to embroider lambs and clusters of grapes as a reminder of Christ's sacrifice, the symbols of Jesus's life, and the cross as a symbol of his martyrdom," he thundered at terrified Kunegunde, "and not—for fuck's sake!—a pagan oak tree under which acts of wicked immorality were performed for centuries!"

Kunegunde had no idea what to say. But she knew that she was the only person at the monastery who knew the art of embroidery. No one else possessed this skill. Or at least that's how it seemed to her. For she was unaware that little Helene had been ardently observing her handicraft while she sat with her in the kitchen, reciting prayers and learning to mend the friars' undergarments and clothing.

Kunegunde had been taught embroidery by her previous benefactress, the wealthy lady from Ferrara, who had followed her son, a cathedral builder, to Neisse. Her son had been invited by the local chapter to design a new church in the town's market square.

Kunegunde had learned from Francesca di Ferrara not only embroidery in its most exquisite form but also oral love, in which the latter engaged at every possible opportunity, lifting her gown and dozens of petticoats in front of cooks, scullery maids, and seamstresses—all women of lower status—paying them generously for these feats and training them in a skill that was rare in the lands of the duchy. And since Kunegunde, who had become quite proficient in this practice, could choose how she wished to be paid, she would always decline money in favor of silk thread of every possible color, including gold and silver, as well as embroidery hoops, frames, and needles. Needles with which, at Francesca's behest, Kunegunde pricked Francesca's buttocks gently during the caresses that preceded further mischief.

Kunegunde was thoroughly rebuked for the pagan artwork and threatened with expulsion from the monastery should anything like this ever happen again. She quietly withstood the tirade but then headed straight to Helene's cell with the cloth in her hand.

This was the first time that she experienced a miracle in Helene's presence. As Kunegunde lifted her hand to slap the girl, she felt it go numb and motionless in the air, as stiff as a tree branch—as stiff as one of the branches on the snags she'd banged with her heavy rod after consuming belladonna berries. She couldn't move her legs either, as if her feet had sprouted roots and grown into the stone floor.

And once again it seemed to her that instead of Helene there was a wrinkled old woman standing in front of her with a thin gray braid reaching to her knees. But she wasn't sure if this was real or some kind of hallucination, for a moment later Helene once again appeared in her usual form.

Kunegunde said nothing. But she was starting to regain feeling in her hand, and she could now move her feet. Speech, however, hadn't returned to Helene—as if, for some unknown reason, her silence was still necessary.

From then on, their relationship changed: Kunegunde no longer embroidered alone. Now they sat at the embroidery frame together and stitched with colorful threads. They embroidered only what was permitted: flowers, birds, ladybugs, butterflies—all of God's creatures that existed in nature and pleased the human eye. And on the liturgical cloths: a chalice of wine, clusters of grapes, ears of grain, and sheep—Christian symbols without any deviation.

Whenever Kunegunde noticed Helene's stitches starting to venture beyond the pattern they had drawn together on the fabric, she immediately snatched away the embroidery hoop or frame—depending on what they were creating that day—and hid it in the kitchen cupboard, which she locked with a key. Helene thus learned to suppress her inner desire to express with embroidery what she was unable to put into words.

The friars were troubled by the amount of time that Kunegunde and Helene spent embroidering together—long hours every day, as if this activity had become an obsession for them, something that absorbed them completely, making them forget about worldly matters. They took care of all their duties as quickly as possible—milking the cows, cooking the day's meals, weeding the garden, doing laundry—and put nothing off for later, so that nothing would disturb the tranquility of their afternoon hours devoted to embroidery.

In the year after Heini Babel's departure, Kunegunde and Helene embroidered so many liturgical vestments and paraments, so many antependia and altar cloths, that they could have covered the entire church with them, and perchance even part of the garden. And the embroidery skills they developed through all this work soon proved to be extremely useful.

Concerning *Atropa belladonna* and Epiphanies

The next two years passed for Helene so swiftly that they felt to her like no more than a month or two. The only peculiarity during that time was her constant silence combined with her pathological urge to embroider—whether on a hoop or a large frame, or even just with her hands when she didn't happen to have any of the equipment nearby.

She experienced no hardships in her daily life, for everyone at the monastery, with Kunegunde Kreppel at the helm, looked after Helene's comfort and well-being. She lived like a saint among the friars, enjoying luxuries that none of them could ever hope for— she slept in a bed rather than on a plank of wood, ate baked goods straight from the oven even though Kunegunde Kreppel strictly forbade it for the friars, and drank fresh milk still warm from the cow's udder. "My little Kreppel," Kunegunde tenderly called her; she'd been showering as much love on the girl as she would have her own child ever since they started spending long hours together embroidering. If it weren't for the death of Helene's parents, one could even say she'd been born under a lucky star. Even the father general sometimes, after consuming too much wine, admitted that the child brought great joy to him as well. The mere sight of her brightened his soul.

And thus life continued until Helene had lived for twelve springs and got her first period. When that day arrived, it was as if the Devil had entered her—this is how the friars, unprepared for such an event, later described it. First, at the kitchen table, having received a bowl of porridge that was too hot, she threw it on the floor and spoke for the first time in over two years. And since the words that exploded out of her weren't "Praise the Lord" or "God have mercy on us," but rather "Go to hell!" in a snarling tone of voice, Kunegunde and the four friars present in the kitchen were overcome by fear, even though deep down in their hearts they were glad that she'd finally spoken. Later, at noon, while picking raspberries, Helene started cursing again, as if the dam that had been holding back her words had suddenly broken, paving the way for nothing but foul language. Among the words that she uttered were some she couldn't possibly have learned in the monastery, hence everyone wondered whence she'd acquired them.

The worst was about to happen, however. In the early afternoon, after the Angelus and dinner, which passed in silence because Kunegunde Kreppel was so distressed by Helene's behavior that she'd begun to sulk and completely avoided eye contact with the girl, Helene set off for the river to catch some trout for supper.

For the first time in her life, she didn't catch a single fish. The agility for which the friars had always envied her seemed to have disappeared. After looking over her shoulder to make sure none of them were nearby, Helene began to spout language foul enough to outdo the nastiest, rowdiest ruffian in the Golden Crab Tavern.

While every word she screamed brought her some relief, it also ignited a fire inside her that only inspired more curses. She hitched up her dress and the apron she wore over it, took off her undergarments, and then stepped into the river, but instead of lying down in it on her back, as she usually did because she loved to float on its current, she began to slam her hands onto the water's surface with all her might, as if she'd become a water mill. She shattered the river's tranquility for the waterfowl and the other creatures that lived on the riverbanks, for she was so angry at the havoc nature had wreaked within her that she had to find some way to vent her rage. And it was a burning rage coming from within her body, which was aching and releasing streams of blood for the first time in her life.

When thrashing her hands against the water's surface no longer brought her any relief and her internal fire continued to blaze like a torch, Helene stepped out of the river and started walking straight ahead, as if guided or driven by an outer force. Pushed through space by something invisible, greater than herself, in an unknown direction. As she walked onward, she noticed the forest becoming denser and darker, as if the foliage were so thick that the sun was unable to penetrate it.

Walking quickly and inattentively, she tripped over a large root and tumbled head over heels. Looking up, she recognized the tree looming above her—the oak under which, two years earlier, she and Kunegunde had eaten the shiny black berries, after which something had happened that she couldn't clearly remember. There the tree stood, no longer alive but not completely dead either. It had split in half after having been struck by a bolt of lightning, and many of its branches were dead and withered, while others still had some leaves on them. It was the tallest, mightiest oak she'd ever seen in her life. She turned and glanced around her.

Yes, this was the same grove of withered trees where she'd been with Kunegunde. The deadwood forest.

Wielding a large stick in her hands, she swung it and struck a dead branch with all her strength. It fell off like a scab from Heini Babel's knee. As Helene's blows became increasingly powerful and unrestrained, the tree scabs fell off one by one, and suddenly Helene felt as if she were peeling the dead layers off of herself— allowing what was alive, what was essential, what was at the core, to emerge finally into the light.

She kept at it until she was completely out of breath. And on the brink of madness. As if something foreign had entered her. Another life, another soul.

Growing impatient as she waited for Helene to return with the trout, Kunegunde Kreppel decided to go to the river herself and bring the girl back with the fish. When she didn't find Helene at the riverbank, she started searching for her in the forest. Her heart was full of trepidation, for there was a silent agreement between them to stay far away from this place.

As she ventured deeper into the forest, she let herself be carried away by her negative feelings. The forest gradually grew denser. A thick fog lay over it, and the trees' sharp tips pierced it like needles embroidering a pattern on a piece of fabric. An ominous sound of woodpeckers tapping tree bark increased Kunegunde's anxiety as she slowly made her way to the deadwood forest.

There she found Helene lying under the oak tree. She was in convulsions, thrashing to the right and to the left, as if some force had enveloped her and penetrated her to the core. Next to her lay a few scattered berries. Kunegunde grabbed Helene's head and began poking her fingers down the girl's throat to induce vomiting.

She tried to revive Helene in various ways. She slapped her face, pinched her cheeks, scratched her back, and bit her fingers, trying to pull her out of the state she'd fallen into, for which she,

Kunegunde, was to blame, for her stupidity and recklessness two years earlier.

Kunegunde trembled with helplessness. She knew that if Helene's soul were wandering somewhere in otherworldly realms, it wouldn't find its way back on its own, since it would be enticed by the unique intensity of the experience. She didn't want to leave the girl like that, although she knew that no help would come. She tried to carry her, but due to Helene's condition, her twitching and thrashing, Kunegunde couldn't make it very far at all. So she laid her down with her head raised on some moss and ran as fast as she could to the monastery, calling for help.

And when the friars arrived at the spot, they saw something they couldn't at first comprehend, and they rubbed their eyes in disbelief. Helene, completely motionless, was floating in the air, as light as a birch or alder leaf. She looked as if she were sleeping, except that she was high up, beneath the trees—as if the Earth wanted to hold her close but Heaven was calling her away.

They began to pray for her so fervently that they felt an intense heat tearing through them, and the fire in which they stood while praying to God to save Helene made them sweat profusely. But it was all in vain. Helene was elsewhere now. She was experiencing the beginning and the end of the world—both simultaneously, for they were, after all, the same thing. Her soul splintered into as many fragments as were needed to permeate every living being that existed in that moment and in the past as well as in the future—human, plant, and animal. It was a communion of all that the Earth had given of Herself since the dawn of time. While Helene's inert, motionless body was levitating in the forest, her soul witnessed the birth of the world, for it arose at that moment completely anew, just as it does every time a human being disintegrates after being turned to dust and no longer resembles what it once was, while at the same time remaining what it has been from the beginning. Just as milk curdles when placed over a fire, completely abandoning its liquid state as it solidifies and becomes cheese, so Helene was becoming at that moment, right before the eyes of Kunegunde and the frightened friars, someone else, or perchance someone in addition to herself, retaining the core of her substantive experiences but also now drawing from other lives. Helene saw all as it truly was. How the world came to be, how God was born. God, who was the all-feeling Mother and Daughter, not the all-knowing Father and Son. How the waters and lands came into being, how the first tendrils of plants emerged from the Earth, how rocks begat light-filled stones, and how animals brought forth their young. How they fed them with milk. How they licked them between their eyes. How, later, humans were brought forth into the world and sat close to the fire. How they began to talk to each other, and before that sang together one powerful song, understood by all. A song of creation, a song of life—in which death was contained. Peaceful. Quiet. Noiseless. Motionless. Different from birth. And yet also very similar to it. Equally toothless, and equally strong in its powerlessness.

After Helene had seen all of this, she woke up as if from a dream—though it hadn't been a dream, for she'd been wide awake the whole time—and fell to the ground with a thud. The friars' prayers had reached her earlier, but only now did she hear them fully. Brother Albert's voice, which was usually gentle and brimming with joy like the warble of a goldfinch or a chickadee, now thundered with a deep resonance that pierced the heavens. It seemed to Kunegunde that she was inhaling his voice with the air, until her head began to spin and she nearly collapsed.

And just when it seemed that Helene's soul would never return to her body, the girl suddenly opened her eyes and looked at Brother Albert, but without seeing him at all, as if she'd lost her sight, and began to speak in a language that he did not know, as evocatively as if she'd always been able to speak it. Her voice was even more powerful than the one with which Brother Albert had prayed. At first sonorous, its tone suddenly changed and became rough, hoarse, and unpleasant, punctuated frequently with a strange, ominous squeak, an unbearable rasp. After a while, the sounds resembled the whimpering of an infant, and then transformed into pearly laughter, a snarling growl, and a gurgling death rattle, all at once and alternating, as if it weren't just Helene's voice but a polyphony of many, all merging with hers and intertwining like a braid.

Brother Albert, terrified out of his wits, struggled to wrest control of Helene from the savage thing that had ensnared her soul, but he was unable to gain any power over her at all, as if the beast that had Helene in its clutches wasn't afraid of the cross on his chest or the Lord's Prayer, which he was reciting again and again.

After the girl regained consciousness, which didn't happen until the Lord's Prayer had been recited five times, and her pupils had returned to their usual size, she saw Brother Albert pale with fear, like the fog as white as milk that often hovered over the monastery orchard at dawn. He begged her to say something. To speak to him in her former voice, which had been as sweet as a nightingale's. But incomprehensible sounds erupted from her mouth, as if all the words she'd known up to that point in her life had crumbled to pieces, and such a great terror overwhelmed Brother Albert that he crossed himself.

He lifted Helene and held her in his arms like a breathless, lifeless bundle of straw. He looked at her but did not see her. Instead of Helene—the lovely, graceful little girl with whom he had once spent so much time—there was a demon. The Church had taught him about demons, of course, but up to this point, he had always assumed that was all just silly nonsense. Now he saw it clearly—the girl in front of him had been transformed into someone else. A stranger. Silent and sullen. She had still been herself the day before, after supper—but that morning, with her first monthly bleeding, she had become a new being who filled him with horror.

When they lifted Helene from the ground and placed her on Brother Albert's back, for she didn't have the strength to walk back to the monastery on her own two feet, he had to hold her in place because her body kept falling limply, like one of the life-sized dolls stuffed with straw that they made in the villages every year to bid farewell to winter, despite the Church's prohibition of this pagan ritual.

As they left the forest, they noticed marks carved into the trees that hadn't been there before. Marks that no single person could possibly have made in such a short period of time . . . Marks that were considered cursed in all the religions of the world because they placed upon a pedestal not the Father but the Mother.

Concerning the Vagina-Womb-Skull and the Embroidered Gospel

"H*ystero-kolpo-cranios!*" exclaimed venerable Brother Hubert, upon seeing the mysterious carvings in the trees on the way back to the monastery from the deadwood forest.
"What the devil?!" Brother Albert blurted out, immediately crossing himself three times and spitting over his left shoulder. "The vagina-womb-skull—the symbol of the Primeval Virgin. The world's oldest religion. The worship of the goddess of fertility, Semele, Mat Zemlya, Magna Mater, Mother Earth, or simply good old Demeter. The mother of all gods, whom we replaced with God the Father, renouncing what is alive, what is feminine. To our own profound detriment."

Right at that moment, Kunegunde thought about banging snags in the forest. She remembered how she'd often done it as a child but had since forgotten all about it. But now she recalled roaming the woods with a rod she'd made for herself from a huge stick and smashing withered branches off the trees. She felt that by doing so she was helping dying trees to survive—she was resurrecting them. Two years ago, while doing the same thing, had she not felt that in order to resurrect a withering religion, she needed to cut away from it all that was dead? And was not the figure who had guided her through the forest—the old woman–child who sometimes seemed to have Helene's face—the Primeval Virgin Herself? Who, then, was Helene? A divine epiphany embodying a deep longing for Mother Earth? The God whom the Franciscans—who loved everything that lived on the Earth but were forced to recite dead Latin phrases in long, boring liturgies—yearned for so intensely that it led them to sin?

"The vagina-womb-skull," Brother Albert repeated to Kunegunde Kreppel. They were whispering very quietly because of their fear and excitement, and thus could barely hear each other.

Brother Albert glanced at Brother Hubert, who was transfixed by the words he'd uttered and so affected by the discovery they'd just made that a transformation could be seen on his face as well. As if, suddenly, upon seeing the symbols carved by Helene on the trees, something had been released in him with which he'd lost connection long ago, and which he greatly missed.

When the friars' gazes crossed, Brother Hubert, without saying a single word, placed his hand on Brother Albert's shoulder and, raising his eyebrows, asked a silent question. Brother Albert said nothing in response. But later that day, after returning to the monastery with Helene and Kunegunde, the two friars gazed at each other again, then they silently returned to the forest. They made their way through the trees and berry bushes, as if searching for something. And when they each found suitable spots— far enough away from each other to ensure privacy—they threw off their habits and lay down on the forest floor with their bellies to the ground (Brother Albert, due to the size of his belly, lay on a slight incline thickly covered with moss), and began to poke holes in the undergrowth with sticks in order to insert their rigid rodkins, which had suddenly become inflamed with lust.

And here they were, not even in the "hungry gap" of early spring, when the anonymous author of the treatise permitted these acts. The two friars felt such an overwhelming desire to penetrate the Earth and moisten it with their juices, but also to moisten their members with the Earth's subterranean moisture, as if they were about to copulate with the entire world. Except that the world was, through these clefts in the Earth, simultaneously copulating with the friars, for while the friars were grinding against the soil, there was also suction emanating from the Earth. Thus, it was difficult to say who was truly grinding whom.

It was as if they were creating the world anew. As if bilberries, willows, and bulrushes would emerge from their seed. They had mutual passion for each other and for all of creation, which is mentioned rarely, far too rarely, in the teachings of the Old Testament and the Gospels.

"Why," Hubert asked Albert one hour later, after putting his habit back on, "should a person love another person but not any other living being, whatever it may be—even a tree, a being of great significance in the Garden of Eden and the Book of Genesis?"

The two men then spent an hour or so in the forest together, looking for anything that might illuminate the matter for them, even just a little. How did it happen that Helene had gained insight into the world's oldest religion, which had been banned by the Church? How had she learned about it? Brother Hubert feared he would never know the answer to this, since Helene seemed unable to speak. All they were able to find in the forest were piles of broken branches lying around trunks gnawed by beavers, as if withered limbs had been ripped off the dying trees. Something else that puzzled them, and which they preferred not to show to the father general and the other friars so as to protect

Helene from suspicion of being in league with the Devil, was the drops of liquid flowing down from the spots where the mysterious carvings had been made. Not of resin but of blood.

"It's as if the trees marked with the symbol of the vagina-womb-skull have begun menstruating along with Helene," concluded Kunegunde Kreppel, who later accompanied the friars during one of their visits to the forest. "As if the trees and Helene have joined as one."

Kunegunde did not reveal to them, out of concern for the girl, that she had also found blood on the stick that Helene had apparently used to hack away at the deadwood with all her might to separate what was alive from what was dead. The girl was bleeding from between her legs more intensely than what normally would be attributed to menstruation alone, just as Kunegunde had two years prior. Although she didn't mention it aloud, Kunegunde Kreppel was almost certain that the end of the stick had been firmly plunged where Helene, under the watchful eye of Kunegunde and Brother Albert, wasn't supposed to bring even a finger near, and that it had been plunged there many times.

She decided to examine Helene herself one week later, by spreading the girl's legs as she slept. The light from the candle's flame revealed to Kunegunde what she feared most: Helene's cleft was torn open. She guessed that her hymen had disappeared without a trace, just like her voice.

From then on, Kunegunde decided never to let Helene out of her sight, which wasn't difficult since they spent a significant amount of time embroidering together. Nevertheless, she now felt wholeheartedly that she should follow the girl everywhere—not to protect her from trouble but for Kunegunde's own well-being. For only when she was near Helene did she feel alive.

She was no longer capable of attending mass; she looked for

any possible excuse not to pray; she could no longer recite from memory the prayers she used to be able to rattle out even when half asleep, suddenly awakened in the middle of the night. Now, to recite the Lord's Prayer, she needed to have her breviary in front of her, for the words kept rearranging themselves in her throat and getting mixed up in her memory, causing ridiculous, meaningless sentences to emerge.

It was the same with Helene—she prayed merely for the sake of appearances, while in truth she was giving praise to the four sides of the world, to all that was under the Earth, not under the heavens. To moss, lichen, fungi, and ferns—the ever-changing and decaying substance of the world. To death in its most life-giving form, because it is death that nourishes everything that lives. To composted humans. And dead animals. The rotting, decaying plant kingdom. Helene wallowed in this death, which at the same time contained new beginnings; after all, it was from death that new life rose in the spring, piercing through the Earth's frozen crust with fresh blades and stalks. Earthworms, moles, and voles brought decomposed matter through the soil and deposited it anew on the surface. And it all blended together, creating an inseparable union of life and death, in which nothing alive or dead remained so eternally.

Kunegunde continued to sit and embroider with Helene, whose speech had returned, though she still rarely spoke. But Kunegunde allowed the girl to embroider more and more often what came from the depths of her heart—or, rather, from the depths of her soul: her epiphanies. Thus, instead of swallows, doves, lambs, olive leaves, and clusters of grapes, Helene's designs increasingly included motifs from the visions she'd experienced while floating above the Earth: moss, roots, rhizomes, mycelia, the decomposing vegetation of the Earth, rotting fruit, the bodies of shot quails and partridges, decaying leaves, and the Primeval Virgin Herself in three forms—as a child, a young woman, and an old woman with a childlike smile on Her face.

She embroidered symbols that came to her on their own, filling her in the same way the sacred host previously had, during the Catholic liturgy, with meanings that Helene didn't know. The things she embroidered were more powerful than she was, and she felt that they expressed more clearly what was inside her than anything she could say in words. Kunegunde was the only person with whom Helene ever spoke, and only when Kunegunde asked her about something directly. Then Helene would show Kunegunde her embroidered narrative. Her religion. Her Truth.

Lest she arouse, God forbid, the suspicions of the father general and the other friars, who had been ordered by the father general to keep an eye on the housekeeper, Kunegunde would recite while embroidering with Helene—first out loud and then in a whisper to impersonate Helene—a litany, or the rosary, while from out of Helene's skilled hand would emerge a scene the complete opposite of what Kunegunde was saying. When Kunegunde said "God the Father," Helene embroidered the image of the Earth Mother in Her three forms—depicted as either the three phases of the moon or the three phases of a woman's development. Belladonna berries and oak leaves appeared beneath Her hand instead of olive leaves, and instead of a white dove, poppies, which cause drowsiness and eternal sleep. And above it all, Helene embroidered the vagina-womb-skull instead of the all-seeing eye.

In the monastery's laundry room, Helene found chasubles and altar cloths that were soiled with candle wax, stained with communion wine, and smeared with goose lard that hadn't been wiped thoroughly from fingers after eating, all swirled together with dirty clothes in washtubs. The garments, befouled with human filth, excrement, and scraps of food, were washed in water with lye soap made from aspen or beech ash, which burned the hands badly.

In addition to the coarse dresses that the friars had brought for Helene from the market in the town of Edelstadt, she also had two old petticoats, and she decided to use them to embroider the teachings. Since she didn't have enough time during the day to embroider everything, she made a dummy out of straw, covered its head with cut locks of her own hair, put her nightgown on it, and placed it under the quilt on the straw mattress where she slept. She hoped that if one of the friars, while making his nightly rounds through the monastery, peeked through the little window in the door to Helene's cell to see if she was asleep, he would see her lying on her stomach, and this would allow her to embroider all night long, in a corner of the cell that was impossible to see through the window, to bring to life on the cloth whatever was occupying her thoughts—whatever was penetrating her soul and radiating outward, as if sunlight were shining inside her, filling all her bones and the flesh that covered them.

Helene described everything that was being revealed to her in the patterns she embroidered, and she was constantly waiting for new revelations. The friars, especially Brother Albert and Brother Hubert, were also waiting. Except, of course, the bishop's spy—the monastery's father general.

Meanwhile, the activity that Albert and Hubert had begun in the forest was becoming extremely popular with the other friars—in complete secrecy from the father general, of course. It became the bane of the monastery. It was precisely this—the "stirring of the earth" proceeding from the Primeval Virgin—that foreshadowed the monastery's final days, which were rapidly approaching.

Especially at dusk.

On Stirring the Earth and Itchy Testicles

Certainly not by coincidence but rather as a repercussion of these events, several months after Helene's revelation, the second part of the treatise "On Fervent Love for All Things Earthly" appeared in the monastery, bearing the title "On Stirring the Earth," which had a significant influence on the friars' lives, especially at night.

Right after the afternoon prayers, in the hours before supper, they would venture, several at a time, into the farthest corners of the garden, which was still covered with frost. When they reached a spot from which they could not be seen from the father general's windows, they would loosen the soil with sticks and pine cones, and sometimes even chisels that they'd managed to steal from the toolshed during the renovation work that had been in progress for many years in the refectory. They would try with all their strength to penetrate the hard crust of the earth and reach its deeper layers. Another group of friars would come after them, several hours later, and gouge into the ground even deeper, since the soil had been prepared somewhat by the friars who had been there previously. This continued for two weeks.

Finally, on the vernal equinox, the friars had loosened up the soil and dug holes deep enough that they finally achieved what they'd been striving for all throughout late winter and early spring.

They lay on the ground and aimed their rodkins into the holes, one after another, and everything proceeded in profound silence and pious concentration, as if they were worshipping God Himself. They took turns copulating with the earth; while one squirted into it, the next was already getting ready to fill the clefts in the soil, the holes they'd dug themselves, with life-giving juice. And the pleasure from this was immense, for the Earth received the warmth of their bodies with gratitude, yearning already for the heat and masculine energy that the sun would give it when spring finally came. Copulation with these men, absorbing their seed, jolted the Earth from its winter lethargy. It was an invitation to spring. A gauntlet thrown to the sun, like a challenge to a duel. And the friars, as well, felt at last fulfilled as they moved their hips, gouging the Earth's cleft. They all had a sensation, however, that they had, for this one night, suspended their vows of chastity, of which, after all, one of the three knots on the ropes used as belts around their habits served as a constant reminder. They were aching for contact with dark, cool, damp matter. For sin fueled by all that is of the Earth. There was no debauchery in this but rather a love for all that was living, which was a wellspring of sin but also of love, for all creatures were begotten of this Earth. As the friars' seed penetrated deep into the soil, they could feel how they were fertilizing it, how they were enriching it, so that everything the anonymous author of the treatise loved so much—every creature in the heavens and on the Earth—would benefit. The elderberry bushes, now naked with their leaves decaying on the ground, in a month's time would bloom and spread a canopy of bright green leaves over the soil they'd fertilized, and the bees would feed on nectar from their flowers in the spring, and then delicious honey would be produced in September. And in the winter the birds would feast here, greedily devouring the berries protruding from the bare branches. The friars thought about how their seed would flow into the depths of the Earth and merge with the moisture there, continuing to flow through the channels created by tree roots and supplying the male element to the entire subterranean world, which in the spring breaks through the Earth's surface to absorb some air and sunshine, and when it emerges in the form of trees, bushes, herbs, and flowers of all kinds, as well as moss, lichens, and mushrooms, it nourishes and heals all the people of the world, although it sometimes also abruptly shortens their lives.

Unfortunately, this mystical practice, revealed in the work of unknown authorship (although everyone in the monastery was quite certain that it had been penned by the same man from whose hand had emerged the previous work, "On Fervent Love for All Things Earthly," thanks to which they had been able to satisfy their lust), also caused them a considerable amount of trouble. The type of trouble that no Franciscan order, and perchance no other Catholic order in the world, had ever faced.

Eventually the friars who had been poking their rodkins into the damp, cool soil began to suffer from a particularly nasty itching of the testicles, along with a hideous scab. In addition to flaming-pink scaly patches, they also began to go bald—by no means on their heads. It looked so disgusting that they averted their gazes while urinating so as not to witness what was afflicting their manhood, and such a profound grief gripped their hearts that they were close to tears. Their testicles were also severely swollen.

Alarmed by the fact that the men under his care were in such a woeful condition, the father general ordered them to take off their robes one by one and stand before him naked, just as the Lord had created them, and began to inquire into the reason for their strange behavior—scratching their genitals during the liturgy, walking awkwardly, spreading their legs wide apart. He thus discovered that some of them had swollen testicles, scabs, and itching.

He resolved to find the cause of this condition, so he began following the friars day and night. He stalked them, ambushed them, and jumped out suddenly whenever he observed any behavior that seemed even slightly suspicious. But the friars were unable to engage in earth-stirring then, anyway, due to the pain in their balls, so all attempts to catch them in the act were unsuccessful.

One day, however, while lurking behind a bookcase in the library, he caught a glimpse of Brother Hubert working on the treatise, whose authorship no one had yet managed to determine.

Completely absorbed by his explorations of knowledge about the veneration of the Primeval Virgin, at that moment Brother Hubert was adding an appendix to the treatise "On Stirring the Earth," titled "An Herbal Cure for Itchy Testicles." He had worked on it earlier with Brother Albert and Kunegunde Kreppel, who had a vast knowledge of herbs. Hoping to help the friars, Kunegunde had boiled a large cauldron of potato peelings, which could cover the balls overnight after they'd been rubbed with an ointment made of badger fat, garlic, marigolds, chamomile, and lavender.

The father general sneaked up on Brother Hubert from behind and grabbed the upper part of his habit, lifting the scrawny man above the ground.

To punish the friars, he ordered them to assemble in the west wing, in a large hall where they often gathered for important monastic events, and he forced them all to undress again. He wished to determine how many of them had preserved their "earthly purity" and how many had defiled divine creation with their carnal weakness. When he saw that even his favorite ones,

Brother Albert and Brother Hubert, had balls covered with scabs and molting like old cats whose fur was falling out along with their teeth, he decided to punish the entire brotherhood.

He ordered the friars to go out to the garden stark naked and grind the soil with their swollen genitals until the sores became completely inflamed, so that they would never forget, for the rest of their lives, that the monastery was a place where one must keep a firm grip on one's rodkin and balls!

So they cried and pounded their rodkins into holes that they'd dug in the soil with their fingers, but instead of pleasure and relief it brought them only unbearable suffering—the scabs spread even more, and the itching sensations burned like fire. The friars yearned for their rodkins and balls to fall off entirely, freeing them once and for all from their guilt and misery.

And since this punishment was accompanied by a thorough search of the entire monastery, with the aim of confiscating all the sinful pamphlets that Brother Hubert had created, Kunegunde Kreppel and Helene Spalt, fearing the discovery of the fabrics they'd embroidered, decided to flee that night. They took dozens of old liturgical cloths and vestments with them that they hadn't yet thrown away and on which they'd embroidered the gospel of the Primeval Virgin.

They were supported in their escape by Brother Albert and Brother Hubert, whom the father general was determined to expel beyond the borders of the duchy. As far from Neisse as possible.

Concerning Marriage to a Blacksmith and the Famous Anti-Rodkin Elixir

Although Helene Spalt wasn't Kunegunde Kreppel's daughter by birth, she was a daughter to her nonetheless. And when Kunegunde decided to give Helene away in marriage, she knew that she was going against the girl's true calling. She was pulling her away from the propagation of belief in the Primeval Virgin, which, though it seemed new, was actually the oldest religion in the world. The word "propagate" was well suited to Helene's calling, for it embodied the essence of how this faith was spread: after all the deadwood was stripped from the trunk, new, healthy branches pulsing with life would grow, and from these, more and more would emerge, shooting up to the sky in a mighty green canopy. In order to sustain life in this trunk, it was necessary to nourish the Earth, the Primordial Mother, with that which was alive in ourselves. According to the teachings embroidered in the gospel of the Primeval Virgin, the only way to do this was by "cleft-sparking"—the act of striking a spark in one's cleft, either alone or in communion with other women, nourishing the Earth by rubbing the moisture of one's cleft into the moss while, at the same time, sucking into it the underground currents of moisture hidden beneath the layer of soil. Rubbing, sucking, yielding vital fluids to the Earth, and receiving its fluids into oneself. A moist circulation of the most life-giving substances, guaranteeing not only a continuation in time but a genuine state of being. No longer existing solely as yourself—a person with a preassigned status and name, a bag of skin concealing muscles, organs, and bones—but as everything alive, everything that's sprung from the womb of the Earth.

Kunegunde Kreppel married Helene off solely so that she would have a place to live and something to eat. Helene herself wished to live in the forest. Only there did she feel at home. However, out of the deep love and devotion she had for Kunegunde, she agreed to the marriage. Despite what her intuition whispered in her ear.

After escaping from the monastery, they'd had nowhere to sleep and nothing to eat except for the leftovers they managed to scavenge from inns and taverns. They were hired as maids, but since they were two mouths to feed instead of just one, they quickly lost their jobs—they were too much of a burden on their employers, especially since Helene could do very little besides milking cows and embroidering. And because she was silent, she didn't win the favor of the townswomen who hired her. Meanwhile, the male townsfolk felt their rodkins hardening at the sight of Kunegunde, who often had to offer herself to the "dickheads" and "hookworms," as she called them, to ensure that she and Helene might be able to stay somewhere a little while longer.

Thus, when the opportunity arose, Kunegunde, with Helene's consent, married the girl off to reap benefits for them both. She struck a deal with Karl Schmied, a local blacksmith afflicted with a serious case of ichthyosis vulgaris that made him look as if he were covered with fish scales. Despite his pleasant manner and great wealth, no maiden in Neisse wanted him, for they were afraid of passing the dreaded disease to their offspring. Before

Helene's wedding day came, Kunegunde made careful preparations to keep the marriage from ever being consummated.

She recalled how once, in order to subdue the lustful urges the friars had felt toward her before they'd become acquainted with "On Fervent Love for All Things Earthly," Brother Albert had boiled a large cauldron full of flaxseeds and spearmint and, after straining it all through a sieve, mixed it with beer, a full jug of which each friar drank with supper. This clever tactic ensured that none of the friars' rodkins stirred in the evening, during the night, or throughout the following morning until noon, which meant one thing: in order to keep the brothers flaccid, they needed to be served the concoction daily. It had only an anti-female effect, however. Later, faced with the lust aroused by the descriptions and illustrations in the mysterious treatise, its effect was weak if not completely nonexistent.

Upon remembering this, Kunegunde brewed enough of the herbs to ensure the blacksmith's impotence until the very end of time, and consequently, now reassured about her protégée's cleft, she decided to settle into the blacksmith's house, which had a beautiful fruit orchard. She and Helene postponed what they'd been planning to do: worship the Primeval Virgin, teach women to attain heights of pleasure not given to them by husbands or lovers who were utterly uninterested in their needs, and become skilled at regulating childbirth—all with the help of what Mother Earth had brought forth from Herself, what She had begotten at the very dawn of time.

Helene accepted the blacksmith Karl Schmied's surname merely as a formality but continued to call herself Spalt, as she always had. From his house, which stood on a hill outside the town's walls, there was a beautiful view of the forest nestled in the river valley. The river called out to her day and night, sending its messengers up to the blacksmith's house. Deer, wild boar, and beavers approached the windows, and Helene would feed them with whatever scraps she could find and look after them.

They would have lived very well together, had it not been for the sadness that began to afflict Karl soon after the wedding when it turned out that he was incapable of possessing his beautiful young bride because his rodkin was defective. A rodkin of which hitherto he had been so proud.

The blacksmith Karl Schmied, who didn't know that he would remain impotent throughout his entire marriage, sometimes wept in a corner of his smithy, suffering from an intense feeling of guilt that he had led this lovely maiden into such a predicament. Helene had lived for only sixteen springs, and since he wasn't very old either, having lived for merely twenty-four, they were doomed, in his opinion, to a long life bereft of carnal love, unless someone could cure him of this affliction.

The poor fellow wasn't aware that he was being plied daily not with beer alone, which he would never have been able to forgo, no more than God, but also with a concoction so strong that even a dog wouldn't have become stiff at the sight of a bitch. He ate almost nothing, drank very little, lost weight, felt constantly distressed, and couldn't sleep. Helene began to feel sorry for him. He was a good husband, so diligent in his work, tender in his daily life, and concerned about her and Kunegunde's well-being. She let him slowly grow closer to her—only when he wasn't fighting against the impotence of his rodkin but rather frolicking with Helene while it remained in a state of total, piteous lassitude. Then she would fondle it with her hands as if she were kneading dough for bread, dip it in a bowl of warm milk, and fling it joyfully to the right and left, treating it more like a lovable animal than a man's body part, and one that should be feared at that.

Meanwhile, the herbs that Helene had brewed with Kunegunde were in ever greater demand among the women of Neisse and the surrounding countryside. She and Kunegunde began to earn a fortune from them, enjoying the adoration of the women they had liberated from oppression in the bedroom.

Kunegunde spread the news of their elixir, which hindered male members from becoming rigid, when she and Helene sold their delicious cheese at the Thursday market. She'd overhear women chatting, mainly about topics connected to the bedroom, and did not hesitate to mention that, in addition to their excellent cheese, they were also secretly selling various medicinal products for women. Beauty ointments as well as remedies for broken hearts, excessive irritability (commonly referred to by men as "having a hissy fit"), and other so-called shameful complaints — discharge, delayed menstruation, unwanted pregnancies, and excess potency in husbands who waited all day for nightfall, so that they could torment their poor wives instead of letting them rest.

And since this last problem dominated the conversations nearly every Thursday, Kunegunde recommended ever more daringly her signature product — the anti-rodkin elixir. She wished to relieve the women of their misery, for they often suffered greatly when their husbands, not experiencing happiness in the bedroom, or experiencing too little of it, directed their attention toward other clefts. How many tears were shed over this! How many hissy fits there were! And hatred arose between the women because of it, as well as jealousy. Kunegunde knew that of all the products she and Helene offered, apart from cheese and milk, it was the elixir that earned the most praise.

And so, instead of preparing delicacies to increase the sexual desire of their present or future husbands, the women of Neisse added drops of the anti-rodkin elixir into their drinks, causing them to become increasingly frustrated. Their limp, flaccid appendages, from which vigor and life had evaporated, dangled between their legs during the day like broken or dislocated squirrel tails, while at night they reposed idly on their owners, waiting for better times, allowing the women to finally have some respite from childbearing and being used by men for physical pleasure. They could shift their attention to the other, nonhuman sexual objects with which they'd become acquainted while cleft-sparking.

Helene prepared the women for these mystical practices, but only after she checked them carefully and confirmed that they were ready, for she took great care not to reveal her methods to anyone who did not have a true calling for them. When Helene was certain the women were ready to be initiated, she and Kunegunde invited them on Friday evenings, just after sunset, to a massive oak tree in a forest glade down by the river, under which they would devote themselves to rapturous prayers, culminating in communal ecstasy and intense physical pleasure that penetrated the heart and soul.

Unfortunately, a scandal that finally exposed the perfidious practices of the local women to the entire duchy unfolded in one of the most popular brothels in Neisse, where a customer—the court feldsher of Bishop Johannes von Sitsch—for the ninth time in one month was unable to make use of a particular service after paying a hefty fee for it, as his rodkin was once again malfunctioning. This time he decided to sneak out of the chamber dedicated to romping and take a peek at what was going on in the brothel's kitchen. When he saw the cook stirring a concoction in a huge cauldron and then ladling it carefully into a jug of beer, he understood everything in an instant and, slamming the door behind him, rushed straight to the town hall to report to the court that men were being poisoned with herbs at the brothel.

It eventually came to light that Helene Spalt, the wife of the blacksmith Karl Schmied—who, despite what was written on her marriage certificate, always introduced herself as Spalt—and Kunegunde Kreppel, who was living in their house in an unknown capacity, were secretly distributing this concoction to women at the market, and hence a decision was made to interrogate them both.

When news spread that it was these two women who had been poisoning husbands in the area for the past few months, causing a sharp decline in the number of pregnancies throughout the duchy, which the Catholic Church considered a sin and an attack against its institution, Helene and Kunegunde were slapped with a hefty fine—twelve ducats each. This amounted to their entire fortune, which they'd been carefully hiding from Karl Schmied.

Further problems ensued. For one thing, they became notorious throughout the duchy. They were no longer mute Helene Spalt and the erstwhile strumpet Kunegunde Kreppel. They became treacherous seed, satanic chaff for Bishop Johannes von Sitsch and the entire canonry, who had been shaking up the duchy and trying, above all, to propagate truly virtuous, bourgeois values among the townsfolk, while instilling in women the duty to bear children and raise them as decent Catholics.

Upon learning of all this, Karl, for the first time since his wedding, began to rant and rave in the company of the men in the tavern who were discussing the scandal, swearing and flailing his arms, cursing his marriage to Helene with all his might, after which, having drunk more beer than usual, he returned home and dragged her to their bed without a word. And when she lay down beside him at his command, she felt, instead of the soft, docile little animal that was usually curled between his legs, a rod as hard and rigid as the sticks she used to bang deadwood in the forest.

She tried to wriggle out of his grasp, but in vain. He possessed her exactly as he'd dreamed of doing for over a year—in every possible way—nearly until dawn. Without rest, without respite, penetrating her again and again, sometimes stopping briefly, but only long enough for the strength in him, fueled by anger, to surge anew.

And Helene, closing her eyes, strove with all her might not to make a single sound, sensing that only by holding back what was pushing its way to her lips, by forcing back into her throat the animal scream that was rising within it, would she transform powerlessness into power and the deepest darkness into a blinding light. And perchance she might succeed in summoning the one who illuminated the darkness and led the way through the most difficult times. As she suppressed her breath to the minimum necessary to survive in a lethargic state, to freeze her body and become utterly motionless, she achieved what the Primeval Virgin had taught her—she was suddenly elsewhere. She had reached this state just once before—after her trance in the deadwood forest, when she had levitated above the Earth or rested on Her as if dead. She had made contact with the Earth, merged with Her as one, and shed her corporeal, decaying husk.

The trees were calling out to her tenderly; she could almost hear her name in their rustling. And then she saw the deadwood glade. In sunshine and rain. Simultaneously. In the glade, a group of women were lying in a circle around a huge oak tree, the one beneath which Kunegunde and Helene had consumed the belladonna. One of the women bore an eerie resemblance to herself. The women's feet were touching each other. Their knees were bent and their thighs were spread wide, as if they were feeding their clefts with rain. As if they were giving their vulvas a drink. The women were soaked to the bone, with their hips raised so that the raindrops, like a man's seed, would enter them and settle in their very depths. There, where life begins. They were as taut as strings, for they found pleasure in receiving the rain into themselves. The oak tree's bark was perforated with small tubes, from which golden sap was flowing and trickling into jugs, drop by drop. One jug for each of them. Twelve women. Twelve jugs. Suddenly the woman resembling Helene transformed into a laughing old woman, and then into a child with the same gaping, toothless smile.

Under the influence of this vision of the Primeval Virgin, Helene began to receive Karl into herself in a completely new way. Like rain.

And when dawn came, having exhausted all his vital energy in that one true night of marriage, Karl Schmied was dead. He had given up the ghost at the precise moment when a new life had been conceived in his young wife, Helene Spalt. A life that was permeated through the air by particles of all living beings begotten since the dawn of time — in water, on land, and in the heavens.

Concerning the Docile Child, Beneficent Bloodick, and Moving to the Forest

How did it happen that a woman as young and strong as Helene Spalt brought forth a child who was unable to enjoy the same things as her mother? Well, that's how life is sometimes. Children are begotten into this world who seem utterly the opposite of their parents. Whether this happens by coincidence or the conscious defiance of the child, nobody really knows. Sometimes the apple falls very far from the tree. And thus it was this time.

From an early age, Ursula exhibited character traits that were quite distinct from her mother's. Meekness and docility. A disregard for her own personal needs. And at the same time an extraordinary gentleness, which, of course, was accompanied by vulnerability to all manner of injury—not only of the body but also of the spirit. Her timid soul was so sensitive that even a callous glance cast her way could hurt her deeply. Thus Helene, unlearned in such sensitivity, had to tiptoe around Ursula and take great pains not to be too forceful, too loud, too fast for her. But that's exactly how she was and always had been. Even as a child. This is precisely why every soul at the monastery had loved her. She had united the friars with her joyous personality. Her boundless energy and inquisitiveness. Her radiant face in the morning. Her enthusiastic greeting of each new day.

Additionally, everything Helene loved bothered the wee girl, triggering in her an intensely defensive reaction. The sun constantly tormented her. The child's eyes watered as a cat's would while being gnawed at by insects. And on days when the sunshine was particularly bright, she sneezed violently. A foul-smelling mucus often oozed out of the child's ears and navel, and her poop smelled so sour and was such an unpleasant shade of green, it was impossible to clean the cloths in which she was wrapped in the river, even with the help of lye. All types of plant pollen caused rashes and sores to break out on her body, and even bathing in potato peelings brought no relief. The nuts that Helene often ate along with berries she picked in the forest made it hard for the child to breathe and caused her head to swell to nearly twice its size. And worst of all were the negative effects that cow's milk and cheese had on her, as these were Helene and Kunegunde's main source of sustenance—particularly since they'd been caught selling the anti-rodkin elixir. It had never been unequivocally proven that Helene and Kunegunde had been the creators of the elixir, which was fortunate because if the Church had declared them as such, they would have been hanged from one of the trees in front of the Breslau Gate alongside other villains and deviants.

But even the threat of death didn't render Helene and Kunegunde idle. Immediately after Karl's death, they invented another product that greatly pleased the women of the duchy—the famous "bloodick" ointment, which they distributed in a much safer and more ingenious way. Made from bloodwort, pimpinella root, and black hollyhock, bloodick was an extremely potent ointment that caused the townswomen to bleed multiple times in a single month: hardly had one period ended when the next one began. Helene and Kunegunde wrapped the ointment up in leaves wound in twine and hid it inside the lumps of cheese they produced. With it concealed in this way so as not to arouse the suspicion of the cassock-clad men who were now roaming the market to ensure that the women of the duchy were not committing some new kind of transgression, the women smuggled the ointment home and used it in secret, without their husbands knowing.

Henceforth the ladies of the duchy could peacefully spend their evenings and nights indulging in other activities—reading, for example, which was gradually becoming popular, for the first printing press had begun operating in Neisse. They also devoted themselves to embroidering textiles, an activity that, thanks to the lady from Ferrara, famous for her proclivity for women, was becoming ever more common. One could earn quite a decent living from embroidering tablecloths for inns and taverns, or elegant dresses in tailors' shops.

Other townswomen had been inspired by the lady of Ferrara to take up not embroidery but baking—specifically the art of baking Italian sweets, which were very different from the local ones because they were made of white flour and sugar instead of honey and spices. They were as light as a cloud, and you could thus eat a greater quantity, but they cost so much that only the wealthiest townsfolk could savor them.

"Italian sugar—best to pass, for it goes straight to your ass!" Kunegunde Kreppel often quipped. She exercised restraint with regard to Italian novelties and continued to bake her beloved heavy gingerbread, the taste of which lifted men up so high they could fly all the way to Ferrara.

The effect of the bloodick ointment was a true blessing for the women of Neisse, for the menfolk of the town listened attentively to the sermons preached by the bishop of Breslau, Andreas Jerin, in the Basilica of Saint James and Saint Agnes, and shuddered at the thought of fulfilling marital obligations on "bloody days," which the bishop described as "cursed." The men of Neisse feared this more than another outbreak of plague, famine, or war. Women were thus finally able to enjoy their long-awaited freedom, even after the supplies for their beloved anti-rodkin elixir had been seized by the Church and secured in the catacombs of the basilica. Their constant bleeding had forced their husbands into abstinence and caused great distress and frustration. And since the trollops practicing the world's oldest profession were also bleeding frequently, to the distress of all the madams running the establishments in which they worked, the Duchy of Neisse was once again facing a catastrophe—both demographic and emancipatory—and was thus setting a terrible example for other cities in Europe.

The case of "the bleeding women of Neisse" was discussed extensively at courts across the Continent and even in the colonies. People wondered why the women there had begun to menstruate so differently from the way nature intended, no longer adhering to the divine order but descending into a state of chaos that offended God.

None other than the pope himself took an interest in the matter and sent his own court physicians to Neisse to examine the bleeding women, which yielded no concrete conclusions but only further grumbling and complaints from the Catholic leaders as well as from ordinary God-fearing husbands.

At the same time, though, the women of Neisse had learned about the pleasure of vaginal rubbing from the teachings of Helene Spalt, who had become, since giving birth, quite loquacious, though only about this and other related matters. The women had also learned from Helene the importance of awakening a love in oneself for plants, including a carnal love, for it was in this way that they could worship the divine child—the daughter of Heaven and Earth, who had merged with the latter to become one unified deity: the Primeval Virgin. This is how Helene expressed it, emphasizing always that a woman's god isn't God the Father but Mother Earth, and insisting that the mission of all women on Earth should be to revive their true religion. The religion that the Church had taken from them. She had received precisely this mission from the Primeval Virgin Herself, when She'd appeared to her and entered her in the deadwood forest.

Helene's lessons took place in secrecy, under the very oak tree where she had consumed the belladonna berries, first with Kunegunde Kreppel and later by herself—that is, the exact spot in which she'd beheld her soul separate from her body on the night her marriage was consummated, one year after her wedding. The night that brought death to her husband, the blacksmith Karl Schmied.

As soon as each lesson had finished, Helene became mute again, unable to utter a sound. As if the language she spoke was meant to serve just one purpose: to propagate a new faith (which was, in fact, the world's oldest faith) and the teachings that sprang from it.

Thanks to the bloodick ointment, Helene and Kunegunde were able to recover quickly from the financial losses they'd suffered, and they used the money to buy fabric, including higher-quality cloth and even silk, on which to narrate the truth of their revelations without the use of words, which are inadequate for expressing such things. To praise the power of the Primeval Virgin. To awaken love, including carnal love, for all the plant life begotten of Mother Earth. From sunny yellow buttercups and calamus rhizomes to soft, tickling pussy willows and intensely veined downy leaves.

The sermons preached by Helene every Friday afternoon were initially attended by only a handful of women who knew her and Kunegunde thanks to the secret products they sold at the market, but soon many more joined them—first about one hundred, and a few months later as many as three hundred. This began to arouse a wave of suspicion among Church authorities, and rumors about Helene and Kunegunde reached even the bishop of Breslau.

Helene arrived early to her lessons every Friday to bang deadwood in the forest and thus achieve union with Mother Earth. For she wished not only to give sermons about the Primeval Virgin but to proclaim Her by allowing the Primeval Virgin to enter and become one with her. It was only through this transformation that Helene regained the ability to speak.

However, this union did not always happen. Only some of the trances were truly fruitful, after which Helene would receive an image from the Primeval Virgin to convey to the women through embroidery or sermon. This was difficult for her, for while she yearned for deeper and more frequent contact with the Primeval Virgin, she was profoundly affected by it each time. The hallucinogenic berries would completely drain her of her vital force for several nights and days. The fatigue made her stagger, and she would lie completely still for a while, as if listening intently to the Earth. She collapsed into herself then, and the exhaustion gradually drained the milk from her breasts. And her affection for her child.

During this time, Ursula was mainly taken care of by Kunegunde, who looked after her as if she were her own child. She lavished attention on her while pushing back against Helene, whose demands were becoming increasingly unreasonable. Instead of trying to decrease her baby's exposure to anything that might be causing her health problems, Helene had decided, contrary to all sensible judgment, to expose the child even more intensely to those very things. She wanted six-month-old Ursula to be placed in so much direct sunlight that she could have gone blind had Kunegunde listened to her. She immersed the baby in tree pollen at the peak of the season, gave her macerates of nuts and nettles to boost her health and eradicate the parasitic worms that frequently infested her, and fed her cheese made from cow's milk every day as her main meal. It later became clear that Helene hadn't been wrong in doing all this. By the age of three, Ursula had overcome all her weaknesses and limitations, although she remained a timid, delicate child living by other people's rules, always meekly following orders.

This worried Helene because she wished, above all, to teach her daughter how to make up her own mind, how to be an independent person. For even in a world as rigid and uptight as the ecclesiastical duchy, women could, with enough determination, join a guild and become trained as artisans, later earning a living from their trade. She wanted to have a child who was rebellious, defiant, curious about the world, and unable to sit still. However, having been conceived by her father as he slipped into death, Ursula carried within her sadness, anxiety, and reticence — feelings that are usually so foreign to children. She agreed with her mother about everything, never causing any trouble.

Hence, when their house was struck by lightning and they miraculously escaped from the fire alive, and Helene proclaimed that it hadn't happened by accident at all, and that they were going to move to the forest, little Ursula accepted this decision without any complaint. And even with gratitude.

Concerning the Purchase of the Deadwood Forest and the Belladonna Trips That Occurred There

The deadwood forest down by the river—the place where it all began—didn't belong, like the other forests in the duchy, to the diocese, but rather to the Franciscan monastery in which Helene had spent the happy years of her childhood under the tender care of Kunegunde and Brother Albert. This was known to Kunegunde, for on more than one occasion she had heard, with her own ears, the friars expressing outrage about the bishop's foresters cutting trees there and accusing them of trespassing on land that wasn't theirs.

Kunegunde and Helene realized that after their house burned down, people might assume that they had perished tragically in the fire, and they decided to seize the opportunity to change their lives. Kunegunde persuaded Helene to use flour and soot to make herself look older and to go to the friars with an offer to buy the forest for a handsome sum. She used her dead husband's name to ensure that none of the friars would recognize her as the local harlot—the "forest hussy," as they called her.

"Remember to sign the contract not as Spalt but as Schmied," Kunegunde warned her.

For Helene, using her husband's surname felt like selling her soul to the Devil. Kunegunde grew impatient with her obstinacy and shouted at her, "Try for once in your life to think with your mind and not with your vulva!!"

Aware that if the friars refused to sell the forest to them, it could thwart their entire plan, Helene gritted her teeth and headed off to the monastery as Mrs. Schmied.

The father general, who had seen eighty-five springs, scrutinized Helene with a penetrating gaze, trying to comprehend how a woman could have amassed such a large fortune. But overcome by greed for the large pile of gold ducats that Helene had placed on the table in front of him, he decided to ask whence she had come. Helene lied that her husband had died in a mine collapse in Reichenstein while digging for gold, and that his body, like those of the fifty-five other miners who had perished with him, had never been found. At that point in the fabricated story, Helene even managed to squeeze a few tears from her eyes and let them trickle down her cheeks, to lend credence to the hoax.

When asked what she intended to do with a forest full of dead trees, which, moreover, Bishop Johannes von Sitsch himself believed to be cursed, she replied, "I will uproot the remaining stumps that might still have usable wood and offer them to the diocese for the construction of new shrines and churches. And after the land has been cleared, I'll turn the soil into agricultural land for pasturing cattle, for there is nothing I know better than how to make the finest cheese."

Reassured, albeit not completely, the father general ordered the monastery scribe to prepare a deed of sale for the deadwood forest, and they signed two copies of it—one for each party.

The rest went smoothly. It took the women only one afternoon to pack their belongings. Apart from their livestock—one horse, six cows, four hens, and a rooster—very little remained after the house had burned down. They hitched the horse to the cart and Kunegunde settled into it with little Ursula in her arms, then they set off for the place that had been calling to them for years—the place where it had all begun.

In addition to the deadwood forest, the piece of land that Helene had bought included the nearby glade with a large oak tree at its very center, under which deadly nightshade grew, covered in shiny black berries. The glade was down by the river, far from the terrain that had been slated for harvesting and, therefore, out of sight of the men who were hard at work every day felling the trees.

It occasionally happened, though, that the woodcutters would sneak up and peek at the two women while they were gathering herbs, milking the cows, or warming themselves by the fire—all of which they did stark naked, just as God had created them, for this was the only way they could physically experience the full breadth of Nature. And come to know its touch on their skin.

Exposing skin to sunshine was more pleasant than exposing it to rain, frost, or wind, but Helene walked naked in the autumn too; only with the onset of winter did she clothe herself warmly, though she remained barefoot even then so as never to lose contact with Mother Earth.

It once happened that the canonry's clergymen, while hunting deer, glimpsed the naked women by the river while they were milking their cows. The priests were stunned, bewildered by the sight. When they started to question the women, Kunegunde spoke for both herself and Helene, explaining to the priests that they had come from afar, from the town of Reichenstein, after Helene had become a miner's widow, and that they didn't need a house because, at least for the time being, the warm Earth and the starry sky were quite enough for them, but that they might begin to worry when autumn came. But Kunegunde was lying to herself too, for due to her age she would really have preferred—and she didn't fail to remind Helene of this at least once a month—to live in a normal house built of stone and brick. Under a roof, not the sky. Even a starry one.

The three of them lived all alone in the forest for over a year, sleeping outside even in the early spring and autumn, despite it being so cold at night that they had to teach Ursula to breathe very shallowly, barely inhaling, to prevent icicles from growing in her nose. At night, Kunegunde would wrap Ursula in two bearskins, having already layered her in all the clothing that they'd taken with them from the burned house. And when Ursula still felt cold, Kunegunde would rub her back and feet with badger fat mixed with various resins and macerates of leaves from bushes and trees. She would squeeze juice from hawthorn berries straight into the child's mouth, and it would warm the inside of her chilled body so much that she no longer felt the cold.

Helene didn't seem to suffer from the cold at all, as if a different kind of blood had begun to flow in her, or she had some kind of internal mechanism enabling her to survive in any conditions. And since Helene's feet never froze, even though she didn't wear shoes, Kunegunde began to eye her with growing suspicion. She resented the lack of thought that Helene gave to the well-being of her child, who was too young for these sorts of experiments. It seemed as if giving birth to Ursula had exhausted Helene, and she now felt no obligation to guide the girl through life among other human beings. She had relegated this task to Kunegunde, without asking whether Kunegunde was willing to undertake it.

Indeed, Helene was inconsiderate toward Kunegunde in everything she did, something that the latter noticed only once it was too late, after they'd settled in the glade. It was as if Helene's thoughts were never truly with Kunegunde and Ursula. As if her soul were constantly drifting somewhere beyond the glade and their everyday life, and only her body, or even just her bare feet, kept her forcibly bound to them.

Helene's selective use of speech didn't help the situation either, for she spoke only when she truly felt like it or when it was worthwhile for her to do so, such as when buying the land from the monastery.

When the first cold nights came, they made a tent for themselves from a piece of waxed canvas and some large sticks they'd found in a clearing where trees had recently been harvested, stacked one on top of another. At night, they lit a fire in front of the tent to keep themselves warm and bake dinkel-fladenbrot, a thin flatbread made from spelt flour, which they dipped in barley malt, honey, and quince preserves that they'd prepared in the summer. They cooked nettle soup, linden blossom compote, and mushrooms with oats, which Kunegunde considered the healthiest of grains. And above all, they simmered large quantities of milk, which, in all its various forms—whether liquid or solid; with added honey, garlic, and herbs; or as cheese—was once again becoming the mainstay of their diet and an essential element of their survival.

One day, when Ursula was feeling mischievous, she dropped some wild garlic leaves that she'd previously picked in the forest into a vat of milk intended for cheese. She was scolded by Helene and Kunegunde for this prank. But after the milk curdled, it turned out to have a wonderful flavor and an even finer aroma. So they began to experiment by adding blueberries to the cheese, then lungwort, then cowberries, then wild mushrooms that had been fried with onions. And when they brought these new varieties of cheese to the Thursday market, they sold all of them immediately, at twice the usual price.

Experimenting with new additives in cheese became Kunegunde's main occupation. During the first year of their life in the forest, before other women came to live with them in tents, Helene and Kunegunde invented over a dozen types of cheese, with various additives—some with wild garlic, some with water mint that grew along the riverbank, some with tree bark that had been scorched by fire, and some with ash and charcoal.

The clergymen were unable to resist this cheese in all its new varieties and secretly gorged on it, for it had no equal. With a perfect consistency that was soft yet firm, it melted in the mouth, revealing its primordial origin from liquid matter, and overnight became the most coveted product on the tables of all the town's residents, the greatest delicacy at the market in Neisse. Everyone—ranging from simple peasants to the town's wealthiest burghers—awaited the arrival of the women with their wooden cart full of evenly stacked lumps of cheese as well as honey with medicinal herbs added to it, birch sap poured into clay jugs sealed with tree bark, and mead, which Kunegunde left to ferment over the winter and then, in early spring, after removing blocks of ice from the vat, poured into kegs bought from Hans Kolberg, a cooper in Neisse. Eventually their goods were exported, which brought them fame outside the Duchy of Neisse as well. They soon became the most famous products that the duchy had to offer.

And when a dozen lumps of cheese preserved in brine ended up in the Vatican, on the table of the pope himself, he locked himself in his chamber after eating it and lashed himself on the back with a leather whip for a quarter of an hour, punishing himself for excessive gluttony, for—in secret from his entire retinue—he had consumed the entire supply, which was meant to last them several weeks.

Henceforth the demand for cheese became so great that

Helene and Kunegunde had to buy more cows to keep up with the orders.

And as for the lumps of cheese with bloodick hidden in them, they sold them and often gave them for free to women in need who came to them in the glade on the recommendation of others. They also began to send cheese with bloodick in it abroad, despite the risk, and thus all of Europe became afflicted with perpetual menstruation, which significantly lowered its population but simultaneously contributed to the intellectual development of women across the Continent. And to the development of their passions as well. Suffice it to say, it was at precisely this time that the determination among women to work in various trades became increasingly apparent. Most often in the field of painting, which at the time included embroidery. But women sought work in other trades too.

Thus, despite living in the forest, in a duchy far from Paris or London, at the time considered to be the cultural centers of Europe, these two women—or rather three, though the youngest hadn't yet lived to see four springs—had a powerful influence on the emancipation of all the Continent's women. Not thanks to their new religion but rather because of their bloodick ointment. This began to trouble Helene, who was envious of Kunegunde's ideas but had her mind set on something greater than practical solutions to women's problems. Helene wanted to give women a faith that, contrary to what was offered by the Catholic Church, would be tailored specifically for them, with special consideration for their needs.

Helene wanted them to worship the Primeval Virgin. A deity for whom feeling joy in life is far more important than anything that happens after death. Orgasmic ecstasy rather than self-mortification. An unbridled trance experienced in communion with other people, and the bliss that arises when one accepts God into oneself, rather than asceticism and fasting and lashes in a cell with a leather whip. The breaking of prohibitions and worship of the deity while in motion, running through the forest naked, rather than while kneeling or lying prostrate in a church.

Helene knew that the anti-rodkin and bloodick remedies could help attract future believers, but she didn't want them to become an end in themselves. Nor a religion, since making love to plants without any deep connection to God would only sate the women physically and defile their souls, and eventually they'd yearn for a hard cock anyway. Unless she could give them something more.

Helene was so consumed by her desire to create this "something more" that she spent very little time with Ursula, didn't milk the cows or churn the milk to make cheese, or even talk to Kunegunde Kreppel, who was as garrulous as usual. And so, it was against this backdrop—of practice and theory—that the first differences of opinion began to arise between them, differences that would continue to take on greater significance in the events to come, and which would eventually have an influence over Ursula, for whom Kunegunde was more of a mother than her own.

Although little Ursula at first clung to her birth mother as any other child would, now, at the age of four, she preferred to grab the hem of Kunegunde's skirt because her mother was usually impossible to grab, walking naked as she did from morning to night.

Meanwhile, Helene, still pondering how to spread the gospel of the Primeval Virgin to more women than the few wayward souls who came to the glade in search of the famous bloodick remedy, or simply out of idle curiosity, wanting to see how one could live completely deprived of any comforts or conveniences, finally thought of a way to propagate the teachings on a larger scale.

After putting a bit of pressure on Kunegunde, she obtained her permission to sell their cheese on their own property, where they could deny access to the virulent priests who were so pathologically obsessed with them, sniffing them out at the marketplace like dogs on a hunt. Helene and Kunegunde established between them that the cheese containing bloodick, unlike the ordinary cheese that they still sold at the marketplace, could only be purchased in the deadwood forest, with a written record to show who had recommended their product to whom, and only on Friday afternoons, when they performed their Earthen rituals. They hoped that an increasing number of women would join them in their ceremonial worship of the Primeval Virgin, which always began with an intense psychedelic trip, brought on by consuming some belladonna berries, or rubbing their juice into their vulvas, which were aching for ecstatic sensations. Once the trip began, they'd bang the deadwood together, the women seemingly shedding parts of themselves as they did, chopping off what was dead to save what was alive, what was new. This all culminated in communal cleft-sparking and a simultaneous moan of delight—a collective orgasm.

Helene was almost certain that these practices would attract townswomen who were bored of living pious, God-fearing lives as well as peasant women from nearby villages. The latter, she was ashamed to admit, were the ones she counted on the most, for their total lack of inhibition while experiencing pleasure was the greatest trigger of delight in the bourgeois townswomen, who were more inhibited and often burned with shame even beneath the marital quilt.

To these abnegators who forbore their own pleasure for so

many years, Helene would give sticks for banging deadwood that she'd lubricated beforehand with an ointment made of henbane mixed with juice from belladonna berries, to intensify the trip.

They used the word "trip" often, for when henbane was mixed with belladonna and applied to the front or back cleft, it gave incredibly delightful hallucinations, as if they were truly flying above the Earth. For some of the women, the rod inserted between their legs and grasped with their hands in front felt like a vehicle carrying them upward, while to others it seemed like the Devil's dick—but all of them knew that the hallucinations were temporary. And that they were caused by the plants they'd consumed and not by Satan, for no one had ever seen him there.

After the women had ingested belladonna or henbane, the Primeval Virgin would frequently appear in one of Her three forms—sometimes as a child, sometimes as a woman in the prime of her life, and sometimes as an old woman—and it was never fully known why sometimes She had the face of a complete stranger, unknown to anyone, while at others She resembled Ursula, Helene, or Kunegunde, as if the three of them had together become the Primeval Virgin. This fathomless topic was a mystery to Helene, although she taught the women that each one of them was and always had been the Primeval Virgin, just like her. They were all Primeval Virgins, for they all originated from Her; from the womb of Mother Earth had they come and to the womb would they return at their hour of death.

Helene was right when she predicted that for the new religion to be propagated, the women would need to be brought to the forest, for it couldn't be done at the marketplace, where the priests and sentries had been watching their every move like hawks, ever since the days when they'd sold the anti-rodkin elixir. The bait of an orgasmic trip, followed by communal cleft-sparking, proved a very effective lure indeed. What Helene and Kunegunde didn't foresee, however, was that these mystical practices forbidden by the Church would prove so appealing to women that they would want more, leading them to abandon their homes, their families, their entire safe, bourgeois, and tedious lives—a way of life that for centuries, intermittently interrupted by epidemics and wars, had guaranteed the inhabitants of the duchy and surrounding areas eternal salvation and the immortality of the soul.

Was this promise of eternal salvation and the immortality of the soul interesting or attractive to the women from Neisse and the backwater towns and villages in the surrounding countryside? Seemingly not, since dozens of women soon came to the forest to live with Helene and Kunegunde, and eventually they numbered two hundred.

Concerning the Early Days of the Congregation

At first, Helene didn't teach the women so much as simply chat with them about their lives, and about how their clefts were either overused by their husbands or else completely forgotten, until they became as dry as ash, withered, cut off from joy and life. Helene proclaimed that a dry vulva is like a living death, a slow and gradual shriveling and calcification. She touched her own vulva every so often, to keep it continuously moist and aroused. Not to prepare herself for men but to better commune with plants and exchange vital energy with them. When she felt her vulva throbbing, pulsing with life, she knew she had just uttered something important, for it had originated not from the truth of the mind but from the truth of the body.

Soon most of the women who gathered around her were placing their hands on their vulvas too, to make sure that the thought they'd had, or the sentence they'd uttered, belonged to the order of the body. The vulva had become their center, their most formidable guide. This was no easy feat for the women, because until recently they'd still been agreeing, out of politeness and upbringing, with whatever the men in their lives were preaching. But their vulvas had no reaction whatsoever to male truths. In church, during the liturgy, they felt this most strongly. While the priest gave his sermon, the vulvas were numb, as if they'd sunk into a deep sleep, although occasionally a stirring rendition of the Song of Songs overwhelmed them with sudden moisture and a shudder would run through their bodies. As if the poem's words touched both vulva and soul. And once again, the women felt love for God and all creation. Including their husbands. It wasn't often, though, that this happened. Most of the time the women's vulvas remained in a state of deep mourning.

The way they kept touching their vulvas through their gowns was quickly noticed by one of the priests, and news of their behavior soon reached the ears of Bishop Johannes von Sitsch himself, sending him into such a state of indignation that he succumbed to an intense fever that lasted three days. And a hideous rash. As if the heat produced by the fury gripping the mind and body of His Excellency had seeped outward and caused his skin to become inflamed.

After that incident, Bishop von Sitsch appointed one of the canons as a "guardian of divine morality," whose job it was to track down and report on any deviant female behavior in the town of Neisse and the surrounding countryside. It was also the guardian's duty to peek through windows at dusk and spy on the rituals of the townspeople's marital lives. He was supplied with a dozen clergymen to assist him, and they would all grimly roam the town at nightfall, dressed in black from head to toe, wearing special masks on their faces so that no one would catch them in their voyeuristic peeping. For if they were caught, none of the women would ever go to confession again if the same priest were sitting on the other side, listening to her sins.

It happened more than once that a woman who was denounced to the bishop after being caught with her hand on her pubic area by one of the guardians was then summoned before him for a lecture followed by a public flogging at the pillory, after which she was forced to pay a hefty fine of two gold ducats. These women were put on the bishop's blacklist, which, in addition to "vulva scratchers," as the bishop maliciously called them, included the names of Neisse's female thieves and prostitutes. The entire list was read out every Thursday at the market by the bishop's assistant, Father Thomas Grunewald.

By bringing together the women of Neisse and their vulvas, and weaving between them a thread of intimacy and understanding that had been severed for centuries, Helene was preparing them for the practice of separating the soul from the body, a skill most easily obtained by making love to oneself. She had long ago embroidered this part of her teachings, so she began to share it with the women who came to her and Kunegunde on market days. Eventually, she'd relayed her knowledge to nearly all the townswomen of Neisse. They started sneaking off to the forest to learn both theory and practice, in sunshine and rain. Even when a thunderstorm was approaching and lightning bolts were slicing the sky in half like a sword, there were always at least six of them down at the river.

The group of women soon formed a congregation that they called the Earthen Ones. It began with Sarah, the daughter of a goldsmith named Joachim Goldberg. At the tender age of sixteen, Sarah left Neisse against her parents' wishes to live in the forest. At the time, Helene had been living in the deadwood forest with Kunegunde and little Ursula for no more than a year. By chance, Sarah had overheard a conversation between her parents about their plan to marry her off to Karl Gropius, the son of a famous doctor from Olomouc. Sarah had met Karl once at the Midsummer's Eve Fair in Breslau, and she would never forget, for the rest of her life, the sight of his face covered in pimples and blemishes; he seemed to her the most repulsive creature in the world. At night, under the cover of darkness, she packed several essential items in her dowry chest and escaped through the window and beyond the town walls, with a clear goal in mind—to live in the deadwood forest with Helene and Kunegunde, whose lives were unconventional but happy, for they were free of all constraints.

Attempts to bring Sarah back to town were all for naught. Sarah had renounced everything she possessed, and accepted without batting an eye the removal of her name from the family will, just to be able to live in the glade. And since news, especially such unusual news, spreads faster than pollen carried by the wind, within one week the entire duchy was gossiping maliciously about the incident. What kind of upbringing had Joachim Goldberg given his only child? He must have been more concerned with turning his accursed gold into pagan effigies than he was with spending time with her! They derided him in their thoughts, instead of sympathizing with him over his loss.

All of this was fueled by people's fear that at any moment, their own offspring might run away from home to join Helene Spalt's congregation, directing their prayers to the Earth instead of to Heaven, and doing God knows what else, for there were already rumors circulating about the obscene, depraved acts being performed in the forest under Spalt's command.

It was even whispered that perchance there was a new religion being created, for while hunting for otters and beavers, men claimed to have seen Helene, Kunegunde, and Sarah lying with their bellies to the ground as if in prayer, and their hair spread around them, making strange movements with their hips and uttering indistinct, high-pitched sounds, as they reported to the alarmed bishop.

And then, less than one month later, Helene, Kunegunde, and Sarah were joined by the wife and daughter of the apothecary Ludwig Zweig. They were soon followed by Irma Grimm, a miller's fiancée who could no longer endure the stench emanating from the mouth of her betrothed, who was perpetually inebriated. She brought with her three sisters: Marie, Hannah, and Dorothe, all orphans. They were joined by Wilhelmina, the widow of an attorney named Hubertus Weiss, who simply wanted to spend the rest of her life in company, rather than in solitude. After a few months, more women arrived with their belongings packed in bundles after leaving their husbands, sometimes bringing their children with them so they could live closer to Nature, and—in the official version conveyed time and again during interrogations by the town's authorities and the Church—closer to God. They claimed that a poor life, devoid of all luxuries, and Franciscan in its more radical form, had suddenly become very important to them.

A year later, there were twenty-two women, and each of them attracted still more. As the years passed, the congregation eventually reached two hundred. The forest glade was filled so densely with tents it became difficult to walk through.

The Earthen Ones were valued in the area because they provided the town with birch sap, a helpful remedy for colds and other illnesses; it revived the body after winter, resurrecting it for spring. The Earthen Ones also supplied the townspeople with milk and cheese as well as potions, macerates, and elixirs, which allowed the eyelids of sleep-deprived townsmen to lower, aching teeth to find relief, and stinking, ulcerous wounds to heal.

In addition to this publicly known activity for which they regularly paid taxes as the "Congregation of the Earthen Ones" in the register at Neisse's town hall, the Clefts (*die Spalten*)—as they were disparagingly nicknamed—conducted clandestine activities known only to a select few women of the town. They expelled fetuses, induced menstrual bleeding so as to impede marital intercourse at the behest of dissatisfied women, and also cured women of hypouresis, vaginal discharge, too much moisture or excessive drought in their clefts. And above all, they showed women how to make love in a way condoned by the Primeval Virgin—with what was soft, delicate, gentle, non-rigid—thereby gradually causing all that was hard to become démodé and passé.

In addition to instructing the women in the mystical technique of cleft-sparking, Kunegunde gave them lessons in embroidery, and both she and Helene taught them how to macerate herbs so that they could find employment in the apothecaries' guild. They also taught them to weave—so that they could make roofs out of twigs and straw. They developed carpentry skills, though they took wood only from trees that were sick or that Mother Earth had knocked down in a windstorm. They never cut down living trees, and they always tried first to cure the diseased ones. They boiled comfrey with resin and smeared it on the trees' wounds. They plastered the affected areas with decoctions made of herbs and their own moisture—sometimes mucus, sometimes blood or saliva—and, above all, they used heavy sticks to bang snags and half-dead trees. Soon the deadwood forest began to heal, and where the withered branches had been smashed away, fresh shoots began to grow.

Apart from their work in the camp for the benefit of their communal life in the forest glade and the health of the environment they'd chosen as their dwelling, the Earthen Ones devoted themselves with great passion to what became the solid foundation of their knowledge of the Earth—they thrust sweetly fragrant rhizomes of calamus into their clefts, and sometimes also its conical flowers, which looked like long, pale green pine cones and had a remarkably pleasant roughness. All the women engaged in this activity twice a day—always at dawn and dusk—to mark the beginning and end of their daily life. They opened their clefts at dawn to receive the morning's golden sunlight, and then again at the end of each day so that the livid light of dusk heralding the star-studded night could enter them, the darkness tingling in their bones and spreading forth. These were considered hygienic procedures, like washing body parts that were otherwise hidden from sight or brushing one's hair, not deemed wicked or indecent in the slightest.

Before a new woman could be bestowed with the title of Earthen One, Helene would test her to see what she had learned from the lessons, and also request that she demonstrate her practical knowledge. Hence, before she became an Earthen One, the woman would be given a rhizome of calamus that had been picked during the full moon in the month of May. Then a spot was found for her in the circle of women sitting around the oak tree where the deadly nightshade grew, and the woman was shown how to rub her cleft with the rhizome until her soul separated from her body and transmigrated, becoming connected by an invisible, luminous thread to the center of the Earth, so that what she was giving would be equal to what she was taking.

And then if the new woman, while cleft-sparking, managed to achieve a state of ecstasy simultaneously with the other Earthen Ones, she was considered initiated, for she had become aligned with the pulsation and the breathing of all other living beings. She took then a solemn oath never to reveal the teachings of the Primeval Virgin to any man, unless Helene herself had chosen one for her to be with. Otherwise, all the Earthen Ones in the deadwood glade could, through her foolishness, end up hanged from a tree or murdered in some other way.

Within their congregation, cleft-sparking was the single most important form of worship, for only then was it possible to spin a single thread with the world—a thread that begins in the heart of the Earth and, passing through a woman's cleft, connects to the very center of Heaven and to the supreme light that shines for eternity. The luminosity pulsing between a woman's thighs must be channeled to wherever it is lacking, to places where only the world's sadness and darkness prevail, though the women must also channel darkness to any place where excessive brightness and joy reign, thereby bringing harmony and order to the world.

Concerning Helene Spalt's Extraordinary Sermons

All of Helene Spalt's sermons remained engraved in the memories of the Earthen Ones. But excerpts of some of the sermons were also written down and compiled into a complete work, so that they could be shared and read again, always in secret. The women who attended Helene Spalt's sermons were not yet members of the congregation (of which there were many), and they therefore lived not in the forest but in their own homes, where they would hide handwritten copies of the sermons inside covers they took from books about the lives of saints, so as not to arouse the suspicion of their husbands, fathers, and pious mothers.

They read the sermons with flushed faces, feeling for the very first time in their lives that someone was speaking directly to them, and to them alone, offering something so extraordinary that shivers ran through their entire bodies. Some even fainted from excitement.

Anyone who wishes to make the sign of the cross before our meeting and raise her eyes to God is free to do so. But remember this: 'Twas the Heavenly Father who created man from clay and bird shit, who ordained that man would constantly desire access to our clefts in order to govern them as ineptly as he does this forest and all the other forests of the duchy. But our clefts shall be protected by none other than Mother Earth, and then only if we also protect Her, and respect everything that is begotten of Her and returns to Her after death, creating fecundity for everything new that is yet to grow. For it was Mother Earth, and not the Heavenly Father, who gave us the vegetation that protects us more faithfully than dogs and offers us more pleasure than any male ever could.

The astonished women listened to Helene's sermons with mouths agape; never in their lives had they heard anything so strange. The plants presented to them by Helene, of various shapes, sizes, and vibrant colors, filled their minds with anticipation of such intense bliss that shivers ran through them. Many became covered with sweat and goose bumps, with cheeks aglow and eyes gleaming.

Thou shalt allow into thyself only what cometh of Mother Earth. Rub thy cleft with a rhizome of calamus, and thou shalt split the starry sky above thee in two and stir the Earth so deeply that it will tremble to the rhythm of thy pulse. Take a young poplar branch and thrust it into thy cleft ever so gently. Do not fear any knots or burls on the branch; they shall only increase thy pleasure, never causing harm to the cleft. And take the serpent root as thy most cherished lover. Do the same with dried comfrey root, but be sure 'tis stiff, for otherwise it may break inside thee when thou art young or hast not yet been with child.

Some passages, though, were more theological, providing the women with a broader perspective on the teachings. For example:

> Let nothing but love for the world and great brightness come forth from thyself; let thyself be so much more than a mere vessel for human offspring. Let the tired, bleeding Earth rest at least for a few springs. Fertilize it with thy inner light. No younglings shall be created from igniting sparks in thy cleft with rhizomes and roots, and this is better for the world. It shall end sooner, and we shall all pass away and return to the Earth's embrace, where a more exciting life awaits us. There, our flesh, skin, bones, hair, and fingernails shall nourish the Earth, allowing Her to give birth to new life from our death. Our debt to Mother Earth shall only be paid once we have become nourishment for Her fruit, and once the Sky receives what He is owed as well. Light and darkness shall return to their rightful places to merge into one, ending the suffering of the world and giving other worlds a chance to emerge. Just as the milk we draw from the teat of a cow changes its form when heated—first it clots, losing its liquid form, and then it turns to curd, which we shape into round lumps and sell at the market, where people worship it almost as passionately as if 'twere the Sacred Host. And thus, we are like this milk from which cheese curd is made, nothing more. But we must protect the light, the aurora, the fire within us, so that it doth not burn out too soon.

And:

> Woman, thou must take care of thy purity—both that of thy cleft and that of thy soul, for the cleft and the soul are one in a woman. Only through thy vulva canst thy soul be kept pure,

and 'tis also through thy vulva that this purity can be defil'd. When the Earth rots and decays, there is a stench but also a chance to fertilize. Just as the Earth undergoes processes of decay in which it decomposes and stinks, while fertilizing everything around it nonetheless, so too must the soul sometimes burn and rot, reek even, for otherwise it would no longer be human—its essence would be too close to the divine. Thou dost carry divinity within thee when thou hast respect for everything that is human. Not only for the beautiful deeds that people accomplish, but also for the shit that is expell'd from people's rear ends, their smelly rotting teeth, the bristles that sprout on the chins of women as they grow old, and their bodies—which only in childhood and early youth bear no trace of decay. Once thou dost understand this and respect every aspect of a human being—even the shittiest and foulest aspects, the ones that repulse and disgust all those who seek only harmony and beauty, and retch at the very sight of old bodies—then and only then shall it be possible to feel this divinity within oneself. No sooner.

The sermons that Helene gave every Friday soon became more famous than the homilies delivered by any priest in Neisse. Each week, several new women came to listen, and many professed their faith in the Primeval Virgin soon afterward and joined the Earthen Ones.

By the time there were two hundred women living in the glade, there were tents everywhere, as far as the eye could see. The voices of children rang out from some—mostly girls, because Helene had proclaimed at the very beginning: "What is for women should remain solely with women."

There were, however, some exceptions. For Helene allowed the Earthen Ones to spend time with their abandoned husbands, if they'd been married. And with their children as well—even those of the male sex. Husbands could visit the women in the glade, but they could not copulate with them. They were allowed to lie with the women tenderly on the moss, as one might with children. Helene showed them how. With tenderness. She let the men feel for a little while that they could also be part of the Primeval Virgin's plan, free from the trap the Church had set for them—a trap that allowed men to believe that they were entitled to subjugate both Mother Earth and all of womankind, to do with both whatever they pleased. And whenever they pleased. Helene managed to dissuade them from this. But there were very few of them. Of the two hundred women who gathered in the deadwood forest, only about forty succeeded in bringing men with them to listen to Helene Spalt preach the gospel of the Primeval Virgin. Helene explained to the men how to love women and Mother Earth without subjugating them, and how to fight the urge to dominate. How, instead, they could love with empathy and provide tender companionship. She encouraged each man to subdue his stiffly protruding, perpetually lustful rod and teach it to sense the needs of the vulva. She explained how to restrain the rod and coax it to find new ways of giving pleasure to women. How to soften their vulvas, allowing them to bloom and flourish. How to moisten and fertilize them, while never wasting their seed.

> And thou, husband and lover—suppress within thyself all desire to stab the cleft of thy woman. For what we need shall sooner be found in stillness than mindless, chaotic movement and stupidity. Anything done in careless haste is incapable of bringing pleasure, but rather brings pain that detaches the soul from the act, until thou dost grind against nothing but

the air around thee or the straw-filled mattress on which the limp body of thy woman doth lie.

One tiny movement, like the flutter of the wing of a bird, and then silence, slowness, stillness, and timelessness. For, verily, thou art not only making love to thy woman, but to Mother Earth as well, who gave birth to all that surrounds thee. Do not offend Her with mindless, passionless grinding. Turn love into a true celebration and observe it as a sacred rite.

Do not treat a woman as property. She belongeth to her mother first—to the Earth. From Her she came forth and to Her she shall return. And if thou art incapable of this, then simply take her in thy arms. Carry her until thou findest the best patch of moss. Plant her there. Then watch her spark her cleft. And while watching, learn for thyself. See how much pleasure she doth derive from the moss. From the rhizomes of plants. From the forest's undergrowth. Learn from the plants how to give her pleasure. How to make love to her. Once thou dost possess this knowledge, thou wilt be ready. Then, thou wilt be the one we await so fervently. Then and only then.

Once a month, during the new moon, when all the healthy women were menstruating together, their cycles having become synchronized, Helene allowed the men not only to accompany their wives while they rubbed their clefts against the moss but also to put their beards under them, as if they were the moss themselves, letting the bleeding vulvas ride them with wild abandon, shifting and shuffling on them without any restraint. They called it their "monthly mysterium"—a name that expressed their celebration of both menstruation and the new moon. Over two hundred women experienced pleasure together. Some with plants and others with their husbands, though Helene allowed them to swap so that the women could have some variety and the men could become more familiar with the women's needs. For each of them sparked her cleft in her own way, at her own pace, and Helene considered this to be a particularly important observation.

Helene Spalt herself, despite her advanced years, was still menstruating, and so she sat on their faces as well. For all that was happening there, in the forest glade, was beyond age—both theirs and hers. It made no difference whether the women were young or old, for they all became one during the great act that connected them. Maria, Hannah, Ingeborga, Ruth, Berta, Sarah, Karoline, Isolda, and dozens of others. It made no difference which of the women was given pleasure by the men—after all, the pleasure didn't belong to any of them individually but to all of them together. For the pleasure was the most intense and meaningful when experienced communally. When a shudder ran through them all at once, when the women fed the men with their clefts and the moisture flowing from them, and the men gushed onto the Earth, fertilizing the Primeval Virgin, it was love on a cosmic level, not an individual one—the kind of love toward which Helene was always striving.

> When thy oafish grinding connects thee not to the Earth beneath thee nor the Heavens above, then it is nothing more than a meaningless release of seed, which sometimes results in a wanted or unwanted child. When wanted, the situation is not so bad, but if not—everything is in vain. The child shall have a wretched life, as shall the woman, and the husband, for everything shall begin to bother him and he shall either leave for another woman or drink his misery away, spewing

bitterness into the world. A bitterness so intense that not only shall it keep smiles from the faces of his wife and child, but it shall make the sun itself lose the will to rise in the morning. Such bitterness depriveth the whole family of the desire to live. 'Tis a path no one should ever follow.

And so to all men I say: if thou dost wish to keep thy woman close to thee, learn to make love to her wisely while connecting with something greater than thyself—something that cannot be grasp'd with either thy rational mind or thy genitals.

Dost thou wish to know how to do this? Let thy woman guide thee. Do not force her to learn what is within thee. What thou hast is the same as every dog, cat, or horse. And verily, because of this, thou wilt bring nothing new to the act of love. Thy grinding is no different from that of any animal. Hence, follow her. Make her thy guide. She shall connect thee to Mother Earth. And then thou shalt not defile her, but honor her, for every act of love with a woman is a sacred rite and a celebration of life on Earth, and only as such hath value. Any physical act that thou yearnest to perform, but does not include this, thou must do alone. And do not show it to us, for there is nothing for us there, only defilement, corruption, and death. And we women—we are life.

These sermons were so important that some of the Earthen Ones knew them by heart and could quote them even if they'd just awoken from deep slumber. Some of the more significant passages were known by the men who were permitted by Helene to join the women, sharing their beards and bodies for the worship of the Primeval Virgin and Helene's experiments in communal orgasm.

By what means some of the sermons that had been written down by Helene Spalt's followers made their way to the canonry, nobody knows. Suffice to say, it was this that led the Catholic Church to wage a war against the women of the Duchy of Neisse, bringing an end to the Earthen Ones. At least for a while.

"This Is War!": Concerning the Conflict with the Catholic Church

Among the men, there was one who was a misfit, a good-for-nothing scoundrel. The nasty bastard ruined everything for the Earthen Ones, simply because cleft-sparking with his beard didn't go well for him. His rodkin didn't react as it was supposed to from beard cleft-sparking alone, so he started rubbing it with his hands, stroking and smacking it the old way, which had been strictly forbidden by Helene, as it delayed or entirely prevented the body from learning to experience pleasure in a manner that honored the Primeval Virgin.

When Helene caught him stroking his soft, flabby rodkin with his hand, she rapped his knuckles with a stick, missing his balls by a mere hair's breadth with each whack. She chased him from the glade without uttering a word, but in her mind she was cursing him and his cock for eternity.

It was shortly afterward that the townspeople of Neisse, while strolling through the market square, heard these memorable words uttered by Bishop von Sitsch echoing throughout the town:

"This is war!" he shouted, after listening to the bitter grievances spewed by the foul, rancorous villain.

"This is war!" shrieked Helene Spalt at the exact same instant, breaking her silence. She grabbed a large stick and ordered the Earthen Ones to do the same.

That was the one and only time these two people were ever in agreement with each other—and they were both right.

There had already been attempts to repress the Earthen Ones, especially when a misfortune of some kind had befallen the town of Neisse or the surrounding countryside. Sometimes it was a flood along the riverbank where the fishermen lived, an ergot contamination in the crops, or the death of a newborn baby in a wealthy, deeply religious family that believed the bishop when he declared that all tragic events were caused by witches. Sometimes all it took was for a peasant's cow to give less milk than usual, or for the milk that had been set aside for cheese for several days to refuse to curdle, and suspicion immediately fell on the women living in the forest glade—the Clefts. So far, however, the Catholic Church's interference in the life of the congregation had amounted to no more than the women being summoned from time to time for interrogations, usually resulting in warnings and fines. They were harassed for what the ecclesiastical duchy could lawfully control— for driving their horse-drawn wagons erratically in the streets on market days when they came into town to sell their cheese; for creating products that were offensive to men and contributed to a reduction in the number of births of little Christians, therefore constituting sabotage of the ecclesiastical duchy; and so on.

But now things were looking considerably more serious, for the slanderous snitch in question, Thomas Kinder, wanted to testify against Helene for insulting religion, and at the urging of the bishop began to demand that she be put on trial as a witch. And since the bishop was anxious to solve the problem of the Clefts as soon as possible, he decided to banish them from the glade and herd them back into normal bourgeois life.

"They will no longer turn our forests into Satan's abode!" he thundered from the pulpit during Sunday mass. "It's high time we brought these Devil's bitches—your children and wives—back to the house of God, at any cost."

He also mentioned that he would announce a decree, in the name of the Catholic Church, for logging to begin on the land where these devilish creatures had set up camp and were mating with each other, and the harvested wood would be used to build a new cathedral. The congregation rose, and for the first time ever, they gave the clergy a standing ovation. This is hardly surprising, since most of the congregation was made up of men left behind by the Earthen Ones: fathers who had lost their daughters, sons who had lost their mothers, and husbands who had lost their wives. All that remained was the matter of the purchase agreement between Helene and the father general, as well as the agreements Helene had made with the Earthen Ones after moving to the glade, offering each one a small plot of land in exchange for their profession of faith in the Primeval Virgin. During the twenty years that Helene Spalt had lived in the forest, she had signed such a contract with two hundred and twenty-eight women, most of whom had taken a theoretical and practical exam in front of her to become an Earthen One. Each woman thus now considered the deadwood forest her home.

The bishop knew that by entering the forest with some armed henchmen hired to guard him, he would be breaking the law, which he was reluctant to do, not wanting to set a bad example for the citizens of the duchy. To solve this problem, he paid a visit to the pope himself, so that he could act according to the letter of the law.

The bishop easily obtained the pope's permission to annul the purchase of land by the savage "swamp demon and swindler"

Helene Spalt, since he was able to provide a good reason for it. For the pope, the disappearance of over two hundred Catholic women from the Duchy of Neisse brought no glory and had long been a source of ridicule and gossip, so it was a matter of honor for him to bring it to an end. Therefore, upon returning from Rome, the bishop resolved to immediately banish the Earthen Ones from the forest.

With the blessing of the pope, Bishop Johannes von Sitsch no longer had to tiptoe around the problem. He could use every means possible to persecute the Earthen Ones. He summoned all the guards from the Duchy of Neisse and the castellany of Ottmachau and ordered their leaders to capture the Earthen Ones, every last one of them, and bring them to his palace that day at dusk.

But merely half an hour after reaching the glade, the armed stooges made a hasty retreat, for the long sticks in the hands of the enraged Earthen Ones—what they called their rumblerods— were more efficient than spears. The men were beaten so badly that the wounds from the rumblerods, which were usually used for banging deadwood, took a whole month to heal. The men said not a word about the incident to either their pals in the Golden Crab Tavern or the women with whom they shared their lives—or men, if it was with them that they shared their lives in secret from the community, which also happened, though only very rarely because of their fear of the divine punishment the priests threatened from the pulpits.

It was then, after the disgraceful failure of his attempt to round up and reform the sinful, corrupted Earthen Ones, that Bishop von Sitsch decided to summon to the duchy the inquisitor Heinrich Babel, a cruel and relentless witch hunter who had made a spectacular career for himself in Franconia. Inquisitor Heinrich Babel had grown up in the Duchy of Neisse and had known Helene Spalt since he was a child—a fact that was discovered accidentally by the bishop, at the Franciscan monastery, when he went there to learn more about the nature of the purchase agreement of the deadwood forest.

Concerning a Visit to Ursula and Some Terrible News

Although the Earthen Ones had been in conflict with the Catholic Church ever since they'd first set up camp in the forest glade, the Inquisition had never been involved. Nor had Heini Babel, whose father had taken him from the monastery and thrust him into the world as far from home as possible. Heini had disappeared for over twenty years and had seemingly had no further dealings whatsoever with Helene Spalt during that time. He had, however, often fantasized about someday meeting both her and Kunegunde again, and had incessantly replayed the scene in his mind, a thousand different versions of it—in each one, the two women met a tragic end.

At the command of Babel, to whom the bishop had given authority to take any measures against the Earthen Ones he pleased, the troops began regular invasions of the encampment. They would drag the Earthen Ones out by their hair and carry them back to the town, where they would insult and defile them in reprehensible ways. In addition to physical abuse and floggings in front of the residents of Neisse, a cross was branded on their chests so that they would forever remember which god they were to serve.

Men were given axes and commanded to uproot all the trees in the glade and throughout the entire deadwood forest bearing the carved symbol of the Primeval Virgin. It thus became increasingly difficult for the women to remain in the glade, and indeed it was only because of Helene's obstinacy that any of the Earthen Ones remained at all.

Two of the women who decided to leave the glade against Helene's will were Kunegunde and Ursula. The latter no longer wanted to live in that manner; she'd never been attracted to such a lifestyle. She was the only young woman living in the glade who had secretly dreamed of leading a quiet life with a kind, decent, helpful husband and bearing him children. She would devote a lot of time to them—holding them, cuddling them, singing to them, and rocking them to sleep, instructing them in everything they needed to know about life—thus giving them everything she had only ever received from Kunegunde, never from her own mother.

A good opportunity to enact her desired future eventually arose when one of the husbands who'd been allowed to join the monthly mysterium brought along a friend named Mathias Bremmel. Mathias was tender, with a slow, gentle manner, so he pleased Helene and all the women who sat on his face that night. And since he had soft, beautiful hair on his chin, not rough bristles like most of the men, the women achieved such magnificent cleft-sparking with him that they remembered it for the rest of their lives.

This fellow was more attracted to Ursula than to any of the others—affection for her took root in his heart from the first moment he saw her. And Ursula, dreaming of a traditional life, opened her heart to his love.

Helene refused to accept this; a daughter who would betray her mother in this way could not be a creature born of her, but merely a viper seeking to buy her way back into a world unfit for women. Not the one Helene had fought for. She and her daughter began to quarrel fiercely in front of the other women, which was painful for old Kunegunde to witness, for she could see how deeply Ursula was suffering while Helene became increasingly harsh and headstrong.

Their quarrels were of a strange nature, for Helene, who rarely spoke—except when she was proclaiming Primeval Virgin doctrine—was incapable of uttering a single sound. So she used her hands to threaten Ursula and began to embroider terrible words aimed at her, sometimes on a piece of canvas from a tent she'd torn apart while upset, sometimes on the thin shreds of cloth they used to press cheese, and eventually even on her own underpants, which she ostentatiously, in front of the entire congregation, took off to embroider with the words "stupid cunt," "ungrateful cunt," and, worst of all, "cocktrap."

She hung her work on trees in the part of the forest where worship of the Primeval Virgin took place, as a warning and reminder to all those who might be tempted to do something similar. No wonder, then, that both Ursula and Kunegunde, for whom Helene's radicalism was slowly becoming intolerable, ran away one night with Ursula's lover to lead a life in town, in a beautiful and spacious home with a view of the church that the man had received from his wealthy father, an amber merchant.

The separation from her daughter and Kunegunde left Helene heartbroken, though she did her best not to let it show. She embroidered even more furiously and preached increasingly passionate sermons, foretelling a terrible end for any who strayed from the path of the Primeval Virgin and returned to the Catholic Church.

"The womb from which we are brought into the world is the

forest. And all the plants growing in it. Not Carrara marble and crypts. Not incense, but smoke from an open fire. Not blood shed in the hour of death, but milk, the most life-giving substance in the world. The vagina-womb-skull, not the cross!" she thundered, drawing her powerful voice from deep within her. It startled the forest animals, even though there were some among them that lay down at her feet like faithful dogs.

It sometimes happened that Helene burned while preaching. Or at least that's how she was perceived by those who took part in the rituals to worship the Primeval Virgin. She looked as if she were standing in the middle of a fire. The flames licked her greedily from head to toe, but she continued to speak as if she were completely oblivious to them. And the women could sense anger in this fire even more intense than the wrath of God. Thus, not all of Helene's sermons appealed to the congregation. And few of them were being written down now. Quite often, once the sermon was over, the Earthen Ones would hide in their tents or in nearby bushes, or deep enough in the forest so as not to risk being overheard, to share their thoughts and doubts freely.

As a growing number of Earthen Ones fled the glade under cover of night, not returning the next day or even the next month, Helene began to soften and slowly accept that perchance she had become too hardened by the war with the Church, and that it might be time for her to embrace balance anew.

She decided to visit her daughter, whom she hadn't seen for over a year, and to hug old Kunegunde too, for she missed her terribly. Even more than her daughter.

Standing on the threshold of their beautiful home, she had the urge to spit three times over her left shoulder at the sight of the cross on the wall, but she refrained. Mathias Bremmel, whom she had met and grown fond of in the forest glade, immediately fell to his knees before her and kissed her hands, asking her to bless him as the mother of his wife. Helene placed her hand on his head and, instead of blessing him, teasingly tousled his thick mop of blond hair and gestured with her hand for something to drink; her mouth was dry from excitement.

Kunegunde also approached Helene, embraced her tenderly, and stroked her cheek with a rough old hand. Helene, deeply moved, was barely able to hold back tears, especially when her gaze fell on her daughter.

At the opposite side of the room, Ursula was sitting in a beautifully upholstered armchair with a footstool, holding a tiny creature to her breast and feeding it.

Helene shot Ursula a questioning look.

"Yes," Ursula said, immediately understanding Helene's silent question. "This is Mathilde. Your granddaughter."

Helene approached them slowly, almost on tiptoe, so as not to disturb the child, and, unable to restrain herself, took the girl from her mother's arms and placed her at her own breast, cuddling her and supporting her with her arm bent at the elbow.

And then something happened that had great significance in the relationship that ultimately developed between Helene and her granddaughter, for the rest of their lives. Mathilde opened her eyes and, seeing her grandmother, instead of bursting into tears, began to smile, staring into her eyes so intensely that Helene was unable to bear the gaze, although she herself had taught the Earthen Ones never to break eye contact with each other, for they were connected in a spiritual dance.

Helene had the sensation that this tiny being, less than nine months old, had won the staring match, which indicated that she already had a stronger and more grounded soul than her grandmother.

After the little one had fallen asleep, Mathias set the table and invited Helene to eat with them, for he had something of great importance to tell her. He had heard something from some clients—two canons who had come to buy amber to decorate a new monstrance.

This is how Helene learned that Bishop von Sitsch had commissioned Inquisitor Babel and his men to hunt down the rest of the Earthen Ones and had given them full freedom to use any possible means to do so. The captured women were to be returned to their husbands, who, in full view of an assembled crowd of all the residents of the town, would have intercourse with them, thus proving that they once again had full control over them, in the name of the entire Church and all of Christendom. And if any of the onlookers also desired to copulate with one of the sinful women—so that she would remember how to make love in a righteous manner—he would be given permission by the bishop himself.

While Helene listened to this, she felt as if a demon had possessed her. A fiery rage engulfed her, and she grabbed at the tablecloth with the intention of knocking off all the crockery and embroidering curses all over it. But Ursula pointed toward Mathilde sleeping in the cradle, thereby urging her mother to get a grip on herself.

Helene eventually released the hem of the tablecloth from her clenched fist so as not to wake her granddaughter. Everyone was greatly relieved, for this was a test of sorts for Helene, revealing whether she was now nothing more than a religious fanatic or still an ordinary human being as well—a member of the family and a new grandmother. Once she'd passed, an outpouring of love once again flowed between them all.

When Helene was standing on the doorstep, about to leave,

old Kunegunde handed her a small bundle and said, "To protect thyself and the other women from being violated, rub this inside thyself before the men come for thee. It shall make their rodkins wither. No harm shall come to thee, and thy cleft shall be protected—for it shall be clenched shut forever. But thou wilt still be able to make love to plants."

In Which the Debauched Harlots Teach Their Husbands' Rodkins a Lesson

The cleft-clenching of the Earthen Ones caused a spectacle so extraordinary that most of the residents of Neisse remembered it for the rest of their lives.

The town set up stalls that night and planned a celebration as merry as the annual Lenten carnival—the townsfolk called it, in jest, the "carnal carnival." An entire bolt of fine, first-rate linen was used to make a massive banner that was hung between the windows of the townhouses on two sides of the market square. The words written on it read: "Down with the debauched harlots!" Pint after pint of cool pilsner beer was poured from oak barrels, and in front of the assembled crowd, chunks of pork loin were sliced from pigs that had been slaughtered that morning. Then they were roasted together with potatoes cut into thin slices. The rabble was satiated. The rabble was happy.

And after stuffing their bellies, the rabble was eager for entertainment of some other sort, so they formed a lively procession and made their way to the Weigh House, where the day before a platform had been built. On the platform stood wooden beds with thick straw mattresses, and next to the beds there were tin jugs full of water and clean linen towels.

When at last the remaining Earthen Ones were dragged out of the forest and brought before the assembled crowd by armed guards, it turned out that there were fewer than two dozen of them. They were the only ones who remained of the more than two hundred women who had lived there, after some had been kidnapped and forcefully returned to their erstwhile lives and others had left of their own volition, either by reason of Helene's deepening radicalism or out of disillusionment with the way of life offered by the founder of the Earthen Ones, which was difficult and fraught with hardship.

When the twenty-one women were ordered to lie down on the beds and set an example to the pious people gathered before them of how one should fulfill one's marital duty before God, they did so willingly, without the slightest resistance. They lay on their backs and pulled up their skirts eagerly, which immediately aroused the first suspicions that not everything would go according to the bishop's expectations. They spread their legs wide, gracefully bending them at the knees, and then invited their husbands, beckoning to them coquettishly.

This gesture by no means helped the husbands feel that the rest of the performance was under their control. Suddenly they felt like little boys, not men who were supposed to show off their virility.

Indeed, nearly all of them began to have trouble with their rodkins, for this was not what that particular body part had expected. At a signal from the bishop, a sharp ring from the bell used to announce daily mass, they grabbed their rodkins and began rubbing them like monkeys, beating them like butter, patting them like a horse's muzzle, and when finally, after a long struggle, they managed to achieve something, they got down to work. Which is when things took a truly comedic turn, for not a single cleft would let them enter, despite repeated thrusts and attacks.

There was only one difficulty that arose for the Earthen Ones—the situation amused them so much that they were barely able to hold back their urine and came close, as a result of their intense laughter, to releasing golden showers upon the tragically humiliated rodkins. But they clenched their teeth and held it back as well as they could.

And when, after a full hour of humiliation and whistles from the mob, the husbands announced their surrender, the bishop, his face flushed with anger, gave the sign to the equally enraged inquisitor to move on to plan B—which nobody but the two of them knew anything about.

Concerning the Tragic Death of Ursula

That night Ursula Bremmel—who signed documents as Ursula Spalt in deference to her mother, despite being married—was tormented by terrible nightmares.

At first, the images were vivid and beautiful—for she dreamed that she was in her mother's forest glade surrounded by all the Earthen Ones, and there were more than two hundred of them there with her. She was standing in that spot not as a human being, born of her mother and father, but as a tree—forsooth, the very oak tree that had been growing there for centuries, the mightiest of all the trees. She stood in the middle of the glade and tried with all her might to suppress the tree's essence, which was spreading inside her, but she could hear, very clearly, the crackling and blazing of life in the trunk, feel how the core of the tree into which she was transforming—the tree that she was becoming or that she had always been—was beginning to pulse in rhythm with the beating of her heart. She felt resin flowing through her temples. She bent her rooted toes firmly, which caused them to grow even deeper into the moist black soil. And then she became perfectly still. She readied herself for gestation. To receive seeds carried by the wind and become impregnated by them. Her foliage rustled, buzzed, and hummed; she felt the tingling of insects swarming inside her, caterpillars crawling on her bark, larvae squirming and coiling beneath it, and slimy snails penetrating her sap; something nibbled at her here and gnawed at her there. As she shed the chewed-up parts of herself, she fertilized an oak stake that had been driven like a totem into the loamy soil that smelled of rot, decay, and death, crowning the horizon. And when, after being penetrated by the wind, she finally released a thousand acorns from which tiny new oak trees would be born, she noticed a noose hanging from one of her largest branches.

This same tree was seen several hours later—in reality, not a dream—by Kunegunde, as she lamented beneath it with wee Mathilde in her arms. Ursula's neck was bound with a thick rope and her face was blue, even though just that morning she had been chattering away so sweetly and cheerfully. *Come to me, my dear Kreppel*, she'd said to little Mathilde, who was taking her very first steps around the table. *Sit beside me, dear husband*, she'd said to Mathias. And then finally, to Kunegunde, she'd repeated like a mantra, for the old woman never listened to her when she said this, *Come, dear Kunegunde, come sit with us at the table instead of serving us!* Now she was silent, dangling from the tree and rocking in the wind that had breathed life into her the previous night, while she'd been asleep. Her body swayed there in the air, as if performing a macabre dance—except that the movements weren't following a repetitive sequence. They came one upon another without any rhythm—jerky, violent, and abrupt.

And the little shoes that Mathias had bought for Ursula at the market in Bremen from the very best cobbler were now lying under the petite woman's lifeless body. Mathias picked them up with tears streaming down his face. He put them on Ursula, then kissed her feet over and over—the tiny feet that he adored nearly as much as her pure heart.

Old Kunegunde's mouth was hanging open, but no scream emerged from it. Just a silent grimace. It was as if she were restraining herself, with every ounce of her strength, from making any sound, so as not to interrupt wee Mathilde's sleep with an outpouring of despair. Under the feet of the dead woman, the Earth suddenly split, and a plant stalk rose out of the cleft. The Earth began to bleed. Still holding Mathilde, Kunegunde leaned over and placed her hand on the crack. The ground clenched shut. All movement ceased. The feet of the dead woman stopped swinging in the wind.

It's impossible to say how long they stood next to Ursula after she'd been taken down from the branch and laid on the grass. When Mathilde woke up from her nap, at the sight of her mother lying on the grass, looking different than usual, like the wax doll her father had given her for Christmas, she called out, "Mama, Mama, Mama!" And she put her arms around the dead woman.

This was the last thing old Kunegunde saw. Her heart broke with grief.

Just before her final breath, she asked Mathias to bury them both not in the cemetery, with funeral rites performed by a priest, but in Helene's forest.

Concerning Helene's Care of
Her Granddaughter

After Ursula's death, Helene Spalt asked herself the same question again and again until the end of her days: whether she was to blame.
And since there was no one to answer this rhetorical question, or to counter her pangs of guilt and console her (except her son-in-law, who, without expressing it aloud, let her know very clearly that the question she was asking herself was valid), she continued to live oppressed by the burden of responsibility for the deaths of her loved ones, with her spirit crushed by guilt, dwindling more with every day. While exposed to Mathias's condemning gaze, she became dependent on his generosity, for after the deaths of her daughter and Kunegunde, the once-rich Helene Spalt found herself standing on her son-in-law's doorstep empty-handed after so many years of providing for her congregation.
She mulled this over in her mind again and again, every single day—whether she had gone too far in the war she'd declared against the Church and the men violently embodying its principles. She wondered: Would Bishop von Sitsch and Inquisitor Babel have dared commit such an act if she'd backed down ear-

lier? If she hadn't become so extreme in her preaching? Would they still have tried to crush her by hanging her only child?

So she went to her son-in-law, driven by a need to repent for all that had happened and a desire to make amends for her child's suffering. Offering to help with the everyday tasks of parenting and housekeeping, she took over the care of Mathilde, who quickly proved to be what Ursula never had been: a copy of Helene.

As Helene observed Mathilde during the first years of her life, she became increasingly vigilant and kept a close eye on her. Helene was so afraid of misfortune befalling Mathilde that she forbade the girl almost everything. But Mathilde didn't concern herself with this one bit and always managed to get her way. As Mathilde grew up, Helene noticed that while the little girl was doing splendidly, she couldn't help getting into all sorts of trouble due to her hyperactivity. She was like a candle burning at both ends. The flame inside her ignited everything around her, transforming her surroundings. And when conflagrations ensued, well, no one reacted too harshly—there was so much vitality and charm in the girl that she was forgiven for everything. Helene was very intrigued by her granddaughter, for she was so different from her dear mother, Ursula, who, as a child, had carried such intense fear of the world within her that she had avoided anything that could lead her into trouble. Even the smallest of things.

While Ursula had done everything to avoid pain, Mathilde seemed to seek it. She leapt across the pain threshold, as if she didn't feel it at all. She would often rub her finger along the wooden kitchen table until the thin skin on her fingertip had been torn off by splinters and began to bleed. When she finally achieved this, she would draw a deep breath of air and, while exhaling, penetrate the bleeding point with her thoughts. Her aim wasn't to dwell within the pain but to pass through it, reach somewhere beyond it, as if the wound were in contact with an unseen layer of the world, its protective outer casing.

Once the pain she'd initially felt had carried her through the wound and through the blood that was dripping from it, all the way to the protective sheath encasing the world, she clung to it as if it were something she'd been longing for, like a mother. And when she reached that point, she no longer felt any pain. Her suffering ceased. The only thing that caused her pain then was the fact that she eventually had to return to the reality that she'd briefly abandoned. As if her natural state was to be intertwined with the cosmos rather than ordinary, everyday life. And when she sometimes went with her grandmother to light a fire on the riverbank and bake potatoes in it, she would take off her shoes and walk barefoot over the embers. The fire hadn't yet burned out, the ashes were still smoldering, and she was already putting her feet in it, telling the fire that she understood its nature and feared it not.

She interacted with all the elements in this way. Every morning, she would ask her grandmother to lower her in a bucket into the well, where she would stay with her head under the water until she was on the brink of death, drawing air only at the last possible moment. And when her grandmother refused to do so, Mathilde would torment her by telling her that she would report her to her father, for she knew that Helene had carved the symbol of the Primeval Virgin on the wall under the crucifix and that she often indulged in strange activities after waking up and before going to sleep, which Mathilde observed through the keyhole.

Mathilde liked to sit inside a cupboard for several hours every day so that her eyes would learn to see in total darkness. Her grandmother pretended not to notice these strange games so as not to encourage such behavior. Helene herself understood the meaning of it all perfectly well, but she was afraid of her son-in-law's harsh criticism. Hence, she preferred not to pay attention to Mathilde's antics, or to do so only very discreetly, so that the little girl wasn't aware that she was being watched.

In truth, Helene was observing her beloved granddaughter intently, meticulously writing down everything she did, and year after year she felt herself becoming increasingly proud. This was the kind of granddaughter she had always wanted to have, and this was what she'd gotten. A girl who would never settle down, constantly venturing to life's outer limits. She was like that herself. All her life she had remained close to death. She had walked hand in hand with it. She liked to smell its foul breath on her neck. Then the desire to live took even deeper root in her. It became firmer. It lodged inside her, growing stronger. Spreading wider.

" 'Tis a pity that such a wonderful child is growing up without a mother," she thought, surreptitiously glancing at Mathilde. She was such a devil that Heaven and Hell combined couldn't have produced a greater one. "She shall get along fine on her own after my eyes have closed for eternity," she prophesied to herself. "She shall find her way among the vermin of the Earth, and then she shall penetrate the constellations in the heavens, rearranging them as she pleases."

Although Helene tried to justify the problematic behavior to Mathilde's father, she failed to kindle in him the kind of adoration she herself had for the lass. Helene believed that one day her granddaughter would abandon the bourgeois way of life to turn her eyes toward the Earth and start living as an Earthen One. For Mathilde had been an Earthen One almost from birth, seeming to understand all the laws of the Earth in a flash, as if she had been born into the world with them carved into her heart. Helene observed that Mathilde, despite still being too young to read, write, or count, understood the principles of the world and knew her place on the Earth, and wasn't afraid of deeply experiencing the Earth in everything she did. When she saw a dead bird that had been ripped apart by a cat, which every passerby would certainly avoid in disgust, she would pick it up and bury it beneath a tree. She would plunge her hands into the rotting flesh of fruits and vegetables, allowing the worms on cabbage leaves to crawl along her skin. She would never kill a spider or mutilate a tree, and at the tender age of six had already learned to collect sap more gently and efficiently than her grandmother, who'd been doing it her entire life. Milking cows came naturally to Mathilde, as her grandmother found out after she paid a farmer to let them into his barn so the girl could try it for the first time. She would certainly excel at making cheese, in which, after all, the whole essence of the world's existence was reflected, just as on the surface of a lake. She would learn to make ointments to clench women's clefts shut when men had the urge to lie with them and create more younglings while the ones already living had nothing to eat and no clothes to wear, due to famine, pestilence, and war.

Helene began teaching her granddaughter about herbs after she'd lived for twelve springs. Helene considered Mathilde to be entering the age of womanhood then and therefore worthy of receiving this knowledge, which should be withheld from children as it concerned adult life. She taught her about the plants that transported women to realms where men could never reach them, for men had no access to that state of the soul. And even if there were a few men who had access to this state, they would spoil it by holding on to this radiance of body and soul and keeping it for themselves, instead of returning it, through a woman, to the world so that it would shine like the stars in the firmament. For one must treat the radiance in the same way one treats a wound; one must strive as quickly as possible to heal the crack from which this luminosity reaches humankind from the universe, so as not to waste any of it. One must absorb the luminosity into oneself, and then radiate it outward and bestow it upon Mother Earth and the entire world, to set the world in motion and propel it toward change of all kinds, so that it doesn't stand still even for a moment. Sustaining the existence of humankind and Mother Earth, as well as the entire world, was, according to Helene, a reciprocal "numinous afflation of love." And only this reciprocal "numinous afflation," as she wrote in her notes, was the rightful way to live on the Earth. "And if humanity taketh more from the Earth than She giveth of Herself, then fires, floods, plagues of leprosy, and cattle diseases shall descend upon it, and grain shall be consumed by ergot, which poisoneth men and womenfolk and causeth them to succumb to hallucinations and madness, often driving them to take leave of this earthly realm by their own hand."

Helene quickly realized that Mathilde naturally possessed what she'd spent many years teaching the Earthen Ones, though it hadn't really been the Primeval Virgin that had inspired them as much as the cleft-sparking . . . That's what they'd had the most enthusiasm for, as if the viscosity of their vulvas had been the most important thing of all. But the cleft-sparking had been, after all, nothing more than a means to an end. A way to worship Mother Earth and Her most sacred daughter—the Primeval Virgin, who was as divine as Her mother. And here she had, clinging to her skirt hem day and night, someone who, although still too young for cleft-sparking, somehow understood everything and—more important—felt it! For it's one thing to grasp something with one's rational mind, and another to feel it inside oneself and thus be certain that *this* is it, that *this* is what it has always been about. And no rational mind will be capable of proving it—only a cleft that responds solely to that greater meaning and what it contains within itself. The cleft is a signpost, marking the way. "*Homo sen-*

tiens, rather than *Homo sapiens*," Helene jotted down in her notebook. She had a premonition that when Mathilde grew up, she would receive these notes from her as well as the entire gospel of the Primeval Virgin, which she'd embroidered on fabric. And she could do with them whatever she wished.

IV

MATHILDE SPALT

On Separation of the Soul from the Body

Misfortune—a faithful friend of all the Spalts—was lurking close by, lying in wait for its next opportunity to pounce. Mathilde's father, Mathias Bremmel, was swindled by his partner in the amber trade. He was unaware that his partner had substituted for real amber a fake made of some kind of cheap material. Bremmel's shop was seized, and to pay off the business partners who had shipped the merchandise from him farther north, he was forced to seek money elsewhere. He therefore had no choice but to sell his house and find a safe abode for his sixteen-year-old daughter. He came up with the diabolical idea of marrying Mathilde off to a man whom he'd met at the tavern and knew nothing about, apart from what people were saying—that he earned a substantial income as a blacksmith, for he shod horses for the bishops of both Neisse and Breslau. But it was also whispered among the townspeople that he had driven his wives to their deaths—for he was already thrice a widower. And since by then Helene had been gone from the realm of the living for over four years, there was no one but Bertha the housekeeper to intercede for Mathilde and try to thwart her father's reprehensible plan.

Hence, Mathilde Spalt was sent off to marry that nasty old scarecrow of a man, Erick Seering, when she had lived for barely sixteen springs. And since she held Helene's love of all living things in Nature deeply within her, she dreamed of resurrecting her grandmother's work and making a new covenant with women—a new generation of Earthen Ones. Mathilde gathered Helene's paraphernalia and kept it all hidden from Mathias's stern eye—the altar cloths she'd embroidered for the Franciscans and later stolen from them, her scribbled writings, and the notes she'd jotted down for her sermons. Mathilde packed it all up in her dowry chest, locked it with a key, and moved into the nasty old scarecrow's house. In this chest she also had remedies that had been brewed by Kunegunde, ointments, elixirs, and decoctions in little bottles as well as the three legendary products that had brought fame to her grandmother and led to her mother's death. Helene had made some of them, for she had known all of Kunegunde's secret recipes. But Mathilde did not know whether she would ever be able to put any of them to use, mindful of what her grandmother had shared with her about the tragic events of the past.

Mathilde had initially resisted the idea of marrying the nasty old scarecrow, but soon she yielded to her father's wish, for she sensed in the union an opportunity to break free from all constraints and live according to the ways of the Primeval Virgin, which would have been completely out of the question in her father's house.

One morning, three months after the wedding, Mathilde waited for the nasty old scarecrow to leave for his smithy, then she ate some porridge cooked in milk and ran to the barn. She knew that an extraordinary day awaited her—that day she would deliver her first sermon in honor of the Primeval Virgin in the nasty old scarecrow's house and spark her cleft in communion with other women.

After aligning her breathing with the cows', just as she'd been taught by Helene, and as Helene had been taught by Kunegunde before her, she drew milk from their warm pink udders and set it for cheese. It curdled in an instant—consolidating and separating as soon as she stirred it with a wooden paddle and her finger. Then she went back to the house, and as she passed the clusters of pale violet wolfsbane that grew along the thick, whitewashed wall, nearly penetrating it in some places, she touched them tenderly, as if she were fondly tousling a child's hair. She'd purposely planted it close to the house so as not to lose connection with it even for a moment. She liked to see it from the kitchen window when she was slicing vegetables, liked how it rubbed up against her like a dog or cat on the doorstep. The plant greeted the other women in the same way when they came to visit while the nasty old scarecrow was away at work. Now that she was married, Mathilde finally had a home to which she could invite them.

Mathilde stroked the clusters of wolfsbane flowers with tenderness. In gratitude, they plunged their roots deeper into the soil and, sheltering from the sun in the shade cast by the steep roof, grew abundantly. The women who came to Mathilde for cheese, milk, and remedies for aching bones, toothaches, and dizzy spells wondered how it was possible that wolfsbane, which always blooms in May, was already covered in flowers beneath Mathilde's windows in the early spring, as if the seasons did not apply to her. It was as if she were living outside of time. Surprised by this fact, one of Mathilde's neighbors, Mrs. Lintzmann, informed Father Hausmann about it during confession so that he would keep an eye on young Spalt; it seemed an evil spirit of some kind lurked around her.

After crossing the threshold, Mathilde bolted the door. She also looked out the window to see if anyone was snooping behind the fence, trying to peek into the house. It was still a few months before strangers began to prowl along the fence like hounds, determined to sniff out evidence of her alleged witchcraft, so she quickly reassured herself and headed toward the pantry at the back of the kitchen. There, behind strings of dried mushrooms and little yellow heads of Saint John's wort as well as chunks of dried venison, which she hadn't taken into her mouth since childhood but which the nasty old scarecrow greedily devoured, there was another room—a hidden one, with an entrance through a trapdoor in the floor that was covered with a striped blanket. The secret room used to belong to the nasty old scarecrow; it was where he stashed all his old, broken tools for shoeing horses, back in the days when his smithy was still at the house. But he'd forgotten about it long ago, and all the tools, even the broken ones, had gone with him when he began shoeing horses closer to the town gate, mostly in the service of the bishop and his entourage, from whom he could earn significantly more than from laymen.

After the wedding, he had grown so fat on the hearty food Mathilde cooked for him that he could no longer squeeze through the hole in the floor. His wife had been intentionally planning meals that would keep him out of the darkest nooks and crannies of his own house, which she was now cleverly arranging for her own purposes. To ensure that the nasty old scarecrow never remembered the hidden room, soon after their wedding she covered the trapdoor with a piece of fabric she'd woven herself and embroidered with colorful thread.

When descending to the hidden room, Mathilde always carried a lit candle, for not a single ray of light entered from outside. The room under the floor was a kind of cellar: on the shelves, where the nasty old scarecrow's tools had once been—

scrapers, tongs, horseshoe removers, sharpeners, and hammers—now, thanks to Mathilde's efforts, flasks and jars were arranged in tidy rows, containing remedies for various ailments, such as premature hair loss, toothache, lice infestation, fevers and chills, excessive heat in the liver that escapes in an explosion of anger from a foaming mouth, and lazy semen that thwarts all attempts at pregnancy. She had tinctures that healed wounds, removed pimples and warts, expelled fetuses from women's wombs, and summoned death.

Most of the remedies had been prepared by Mathilde, under Helene's watchful eye. From a very young age, Mathilde had been more sensitive to plants than people. She had a natural aptitude with them. She was able to restore life to all dying plants—even flowers in a vase, with wilted leaves and falling petals. While concocting remedies, Mathilde followed the secret recipes created by resourceful Kunegunde Kreppel, who now lay in the deadwood forest, fertilizing it with her stocky body, which in her youth had been the object of such lust. Next to her lay Mathilde's mother, Ursula.

Some of the concoctions were the very ones that had brought Helene and Kunegunde their greatest fame—the anti-rodkin elixir and the bloodick and cleft-clencher ointments. These stood separately in little colorful boxes. Until the day of her wedding, Mathilde had never touched any of them. She knew that without them, and without the teachings about the Earth that her grandmother had embroidered—known as the gospel of the Primeval Virgin—the congregation of the Earthen Ones would not exist, but also that these concoctions had been the primary reason why the Earthen Ones had been so brutally targeted. Mathilde also knew from her grandmother that Ursula had been hanged as an act of revenge against Helene—for having made a mockery of the Catholic Church and men.

Mathilde understood that these remedies had to wait for a time when they could—as her grandmother had taught her—serve a greater cause. But after she got married, she began relying on one of the ointments nearly every day. She needed it. And once she started to use it, she understood that she would have to replenish her supply.

Thus, every time the moon was full, she sneaked out into the woods in search of damp places—spots where the water was the deepest on rainy days and, like the breath of animals, evaporated in the morning, forming a connection between Heaven and Earth. She avoided bogs and marshes, for fear gripped her when she remembered what her grandmother had said about them. That once, while she was leaning out to reach a marsh marigold with a long stick so that she could save the liver of her son-in-law, who indulged heavily in strong liquor, the mud gave way beneath her feet and she began to sink, no longer able to touch the bottom with her stick. And the muddy water turned into vipers that began to coil around her body and drag her down, as if she were about to plunge into the ground, which she no longer could even feel beneath her feet. It was only when she grasped a long wooden rod that lay within reach and started wildly banging it against the branches protruding from the trees around the swamp that the pit of vipers released her. They disappeared as if they had never even been there.

Mathilde thus steered clear of the swamp, choosing other marshy terrains instead. And since there was no shortage of comfrey there, she always returned home with a large pile of the herb in her arms, covered with a linen tablecloth. She added viper's grass and oak bark to the comfrey, then she simmered the mixture over a tiny fire; the brewing process would last from one full moon to the next, exactly one month. She had to add fresh water to the concoction every day from the well, and only water that had never reflected light from the moon or the stars. Thus, Mathilde kept her eye on the nasty old scarecrow to make sure he never uncovered the well, and always went to fetch their water herself. She would tilt the wooden well cover only slightly so that the water's surface was always kept in shadow, with not even a sliver of light falling upon it.

After one month of brewing, the mixture turned into a sticky ointment that was so thick it could barely be stirred, and the ladle would stand straight up in the pot. Mathilde would then apply the ointment, rubbing it into her cleft until it became protected from the entire world, completely impenetrable. After several months of applying the ointment, her cleft was so tight that it became difficult to insert much more than a few blades of grass into it.

Since news of this kind, concerning violations of natural law, spread like wildfire, soon all the men at the tavern were aware that Mathilde's cleft was clenched shut so completely that she couldn't be taken even by force, and a short time later, the whole town knew about it. They were quick to blame the devilish tricks that Mathilde surely had been taught by her swamp demon of a grandmother. Eventually the news spread to the town hall and the bishop's palace. It outraged the townsmen, resulting in the public prosecutor of Neisse himself, Franz Zacher, and his henchmen issuing a search warrant for the blacksmith's house to see if they could find any of the prohibited remedies that Helene Spalt and Kunegunde Kreppel had become famous for concocting so many years before.

It wasn't just the townsmen who became agitated by the news but the women too, thanks to Gretchen, the tavern keeper's wife, who had a keen sense of hearing. A certain thought dawned on her: an opportunity was presenting itself once again for them — the women of the town — except this time, instead of clenching their clefts completely and bringing the wrath of the Catholic

Church down upon their heads, they could play it more wisely, let their lovers and husbands enter them only as a reward, when the women had achieved a desired goal, and refuse them entrance as punishment if they prevented them from achieving it.

A new satin gown, a new silver brooch with a ruby in its center, a chamois pouch stuffed with ducats so that she'd "always have enough for the Sunday collection tray at church," and then lo and behold—the clefts would open. No pouch, no dress, no brooch with a little red eye—no penetration. None whatsoever. Nothing for free. This was Gretchen's motivation, though she declared something quite different to Mathilde. Mathilde assumed that her remedies were only going to be used by women who were in great need, ready to rekindle the faith in the Primeval Virgin that they had either experienced themselves long before, while living with Helene in the forest, or heard about from their mothers, older sisters, and sometimes even grandmothers.

Moving out of her father's house had allowed Mathilde to devote herself to what she had always loved most—herbal medicine and the propagation of Helene's teachings, which for so many years had lain fallow because her grandmother, after losing her only daughter and beloved Kunegunde, had feared exposing her granddaughter to the same danger, and thus had stopped preaching, as the Church had ordered her.

Mathilde gave decoctions to the women of Neisse to cure them of many things, such as hypouresis, uterine prolapse after childbirth, abscesses that grew in their breasts from feeding new babies year after year, toothache and decay in the roots of their teeth, ichthyosis vulgaris that caused their skin to become so dry their entire bodies appeared to be covered in scales, excessive lust for other people's husbands or wives, and violent torrents of thoughts that were impossible to calm by any means and kept them awake at night, often causing them to fall victim to madness or somnambulism. And while taking care of these needs, Mathilde could not, after all, overlook the women's clefts, from which every single breath, even the slightest one, originates. From which life springs, and through which the soul returns, not to Heaven—as the Church teaches—but to the black soil of the Earth. The very soil from which purple-hued wolfsbane grows and worms crawl to the surface after rain falls. Hence Mathilde shared her cleft-clencher ointment with the women she considered kindred souls—those who loved the Earth far above Heaven, who embraced the Earth as if they were lovers. So far, however, none of the women except Mathilde had learned how to clench their clefts shut without depriving themselves of sublime pleasure.

And now Mathilde was going to not only reveal this knowledge to the women she had chosen—knowledge of how to achieve pleasure from that which is not hard, stiff, or rigid—but also demonstrate it to them directly. By clenching her own cleft shut to men once and for all and opening herself up solely to plants—to all that arises from the Earth.

When Mathilde descended that day to the secret cellar, there were women already waiting there for her, the ones most desirous of a complete and irreversible cleft-clench: Councilor Gerbauer's wife, Brunhilde; Hedwig, the housekeeper at the canonry, who was aggressively pursued by a considerable number of men from the bishop's entourage; Inga, the apothecary's daughter, who was eligible for marriage but whose eyes lingered more often on women than men; plump, rosy-cheeked Frieda, whose belly became swollen and huge year after year; and highborn Bernadette von Klisch, who already, at merely fifteen years of age, knew that she would never allow any man but Jesus to enter her, and had already chosen a monastic path in her heart, against her parents' wishes.

They sat in the middle of the room, which was dimly lit by

flickering candles. Each woman had brought a candle with her, at Mathilde's request. They'd come at dawn, before the nasty old scarecrow awoke. Mathilde had left the door open that night so they could enter freely, and they'd been waiting there for her, excitement visible on their faces.

They all rose to their feet as Mathilde entered. She was pleased to see them—none had lost her nerve. Acknowledging their courage and the willpower that had allowed them to make this irreversible decision, Mathilde went up to each of them and embraced them individually, her breath aligning with theirs one by one. And when, through their rhythmic breathing, they had aligned themselves with each other like a single vessel, they perceived all at once that, not with their minds but from the desire of their bodies, they had unconsciously formed a perfectly even circle. And they sat in this circle, in complete silence, afraid to disturb the connection that had emerged from their breaths.

Mathilde was the first to break the circle. She turned toward the shelves and took a massive pewter jug from one of them. She set it in the middle, encouraging the gathered women to sit on the floorboards around it. She handed the jug to the woman on her left, Brunhilde. After drinking the sap, Brunhilde immediately handed the jug to the woman next to her, Hedwig, who then passed it to Inga. Inga handed it to Frieda, and Frieda to Bernadette von Klisch, after which there was a moment when the jug returned to Mathilde. The sap they were drinking had flowed from birch trees in the springtime, had been called the "water of life" by Mathilde's grandmother. The women consumed it with such intense concentration and silence, it was as if they were passing the blood of Christ in a golden goblet during the Last Supper. There was deep devotion among them. They were breathing so lightly that their inhalations and exhalations barely disturbed the air. As if they didn't exist at all.

This kind of focus and devotion greatly pleased Mathilde, though she gave no indication of it and instead concentrated all her attention on preparations for the next part of the ceremony. She stood and began to take off her garments. Once she was completely naked, she scooped sap into her cupped hands and brought it close to her vulva, spreading her thighs apart slightly, then made a gesture as if she were offering it a drink. As if she wished to quench its thirst. With a nod of her head, she instructed the other women to do the same. And they all did so. They stripped off their garments as if their bodies were burning and gave their vulvas some of the sap to drink, gently bathing them as if they were a precious treasure or jewel. Then, at a signal from Mathilde, they sat down again in a circle, while she, with very slow movements so as not to disrupt the glow of the candlelight or disturb the flames, began to spread out in front of each of them on a piece of blanched linen the roots and rhizomes that lay among other herbs next to one of the walls. Everything that Mother Earth had ever brought forth from Herself was there. Amber-hued poplar buds that looked like the claws of a wild beast, the golden flowers of Saint John's wort, oak bark, greater celandine, lungwort, bloodwort, hawthorn flowers, violets, daisies, cornflowers, poppies, and elderflowers, and farther back there were hagberry blossoms, alder buds, chamomile heads, and intoxicatingly fragrant linden blossoms, while in the far corners there were all manner of poisonous plants—from deadly nightshade and pale blue foxglove to larkspur and violet-hued wolfsbane, the darkest plant in all of nature, and even black henbane, which Mathilde loved the most, like Helene. Although both the grandmother and granddaughter most often used the root of viper's grass for the actual poking and prodding, a fresh calamus rhizome was best suited for tickling and titillating the cleft—the activity Mathilde's grandmother had called "cleft-sparking." When the rhizome was squeezed tightly between the thighs or slid slowly up and down, it made the vulva so wet, it often gushed like a mountain spring bursting forth from the rocks.

Mathilde set one rhizome of calamus and one root of viper's grass in front of each woman, adequately dried and cleaned of soil but with all their bumpy unevenness left intact. After laying them out with reverence befitting royal insignia, she turned toward the shelves along the wall, on which stood dark bottles of various sizes. When they were held up to the light, one could see that each was filled to the brim. Slumbering inside them, or rather leading hidden lives within, were elixirs, potions, decoctions, and tinctures. Their secret contents buzzed, fervently waiting to be used for the purpose that Kunegunde had described in her lopsided, barely legible handwriting on their labels. Some of the dark bottles and flasks were covered with such a thick layer of dust, they looked as if they'd been sitting on the shelves for decades. Lying next to them were aromatic dried plants in linen pouches and tree buds resting on little scraps of cloth.

On the topmost shelf, there were beautiful little boxes full of Kunegunde's most secret remedies. Some of the boxes were such a dark shade of green they were nearly black, while others were an intense hue of purple that pulsated even in the semidarkness of the cellar. When Mathilde had been a child and her grandmother had still been alive, they used to buy the boxes every year at the Christmas market in Breslau, where they'd sold hot drinks made of brewed herbs and roots, earning more in one day than Helene's merchant son-in-law was able to earn in one month, since his main occupation was squandering ducats at the tavern. The little boxes had contained medallions of the Virgin of Carmel, all of which Mathilde, at her grandmother's request, had removed and thrown into the snow before they returned to Neisse by horse-drawn cart—a journey that took at least a day. At home,

Helene had given the boxes a new purpose, filling them to the brim with ointments made in secret from her son-in-law. The boxes were always kept out of sight; Helene hid them carefully so that only Mathilde knew where they were. Helene would get the boxes out, for example, when a grieving woman came to her, asking for herbal remedies to help relieve her suffering. She helped someone in this way no more than ten times or so, and usually used other means—either a mixture of herbs ground in a mortar, dried plant buds, pulverized berries, or leaves from little plants growing in jars on the windowsill that Helene pretended were herbs she needed in the kitchen.

Helene had told Mathilde nothing about the contents of the boxes apart from the fact that the dark green ones contained an ointment that could be used to clench the cleft shut forever, while the ointment in the purple boxes made the soul depart from the body.

Mathilde now reached for several of each kind of box and handed them out to the women, who were still waiting in pious silence.

Brunhilde, who was menopausal and thus suffering from hot flashes and recurring hypouresis; Frieda, who was excessively plump following multiple pregnancies and suffered from back pain as a result of carrying around so much extra weight; Inga, who was aroused only at the sight of women and felt repulsion toward men; Hedwig, whose gown one of the canons tried to lift nearly every day; and young Bernadette von Klisch, who desired no man but Christ with both her heart and her cleft—all of these women nearly fainted at the sight of the little boxes. They knew from Mathilde of their existence, but they couldn't believe that they'd have a chance to experience the effects of their contents firsthand.

Back in the days when Helene was still living in the forest, some of the women used to go to her for cheese and herbs, and later also to hear her Primeval Virgin sermons on how to transform oneself, the way milk is transformed into cheese—remaining oneself to a certain extent while simultaneously becoming someone else, living in an altered state. As if breaking away from the flesh toward that which exists beyond the flesh, that which belongs not to God the Father but to the Earth. They knew that the new bishop of Neisse, Johann Balthasar Liesch von Hornau, sternly forbade these teachings and tried to punish any woman who, instead of worshipping God the Father, focused her love and attention on Mother Earth. However, the women also knew that anything temporal, anything of the Earth—contrary to what the Church taught them and what the new bishop vigilantly enforced—ignited them like a flame and brought them truly to life, unlike the hazy promise of a life after death, the crowning glory of which was said to be a place at the throne of God the Father, right at His feet. And this would turn them into God's bitches, something they adamantly did not want to be.

It was also from this place in their souls that arose their desire to experience, here and now, intense feelings that later, at the feet of the Almighty, they might never be able to experience again. They believed, as Helene and Mathilde did, that one could free oneself from one's body before the hour of death and direct one's soul toward Heaven through the pleasure that came from cleft-sparking—an intense pleasure impossible to express in words. And when a great fire was begotten from this act of cleft-sparking, one's entire body began to tremble as if a lightning bolt had entered through the toes and exited through the eye sockets, a flash of light that filled the body so brightly that stars appeared and suddenly one ceased to exist, only to be born again a moment later. Among themselves, they referred to this intense sensation of body and spirit as "the separation of the soul from the body," or "omni-sparking." And they would yield their souls to the divine and their bodies to what belonged to the Earth, nourishing both at once.

In the tiny cellar, sitting naked in the silent circle of women, Mathilde reached for her viper's grass root and applied a bit of ointment to it from one of the little purple boxes. She smeared it thickly onto the tip and then rubbed a smaller amount of it onto the shaft. She nodded to the other women to do the same. And when they'd all done so, she leaned back slightly and spread her thighs, and then reached not for the root but for a calamus rhizome, which was swollen from the moisture retained in its leaves. She began to slide the rhizome gently up and down between her thighs, giving herself indescribable pleasure. At first, she merely nudged and brushed her vulva gently, but soon she was rubbing it with the rhizome and its branching, hairlike roots. Then, with the help of her other hand, she spread the cleft with her fingers so that she could rub the rhizome on the protuberance above it, bringing forth ineffable pleasure, foretelling the imminent approach of the lightning bolt.

It was then, when they were poised at the edge dividing the earthly from the divine, that Mathilde lifted her fingers with a decisive gesture, as if to break the silence, which was already laced with sighs and rhythmic breathing, and sometimes even soblike sounds, and gave the signal for each woman to reach for their root. They did so simultaneously, fervently grabbing the viper's grass roots and sliding them into themselves again and again, delicately inserting just the tip, poking themselves with it slowly, then quickly, then gradually pressing the entire shaft into their clefts more deeply than they had ever been penetrated by any man.

Covered with ointment, the roots began to lead the women into an altered state of pure rapture beyond any comparison; there are no words in any language of the world with which to describe the moans of pleasure and the murmurs that emanated from their throats and their vulvas—for they too, while spurting their inner juices, produced sounds akin to those that flowed from the viscera of the Earth when She begot the very first fish and birds, when the first rain fell, and when, after the rain, earthworms crawled into the world with fat little bodies fragrant with soil, when the wind blew, and the very first spring came.

And when the moans subsided, Mathilde lay face down on the ground, and on top of her, silently, guided not by words but by a profound premonition, the women began to lie down on top of each other, like pancakes piled up on a plate, their naked bodies tightly clinging to one another. Once they were settled comfortably in a pile, Mathilde wiggled her big toe, and that's how it all began. When Mathilde wiggled her toe, it triggered a movement in another body part in the pile—the ankle of Brunhilde, who was lying right above her; this caused Hedwig, lying above Brunhilde, to move her hips; this caused Inga to change the position of her pelvis and lower abdomen; this caused Frieda to shift her large breasts, which were temporarily not full of milk; and, finally, this caused Bernadette to rub her lips together. A powerful tremor rippled through the women's bodies as they lay in the pile, tightly embraced in each other's arms, and this lightning bolt coursing through them caused a physical sensation that none had ever experienced in their entire lives.

The tremor seemed to last an eternity. They were omnisparking. They felt as if they were flying over the town, admiring the pointed roofs of its churches and opulent houses, passing over bridges, the river, and the treetops in the forest that surrounded the town, as sharp as the tips of the viper's grass roots. As they flew over the river, each saw her own reflection in it, but upside down. Mathilde was the only one who couldn't see anything, as if she had no reflection, or didn't exist at all, or perhaps existed outside the laws of the world's existence, but this worried her not at all, for after a while, like the others, she could see once again what was below: forests and meadows with grazing cows, and her own house, and even the kennel with the dog in it that always barked at her—a stupid beast that was obedient to its master, though the latter didn't spare it any kicks to the ribs or other forms of malice and ill treatment.

"Stupid mutt," she thought, mixing a worldly thought into the otherworldly experience, which immediately ruined her flight. She began to fall.

As she fell, she screamed, and then all the women landed next to her, unable to believe what they'd experienced and where they'd just been.

Mathilde broke the silence: "If thou art certain that thou dost wish to clench thy cleft shut once and for all, never again to open up thy inner self to men, thus rendering thy cleft eager only for roots and rhizomes, then take some of the ointment from the green box on thy fingertip. Put as much of it as thou canst inside thyself. Once it hath dried inside thee, thou shalt be sealed shut forever. And no creature—neither man nor beast—shall have access to thee. Thou wilt thus experience pleasure solely with plants of sundry kinds, or with women; nothing hard shall penetrate thee ever again, only the soft, thin roots of plants. Thou shalt caress thy vulva with rhizomes, twigs, plant buds, and roots. Thou shalt tickle it with dried bunches of elderflowers, tuck acorns into the center of the dried flowers, thread walnuts and chestnuts onto a string, all so that they will please thee sweetly and sway inside thee as thou dost walk, bringing thee indescribable ecstasy all day long. And if thou dost become afflicted by longing for that which only men can give thee: teach them to love thy vulva with rubbing and stroking, rather than stabbing. For only then canst thou rule over them—when they no longer conquer thee with their genitals but engage in a new and better form of love. One that floweth from Mother Earth. From Nature. A form of love derived from the life of plants, not animals."

Helene's spirit was floating above them as Mathilde spoke. And as she looked down upon her granddaughter from the afterlife, her pride lifted her ever higher above the world.

Concerning the Nasty Old Scarecrow and the Benefits That Come from Crafty Cleverness

---

Several days later, Mathilde checked her cleft immediately after waking up in the morning. It was throbbing more intensely than usual. Perchance by reason of a dream, one of those dreams in which she sat astride mossy, windfallen tree trunks and rubbed her thighs against them. Warmed by the sun, the damp moss looked to her like the beard of the underground forest, protruding above the soil. The moss concealed the secrets of the forest's hidden life: a life that was filled with the movements of bark beetles and ants, the soundless decay of organic matter, the trickle of intoxicatingly fragrant, life-giving sap and resin. Glittering raindrops on bright green leaves. Pearly beads of dew. She held her breath and penetrated herself. Not with her fingers but with the thin sprigs of flowers that always stood in a vase on the table, freshly gathered from her garden. She slid them gently into her cleft and what was hidden behind it, until her soul detached from her body and floated beyond the house, the garden, and the nearby forest, and then beyond the town of Neisse, even beyond the city of Breslau, which she scarcely knew—only as much as she had managed to see when traveling there once a year with her grandmother to purchase the little boxes in which they would later keep their concocted ointments.

Since her marriage to the old scarecrow, Mathilde had regularly used the cleft-clencher ointment brewed by mixing comfrey with oak bark and viper's grass root. It would clench her cleft shut for several hours, so that nothing but a few blades of grass or twigs could enter. She liked to do this with sprigs of elderberry and alder, and most of all with willow branches, which her cleft found most pleasing. She slid them into herself unhurriedly, as if they were beads threaded onto a string, nourishing her cleft with pleasure so intense it was nearly impossible to bear. She also liked to penetrate herself with a feather from her pillow. Something so tiny and supple it was almost imperceptible, as if it didn't really exist. Sliding one feather in and out of her cleft at the front, and another in and out of the little hole at the back, before long she began to rustle, grow branches, and blossom. She rooted herself back into the essence of her being. And while she was still pulsating from this rapture that had permeated her entire body to the core, she would reach under her pillow to retrieve the little box that she'd hidden there. She placed it next to the beautiful purple wolfsbane that was in a vase on the table. Her fingers moist with water, she would open the lid, scoop out some of the greasy substance, and rub it into her cleft. The oak bark that it contained was from the same tree on which her mother, Ursula Spalt, had given up the ghost sixteen years before, hanging from a branch with a noose around her neck. Bark ground to dust, then mixed with comfrey and viper's grass. Just as her grandmother Helene had taught her to make it. So that evil could not enter her. So that she would become tightly clenched, and no undesirable men would be able to pick the petals from the flower inside her—not forever but for a day and a night, in the hope that the old scarecrow would die before he could possess her.

But she no longer needed to apply this remedy since the fateful decision she'd made with the other women to use the lifelong cleft-clencher ointment that had been stored for so many years in the little dark green boxes in the cellar, brewed long ago by Helene. Helene hadn't taught her granddaughter to make the lifelong cleft-clencher ointment, which had been given to the Earthen Ones before the public attempt to force them to return to their pious lives, for fear that Mathilde would make use of the concoction and end up hanging from a tree, like Ursula. This was the only recipe that Helene had never disclosed to Mathilde, and she herself had almost forcibly extracted it from Kunegunde.

The old scarecrow was wheezing in his sleep, grunting, coughing, and drooling like a wild dog poked with a stick. Seeing him like this, Mathilde closed her eyes to preserve her peaceful mood. She walked down the stairs to the kitchen barefoot, placing her feet in such a way that the silence wouldn't be disturbed by the slightest rustle.

She was pleased by her own cleverness. And by the knowledge that her grandmother had passed on to her. Knowledge that now she—Mathilde—had to bring forth to the world so that the covenant could be renewed. So that the congregation of the Earthen Ones could be restored and Mother Earth worshipped once again.

But she didn't know how to accomplish this with Bishop Johann Balthasar Liesch von Hornau and his men watching her so intently that she was unable to take a single step without a pair of eyes following her from the other side of the fence surrounding her farmyard. Eyes that never slept. Eyes that voyeuristically watched her every move.

She didn't yet know how, where, or when she would be able to continue to preach the gospel of the Primeval Virgin. How could she preach it to women who were still uninitiated? For the connection with the former Earthen Ones, apart from those with whom she had recently managed to enter into a covenant in the blacksmith's erstwhile storeroom, had been brutally ruptured by Ursula's death and the attempted rape of the Earthen Ones in front of the entire town of Neisse. How should she select them from the crowd at the market? After all, that was the only place where she had direct contact with other women, while selling cheese and milk. How could she invite them to come to her when the bishop and his men wouldn't let her breathe in peace, making sure that apart from giving prices and thanking women for buying her products, nothing more ever came out of her mouth? How could she show them her grandmother's fabrics hidden underground, fabrics that had been embroidered to honor Mother Earth and the Primeval Virgin? All this troubled her greatly, although she believed that life would eventually present her with a solution. She felt deep down that she just needed to wait patiently for the sign that her grandmother had told her so many times would come, but only when Mathilde was ready.

Thus, instead of fretting endlessly over these problems, she focused on what she had to face every day in her marriage. She congratulated herself on being able to put the nasty old scarecrow into a sleep so deep that he was close to death. Not even the blacksmith's mother had been able to soothe him as well as Mathilde could now.

Shortly after the wedding, Mathilde had observed that the old man liked to indulge in something stronger in the evenings than the beer he drank in the tavern after work, so she contrived to give him something extra that would make him fall asleep before he even reached their shared bed. And since she would have sooner allowed a dog to touch her than him, she poured various homemade concoctions into his mouth with a devilish smile. It was not difficult to please him, as far as alcohol was concerned, as the blacksmith drank excessively. And he never even asked Mathilde what he was drinking. She knew a thing or two about brewing potions from herbs. She had a knack for it. The old man couldn't smack his lips enough to express how impressed he was by her brewing skills. She was able to concoct an exquisite beverage out of anything. And then, warmed by the drink, he would become so incapacitated that he could barely feel his hands. Sometimes he lost his sense of hearing temporarily; other times his whole body became as heavy and inert as a log. After knocking back a mug of Mathilde's brew, the world he knew, which in his case extended between his home and the tavern in Neisse, flipped upside down and whirled strangely, and his eyes fogged over like those of the fish that Mathilde had seen in the river near the mill. His mouth would gape open and he stank so badly that all the windows had to be flung open to air out the cottage. A demon of a man. All he lacked was horns and a tail; Mathilde would swear that if the Devil existed, it was certainly in the form of her husband, the nasty old scarecrow. Thanks to him, she learned to brew much stronger beverages from anything she had at hand: potato peelings, turnips, plums, apples, and breadcrumbs. And since she added small amounts of belladonna, viburnum, and mezereum berries to everything, the old man's health began to deteriorate rapidly.

But all the same, compared with other men, he was hot-tempered and lustful. Despite having already been in the world for more than seventy years, his foolish mouth still gaped open at the sight of his customers' wives. He exuded the stench of fermented drink as saliva dripped from his muzzle. Mathilde couldn't poison him too quickly, for it would raise suspicion for a man as strong as an oak tree to collapse suddenly, as if struck by lightning. So she poisoned him slowly. Not enough to invite death into the house, but just enough to make him lose his desire to lie with his wife in the marital bed.

Suffice to say that the old man, even after such a long life, was still left without an heir. And it was for this very reason that he'd taken Mathilde as his wife, despite the warnings he'd heard from every direction. Now he was cursing himself for listening not to his drinking buddies at the Golden Crab Tavern but to that bankrupt fraudster Mathias Bremmel, who'd assured him that his daughter, Mathilde, was the most hardworking, resourceful, virtuous, and beautiful woman in town. Of all these qualities, virtue had been the one that had pleased him the most—but now it caused him immense grief. Since the nuptials, a winter and a spring had already passed, but still he hadn't even touched her. He had never experienced her body, nor had he even seen her naked—only clothed. She seemed skittish to him. And quick. Whenever he tried to catch hold of her and take her on his knee, she would run to the hearth to add wood to the fire, or over to the window, saying that there was a draft, or that the wind would carry away their souls before she'd managed to cook their supper. At first he laughed at Mathilde's tricks, but now he found himself laughing less often. In late winter he'd tried for the first time to take her by force, but she wouldn't open up to him. He tried to talk her into it at first, then he didn't hesitate to use violence—and yet he failed to unseal her cleft.

This was why she got him drunk—so that he would never be able to have her, and so that he would die faster. It was why she had clenched her cleft early every morning, before he woke up.

It was thanks to the cleft-clencher ointment that she was able to prevent the nasty old scarecrow, or anyone else, from entering her. Apart from plants—which her grandmother had called "the best lovers among all living things"—she had never wished to receive anything into herself. She denied this pleasure to the miller, who winked at her as many times as there were stars in the summer sky, looking lovingly into her eyes every time she came to the mill for flour.

And to Mr. Lintzmann, a neighbor who stared at her, drooling like a rabid dog, whenever he saw her on the road. He once hunted her in the woods, when she was picking mushrooms, crept up behind her and grabbed her by the waist, trying to lift her skirt, but she wriggled out of his grasp and got away. She was faster than him and ran straight to Mrs. Lintzmann to complain that her God-fearing husband had caught her in the woods, clearly with lecherous intentions.

And to Petrus Gerbauer, a chapter councilor who had also tormented her grandmother, for he'd been the previous bishop's right-hand man and had advised him on many matters. He was said to have been the one who suggested to Bishop von Sitsch that it would be a good idea to bring the nasty teat-sucker Heinrich Babel back to the duchy to solve the problem of the Earthen Ones. And he once sneaked into the barn where Mathilde was milking her beloved cows and grabbed her, using all his strength. But still she refused to open herself up to him, even though he was a brawny fellow.

Mathilde shuddered, remembering those incidents and all the other times when she'd had to defend herself. She walked down the stairs from the bedroom to the kitchen and tossed some wood onto the fire in the hearth. She sipped from a jug of milk that had been set for cheese. She ate the heel of a loaf of bread thickly smeared with butter. She opened the windows to let in some fresh air. She glanced upward and waited for the cloud that was covering the sun to drift across the sky. She squinted her eyes in the rays of sunshine and slowly opened them so that the brightness spread across her eyelashes, and for a moment she could see nothing but this golden luminosity. As if the entire garden and orchard were about to emerge from this brightness and come into being. She successfully accomplished this trick, as she always did on sunny days.

Feeling very satisfied, she ran to the barn to feed and milk the cows. She wanted to set more milk for cheese so she could earn money at the market on Thursday and hide some of it, as usual, from the nasty old scarecrow. No one else in Neisse or in the castellany of Ottmachau charged as high a price for cheese as she did, but for the past several decades the entire duchy had been aware that this was no ordinary cheese. Legends of the cheese that had been made long before by the Earthen Ones added value to Mathilde's dairy products, for everyone knew that she was the granddaughter of the congregation's founder. She always sold everything she took to the market, down to the very last lump. For no cheese could compare with hers. Firstly, the cheese that Mathilde made—just like her grandmother's—never cooled down. It always remained as warm as milk freshly taken from a cow. Secondly, it solidified in such a way that if you tore off a piece, you could press it back onto the lump to form a whole again, as if it had never been torn off at all. Other kinds of cheese, after a piece was torn or sliced from it, could never again connect with what they had been separated from. Some tried to explain it by saying the cheese had been made with black magic; since the grandmother had been a heretic, surely the granddaughter was as well, and was striving to entangle them all with the Devil and drag them into the infernal abyss. Especially those who, like Berta Lintzmann, were fed up with all three of the cursed Spalt women: the wild swamp demon grandmother, the suicidal daughter dangling from the oak tree (it was still generally believed that Ursula had taken her own life, despite Helene's insistence, while she was still alive, that her daughter would never have put a noose around her own neck, and certainly not after giving birth to her child), and now the insolent wench's granddaughter, who had been living in the house next door ever since she'd married Erick Seering and was leading Mrs. Lintzmann's husband into temptation.

Mrs. Lintzmann had decided to investigate matters more thoroughly. She started creeping into the neighboring farmyard when the gate was unlocked to spy on Mathilde, and one time she overheard her, through the barn door that was slightly ajar, speaking to her cows as if they were people, but more tenderly, as if she were lulling children to sleep by whispering sweetly. And with strange, unintelligible words. Hidden behind a pole supporting the roof of the barn, Mrs. Lintzmann also saw that the wench was standing nose to nose with each of the cows and breathing the same air as them. As if she were sharing her own breath with the cattle. And what displeased Mrs. Lintzmann most of all was that the animals were staring at the young woman as if they were bewitched, without blinking. Hence, she felt it was her obligation to run as quickly as possible to the palace and report what she had seen to Bishop Johann Balthasar Liesch von Hornau.

A few weeks before this happened, the nasty old scarecrow himself had observed his wife doing this very same thing and had given her a good flogging for it. She hadn't even flinched when he'd whipped her with willow branches bound with twine. He beat Mathilde not only for this but for all the strange things she did. He beat her blindly, as if he were punishing her for every wicked act that he'd ever attributed to her. For the fact that her grandmother had been the wild swamp demon Helene. For the fact that he hadn't been able to defile her after marrying her. For the fact that other farmers were always following her with their hungry eyes. For the fact that, when he was at the tavern, the miller would start boasting, after two jugs of beer, that he was more intimately acquainted with Mathilde than her husband was, by reason of her having performed acts with him of which the blacksmith could only dream. And he would say that Mathilde's eyes looked as if the whole world were reflected in them—not only the town of Neisse but also the sky, rivers, stars, moon dust, distant lands and seas, ships full of treasure, and mines full of gold. All a man had to do was gaze into Mathilde's eyes and then all of this would reveal itself to him, but upside down. The miller babbled at the tavern that these visions would come to anyone who looked into Mathilde's eyes, as if men could become infected by how she perceived the world. At first the world would flicker slightly, then it would lose its sharp contours, dissolve, and merge back into one, though not the image of the world that everyone knew—like Mathilde's cheese, the world would transform into something new and different. And so, the nasty old scarecrow beat his wife for the way she looked at the world with the miller, but also for everything else that came from her—rotten and decayed, like fruit devoured by maggots. He beat what was close to him but still so distant: her narrow waist, which he could never hold in his hands, and her little round buttocks, which never sat on his lap for more than a moment. And he pulled her long hair, which, even when it was tied back, fell sinfully on her white neck and shoulders, twisting into chestnut ringlets. But most of all he beat her for the fact that, although he himself had looked at her so many times, he saw only darkness in her eyes, and nothing more.

Now, after going to the kitchen and setting milk to make cheese, Mathilde looked out the window, for she heard the thud of hooves on the road. Seeing horsemen, instead of going to the barn, she grabbed a broom and began sweeping the farmyard. She did this impetuously, trying to quell the anxiety she felt and dispel the darkness they were bringing with them. As if she were rearranging the sky by pushing the sun and stars around with a broom and creating new constellations from them. As if she were sweeping all the evil of the world out from under the oak bench in the garden. As if she were tickling the Earth's back to cheer Her up. So that She would sleep soundly all winter and then yield abundant crops in the spring. So that the rain falling on Her in the autumn wouldn't wash away ancestors' graves. So that life would throb in the tangled roots of shrubs and trees beneath the layer of frozen mud.

After Mathilde finished sweeping, she glanced up surreptitiously to check what was happening with the horsemen, for the thud of galloping hooves had suddenly ceased. When she saw that they'd stopped some distance away and were watching her, not hiding at all, she began to braid her curly hair and pinned it on top of her head so it wouldn't fall in her eyes, threw on her sheepskin jacket, and hurried over to the animals, as usual, just as on any other day. She didn't want the men to sense that she was afraid of them. She tossed some grain to the ducks and hens and then fed the dog, who, as usual, greeted her with loud barking, as if he didn't like her or was afraid of her, even though it wasn't Mathilde but the nasty old scarecrow who was always beating the dog for no reason. The dog never barked at him, even when the old man kicked him in the ribs, though he always lunged viciously at Mathilde, the copper-brown hairs on his back bristling. As if he felt threatened by her and sensed something in her that his master was unable to perceive.

"You silly beast, you're going to miss me someday," Mathilde scolded the dog, not even really knowing why.

The cows began grunting and mooing joyfully before she'd even reached the barn. They'd picked up her scent. Hearing these sounds, she smiled to herself. Her grandmother's wish had come true, hadn't it? That her granddaughter would not only be capable of enjoying life but would bring joy to life itself, through the way she ate, slept, and breathed. She greeted the cows, inhaling and exhaling with them.

She'd barely finished calming them when the strangers entered the garden. They'd been appearing outside her house for a long time but had never stepped inside the gate. They would linger outside the fence just long enough to make sure she'd seen them, always when the old man was absent and she was at home alone— when the blacksmith was working in other parts of the town or off in the countryside. But never before had anyone entered the garden.

So when Mathilde saw the men standing in the doorway of the barn, she became frightened, for she knew that this time she might not get away from them so easily. But she'd done nothing wrong, apart from tempering the nasty old scarecrow's lechery. She lived her life as she'd been taught by her grandmother, who, after the death of her daughter, had been harassed relentlessly by Bishop Johann Balthasar Liesch von Hornau and Chapter Councilor Gerbauer, both of whom insisted that she cease worshipping the Evil One.

Helene likely would have agreed to their demands, had she ever truly worshipped the Prince of Darkness. But this simply wasn't the case. She didn't believe in the Devil's existence at all, which further enraged the bishop. It had been impossible to force a confession out of Helene, even when the bishop and Heinrich Babel poured holy water over her, made the sign of the cross on her forehead, and forced shoes onto her feet to break her connection with Mother Earth. She needed to have her feet constantly touching Her. Even after she'd moved to town. Until the day she died, she'd never otherwise lost contact with Her. Just as the Primeval Virgin had preached.

Furthermore, Helene had once recited to Bishop Johann Balthasar Liesch von Hornau and Chapter Councilor Gerbauer a version of the Lord's Prayer that was so strange they never forgot it for the rest of their lives—the words were tangled up with each other and some of them disappeared. And if they reappeared, it was in a fragmentary form—as single, disjointed sounds and syllables that made no sense. Listening to the prayer was like observing the wreckage of a massive ship that had smashed against the rocks.

When now, years later, they invaded not Mathias Bremmel's home but the home of the blacksmith—and specifically his barn— fear overwhelmed Mathilde. She immediately remembered what the miller had told her a few days earlier. He had seen, while carting flour to the Lintzmanns, some guards with their noses to the ground looking for traces of devil hooves on the road leading from Mathilde's house to the forest. He supposedly heard at the time that papal envoys had arrived from Rome, at the behest of Bishop Johann Balthasar Liesch von Hornau, and were being entrusted with the task of catching witches in the area and burning them in a huge furnace, under the command of Inquisitor Babel, who was already old at the time, though still skilled at catching and torturing witches as no other inquisitor before had been. Two of the five men, among whom Mathilde recognized the bishop himself, Chapter Councilor Gerbauer, and Judge Gombrich, were wearing garments she'd never seen before. Their coats were so wide they could cover four people of her size, with enough fabric left to clothe a child. They were about a dozen paces away from her, and from this distance they looked like human-sized rooks. They had hats on their heads unlike those worn by the men of Neisse or the councilors from the town hall. These hats were much taller, ending in a pointed tip cropped at the very top, like the chimney in which Mathilde baked bread and broiled meat. And they were worn in a strange manner, for they were tilted downward to obscure half their faces.

Instinctively, Mathilde tightened her grip on the udder of a heifer that had recently calved, until the heifer, instead of squirting milk, began to kick, letting Mathilde know that she'd hurt her. To apologize for her carelessness, Mathilde rubbed the spot between the heifer's eyes, for she knew cattle loved to be stroked in this way. As if they had a third eye hidden in that spot, beneath the hair—a secret eye that was concealed from the world, giving them a different perspective on everything.

The animal must have sensed something, for it behaved differently than usual—instead of standing still in one spot, it began to turn in circles. Mathilde stroked its side, but all for naught, for the beast remained agitated. And the milk that was dripping from its udder, instead of soaking into the ground, condensed into a strange shape that looked like a simple blotch to Mathilde but seemed to stir some feelings in the newcomers, for they immediately left the barn to confer with one another, which worried Mathilde even more. After they left, the heifer, having been patted on the back, once again started producing milk, and so much that a second bucket had to be placed beneath her udder. Mathilde kept glancing surreptitiously over her shoulder to see if the men had left for good or were coming back into the barn.

And suddenly a miracle happened. She saw the nasty old scarecrow on the doorstep of their house, in his nightgown and sheepskin jacket, gripping a scythe.

"Get away from her, or I'll whip you like a dog!" he shouted.

For the first time, the sight of the old man aroused not revulsion but gratitude. As soon as the men were gone, Mathilde threw her arms around his neck. When he started to claw at her body, she tried to escape as usual but this time didn't succeed.

He grabbed her firmly by her long dark braid, and she would have screamed in pain if her body hadn't still felt numb from the fear that had overwhelmed her in the barn. And since she was small and light, her shoes barely touched the floor as the old man dragged her by the hair down the hallway, to the bedroom.

She was unable to squirm out of his grasp, and so with all the strength she had in her, she separated herself from her body so that her soul, and all the feelings deep in her heart, could not be touched by his lust and defiled by it.

He didn't even carry her to the bed. He flung her to the floor. When she felt his rough hands on her hips and thighs, she shut her eyelids tight so she wouldn't have to look at him, not even once. And so he wouldn't be able to gaze through her eyes into the depths of her.

Even when the nasty old scarecrow tugged hard on Mathilde's hair, when he bit and pinched her until she bled, she didn't open her eyes for a second, forbidding him access to her inner self. And since her cleft, sealed with ointment, refused to open, the old man decided to penetrate what he'd previously known only with animals. Although it was so tight that he could barely move inside her, she didn't even flinch. With her eyes still closed, as if she were blinded by the sun and the full moon and all the stars in the sky simultaneously, she began to breathe less, feel less, exist less. She became the floor on which she was lying, and the air surrounding her and her nightgown, sheepskin jacket, and shoes. And the ribbon in her hair, given to her by the miller, with whom she had nothing more in common than a certain way of gazing at the world. While the old man grunted and wheezed on top of Mathilde, shattering the silence with his panting, the slapping of his flesh against hers, and the shuffling sounds of his filthy feet against the floor as he gripped her body with his rough hands, Mathilde gradually ceased to be Mathilde Spalt, the daughter of Mathias and Ursula. With each of the old man's movements, it mattered less and less who her parents had been. Her facial features started blurring together, becoming the faces of every woman he had ever known; as if she were becoming his wife while he copulated with every woman he had met in his life, while also being none of them. But there was a core, some kind of underlying essence, shared by Mathilde and all the other women. As if they were one and the same, a single entity. By possessing her, he was possessing all of them at once—ever more violently, ever more vigorously, until they suddenly began to slip from his hands, crawl out from under his body, and disperse into the air like phantoms.

He pulled her hair several more times, trying to force her to turn her head toward him, and he ordered her to open her green eyes so that he could peer into her soul with his own and suck all the light out of her. She ignored his command. Despite the pain that throbbed under her fingernails, in her teeth, and on her tongue.

When he looked at her, he saw that she was no longer beneath him, as if his spouse, suffocated by his weight, had vanished into thin air.

And even though he was never certain if it really had happened, or if it had merely been a hallucination, he would still testify against Mathilde in what was soon to be the most famous trial in Silesia.

Concerning the Miraculous Properties of Birch Sap, Cultivating a Forest in a Vase, and a Prophecy

―――

The first time Mathilde had detached herself from her body, she'd had a vision that was consistent with what her grandmother had predicted long before her death. A vision that would lead her on a path toward the Primeval Virgin, though it seemed impossible to her at the time. This puzzled Mathilde—how was it possible that during Helene's life, while mute most of the time, she always managed to use her tongue in matters concerning the Primeval Virgin, and even after death had somehow found a way to communicate with her granddaughter? And then, when that nasty old goat of a husband of hers had grabbed her from behind, just as a ram mounts a sheep, a stallion a mare, and a mongrel a bitch, she once again led her soul far away from her body, so that he couldn't defile her. So that her brightness and luminosity would be protected from him.

And just as Helene, many years before, while her husband was forcing upon her the consummation of their marriage, had received a vision of what she should do in order to worship the Primeval Virgin with other women, so Mathilde also beheld a magnificent forest in which there were dozens of trees, or perchance even hundreds, from which women were draining sap into large jugs. In this vision, the sap in the jugs suddenly began to overflow, flooding the ground and flowing into the river. And then the river became so swollen that it burst free of its banks and consumed everything—the jugs of sap, the forest, and even the entire town in the valley off in the distance.

When Mathilde had been a child, she'd learned from her grandmother how to release sap from birch trees. They would go out walking together, but not to the forest. They would walk along the stretch of land next to the river—a terrain with which the canonry didn't meddle, for it was deemed too far from the town to be of interest to anyone, especially since the river was meandering and dangerous, and the only trees that grew there were birches, willows, and poplars, which weren't suitable for constructing churches.

Helene and Mathilde went there together two or three times per week throughout Mathilde's childhood, even though it was an exhausting distance for her little feet. It took about an hour to get there, sometimes even longer—depending on how fast they walked on a particular day.

While teaching her granddaughter how to puncture birch trees so as not to cause them any harm, and how much sap could be extracted from their trunks, Helene felt once again as happy as she'd been at the very beginning of her journey, when the first Earthen Ones had come to live with her in the forest glade: Kunegunde Kreppel, little Ursula, Sarah Goldberg, and Irma Grimm with her three sisters. She carried them all in her heart, although toward the end of her life she had no idea what had happened to most of them. There had been over two hundred women in the congregation. How were they living now? How did they pray? Whom were they allowing into themselves, and how? Did they remember that they had once emerged from Mother Earth's womb and would one day return to it? Were they taking care every day to remain constantly connected to Her, never losing contact?

These questions kept troubling Helene before her death. For she was unable to free herself from the past. Mathilde was her only salvation. The little girl kept Helene planted firmly in everyday existence, which had otherwise become unbearable, devoid as it was of everything sacred. This wasn't an easy task, for Helene, like a kite in the wind, constantly jerked at her granddaughter's hand to escape from her into the air. The child thus had to adjust the length of Helene's string constantly.

During all her years in the forest, Mathilde's grandmother had not acquired the usual practical skills that other people pick up along the road of life. She knew how to consume just the right amount of belladonna berries to have first-rate visions and hallucinations without giving up the ghost, how to bang deadwood in the forest, how to rub her cleft against the moss to ignite a flame within herself. But when it came to tasks such as cooking meals, washing clothes, and tidying up—all these things seemed impossible for her. Thus, in their relationship it often seemed that their roles were switched—the granddaughter became the grandmother, and vice versa.

But collecting birch sap was one of the activities in which Helene remained the grandmother while Mathilde remained the granddaughter—it was the older one who taught the younger the laws governing the lives of plants. She brought her as close to Mother Earth as the girl desired. And the girl desired it more than all the Earthen Ones Helene had ever known during her long life. Mathilde absorbed the knowledge conveyed to her by Helene very quickly, and she displayed extreme gentleness and compassion while making incisions in the trees, gratefully extracting as much sap from them as the jugs could hold. Then they poured the sap into smaller vessels to sell at the market—not in person, but with the help of Bertha, Mathias's housekeeper, to whom Helene gave one-third of the earnings.

The health benefits of the sap were soon discovered by the entire canonry, the members of which often died of heart attacks from the rich food they consumed and their complete lack of exercise, sequestered as they were within the palace, which was lavishly decorated and upholstered with the most expensive and exquisite Italian fabrics.

And when the plague returned to the Duchy of Neisse, at the recommendation of Helene, who had already survived one epidemic, birch sap started to be administered in the infirmaries, which, also at Helene's suggestion, had been moved out of the town and deep into the forest. Helene had a personal interest in all of this, which not a soul suspected at the time. Combined with the ointments that she had begun to prepare at the behest of Bishop Johann Balthasar Liesch von Hornau, the birch sap worked wonders. Consequently, Helene was finally regarded in a slightly gentler light, and some people even began bowing to her in the streets.

The bodies of those who died before they had a chance to be cured with Helene's concoctions were burned in a huge pit, stacked one on top of another—men first, women on top of them, and children last. Their corpses were fully dressed so that the fire would consume the plague that had also permeated their clothing.

The ash settled on the bark and branches of the trees in the forest, penetrating deeply into them. And then, after the plague had passed, Helene and Mathilde once again collected sap from these trees, for it was then that they produced the most, as if they were shedding tears for the people who had fertilized them with their ashes.

Helene's cooperation with the Catholic Church meant that

she could finally spend time in the forest again, as long as she obeyed the bishop's written injunction to stay away from the deadwood grove and the glade where the Earthen Ones had lived. And now that she was allowed back into the forest, she could see for herself the harm caused by the Church's logging.

As Helene looked for new trees from which to harvest sap, she saw that the forest was being felled blindly and indiscriminately, without any kind of plan. After the plague ended, the bishop had made the worst possible decision—to clear-cut the section of the forest from which the sap had been extracted in order to obtain timber for a church dedicated to Saint Roch, an offering of gratitude to him for having saved the town. "What a savior," Helene Spalt spitefully thought. "Half the duchy's population wiped out in a fortnight, and who lifted a finger to stop them all from biting the dust? Certainly not Roch." The survivors of the plague should not thank God for sparing their lives but rather the Primeval Virgin, for it was birch sap and medicinal ointments that had saved them.

But there was one thing of which she was absolutely certain, and she passed this knowledge on to Mathilde in her writing and embroidery: that the Church's felling of trees would one day lead to a great calamity that she called the Deluge. Helene had urged her granddaughter, when she was still a very young girl, to concern herself with this problem after she was gone and Mathilde had reached adulthood.

What they could do now was grow as many new trees as possible and plant them in the areas that had been clear-cut. Thus, they would sneak out of Mathias's house at night, in the silvery light of the moon and stars, to break branches off fallen trees and use them to propagate new ones. Helene and Mathilde would return in the morning carrying wicker baskets on their backs full of willow and poplar branches, from which life had been taken in order to later be restored. They kept the branches in jugs and vases for many weeks, and Mathilde explained to her puzzled father that they were to honor the memory of Ursula, instead of flowers.

Many weeks passed before the first threadlike roots began to sprout. Helene Spalt was slowly beginning to lose faith that this could work, as no one had ever done this before in those parts.

Here, in a solid bourgeois townhouse built of bricks on prestigious Burggasse, a forest was growing in vases and jugs thanks to Helene Spalt, an erstwhile Earthen One, and her twelve-year-old granddaughter. Then they planted the new trees where the forest had been clear-cut, returning to the Earth what had been taken from Her. What She had lost as a result of policies that had failed to include Her.

One day, while Helene and Mathilde were planting willow and poplar branches, they wandered deeper into the forest until they found themselves next to the erstwhile glade of the Earthen Ones and the deadwood forest. Whether this happened completely by accident or Helene led them there deliberately, there's no way of knowing. Suffice to say that as soon as she and Mathilde reached the massive oak tree around which she and her congregation had so often sparked their clefts in worship of the Primeval Virgin, she spied a bush of deadly nightshade growing beside it—as she had long ago, when she and Kunegunde Kreppel had come hither—laden abundantly with shiny berries.

It was not that Helene had lost her rational mind, but the flame that had burned inside her for all those years when she'd lived in the forest and preached the gospel of the Primeval Virgin suddenly struck her again, like a blazing thunderbolt. It engulfed her and spread through her body—every one of her body parts—taking possession of her in such a way that her granddaughter no longer recognized her. And when Helene motioned for Mathilde to sit down next to her, she did so, afraid for the first time in her life to disobey her grandmother. For she had never seen her like this before.

And verily, that was when it happened. Seven little black berries for Helene, three for the child. They washed the berries down with sips of water from the goatskin pouch hanging from Helene's belt.

A quarter of an hour later, they were running through the forest with huge sticks in their hands as if it were the most natural thing in the world. The little girl wielded the stick just as well as her grandmother did. She banged the snags—smack! whack!—with full force, even though it was the first time in her young life that she'd ever done it. And it was then, during her very first trance, that twelve-year-old Mathilde beheld the Primeval Virgin. Mathilde recognized Her immediately, thanks to the images her grandmother had embroidered on old, worn-out tablecloths and kitchen rags.

During that first appearance, the Primeval Virgin didn't say a word, but stood opposite Mathilde and loosened Her thin braid. Then She put Her long hair, which seemed to Mathilde to be made of silver and gold, over Her face to hide it, and raised Her hands, which were glowing as if someone had melted the gold from a monstrance and turned it into streams of light. Clear water was flowing from them, and sometimes also blood.

Mathilde drew close to Her and merged her breath and hands with Hers, so that they began to share the same air, and the insides of their hands came into contact—light, water, and blood mixing together. And then something else happened. After the two pulses had aligned, creating a deep harmony between them, no gestures or words were needed; they understood each other entirely through pneuma. In their slow, aligned breathing. And in this slowness, this unhurried stillness, the blood coursed in the two bodies from head to toe and back again, creating a circular flow of life that prevented death, banished it, removing part of existence from this circuit. They became connected to everything that lived and breathed, for after a while everything that existed had aligned its breath with them and the entire Earth throbbed with one and the same pulse. And something else flowed from this alignment of the breath of all living beings—all humans, plants, and animals. Everything in which this breath was present began to murmur, whisper, whimper, wail, coo, chitter, and chatter with one another—all without words, of course. In one harmonious language, which was breath itself. Nothing more. For what they were inhaling and exhaling was the breath of the entire world.

And when the vision ended, Mathilde, just like her grandmother Helene so many years before, fell to the ground completely drained of strength, for so much of her life force had been consumed by her connection with the Deity.

Helene was lying next to Mathilde, with her long wooden rod in her hand and a mysterious smile on her face, radiating victory. The end of the rod was still warm, with Helene's moisture covering it, mixed with the juice of crushed belladonna berries to intensify her very last experience in this world.

And thus they lay a mere foot away from each other on the ground—grandmother and granddaughter. One dead and the other alive but with the appearance of death on her countenance.

After some time, when Mathilde saw that her grandmother was still completely motionless, she went closer to listen for a heartbeat. When not a whisper of a pulse could be heard, she realized that Helene had died a beautiful death, the kind she'd always dreamed of—in nature, which she loved so passionately, and without a priest. Helene had even once embroidered this moment of her own life on a piece of fabric, predicting exactly how it would be.

In Which Arrives the Deluge That Was Foretold

Was it the Deluge that had been predicted by Helene long ago—a flood the likes of which had not been seen in these lands for over two hundred years, and which claimed the lives of more people than could fit inside the Basilica of Saint James and Saint Agnes, and so much property and wealth that it would be enough for the inhabitants of three towns less prosperous than Neisse—that became the turning point for Bishop Johann Balthasar Liesch von Hornau, leading him to attack women once again and accuse of witchcraft yet another Spalt, the granddaughter of the famous Helene, who even at the hour of her death had refused to turn her eyes toward God and instead had departed this world in a vile state of obscenity and blasphemy? Suffice to say that the grandmother's prophecy, for which it had not been necessary to be a clairvoyant but simply to have a deep knowledge of the forest and thus understand that cutting it down would mean that nothing would stop the river from overflowing its banks when disaster struck, was about to come true, for it had been raining continuously for seven days and seven nights.

And since Mathilde also knew a lot about the forest, having

grown it at home with her grandmother when she was a little girl, and having begun at the age of four to gather birch sap with her too—and, moreover, because of a vision that had come to her in which she had seen what was about to happen—she went straight to the bishop's palace to report it to His Excellency. She knew that he wouldn't believe her. For of what possible value to him was the fact that, while being violently penetrated against her will by the nasty old scarecrow, she'd had a vision that foretold an impending calamity? A calamity, moreover, that she'd been trying to tell him about since she was a child and her grandmother had bestowed this responsibility upon her? She wondered how best to explain it to him so that he might actually listen this time.

Simply casting an eye on the granddaughter of that wild swamp demon, Helene Spalt, was torture for the bishop. He recalled how, four years earlier, when she was still a child, after the death of her cursed grandmother, the girl had begun visiting him in the company of other children (with whom, against the bishop's order and without their parents' knowledge, she used to go into the forest to collect birch branches to propagate in jugs and vases, in order to transplant them, releasing the water of life from them into the soil, just as her grandmother had taught her) to request that the woodcutters the bishop had hired not fell so many trees. Mathilde prophesied that cutting down so many trees, with complete disregard for the laws of Nature, would bring misery to the Duchy of Neisse, as nothing would remain to contain the river within its banks during heavy rainfall.

Looking at Mathilde now, he recalled how much he had feared her in the past. There had never been such a child in the bishop's palace before her. A child who'd looked at him with an insolent gaze, questioning his decisions and challenging his orders. He would have eagerly thrown her over his knee and given her a good spanking to instill some discipline in her, which her father had clearly failed to do, not to mention her grandmother. The stupid bitch wouldn't have taught the child anything good anyway; it was for the best that she'd expired in the forest like an animal.

Verily, the prophecies that Mathilde presented to the bishop soon became reality, including the sores that broke out on his tongue after proclaiming derogatory words about women from the pulpit. He knew not what to do with her. She was too young to be put on trial, too old to be bent over his knee and whipped, and he did not have the freedom to smack her across the face, for she came with other children, as if she were using them as witnesses in case a single hair were to fall from her head.

Assuming that Mathilde's warning about a flood was merely a hoax, and suspecting that the child wished to put a curse on the Duchy of Neisse and all the surrounding lands, the bishop issued a decree forbidding women and children to enter the forest. This was punishable by flogging, and even by death in some cases (as for which ones, the proclamation published by Erasmus Grunn's printing house did not clearly specify).

Disobedient Mathilde, however, continued to go to the forest with the other children, and they all swore by the moon and the cross simultaneously that they would never breathe a single word about it to a living soul. For they were doing forbidden things in the forest, in accordance with the rules embroidered by Helene and later written down by her and the other Earthen Ones.

And so, they would often venture into the forest together in secret. It was there that Mathilde first taught the laws of the Primeval Virgin to others. They learned the arcane secrets of coexistence with each other and with all that exists in Nature. They cautiously ate shiny black belladonna berries and began to experience what Mathilde had first experienced with her grandmother on that day long before, when they'd strayed from the path together and ended up at the deadwood forest. The children had similar epiphanies and visions while banging deadwood with long sticks. Mathilde knew how to speak to them in a way that allowed them to gain understanding of the Primeval Virgin and inspired them to abandon the religion of their fathers and return to the faith of their mothers. The faith followed by the Earthen Ones, derived from Mother Earth—feminine, intimate, and tender, based not on suffering but on wild, unbridled joy.

Now, faced with the ringleader of a new generation's heresy, the bishop lost his patience. "Flee from here before I set the dogs on thee! And stop spreading ridiculous rumors in my duchy! Stop sowing fear! Thou hast spoken of a flood for many a year, and yet somehow God hath protected us from it so far. He shall do the same now. Mathilde Spalt, thou shalt finally receive what thou deservest!"

There was nothing more Mathilde could do. She left the bishop's palace, slamming the door as she always did, and the flood that came in the night submerged the town of Neisse in water five feet deep.

In Which, Several Months After the Deluge, a Furnace Is Built in the Market Square

---

Mathilde became aware that a furnace had appeared in the market square when she stopped at the tavern one day to sell milk to Gretchen, the tavern keeper's wife, who preferred Mathilde's dairy products to all the others. But at the sight of Mathilde, Gretchen crossed herself and spat over her shoulder three times. She'd noticed her husband looking at her and was afraid that he might accuse her of witchcraft by association. She waited until the tavern keeper had ducked his head back inside and closed the upstairs window, and then, making sure that no one could see them, she looked into Mathilde's eyes and said, "Hast thou heard that a furnace for burning witches is being erected in the market square? And that they intend to burn women like us?"

"Like us?" Mathilde asked. "What dost thou mean?"

"The ones who know how to clench our clefts to keep evil from entering, who pleasure ourselves with bulrushes and separate our souls from our bodies. Just as thou hast taught us."

"I teach no one," exclaimed Mathilde indignantly. "Thou dost present me with questions, and I merely tell thee what I learned from my grandmother. Verily, I say to thee: Come to me no more for cheese or herbs, if thou art so holy. And never again shall I help you expel a fetus."

After the flood, tension had increased throughout the Duchy of Neisse. Its inhabitants felt that someone ought to take the blame—after all, such calamities don't just happen out of the blue. Someone must have brought it upon them. There prevailed a conviction that women must be behind it, not the pious men who worshipped God the Father and conscientiously paid their tithes to the Catholic Church.

Filled with bitterness after their unpleasant conversation, Mathilde and Gretchen returned to their respective homes. Fearing the worst, Gretchen decided to serve the customers at the tavern's most honorable table herself so that she could eavesdrop more easily. The bishop laughed the loudest that evening. If all went well, the furnace would be finished in a few days. The very first furnace of its kind in Silesia, built for the glory of Heaven. Beaming with pride, the bishop raised a toast to valor. The valor of the duchy's inhabitants—more specifically, the valor of Christians and the valor of Silesia! Neisse would soon have a furnace more powerful and efficient than the one in Bamberg! Highly inebriated, he kept demanding more tankards of mead. He was accompanied in his drunkenness by Judge Gombrich and a group of men in black hats. The only person missing was Chapter Councilor Gerbauer, who had returned from the market square to the bishop's palace, where he was staying at Bishop Johann Balthasar Liesch von Hornau's invitation, and was now kneeling beneath a crucifix hanging on the wall and beginning his evening prayers.

On Somnambulism and Invocations

Mathilde foresaw that the only way to oppose the Church would be to find more believers in the Primeval Virgin — ones who were courageous enough to join her in the battle. On the last Friday before the Church planned to carry out the terrible deed of which Gretchen had informed her, Mathilde told the rest of the women in her small congregation to bang deadwood as usual and enter into a trance. But instead of cleft-sparking, she led them in a different kind of ceremony, for the very first time since they'd started meeting. She asked all the women to lie on their bellies and surrender their weight to the Earth. And to exhale their breath into Her. Then they linked hands, forming a circle. When their bodies were arranged in a radiating shape, they began to breathe together steadily, in rhythm with Mathilde, who inhaled and exhaled so slowly and deeply that at first it hurt their lungs, and then faster and shallower until there was hardly any air in their lungs at all. And as they shifted from slowness to a frantic pace, they could feel their souls separating from their shell-like bodies and beginning to wander out of the forest, toward those whom they wished to attract and to their beloved, sacred glade.

They succeeded. They simultaneously entered a trance and released their souls so that they could wander and attract others to them. They called the ones they pulled toward them "sleepwalkers," for they arrived from the border between dream and reality, neither awake nor asleep. As if their souls, hungry for adventure and a different life, were roaming somewhere in the vast cosmos, waiting for such a chance.

Those who were willing to be summoned by the group experienced what felt like a confusion of the senses, as if they had suddenly become overwhelmed by a state of frenzied madness. In an instant, they were transformed to such an extent that their family members and loved ones grew numb with terror, for they no longer recognized them. For instance, Karoline Klausberg, the seamstress at the bishop's court, suddenly threw herself to the floor while handing a cassock to the bishop that she'd widened at the waist for a canon who had gained twelve pounds in less than three months after overindulging in sumptuous dinners, and began to grope at her breasts, screaming that they were burning, and that she felt as if she were engulfed by flames.

And when Karoline put one hand under her skirt and began to make strange movements with it, the bishop called the guards and ordered three buckets of cold water to be poured over her, to cool her down. When that didn't help, the bishop ordered his guards to throw her into the dungeon without food or water for two days, after which she would be released—if she showed improvement.

This is precisely what happened to Anna Frenza. For it was then, during the great summoning, when Mathilde and the women she loved needed tremendous support, that the CEO of the national oil company dashed naked through the park and straddled a mossy tree that had fallen in a windstorm, changing the course of her life forever.

Concerning a Trial
and Torture

When Franz Zacher, the public prosecutor, was requested by Inquisitor Heinrich Babel to read the notes that had been found among Mathilde Spalt's belongings, which Babel claimed had been written by both her and her grandmother, he felt that he would rather be anywhere else than where he was, the town hall, where the public trial against Mathilde had commenced.

For he felt not completely at ease there. First, he didn't believe the flood that had inundated the town but receded quickly, in a single night, had been caused by the accused. There was no evidence to prove it. Second, he doubted whether the notes had truly been penned by Mathilde, for the handwriting seemed to suggest (after an analysis of the signature on the contract with the Franciscan monastery) someone else: Helene Spalt. Third, he knew that the young woman had done nothing wrong—she had simply reforested some terrain where trees had been felled, using a common propagation method. As for her intention to poison her husband, the prosecutor didn't believe it, since the old man could simply have eaten some cheese that had turned rancid and become afflicted by a stomachache in this manner. Franz Zacher tried to worm his way out of reading the notes, but the bishop and inquisitor instructed him to do so aloud, in front of the crowd that had gathered in the town hall.

Thus, he began:

> There is one God—Heaven—and one Goddess—Earth. The Universe was born from their union. A man is an emanation of heavenly energy, while a woman is an emanation of earthly energy. At God the Father's side doth stand His Son, Jesus Christ, who is one with His Father, while at Mother Earth's side doth stand Her belov'd Daughter, the Primeval Virgin, forming a sacred unity with Her. Each and every man and woman in the world is a divine vessel, but a man, by reason of his tendency to be distracted by his rodkin, is a vessel far more breakable indeed. 'Tis wherefore there are so many shatter'd and bruis'd menfolk in the world, who contribute nothing of positive value with their minds or any other part of them, but rather just burden it with their stupidity.

At this point, the crowd in the town hall burst out in thunderous laughter, which gave the court a moment in which to catch its breath and then declare that the quoted passage from the notes allegedly written by Mathilde was merely a jest of some kind, and not a sin for which she must pay with her life.

The prosecutor continued reading:

> Heaven is position'd above Earth, and Earth doth rest at His feet. These two deities touch each other, just as a man and a woman unite their bodies in acts of love. Although Mother Earth—who doth nourish and support us, and, after our deaths, taketh us into Herself and embrace us—doth lie beneath Heaven, She is not subordinate to Him. 'Tis not

Heaven that doth exert influence over Earth; 'tis rather Earth that doth exert influence over Heaven. By underestimating Earth's power, or by attempting to conquer and exploit Her, as if She were just some corrupt wench, we bring upon ourselves great calamities and misfortune. Verily, to compensate for the evil that humans inflict upon Mother Earth, 'tis necessary to do that which bringeth Her the greatest joy and benefit—nourish Her with our breath and our moisture, so that the juices flowing within us feed the soil, which doth yearn for fertilization. Hence, menfolk are encourag'd to sow their seed deep in the Earth, preferably in orchards full of fruit trees, vegetable patches, and fields where wheat, rye, and barley grow, while womenfolk are encourag'd to engage in cleft-sparking every day, igniting not only their clefts but also the entire world.

At that moment, a murmur of surprise rippled through the room, while expressions of disbelief and disgust began to appear on some faces.

Zacher continued:

Cleft-sparking occurs when womenfolk, instead of receiving menfolk's bruis'd rodkins unto themselves, derive inexpressible pleasure from plants, which are not hard at all, but soft, so that instead of inserting what is as hard and stiff as a bodkin into their clefts, they stroke them in various ways and rub them with things that do not force them open, nor stretch nor tear them. The Earth doth begin to tremble with every act of cleft-sparking. 'Tis a trembling that stirs the heavens and the Earth, awakening the world with a spark of life and a renewed creation. As if 'twere being born for the first time, emerging from the womb of the cosmos.

As he finished reading this passage, Franz Zacher struggled to make himself heard over the thundering roar of anger in the room. But Bishop Johann Balthasar Liesch von Hornau ordered him to continue reading everything that he, the bishop, had prepared for Zacher to read the day before, having selected passages that he knew would be the most insulting to the men gathered in the town hall. And the most odious.

When the cleft is rubb'd and strok'd, it should be done as firmly as if thou were striking stones together to kindle a fire, and as gently as the flutter of a butterfly's wing. The Earth is happiest when womenfolk do this not alone, in their own homes, but in groups, lying down together, kneeling, sitting, or squatting—or even standing, for there are women capable of rubbing their clefts while standing, even at very unexpected times, such as while killing flies with one hand, or kneading dough for bread, if they have already become so adept at it that only one hand suffices, and their spouse is so absorb'd by the food on the plate in front of him that he notices not what the woman is doing, while she pinches her cleft ever so lightly, then caresses it ever so gently, though of course this must be done more forcefully through petticoats and dresses than when naked. Verily, 'tis essential not to let the broken man out of thy sight, for if he perceiveth what doth transpire beneath thy dress, he might slay thee out of jealousy.

The outrage triggered among the men by the last passage rivaled the uproar caused by the sale of the anti-rodkin elixir at the market, and later the bloodick ointment. But what provoked the loudest whistles, stomps, and furious threats against Mathilde were the words that Franz Zacher read at the very end:

'Tis recommended that women cleft-spark together, in secret from their husbands, for only then shall Mother Earth be revitaliz'd, as She doth desperately need after an onslaught of misfortunes—wars, droughts, floods, the Black Death, and ergot. Through cleft-sparking, the connection between the Earth and these women shall expand and grow, just as the roots of the trees beneath the Earth, forever entwin'd even after they are cut down, even after Death.

After reading the excerpts from the notes and sermons, Franz Zacher already knew what would happen next. And everyone else gathered in the town hall was certain of the events that would unfold. After all, similar trials were taking place with increasing frequency in the nearby towns of Mährisch Schönberg and Freiwaldau. Moreover, they were in the presence of the master himself—one who was rivaled at that time by very few inquisitors on the entire continent.

Two hours later, her head had been shaved. She was filthy. Bruised and battered. Her eyes were full of terror. She was on her knees in a dungeon, in front of three men clad according to the rank assigned to them in the ecclesiastical duchy: one was wearing a black hood that obscured most of his face, and his shirt and trousers were soaked with sweat and splattered blood; the second was dressed in a long bishop's robe with a huge golden cross on his chest; the third, at first glance, judging by his conical black hat with a wide brim and black leather gloves, was the inquisitor.

One of them clamped iron rings spiked with nails around her ankles, then began to rape her from behind. Every time his hips collided with her emaciated buttocks, the spikes penetrated deeper and deeper into her skin. The man with the huge golden cross on his chest held a burning torch so close to her back, which was already bent over with pain, that it scorched her. Mathilde screamed, trying to break free from the iron shackles on her feet and the strong male grip, but to no avail. She was held down by yet another tormentor, who had emerged from the shadows of the dungeon. He had a terrifying face, etched with acts of violence. The left cheek was sliced in half by the scar of an old wound. Despite his advanced age, he stood tall and erect, with his large hands hidden in gloves. He adjusted his trousers, shifting the loosely tailored material to conceal his swollen member — the only part of his body that refused to obey him during interrogations and executions, unlike his dexterous hands, with which he could quickly (and always accurately) toss a noose around a condemned man's neck, or light a fire beneath yet another stake. His member no longer responded to his wife on the nights when she freely surrendered her body for his pleasure. Her body no longer aroused him. Not a single spark of desire flared inside him, even though his wife lacked nothing. In fact, a fair number of men eyed her hungrily in the town of Edelstadt. She was a God-fearing, docile bitch who groveled at his feet and inspected every nook and cranny of his clothing to see what gifts he might have for her. Didn't he bring her a li'l sumthin' today? To cheer her up just a li'l bit? Of course! An amber pendant set in silver, perchance with a hint of gold. A fashionable French shawl with such thick and detailed embroidery, it would soon be the envy of all the maidens in the town. And the key to the chest in the Neisse tavern keeper's attic? A chest whose contents he knew well from the tavern keeper himself, who had often boasted proudly of how generously he rewarded his wife for her care of the tavern. Oh, what wonderful things were in that chest! Gorgeously decorated gowns and bonnets adorned with precious gems, kept for the eldest daughter's dowry. One only had to find a reason, create an opportunity. The property and possessions of the women on trial were at his fingertips. It would all have to be fairly divided, of course, but there would still be plenty!

The tavern keeper's wife, Gretchen, had aided them considerably in their efforts by telling them about Mathilde's knowledge of herbs, and her ability to brew various potions from them, knowledge that had been handed down to her from her grandmother. She informed them of Mathilde's sinful inclinations as well, such as how she often pleasured herself while lying on moss in the forest like some kind of wild animal, and how she'd corrupted the local women and encouraged them to engage in sinful activities with her. It was Gretchen who swore that Mathilde was sleeping with the Evil One—a version of events, clearly indicating Gretchen's treachery, that was relayed to Mathilde by Heinrich Babel during the first day of torture.

At the sight of Mathilde bound in shackles, singed by the bishop's torch while he searched her body for the mark of the Devil, Babel could barely restrain himself from reaching into his trousers to stroke his member, which was beginning to swell. The labored, wheezing gasps of a wild animal being chased by hunting dogs, its howl after being struck by a well-aimed arrow, gave him a thrill that he could find in no other profession. No one but him—Heinrich Babel—was capable of coming so close to death. He stood on the border between life and death, where his victims could feel that their torture was not over yet, though the end was near. And though it seemed impossible for the pain to be any more excruciating than it already was—it could be. Heinrich Babel would always find a way, somehow, to make impossible-to-endure pain endurable, for lurking beyond every level of pain was a new form of torture that no human on Earth could ever imagine. Except, that is, for Babel.

The inquisitor asked Bishop Balthasar and the other men to leave the torture chamber, for he wanted to make one final attempt at crushing the prisoner. It was no easy feat for him to refrain from raping what was no longer possible to rape. From annihilating something that was already nothing more than a sack of bones—something from which the soul would depart very soon, lying as it was now in a state of dormancy, the body it inhabited having been rendered unconscious. Babel, of course, knew precisely how to summon such a soul back to the body, how to keep it from escaping.

He glanced behind him to see if the other torturers had left. Reassured that he was now alone with the victim, he approached her limp body, knelt in front of her, and started whimpering, whining, howling, and snarling. He paced in front of her on all fours like a wild beast, sniffing at her battered flesh, at her crotch and anus, from which blood and other fluids were seeping, for her body no longer had control over anything, the pain above all. This "hunting of life"—as Babel described the practice in his discussions at the bishop's palace—helped him to penetrate deeper into the essence of Satan, with the aim of extracting a final confession from the woman suspected of witchcraft.

Anna Frenza is overcome by excruciating pain in every particle of her body. She feels as if she were nothing but a thousand wounds from which blood is trickling, drop by drop. She touches her face and head, wanting to make sure she's still whole and hasn't crumbled to pieces. The rough texture of her shaved head leaves her perplexed. Who is that woman she's looking at on the TV screen? Could it be her?

She realizes that she's completely naked, but the body belonging to her bears no resemblance to the one she had just a moment ago. And yet she's able to move its limbs. She's the owner of this body. Where has her former body gone? The one without any wounds or bruises? Where have her fingers and toes gone that were once intact and strong, without crushed bones?

V

THE REVIVAL

Encryption of Madness

Although five weeks have passed since she was taken to the locked ward of the psychiatric hospital in Tworki, Anna Frenza still feels completely cut off from everything around her, as if she were trapped behind a thick pane of glass. None of the hospital staff are able to get through to her. Despite constant medication, she's slipping deeper into herself by the day. But in the silence of the cellophane-wrapped night—the kind of silence that exists solely in hospitals, silence that resounds so deeply and intensely that it turns a person's skin to bristly gooseflesh and the brain shatters as it strains to detect the slightest noise, even one as quiet as the scratching of a rat or mouse in the labyrinth of musty, mildew-covered objects and medical equipment—only one resonant, melodious syllable reaches her, repeated over and over again by Halina Rutczyńska-Łemka as she obsessively calls out for her drowned dog: "Tin tin tin tin tin!"

Once in a while, Frenza grunts or growls a certain sound, one that seems completely meaningless, interspersed with other grunted and growled syllables with unbearably long whistles and pauses between them. At first, none of the ward's staff members pay any attention, but as luck would have it, the hospital has recently hired a new employee—a university student named Adek, who's doing a master's degree in German language and literature. He very quickly notices that the German words *"die Spalt"*—"cleft"—are frequently repeated in Frenza's outbursts. A few days later, after mopping the floor and washing the barred windows so that the patients can see out to the beautiful park with its romantic little bridge over the Utrata River, he sits down with a notebook next to Frenza, who is strapped to her bed, and begins jotting down everything spewing out of her throat. And when he discovers that there might actually be some sense in the combination of these gibberish words tumbling breathlessly out of her mouth, in between long inhalations that seem like a ravenous desire to draw life-giving air into her lungs, as if she were on the brink of suffocating, he starts treating her differently than the other patients.

He begins to piece her syllables together, eagerly waiting for each new pause. And eventually he's struck by a stunning realization: The syllables that follow one after the other form a nearly coherent sentence. All he has to do is wait through the pauses and then write down the sounds that are draining Frenza of breath. Again. And again. And again.

alt-es-vibe-yung-frow-shy-da-ge-bear-moo-ter-heern-sha-la-ge-er-det-shpalt-alt-es-vibe-yung-frow-shy-da-ge-bear-moo-ter-heern-sha-la-ge-er-det-shpalt-alt-es-vibe-yung-frow-shy-da-ge-bear-moo-ter-heern-sha-la-ge-er-det-shpalt-alt-es-vibe-yung-frow-shy-da-ge-bear-moo-ter-heern-sha-la-ge-er-det-shpalt-alt-es-vibe-yung-frow-shy-da-ge-bear-moo-ter-heern-sha-la-ge-er-det-shpalt-alt-es-vibe-yung-frow-shy-da-ge-bear-moo-ter-heern-sha-la-ge-er-det-shpalt-alt-es-vibe-yung-frow-shy-da-ge-bear-moo-ter-heern-sha-la-ge-er-det-shpalt-alt-es-vibe-yung-frow-shy-da-ge-bear-moo-ter-heern-sha-la-ge-er-det-shpalt-alt-es-vibe-yung-frow-shy-da-ge-bear-moo-ter-heern-sha-la-ge-er-det-shpalt-alt-es-vibe-yung-frow-shy-da-ge-bear-moo-ter-heern-sha-la-ge-er-det-shpalt . . .

Adek

Adek notices that Frenza seems to be slipping into the darkness, and with a firm grip on her wrist he tries to keep her afloat.

Even here, in the locked ward, Adek didn't expect to encounter anything as wild as this. He struggles somewhat with his own identity—a gay German literature student from Pruszków who spends his free time hooking up online with the whole queer world in the swampy quagmire of Grindr. These adventures clash uncomfortably with the Catholicism that he suckled in his mother's milk. Right off the bat, Adek had been given a golden devotional medal of the Virgin Mary to wear around his neck, then a computer for his First Communion, and then a Yamaha keyboard for his Confirmation, in front of which he still often sits and pumps out tunes for the cloud. He gets some positive feedback about his music from time to time. Songwriting comes easily for him, especially when he's high on shrooms. His ears, which have platinum tunnel piercings in the lobes, pick up new sounds and harmonies right out of thin air, which, during his hallucinations, undergo amazing transformations and reverberations, and it feels for a while as though God, whom he encountered during his Baptism, First Communion, and Confirmation, is speaking directly to him. But Adek (known as "Adell" in the cloud) doesn't yet understand what God is trying to tell him. It's as if he were an epic bard, like Słowacki, Mickiewicz, or Norwid, though they used a familiar language to convey what God had to say about Poles and Poland, while he has a more difficult task—he's forced to communicate in a language he doesn't know, because he never learned it. He's a *flat*-out genius with *sharp* observations making *signature* moves—even though he never learned to read music. He's a Saint John the Evangelist of composition. A musical illiterate who will nevertheless leave behind an MP3 gospel. Several hundred songs in a cloud to be enjoyed for free by listeners around the world. And it's this creativity of his that makes him special among all the plebeian residents of Pruszków.

His most devoted listeners are the female patients in the locked ward of the psychiatric hospital in Tworki. Thanks to Wanda from room number two, they even exercise to Adell's tunes—with intense, feverish routines they call "witch aerobics" when none of the hospital's staff members are within earshot, and "Slavic yoga" when they are. Last week, during one of Adek's night shifts, they exercised to his newest tune. They were all in a position with their elbows on their knees, breathing in such a strange way that he got a hard-on while watching them. That's how intense it was. Guided as if on a leash by Wanda's hypnotic suggestions, he imagined a beam of light penetrating him like a sword (one that wasn't too sharp, just a plastic one—like a toy version of Master Yoda's lightsaber), straight into his rosy anus and staying there, stabbing that cute little hole, no bigger than a snag in a pair of pantyhose, as gently as if a sparrow or blackbird had landed on it. Being poked in the asshole with light was such a delicate feeling that it was nearly unbearable, little more than a tickle and yet it induced spasms of delight. This surprised Adek, who was more accustomed to a hard pounding in the ass than the soft touch of a bird's tiny claws.

He has to admit that the witch yoga is an extremely effective type of exercise, especially if done with an imaginary lightsaber. All Adek knows about Wanda is that people say she was committed to the psychiatric hospital after her exercise routines gave women in Podkowa Leśna such an increased libido that their husbands, accustomed to their wives not having any sex drive whatsoever, started suffering from post-traumatic stress disorder after being relentlessly attacked by them. The men had, in fact, gotten out of the habit of having sex with their wives shortly after their weddings—those, of course, who'd had the chance to develop such a habit at all. The same was true of Wanda. By arousing the libidos of her female clients, she was depriving their partners of the comfort they'd had up until then of not fucking their wives (not to mention making love to them, an even higher level of initiation) but instead fucking themselves wildly, without any restraint. Not to mention girls from dating apps and porn sites, with whom everything always proceeded smoothly. There was no need to kiss and spread germs, no need to moisten suspicious-smelling clefts.

And then, suddenly standing in the way of their sex life, which they pursued every night in secret from their libidinally dormant amoeba wives, came Wanda, who was fixated on causing a great awakening of women's sexual energy.

"Real sex isn't for idiots," she'd say, kneeling with her rump sticking straight up, swinging her pelvis, and reactivating her ovaries. Her huge breasts, which were nearly exploding with love for the world, bounced up and down as if to prove this thesis, and her butt did the same while harnessing an invisible broomstick, which they were supposed to imagine was sliding into their front cleft, then into their back cleft, picturing themselves flying over the tops of century-old trees in one of the parks in Podkowa Leśna, whereupon they usually experienced such an orgasmic epiphany that it was difficult to bring them back down to earth afterward.

No one knows exactly how Wanda, who seems completely of sound mind, ended up in the locked ward of the mental hospital. She herself eventually stopped blaming it on the "patriarchal conspiracy in that conservative Catholic shithole," as she calls Podkowa Leśna, and instead started putting her skills to use and propagating pagan practices among her new female disciples.

There's no shortage of feminists and environmentalists in the ward who, out in the real world, strapped themselves to harvesters and were determined to die for their homeland—which wasn't Poland for them, but the forest! Or those famous River Sisters—a hydrofeminist collective of women who organized activist campaigns to save Poland's natural bodies of water. And the mothers who staged protests in clear-cuts by sitting on tree stumps while cradling their babies. On orders from the prime minister, all of these women—every last one of them—were caught by scoundrels from the city guard and taken straight to the psychiatric hospital. Goddamn river nymphs and fucked-up mermaid nymphomaniacs. Why the fuck would someone want to endanger one's own family—one's husband and children!—just to defend some old oak or pine tree?

It's all beyond Adek's comprehension. All the attempts he makes to grasp this topic intellectually result in the abdication of the cerebral cortex responsible for complex thought operations and a swishing sound in his ear canals. His thoughts escape into the distance, far away from the climate problems of the contemporary world. He already decided long ago to join that "fucked-up soyhead" club, to become Adek of the Tofu Coat of Arms—but veganism is his one and only link to the eco-friendly universe. And his veganism does not stem from a concern for the planet but is rather for the purity and cleanliness of that little cave of his, which so often is explored by his numerous lovers. Of course, he doesn't support killing animals. He doesn't eat them. And he has vowed to himself that he'll never rent a room with a stuffed bird on the wall, or step across the threshold of any house with the skin of a bear or wild boar on the floor. Absolutely not! But the role he's playing in the theater of eco-conscious living ends there. Isn't that enough? Doesn't he have a hard enough time already, spending eight hours a day in this circus, Monday through Friday, for a lousy paycheck that, if it weren't for the opiates he frequently swipes from the hospital's supply, wouldn't even be enough to pay for a bachelor pad in Pruszków?

It's only thanks to Anna Frenza, and Adek's interest in her Old German utterances, that he begins to notice the significance of his daily drudgery, work that so thoroughly wipes him out, he doesn't have the strength even to tap the screen on his phone with his finger when he gets home. Since being hired in Anna Frenza's ward, he hasn't slept with any Twatville boys from Grindr, or any other app, since all of his attention has been absorbed by trying to decipher the notes he's been scribbling down as he listens to her monologues. It's not until he reaches out to his favorite professor, a specialist in Old High German, and shows him his notes, that the meaning is revealed! His professor sounds out the words Frenza has been repeating: *altes Weib, Jungfrau, Scheide, Gebärmutter, Hirnschale, Geerdet, Spalt.* His eyes grow wide. "I believe she's talking about the Primeval Virgin, the vagina-womb-skull, the Earthen Ones, the Clefts." Adek writes down the professor's words, trying to piece them together—but the message is still far from clear.

The Writing on the Wall

The water faucets in the hospital sink are the same as those in the block of flats in Mszczonów where Anna Frenza lived as a child. Impossible to turn off completely. Water constantly drips against the porcelain surface, as if gouging away slowly at a rock. As if washing away eternity. The endless tapping sounds make Frenza feel as if, in this room where the doors have no handles, there weren't any walls either—just the Himalayas stretching all around her.

A shapely blonde in a white apron and white Crocs enters the room to which Frenza has been transferred thanks to the new orderly, Adek, after a few months in isolation.

"Some pills for you, Ms. CEO."

Frenza shudders at the thought of swallowing anything more than her own saliva.

"Come now, let's stick out our tongue like a good girl and swallow. There we go. All the pills at once. And here's some water to wash them down. Not too much. So you won't pee as much as last time."

Frenza's consciousness is perforated like a sieve. She doesn't know when she changed rooms, but she has noticed that a cute, colorful boy with tunnel piercings in his earlobes is often hovering nearby. In her mind, she calls him Akhenaten because he reminds her of a pharaoh. When she stares at those holes in his ears, she feels as if by staying close to him, she might somehow travel far from this place. But for what purpose is Akhenaten hiding his real name? Perhaps Adek, the name he uses in his daily life, is a hidden message directed only to her? A+D+E+K. He's sending it to her, Mathilde Spalt. A secret message about vitamins. He's telling her to take them. To stop resisting. If she takes the pills, she'll be fine. She trusts Adek, so she stops fighting with the staff. She starts cooperating. Especially with him. With Akhenaten from Mazovia with the body of a California surfer. Beautiful round buttocks packed into shorts, a massive chest spreading out above, reminiscent of the vast Atlas Mountains, and a classic American jaw, strongly outlined thanks to his habit of chewing gum. He's the object of desire of nearly all the patients in the ward.

The multicolored pills annihilate the calendar. Frenza completely loses track of time. Her thoughts constantly wander to the edge of reason, searching for some kind of impassable limit so that they can finally rest, adjourn, surrender. But no. Her mind refuses to lay down its arms; new images and ideas, each stranger than the last, keep swarming through her brain, causing traffic jams and fender benders on her neural pathways, which have now become high-speed freeways. After about a quarter of an hour, the medication starts to kick in. Reality becomes shallow and compressed, the only kind of reality in which she can safely immerse herself. Before the pills take effect, she must endlessly rearrange the puzzle pieces so that some sort of clear image can finally emerge from the shards of reality, from all the shattered glass scattered across her consciousness.

Frenza swallows the drugs, though they make her feel like she's about to puke. Her body aches as if she's just been beaten up.

Every single muscle and bone hurts. She doesn't know, doesn't understand, how ordinary vitamins can have such a bad effect on her. But she trusts the pharaoh. She has to trust someone. After all, she doesn't want to be sent back to the previous room. She remembers the hell that reigned there. The overhead light that was never turned off. Straps for restraining unruly souls attached to every bed. And the fly-specked windows. As if those goddamned creatures that thrive on human shit had become fixated on the exact room where she was lying. Strapped down because she was constantly fighting with everyone, she spent endless hours staring at the fractal patterns of fly excrement on the windowpanes. What else could she do? When, at her request, she was unbound so that she could move her hands or read, some unpredictable detail would inevitably plunge her into the dark abyss again.

The worst was when the nurses decided to weigh her so that the doctor in charge of her—the famous Dr. Charcot—could more accurately determine her medication dosage. When the nurse ordered her to take off her nightgown and clogs and stand on the scale, she once again saw before her Chapter Councilor Petrus Gerbauer, Bishop Johann Balthasar Liesch von Hornau, and the prosecutor from Neisse, Franz Zacher, along with the investigating prosecutor, Martin Lorenz, all questioning her. They sat at a high table, staring at her naked body as if weighing it with their eyes. At the order of the prosecutor from Neisse, a scale for weighing livestock was brought into the stately chamber of the town hall. She was told to stand on one side, while a Bible was placed on the other. A heavy one, bound in leather by Johannes Krucht, a Franciscan friar whose bookbinding skills were renowned throughout the Duchy of Neisse. It was the Bible on which Heinrich Babel, who was a witness to this scene, swore that if the Devil turned out to be dwelling in this woman accused of attempting to poison her husband and of causing a flood in the

Duchy of Neisse, he would drive him out of her even if she had to pay for it with her life.

"Twenty-six innocent souls drowned, through no fault of their own! Cows as well! An entire herd of them! But as for these women standing before us," Heinrich Babel declared to the crowd and the jury, pointing to Mathilde and the other women standing next to her in a tight row, "their lives were not claimed by the floodwaters, and thus their guilt is clear for all to see!"

The sun had been sinking in the west when, like every Friday, the women secretly made their way through the forest to the glade where the great oak stood and belladonna grew, in order to gather birch sap, just as Mathilde had taught them. And above all, it was the perfect time to listen to Mathilde speak about the Primeval Virgin, whom every woman carries within herself from birth to death, and even beyond. The Primeval Virgin is simultaneously Mother Earth, a cleft, a feeble child, and a woman in her prime, as radiant as the full moon. But She is also a toothless, hunchbacked old woman who wanders through the forest seeking things to mount and possess with Her body—not to experience pleasure but to preserve the Eternal Order. Now, standing in front of a jury and a mob of townspeople gathered at the town hall, Mathilde doesn't understand why she triggers such emotions when she hasn't harmed anyone or anything on Earth and has merely sparked new life in the world. She tries her best not to look into the eyes of the people gathered, all of whom seem incapable of understanding that there's nothing wrong in what she did. Nothing that would pose a threat to God in Heaven or humans on Earth. And she uses her hands to cover what everyone is staring at. The prosecutor from Neisse, Franz Zacher, orders her to stand on the scale to determine, in front of the crowd of people in the chamber who didn't hesitate to pay for the spectacle with fistfuls of ducats, what will be heavier—a woman suspected of witchcraft, or the Bible.

Damnation! Franz Zacher curses under his breath as the scale begins to tip to her side, but so quietly that no one can hear him. He wanted to take the day off from work today. After a night spent hunting, he's not feeling great. He's overcome by drowsiness, as if he has just drunk an entire keg of monastery beer. In order to speed up the weight test, he removes the Bible from the scale and orders his assistant to arrange some weights on it instead.

At first it seems that the result of the weighing—forty-nine kilos and ninety dekagrams—once again jeopardizes Zacher's afternoon, which he would rather spend with his family than inflicting torture. After hoping that the woman standing on the scale, who apparently was caught by the bishop himself, will turn out to weigh at least fifty kilograms, which will dispel, at least for a while, the suspicion of witchcraft, he begins to sweat. He feels like he's suffocating in his overly tight collar. A moment later, however, a glimmer of hope enters his mind, for behold—the clerk performing the test declares that the woman suspected of witchcraft weighs exactly fifty kilos!

Mathilde can finally breathe as deeply as she did the day she came into the world, when she took such a huge gulp of air that it caused her to cry out in pain. The prosecutor closes his eyes for a moment and exhales a sigh of relief along with her. In the depths of his soul, he's genuinely pleased that this pretty, innocent girl won't be beaten to death or burned in the furnace.

But then, just as she's about to step off the scale, the inquisitor approaches Bishop Johann Balthasar Liesch von Hornau. He leans over him and says something in his ear. The bishop then indicates to the others that he has something to tell them, and that the matter may yet take a different turn.

At the bishop's command, Franz Zacher slowly approaches the woman and unfastens the clasp holding her hair above the nape of her neck. And then something happens that can't be stopped or reversed. As the scale slowly begins to tilt, lifting her up slightly, Mathilde Spalt realizes what awaits her. The silver clasp, a wedding gift from the nasty old scarecrow—the only thing he ever gave her that she truly liked—seals her fate.

Connected

When Eliza Reszke and Joanna Draka, nurses at the psychiatric hospital in Tworki, see Anna Frenza convulsing on the hospital floor, yanking something invisible off her head, they're terrified and call security for help. By the time Euzebius Mruk and Andrew Plona, the hospital's security guards, reach the second floor of Ward X, Frenza has savagely bitten Joanna and nearly strangled Eliza as she leans over her in a desperate attempt to save her colleague. And it will take the security guards more than a quarter of an hour to subdue Frenza firmly enough that she can be injected with a quadruple dose of hydroxyzine to calm her terrified soul, at least for a few hours.

How could they have known that the weighing procedure would cause such a reaction in the new patient? "Post-traumatic stress," explains Dr. Charcot, the director of the hospital and head of the ward, to the nurses after they come to his office and complain about Frenza. He's been trying for several weeks to decipher the notes that the orderly, Adek, has passed along to him and has just come across a reference to Helene Spalt, the founder of the Earthen Ones—a female congregation that existed in the ecclesiastical duchy of Neisse in the late sixteenth and early seventeenth centuries and worshipped the Primeval Virgin, the daughter of Mother Earth. But nothing more.

"Connected"—this is what the hospital's staff calls such women. Except that in Frenza's case, something else is happening. The current that's been flowing through her ever since she was "rewired" has nothing to do, for instance, with the patients struggling with delusions, who plug themselves into whatever their superego suggests. For Frenza, this connection seems only to have led to suffering, not any sort of extraordinary power or exceptionalism.

The attempt to weigh Frenza caused her to collapse into a state of extreme anxiety. And unbearable pain. Her body has become little more than a carcass, every inch of which feels like it has undergone excruciating torture. Such intense pain has been inflicted upon it, and it has been brutalized so many times, it's now begging its soul to abandon it because every second that it continues to live is unbearable. At least until—as Dr. Charcot surmises—the optimal treatment can be determined, which is precisely why it's so important to determine her exact weight.

Cowering on the cold floor of the nurses' room, Frenza pisses herself from fear. She floods the floor with urine and then voraciously licks it up. The nurses decide to bathe her so she won't stink. But bathing Frenza causes the nurses even more trouble than weighing her. As bad luck would have it, the showerhead broke two days ago after having been incessantly used for masturbation, heavily rubbed against patients' clitorises that had been yearning to be caressed. This means that Frenza has to be plunged into the bathtub.

They struggle with her again, but—after checking to see if Dr. Charcot is sitting in his office, as he often is at this time of day—they call Adek for help. He always somehow manages to get through to Frenza. As soon as Adek appears, Frenza steps into the tub without protest. She's unaware of what's going on because she's been given her daily dose of risperidone. She drifts off into her own world. But the question arises whether that world is, indeed, her own.

A few minutes later, when the nurses try to submerge Frenza's head in the water to wash her hair, memories rush into her mind.

Surging after the flood, the river is flowing so fast now that even those who know how to swim must catch hold of willow branches hanging over the bank to keep their heads above the surface as they're submerged in the powerful current. Water fills their mouths as they gasp for air.

They can't see each other. They only know that the ones who can't swim, for whom water is a hostile element, have remained in the glade. They're stranded on the riverbank, facing certain death—along with the cows they've just milked so they can make some cheese before the Thursday market. When Mathilde sees men on horseback approaching, she recognizes one of them immediately, despite the considerable distance that still lies between them. She would recognize him even if she were awoken in the middle of the night. A year ago, when he came across her gathering herbs in the forest, which was strictly forbidden to all women in the duchy—as was simply being in the forest—she knew there would be trouble. Even though she hadn't given birth, milk had begun to flow forth into her breasts and soaked her gown, which, of course, did not escape the attention of Heinrich Babel, who believed he could sense the Devil's seed in her. What he didn't know was that a few hours earlier, before she'd entered the forest in search of herbs, one of her beloved heifers had given birth to a calf in the nasty old scarecrow's barn, and for some reason the milk hadn't started flowing into her udder, leaving the baby with nothing to drink and wailing in distress. So Mathilde had stood next to the heifer and, putting her nose right up against its nose, had begun to breathe with it, causing their breaths to become steady and aligned. Then her breasts had filled with milk, and she'd fed this milk to the newborn calf so that the heifer could rest after the difficult birth. Hence to the forest she'd gone to fetch some herbs so that the cow's udder would fill with milk, and it was at this moment that Babel had managed to hunt her down.

And when he'd dismounted from his horse, she'd approached him and gazed into his soul in such a strange way that all at once, without uttering a single word, he'd leapt back onto the saddle, frightened by what he'd glimpsed in her pupils. He'd ridden away, and the thud of his horse's hoofbeats had echoed through the woods for a long time.

She'd considered the encounter a victory for herself. However, what she'd seen in his eyes had terrified her to the depths of her being. To dispel the fear and gloom that had descended upon her, she'd made a fire larger than any she'd ever kindled before, with elderberry and alder branches. Her grandmother Helene Spalt had been right to defend the reputation of her daughter, Ursula, Mathilde's mother, to the very end of her life, while vociferously denying her alleged suicide. Ursula's death hadn't been a suicide. Everything was reflected in Babel's pupils. Even the color of the sky that day when he'd hanged her in order to drive the Earthen Ones out of the forest once and for all. Mathilde also saw her own death in his eyes, hence she tried to keep the women away from the forest and closer to the river—in a stretch of land that the Church seemed to have forgotten about. In any case, there was no certainty that the terrain along the river had ever belonged to the Church at all. There she hid everything that Helene had left behind and that Mathilde had been guarding vigilantly for the past few years, to ensure that it wouldn't fall into the wrong hands before she had a chance to sow the seeds of these teachings among women and propagate faith in the Primeval Virgin.

This time, however, at the sight of Babel and several other men approaching on horseback, followed by a whole army of the bishop's henchmen, she, along with some of the other women who weren't afraid of water, threw herself into the river's swift current in a desperate effort to escape the men and save their lives.

The New Deal

Despite triggering painful memories of witnessing her companions being chased into the river, the bath eventually has a sobering effect on Frenza.

Back in her room, she blinks her eyes to acclimatize to reality. Instinctively, she plugs her ears to shut out the horrible sound coming from the faucet, gnawing away at the silence. Her mind begins to register the image that slowly emerges in front of her: white walls, a window, and a windowsill, on which there are some fruit peelings, wilted flowers, pine cones, and moss. Sitting on a hospital bed straight across from her she sees a greasy old hag with curly, waist-length black hair. She looks as if someone poured tar on her head, smeared her with asphalt, and sprinkled her with ash from the wings of a burned raven. The hag smiles brazenly at her, reminding her of someone. But who?

Frenza's brain has become a dead fish floating near the shore of the Baltic Sea, poisoned by an oil spill. A spill that, according to the fucked-up environmentalists—oh yes, now she's finally starting to glue the shards of glass back together from the mirror that shattered—was caused by her own decision to drill there. Environmentalists, yes! Environmentalists. Isn't the fat old hag the high priestess of that mob? What's her name? Grażyna Kło . . . sińska? Kło . . . sowska? Frenza gives up because she can't follow the thread of her own thoughts. She can't remember names, faces, addresses, or events. It's as if the drugs have scrubbed her brain completely clean, and now instead of a neural network she has a stiff, bleached-white tablecloth stretching across the interior of her skull.

Next to Frenza, on a bed parallel to hers, there's a scrawny creature with hunched shoulders, clad in an oversized T-shirt with *PEPSI* written across it in huge letters, beneath which the outline of sagging breasts can be seen, hanging down so low that they must've been suckled for years on end, not only by throngs of human babies but also canine, feline, and rodent. It's not the breasts that are the most monstrous, however—it's the face, which is thickly covered with bristles.

A short, corpulent fellow with a bald spot on the top of his head surrounded by a halo of gray hair enters room number seven with a sprightly gait—Dr. Charcot, as his ID badge reveals.

"It's high time you ladies got to know each other," Dr. Charcot says. "Let me introduce you to our new patient, Anna Frenza. Ms. Frenza, on the bed across from you is ecoterrorist leader Grażyna Kłossowska, and on your left is our Miss Vanitas: the Bearded Woman."

The crow lady peers intently at Frenza and, raising the thick eyebrow stretching across her face, croaks out, "Didn't I tell you?! What a shame you didn't join us in the Białowieża Forest. It was worth it!"

"Ah, what a wonderful trio!" Dr. Charcot concludes, rubbing his hands together and leaving the room.

Frenza can't believe her bad luck. Stunned, she stares at a hand ending in claws curved like a parrot's, painted blood red. A hand extended to her in a gesture of greeting. When the owner of the hand, Grażyna Kłossowska, laughs, the folds of fat on her belly shake, slamming into each other like waves on a river of flowing melted butter. The bulky body, the clawlike, crimson-hued nails—there's something appealing about this character. Something atavistic and therefore electrifying.

"I don't know, Frenza, I really have no idea how you did it—how you got so much pleasure from sex with that tree! After you did that, we lay naked on some fallen trees too, trying to get off on them, but—a tree trunk is just a tree trunk, after all. Covered with burls and rough bark. We didn't get any pleasure from it at all. I swear to God, we tried. We had to fake orgasms for the cameras."

Frenza fixes her gaze on the high priestess of ecology because she doesn't understand what the old crow is saying to her, silence that Grażyna perceives as encouragement for further discussion.

"To make a political act out of it, of course," she continued. "So they'd finally get the fuck out of the Białowieża Forest. But when they eventually dragged us out of there, our pussies and thighs were bruised and battered, we were bleeding like crazy, and it hurt so bad it was like we'd been raped by a battalion of soldiers. Maybe you could teach us someday? That video of you has about ten million views." At this point, Grażyna takes a phone out of a pocket in her bathrobe to check if this number is still accurate or if Frenza's popularity is still growing. "There was so much passion in you! It was obvious to everyone who watched it! That's how we all need to show our love for the Earth."

Frenza turns her head. She doesn't want their eyes ever to meet again. All she wants is for the onslaught of painful memories to stop. Memories of everything that triggered the tragic series of events that brought her to Tworki. Unfortunately, Grażyna's directness restores her awareness of past events. Vigorously riding the trunk of a fallen tree in a park in Podkowa Leśna. "Oil company CEO fucks nature again, but in a whole new way!" proclaimed the caption under the video. Frenza lies down on the bed and closes her eyes, which creates an opportunity for even more memories to invade her hippocampus.

When she opens her eyes again, she sees a window. Without handles, of course. Outside the window, there are bars that have been painted white. The white bars make it seem like there aren't any bars there at all. They merge with the sky. Everything the color of milk. Milk and butter. The buttery belly of Grażyna Kłossowska across from her—a caricature of a woman, with a huge cunt sticking out from under her bathrobe, which is too short for her.

When the drugs stop working, Frenza starts noticing tiny holes in the screen created by a substantial amount of psychoactive and sedative substances that separates her from the world, through which shines a different world, one that she recognizes. A world that she lived in very recently—or at least pretended to live in, a charade that generally had worked out quite well for her. At least when she was diligent and regularly ingested lithium, keeping her madness on a leash.

But what did she ever get out of it? Orgasms from masturbation and a husband who'd been deceiving her for years. A weekly dinner with priests from the Club of Catholic Intelligentsia that she had to cook herself. Peacocks squawking in the churchyards. Parents who had loved her only when she was a child. A job in which—in order to keep it—she had to act even more masculine than the men around her. A prime minister who deprived women of their right to an abortion. A Polish Gilead, but without any of the well-tailored red dresses and cloaks. And a reality so absurd that most of her dreams seemed to make more sense.

After a month in room number seven, Frenza is starting to feel better. All thanks to Adek. She's been improving since she started listening to him. Secretly, without the other staff members knowing, Adek suggested to her that she stop taking drugs and take herbal psychoactive substances instead, which he often takes himself. He's noticed that after Frenza consumes some cannabis, it's easier for her to channel spirits—the women she refers to in her trances as *Geerdet*, the Earthen Ones, who have been speaking through her in German. After working with his professor to translate and modernize what he's heard Anna say, he's made some sense of it. It's some kind of message for the modern world. Maybe he will even write his master's thesis on it.

> The rubbing must happen simultaneously and collectively, ideally during gatherings of a solemn, sacred nature. It can be done with your fingers, metacarpus, or entire hand, as well as the upper or lower limbs of the other women present. But the most sublime form of this act is CLEFT-SPARKING, which leads to a complete union with Mother Earth. It's achieved by firmly and vigorously rubbing the cleft against plants—particularly angelica root, calamus rhizome, burdock root, comfrey root, valerian root, viper's grass root, and the tubers of sunchokes. It's also recommended that the cleft be caressed with alder branches, elderberry, ivy, and wild mushrooms, which, when properly used, can successfully replace a man's rodkin. At the same time, it must be made clear that rubbing a rodkin against a cleft has nothing to do with SPARKING LIFE INTO THE WORLD, as it only contributes to populating an already overpopulated planet. In order to save the world on an ethical and ecological level, women should copulate solely with living matter of botanical origin. In this way, they will offer their fertility to Mother Earth, thereby creating the resources needed to revive Her primordial fertility and abundance with their sexual energy, which has been sti-

fled and suppressed by destructive male sexual energy, which revolves around violence and pornography.

[. . .] Without CLEFT-SPARKING, which is the conditio sine qua non of RENEWING THE SPARK OF LIFE IN THE WORLD, the Earth's resources will eventually die, leading to the demise of all flora and fauna, including humans, whose way of life on this planet is contributing to its annihilation like no other creature ever has [. . .]

When, at night, Adek prints out a pamphlet that he's compiled and titled *The Earthen Ones*, he has no idea that he's about to inspire a new page in the history of the psychiatric hospital in Tworki. And that, thanks to his help, the patients will soon achieve what no one else in their country has ever been able to.

The Bearded Woman

After Adek makes copies of the pamphlet on the hospital's photocopier, it finds its way into the hands of the patients in the locked ward and causes quite a stir. Additionally, what Adek tells them about Frenza inspires reverence. They treat her like an enlightened being. A saint. They pray to her because, just like Adek, they perceive in her a new hope for the world. And she sees something in them—new Earthen Ones.

Grażyna Kłossowska wishes to be Frenza's greatest ally, after Adek. She knows that no one else can do as much good for the EcoDivas—the women's faction of the Green Party. It would be amazing PR! Frenza senses this self-interest, so she keeps Grażyna at a distance. For this reason, it's not her but the woman with the facial hair who becomes Frenza's right-hand woman in the group that she and Adek form.

Of all the patients in the ward, the Bearded Woman is the one who interests Frenza the most. She has something that Frenza has never had in her entire life—a means of provoking her environment, of interacting with it in her own unique way, enabling her to push boundaries. To test how far she can go.

Frenza keeps a close eye on both women—Grażyna and the

Bearded Woman. She watches as Grażyna inserts a toadstool she found in the park outside the hospital into her vagina, and after climaxing under a blanket with a grunt and a squeal, she hands it to the Bearded Woman, who's panting with excitement. She observes too how the patients, familiar with the pamphlet Adek created from her cannabis trances, bring moss in from outside as well and rub themselves against it shamelessly, ignoring her presence and even encouraging her to do the same. The other patients start imitating them. In the hospital's park as well, during walks. To the annoyance of the staff, who have to drag them out of the bushes.

And to top it all off, all those dreadful things on the windowsill! The sticky roots of the viper's grass. Potato and yam peels. Decaying strips of leeks. Cabbage leaves wrinkled like an old man's face and voraciously consumed by maggots and flies. Wilted flower petals from the hospital garden. Lilies smelling of death. Snapdragons, phlox, and tea roses. They've all been brought here because of her and for her—the new Earthen One, as Adek calls her. There are rumors in the ward that the Bearded Woman ended up here for public indecency and copulation with decomposing matter—things that the wealthy residents of another nearby garden town, Milanówek, discarded in compost heaps or the rubbish bins in front of their houses. And for orgies with vagrants.

Sixty years old, covered in bristles and dirt, the emaciated woman stuck in the town's flesh like a splinter. Her house—a dumping ground for all manner of filth, dust, and garbage—attracted vagabonds like a magnet. They were looking for trash, but unlike the Bearded Woman, they wanted it not for copulation but for consumption. They could sense something familiar in her, for these starved wanderers weren't just hungry for food but for human touch and warmth, which the Bearded Woman was very happy to give them. And so, after robbing the home of some notable local resident, these amateurs of lunar peregrination would end their nocturnal adventures at her house. And the Bearded Woman would share with them the most precious things she possessed: composted food and access to the Cleft of Existence. Both *per rectum* and *per vaginam*. She led them to a place without shadows, where time doesn't exist. Where rivers are inhabited by mermaids whose scales, shimmering in the sunlight, form a hologram of Eternity.

Despite what has been said about her in the ward, and what her appearance may suggest, the Bearded Woman has, in addition to the lewdness that was nothing more than a social game played with the world, a great deal of tenderness for everything that has been cast aside and branded as useless—for waste of all kinds. Not only waste from the world of flora and fauna but human waste as well. After all, it belongs to the same cosmos.

And so, when she copulated with the rotten roots of horseradish, carrots, or viper's grass, she felt exactly the same joy as when she copulated with vagrants and beggars—a social element that was unwanted in the garden cities. In the spring, summer, and early autumn, she would lounge with them on the grass, nibbling wild apples and gazing at the sky through shards of glass from broken bottles. She would whip them playfully with the stems of irises growing in her garden and ask them to do the same to her. To scratch her back or relieve their sexual urges on her. They would amuse themselves in this way for hours, in greater or lesser configurations. They put their bare feet together and rubbed them against each other, bringing relief to their filthy, itchy skin. And from their observations of the sky through shards of glass, and from this tenderness flowing from the friction of dirt against dirt, skin against skin, a desire began to grow—pulsating only very delicately at first. A desire to dissolve into the universe, to lose one's own contours, to erase individual existence and become unified as one. This desire was completely nonpornographic. It was the purest kind of desire possible, though utterly filthy at the same time.

She recalls beautiful moments from the past when she was bent in great concentration over a decaying bird that, as with all transient things, had aroused in her a desire that was mixed with the ardent wish to bring the creature back to life. Despite being aware that she's being watched by the nurse and by Frenza, the Bearded Woman begins to moan quietly and rock her hips back and forth, back and forth, transferring her energy to her invisible lovers. And they, after a while—in accordance with the law of energy conservation, propelled by the bold movements of the Bearded Woman's bony yet nimble hips—begin to unleash from their loins a type of desire that has nothing in common with love made quickly under a blanket and serving no purpose beyond the release of excessive aggression from oneself or a brief escape into illusory bliss from the painful, agonizing disease that is life. It is, instead, a transcendental movement uniting the pulse of Existence itself with the existence of human beings—not in an individual sense but rather a communal one. With her imaginary lovers, the Bearded Woman ceases to be merely a bearded woman, the hospital janitor ceases to be merely a janitor, and the doctor ceases to be merely a doctor, confined to a specific existence by means of a particular name and background. They're transformed into representatives of the entire human species, with its inherent beauty and decay—living beings who will one day disintegrate on the compost heap, just like the carcasses of cats and hedgehogs that have been run over in the road.

The Bearded Woman's orgasm, reached right before the eyes of a voyeuristic nurse who is both terrified and aroused in equal measure, shocks Frenza and is heard by the entire hospital. Her moans of delight fill every nook and cranny, penetrating where not even the cleaners' brooms could reach.

"Room number seven. Intuition as deep as a pussy," Dr. Charcot remarks under his breath as he lights a cigarette in his upstairs office and zips up his fly.

The Covenant

The registry of patients in the locked ward overseen by Dr. Charcot contains a list of only twelve names, though some of the patients have multiple personalities.

In addition to Frenza, the Bearded Woman, and Grażyna Kłossowska—the high priestess of environmental activism who straddles the gap between the EcoDivas and the Earthen Ones—the ward is swarming with patients with schizophrenia, bipolar disorder, paranoid personality disorder, cyclothymic personality disorder, and so on; thus between the twelve of them, sometimes there are as many as one hundred personalities! These are the women who form Frenza's gang. Their personalities proliferate and multiply, especially on days when the weather turns stormy—not to mention during the full moon, when they all lie down in an empty corridor flooded with silvery light and summon still more women to join them. No matter how ignited they are by their newfound faith and the principles of making love with all that is supple and soft, some of the women still yearn, deep down, for a cock. For a stiff rod. It's easy to single them out because, in their spare time, when the nurses aren't observing them closely and they dive into the bushes to cleft-spark with Frenza, they wait until she closes her eyes while sinking deeper into her trance—then they grab branches and jam them deep into their clefts, right up to their throats. Caustically referring to them as "rod-whores" in her mind, Frenza loses patience with them and relies on her right-hand woman, the Bearded Woman, to give them a sharp whack with a branch. The worst of them is Grażyna. No wonder she had to feign pleasure, back in her protest days, while making love to trees in the Białowieża Forest.

And so Dr. Charcot's ward, a four-hundred-square-meter space that was consecrated three years ago by a Catholic priest, is under siege. With acoustics enhanced by thick brick walls, it frequently resounds with moans of pleasure emanating from under the hospital-issued blankets. Even the density of the air has changed, thanks to the invisible web of emotions and unbridled madness (restrained only to some extent by psychotropics) that has enveloped the entire institution like ivy or woodbine, its tendrils creeping along and burrowing into the building's brick façade, which still holds memories of the nineteenth century, when psychiatric hospitals were turned into a panopticon or peep show for a few hours every day. And all this is happening because of the revival of the congregation, which Frenza, while smoking weed almost daily, is infiltrating and becoming better acquainted with.

Aniela Żarska, for example, from room number eight. She's a seamstress from Milanówek who knocked out her common-law husband with a huge cast-iron frying pan and then sewed his mouth shut after he'd left rehab for the umpteenth time and then made his way to the nearest liquor store before even going home. Aniela had four women right at her heels, ready to help her: her daughter, her mother, her grandmother, and her great-grandmother—all man-haters, every one of them. They're not alone in this. It's a common case of women's loyalty to others who have been hurt by men. Although they don't live under the same roof, and two of them are no longer alive (her great-grandmother and grandmother), the women are nonetheless attached to her in the immaterial, noncorporeal sphere, feeding on her life and gaining nourishment from each of her acts of violence against men. And although it seems that they're merely passengers in the ship that Aniela is sailing across this troubled ocean, if she dozes off for a while or goes to the bathroom, they grab the helm. They fight over it, clawing at each other's throats, even though they have the same goal—to stay on course in their hatred of members of the male species.

And then there's Aneta from room number nine. She's a film producer who worked with some of Poland's best directors. She made challenging cinema. Everyone in showbiz adored her. A statuesque blonde with such an excellent sense of humor that the greatest court jesters of the past would have been no match for her. And fate smiled upon her private life too. A rich husband who treated her well, two wonderful children, and a beautiful apartment—with a huge mortgage, but at least they had some valuable artwork in it. Things were going along nicely in their family life until, in the year 2020, the idyll was interrupted by the pandemic. Everyone knew that the coronavirus had to come and devour the oldest section of humanity, which Western societies didn't revere as guardians of the past and its secrets but rather as leeches sucking social security dry. But for Aneta, the quarantine imposed by the government meant that she had no way to produce films.

After two weeks of sitting at home with her kids while her husband worked all day, then drove to the shop to buy cat litter, dog food, and grain seeds to sow on the large terrace of their flat in Warsaw's Powiśle district (pampas grass was already passé by then, as was Morrow's sedge and other grasses of exotic provenance), Aneta nearly went nuts. The hitherto cute high-pitched voices of her children had transformed into poisonous, brain-crushing messages sent by an enemy from an alien civilization.

"My three-year-old son's completely fucked up," she lamented to a friend the day before the incident that landed her in the psychiatric hospital. "He keeps jumping around. I tell him for the hundredth time: 'Stop that goddamn jumping! You don't know how to jump and you keep falling on the ground, and the ground is dangerous now, you can catch the virus from it.' Nothing! It's like talking to a brick wall. And all the time I just keep hearing *Mommy Mommy Mommy*, from one room *Mommy*, from the other room *Mommy*, from the bathroom *Mommy*, always just fucking *Mommy* endlessly in that high-pitched voice. I'm going to forbid him from shouting *Mommy Mommy Mommy* ever again, I just can't stand it anymore!!!"

The next day, her son stopped saying "Mommy." He fell completely silent for a long time. As Aneta's neighbor Karolina Burska testified before the court: "The last time my husband and I heard the word 'Mommy' was around eleven o'clock, after which there was silence." Concerned by the sudden absence of Aneta's screaming, which they'd heard relentlessly for the full two weeks of quarantine, they decided to contact Aneta's husband to tell him they thought something bad might have happened.

Her husband, Andrzej, worked as a doctor in an infectious disease hospital and was unable to leave work for many hours as he fought to save the lives of his patients. He didn't get home until late that evening, as he testified during the interrogation—around nine or ten o'clock. He found Aneta asleep in an armchair with an empty wine bottle in her hand and a smoldering cigarette. The television was oozing facts like poison about the latest victims of the pandemic. It was only when he looked around the flat and saw his children's toys scattered everywhere that he remembered the phone call made that morning by the neighbors who were concerned about the funereal silence.

He managed to revive his wife, who'd drunk herself into a stupor. As he later testified to the court, Aneta tried for at least half an hour to remember what she'd done with their two young sons. Unfortunately, to no avail. They struggled with each other and he pushed her so hard that she fell onto the sofa. It was then that they both heard something that sounded like the whimper of a newborn baby and Aneta had an epiphany. She triumphantly lifted one of the cushions on the sofa, and a sight appeared before their eyes that Andrzej would never forget. "The children were bound with skipping rope, numb with terror. Their little mouths were gagged with kitchen gloves," was how he described it to the court. "But fucking silent at last," quipped Aneta in her mind.

Her parental rights were swiftly terminated after the incident.

When asked by the journalists thronging outside the courtroom for her views on the verdict, Aneta replied, "Freedom prevails! At last!" The expensive lawyer who had represented Aneta succeeded in having her declared "not criminally responsible" due to insanity, thus guaranteeing her a one-year stay in a psychiatric facility rather than imprisonment. Aneta did not request permission to see her children.

However, Aneta didn't feel free at all, as demons began to torment her in the form of children's voices—not two this time, but thousands. A powerful chorus of them resounded in her head, repeating that one accursed word. A word that triggered her gag reflex. A word that sliced her brain in half. A word that seeped into her like arsenic, condemning her to die a slow, agonizing death every day. Thousands of little voices screaming "Mommy"— crashing against the white walls of the hospital cell.

Thus, she wasn't alone at the psychiatric hospital but in the company of a thousand little brats who were firing those two syllables at her like salvos from the *Aurora* battle cruiser. It was the worst word in the world—a word that had served as the foundation (because of the fucking patriarchy, Aneta assumed) for the edifice of Western civilization, a civilization of death. The death of mothers tormented by their children.

Aneta shares room number nine with Danuta Klawa, known as the Pigeon Lady. She got this nickname because in her imaginary world, she's accompanied constantly by pigeons flying in circles around her—pigeons from the coop that her deceased husband kept, her husband on whom she'd exacted revenge by digging up his coffin and cutting off his dick. She'd done this because, during his funeral, an attractive woman had been standing opposite her, passionately weeping. When Danuta approached the woman to ask how she'd known her husband, the woman replied that she'd been his lover for over thirty years.

This was something Danuta couldn't forgive him for. The next day she went back to the funeral parlor that had taken care of the burial at her request and with her money. Complaining about the grave and insisting that the soil on it was uneven, she asked the undertaker for the gravedigger's phone number. She discussed further proceedings directly with him. The libretto was unusual but simple. For the sum of 1,500 złoty, the gravedigger unearthed the coffin, lifted the lid, and then cut off the lecherous rogue's member, replacing it with a dead pigeon from the man's own coop. He sent a photo to the Pigeon Lady documenting the accomplished task, after which he got completely pissed, drinking himself into a deeper oblivion than ever before in his life, for he was unable to shake the feeling that by committing such a grotesque assault on a dead man, he had lost the privilege of calling himself a human being. From that day onward, he spat at his own reflection in a store window or mirror and was unable to look himself in the eye. However, it wasn't him, the contracted gravedigger, who spiraled into madness, but her—the vengeful contractor of the grotesque deed, the penis snatcher, who soon after the incident began to hear the cooing of pigeons everywhere, pursuing her, and the brazen flapping of their wings.

In the same room, there's a woman named Milena, whose perception of reality completely changed after a vacation in Tenerife with her lover from Warsaw, a second-rate theater director. Her lover had bought some sort of drug from the locals. After taking it, Milena became convinced that her entire life up until that point had been a mistake. She decided that she wasn't really a public relations executive in a major corporation but—all along, since birth—a shaman and healer.

The same is true for Natalia Połabska from room number one—a math teacher who, whenever she puts on a white terry cloth robe, immediately heals the entire ward miraculously, with such subtle movements that almost none of the staff notices. She simply slides her hands over a person's shoulders, and voilà, they're healed. The person instantly—in Połabska's eyes, of course (and, interestingly, in the eyes of the other patients as well)—recovers and becomes capable, according to the teacher, of living independently. She and Milena are rivals and hate each other. They keep a tally of how many patients they've healed, jotting down their scores on pieces of paper.

There's an astronomer too—Xymena Zdun, who stands at the window every night holding the cardboard tube of an empty toilet paper roll up to her eye as if it were a telescope, staring at the star-speckled sky. While doing so, she's convinced that she can't let the sky out of her sight even for a moment, or else it will fall. She must, therefore, use all her willpower to hold the sky up, to prevent it from crashing down and shattering the world. She does so with such intense concentration that she often utterly exhausts herself. No wonder. To keep heaven and earth in their places—what a responsibility! On one occasion, wanting to relieve Xymena at least for a while from this dreadful responsibility so that the patient could get a few hours of rest, Dr. Charcot ordered some members of the staff to take turns "keeping an eye on the sky," to make sure that it didn't fall on her head or anyone else's while she was asleep.

And so, these are the women who have become Anna Frenza's army of Earthen Ones. There's also one man in the group, who enjoys making love to the Earth as well, especially when he's high—a man to whom Frenza owes more than anyone else. And trusts more than anyone. Adek.

Frenza doesn't understand why the hospital's patients are all women. From the beginning, she senses that something is wrong with the place. When she first arrived at the hospital, she tried to pinpoint the precise source of the uneasy itch of anxiety that had begun tormenting her, drilling into her brain, and after a week she realized that the unease she feels stems from this: the total lack of men among the patients.

When she looks out the barred windows of her room, the common room, or the cafeteria, all of which have a view of either the hospital's park in the front or the courtyard in the back, she never notices any male figures dressed in hospital-issued garments. It's as if there were a binary division: men are granted the status of employees in the hospital, while women are the deranged patients. Except for orderlies and nurses, although the latter are also slowly being replaced by men. Could it be that at some point in the past (which she must have missed) insanity was assigned only to one gender? When she poses this question to Dr. Charcot and the hospital staff, she's met with an indulgent smile and no answer. Sometimes the doctor seems to mumble something like, "That's the way it is these days. Just the way it is." But she's not sure. One patient, who claims to be a lawyer, starts citing a legal clause; she recites it in the hallway every night until she's finally injected with a tranquilizer—"something to help her sleep," as the nurses call it. Her acts of madness have a fixed pattern that repeats every night around three o'clock. First, she lets out a bloodcurdling scream in her sleep—most likely during a recurring dream. The scream is so startling that it jolts all the other patients out of their sleep, some of whom begin to tremble with fear, while others laugh, and others scream along with the lawyer, until it all turns into an extraordinary polyphonic fugue— except that it's based on dissonance instead of harmony, thus bringing restlessness and agitation instead of tranquility to all the poor souls locked up in the hospital. And it soon escalates to such an extreme pitch that the nurses begin to swarm throughout the rooms and corridors like bees in a hive, distributing stupefying pills as generously as Santa Claus gives presents at Christmas. Before the agitator can be caught and restrained, she usually manages to recite the content that sits like a lead weight in her heart: "Men are bloodsucking fleas: Article Thirty-Three!" and "Our bodies belong to us, not you! Article One-Fifty-Two!" All of it is accompanied by a spectacular display of expletives and vulgarity: "Motherfuckers! You're unbelievable! May your dicks and balls shrivel up and die!"

Of course, her catchphrases are picked up in a heartbeat by her awakened and highly stimulated comrades in misery, and together they create the illusion of a powerful protest outside parliament, or some such thing. Sometimes the lawyer, seething with anger, tears open the white hospital gown she's wearing, exposing her ample breasts, and then, like Lady Liberty leading the people to the barricades, she leads all the other patients straight to the office of Dr. Charcot, who often spends the night at the hospital. He and his staff take refuge in his office, managing to shut the door in the nick of time, sliding into place all six of the bolt locks. In such situations, Charcot never tries to pacify the women, for he knows he'd never succeed at subduing this wild fury even with the stun guns his predecessor added to the hospital's equipment. So he prefers to wait out the disturbance until morning, hoping that the lunatics will eventually collapse from exhaustion and surrender the Bastille by midday, as they've done so many times before. In the meantime, he and his staff will enjoy some refreshments delivered from the Ministry of the Interior (not the Ministry of Health, by any means), sent in gratitude to them for "solving the woman problem"—exquisite molecular cocktails in the form of little balls, just a tad larger than sturgeon caviar, flavored with the purest vodka and a dash of Lugol's iodine to compensate for the fact that iodine is nearly absent from the atmosphere, due to air pollution.

The little balls are supposed to be distributed to the staff only on days when the hospital is informed by e-mail that there are dangerously high levels of CO_2 in the air, but Dr. Charcot dares to assume that the Ministry of the Interior must have more of the goods on hand, ready for an emergency, and will deliver an additional supply to them if necessary. There's also always the possibility of resorting, in such an emergency, to the modest but still intact stock assigned to the patients, which hasn't yet been issued to them despite the alarms. Dr. Charcot has thought this through carefully. He's fond of his patients, in a certain way—the way one likes monkeys in a circus. He has a pleasant life in the village of Komorów, just outside of Warsaw, in a nicely furnished villa that was seized from a certain family involved in environmental activities. And running the famous psychiatric hospital in Tworki, which now has only female patients (some of them quite attractive), gives him satisfaction and fills him with immense pride, for what an interesting job it is! From both a professional point of view and a strictly male one. It's incredible what he's witnessed here. Many a man would dream of having the opportunity to observe the female patients, especially during manic episodes when their libidos are as high as the ceiling. As Dr. Charcot has remarked at the all-male banquets in the Ministry of Health: "This is the new porn."

Frenza's questions about the lack of men among the patients are ignored by the entire staff. They pretend not to hear her when she brings it up. At night, Frenza sneaks into the hospital archives, after Adek steals the key for her. She studies the medical records of female patients and discovers that they read like a mantra: lewdness, excessive sexual urges, verbal aggression against police officers, physical violence against men, excessive irritability (especially in response to stimuli of a political nature), unhealthy arousal, hypomania, obsessive-compulsive disorder concerning nutrition and ecology, love of rivers, sexual harassment of men, nymphomania, hysteria, and dendrophilia.

It's precisely these patients that Frenza rallies together into a powerful army. She knows what must be done. The necessity of sparking a revival of the Earthen Ones has been dawning on her for quite a while now.

Her newfound clarity came during a therapy session with Dr. Charcot. It was then that she remembered the dream. The missing piece of her puzzle. She knew that some of the Earthen Ones, led by Mathilde Spalt, had managed to escape by letting themselves be carried away by the river's strong current. She also knew that they'd returned to the place where the bloody massacre had occurred. Essentially, the dream was all about her—Mathilde. An Earthen One. *Geerdet.* A person in whom dwelled an ancient deity—the Primeval Virgin. She helped the other Earthen Ones understand that the Primeval Virgin dwells in each of them. In the enraged ones. The rebellious ones. The ones scorned by the system governed by God the Prime Minister and God the Father.

Mathilde was tortured and burned in a furnace built in the market square in Neisse, the first in Silesia designed for this purpose. A similar one had been constructed in the city of Bamberg, and the heat it generated as women were burned inside it was piped from the chimney and into the nearby tenement houses.

It was with the certainty of this vision that Frenza found a new confidence in her mission. And a new sense of urgency. She knows she doesn't have much time to achieve what the two Spalt women summoned her to do.

A Session with Dr. Charcot

You demanded sex from your husband in a straightforward manner, and by doing so you castrated him. Men *en général* don't like to be put in situations like that. We're the ones who demand sex from women, according to the laws of nature. Otherwise, everything—please forgive the lapidary expression—gets totally fucked up. It's no longer clear who's the guy and who's the gal—it's precisely this conflict that's caused homosexuality, by the way. Men have been subjected to an onslaught of femininity."

While pronouncing this hypothesis, Dr. Charcot blinks so quickly that Frenza, who is staring at him, almost becomes hypnotized.

"Your task," Dr. Charcot continues, "when you wanted sex, was always to resist and deny it. It's only when you exhibited that famous female unavailability that you'd be attractive to your partner. No one wants to have sex with someone who's always in the mood for it. A man must conquer. For each of us, deep down, is a Viking, madam, a barbarian who only pretends to be civilized. We men fuck, impregnate, burn, ravage, and then sail on, into deeper waters."

Frenza clenches her teeth. She sticks to the plan, but she can already feel a flame of anger tickling her feet. She's unable to sit still. Dr. Charcot offers her some candy. To sweeten her mood. He serves her tea brewed in a teapot sitting on his desk. He offers shortbread cookies sprinkled with sugar crystals. Nothing sophisticated, and yet it builds a bridge between them, making Frenza feel that perhaps it would be safer to pretend to agree with him. For the sake of the cause, so as not to screw up the plan she's been intricately weaving at night. So she tries to subdue the rage and demonstrate her faith in progress concerning the existence and functioning of humans, the condition of Western civilization based on the power of reason and the power sanctioned by that reason. Reason, which is constantly threatened by women, their menstrual cycles, their hormonal changes, and their manipulations—in short, their total unpredictability, a fucked-up shitshow that's been passed on from generation to generation.

One week later, on September 30, 2026, during her next session, Frenza deliberately refers to her condition as exactly that—a "fucked-up shitshow." She feels it perfectly. She picks up crucial themes, giving vent to her innate dislike of women. Dr. Charcot, listening intently to the patient's radical discourse, is charmed. He likes her more and more by the minute, and while he gazes at her rational head nodding politely at him, his smile grows increasingly radiant. Never before has he met a patient in this hospital with such a levelheaded view of reality. A patient who was almost like a daughter spawned from his own mind. So different from the flock of fucked-up crows he handles in the ward. As soon as they stop taking their pills, they'll be lost to society again! And dangerous. Especially for men.

"I'll tell you, though it's perhaps not entirely professional, that what happened to you is just a slipup. At least that's how I see it. You're very lucky, because you're guided by reason in your life, unlike all those"—here he lowers his voice to a conspiratorial tone—"madwomen. You and I—we think in similar ways. It's why we've come so far. We're both in leadership positions. But while you've fallen from your throne, I'm still sitting on mine. Please don't worry, don't stray from the path you're on, don't unbuckle your roller skates as you roll along, and in two or three weeks we'll try to get you discharged. Provided, of course, that your behavior is irreproachable, you take your prescribed medication, and you have a monthly checkup here, in this office."

Frenza bites her tongue because she wants to ask something, but reason tells her to stay silent. The doctor reads her thoughts as if he's just taken an X-ray of her mind, and he answers her unasked question: "No. They'll never leave. They're all profoundly messed up. And no amount of psychotropics, brainwashing, or lobotomy will change that. They all have the same defect, which manifests itself in different ways. They think with their cunts instead of their brains. And it's the cunt that's the very foundation of insanity. When someone chooses *encuntment* instead of enlightenment, these are the consequences. Out in the world, away from the institution, they stay in control for a week, two at the most. Then they immediately begin to exhibit antisocial behavior driven by their unbridled libido and chaos. A libido that's resistant to medication. We've tried many times. Lithium, bromine, quetiapine. No chemicals have any effect on their rapacious cunts. Therefore, we catch them, like dogcatchers round up bitches. Decent citizens who, even in our present times, continue to defend the values that are the foundation of our Christian civilization, call us and report a problem, and we show up and solve it. We catch them and isolate them from the healthy fabric of society, so that this gangrene doesn't spread any further."

Dr. Charcot continues with his telepathic dialogue, which only seems like a monologue on the surface. He's sensing the questions that he knows are arising in Frenza's mind, even without her expressing them aloud, and answering them.

"What did these women do? How did they end up here? It would take a long time to explain. Some of them have always been alone—who would want anything to do with them? Well, maybe to get laid. Some of them are so hot we get hard just looking at them, though we're ashamed to admit it. Others had husbands but left them after becoming infected by the heresy preached by the rest. You understand, madam, they abandoned everything they had—everything they'd acquired not through the work of their own hands but through their husbands'—and ran off into the forest like wild creatures, fleeing civilization. And culture! Exactly like you, in that video! That's why we had to catch you too! It was necessary to cut off the hydra's head preemptively! The City Guard thought you posed the same kind of threat—that you were one of those goddamn bacchantes. And this was something we simply couldn't allow. Men's frustration was at an all-time high. The destabilization of the family unit had led to the destabilization of the entire town and even the surrounding areas—all the magnificent garden cities, which had been known up until then for how well run they were and for the conservative Christian values of their residents. Because of these women, we began to deteriorate—first the Catholic Church, and then all of society. We had no choice but to catch them and shun them and banish them to the periphery."

After hearing all that, Frenza spends an entire week in deep contemplation. How can she fire up her army so that they'll believe in her plan and want to escape with her? How can she bring about a revolution that will heal the world?

The Rebels

Frenza knows that she must inspire the Earthen Ones to rebel. First she has to instill in them the necessary mindset so that she'll be able to convince them more easily of the plan that she's plotted with Adek.

Influenced by the sermons about the Earth that Adek scribbled down while listening intently to Frenza's trancelike exaltations, the women stop washing themselves. They begin to perceive a state of filthiness as consistent with their radically ecological way of life. The same is true of their clothes, which need to be thoroughly worn, soiled, and drenched with sweat. They explain over and over again to the nurses trying to take away their dirty clothes that union with their natural scent is a vital condition for them. And that the evaporation, respiration, pulsation, and production of secretions by their bodies is genuine proof of their existence. They begin to regard deodorant as a mortal enemy, even if it's made entirely of natural ingredients. Since they're under no obligation to wear hospital gowns in the ward, they all dress similarly—they wear loose T-shirts over their busts, which aren't restrained by bras, and wide ankle-length skirts with exotic patterns on them, under which they unashamedly let thick fur grow. What also makes the Earthen Ones stand out from the other women in the ward is that they walk around barefoot in order to be closer to Mother Earth. Moreover, all of them—the High Priestess of Ecology, the Bearded Woman, and the other nine Earthen Ones in the ward—wear their long hair loose and smell of sweat mixed with sandalwood and patchouli. They make a very strong olfactory impression wherever they go.

They refuse to have their clothing washed by the staff. They do it themselves, washing the garments only in the traditional way—in the Utrata River, not far from the hospital cemetery, where four generations of women like them, those who deviated from the generally accepted norm, are buried. They wash their clothes by rubbing them on pebbles, not using any soap for this ceremony, so as not to poison the river with suds. While doing this, they sing folk songs in strong, clear voices, lulling themselves into a trance that spreads throughout the hospital. Crouching over the stream, they sway from side to side, sometimes even falling over, and Dr. Charcot, who was opposed to the practice at first, eventually relaxes into their singing too, and comes to recognize it as an essential part of the institution's atmosphere.

The Earthen Ones are known for other quirks as well. They don't eat anything that didn't originate from the Earth. Their main sustenance is root vegetables—potatoes, Jerusalem artichokes, parsley, carrots, radishes, and turnips, which they cultivate, with the hospital's permission, in a greenhouse specially set up for this purpose. They also grow hallucinogenic herbs in the greenhouse, in secret from the rest of the hospital. Between rows of tomato plants, covered by their leaves, grow belladonna and henbane, known in folk medicine for their psychoactive properties.

They've brazenly planted jimsonweed—the poison of all

poisons—at the entrance to the greenhouse. The hospital's staff has clearly never heard of it, especially under its common name, "devil's trumpet." Additionally, the women drink only spring water and sap, which they extract from the birch trees in the hospital park with traditional methods. Administering the women's daily medication is extremely difficult for the nurses, and so, every morning at dawn, the nurse on duty collects a small amount of sap from the birch trees that have been punctured by the Earthen Ones and mixes their medicine into it.

Collecting sap isn't the only activity that causes the hospital's staff to look askance at the women. In addition to their aversion to traditional methods of maintaining hygiene, they have other peculiar habits—such as brushing their teeth with soil or compulsively peeling potatoes as a way of dealing with stress, which they call "instant grounding." This ultimately results in the entire ward needing to be swept multiple times per day, as potato peelings are scattered everywhere, not to mention the other plants and weeds that are constantly being brought inside—bulrushes from the banks of the Utrata River, calamus rhizomes, moss, ferns, and comfrey, as well as roots and bulbs cultivated in the greenhouse and used for self-pleasure in secret from the staff.

They peel the potatoes in silence. The knife for peeling the vegetables and the bowl for catching the peels are their thread and spinning wheel, with which they spin the destiny of the entire world. Each morning, after eating breakfast in the hospital cafeteria, half the patients go downstairs to the common room to watch mushy soap operas, while the Earthen Ones congregate in the kitchen to start playing with knives under the watchful eye of the nurse on duty.

The way the Earthen Ones enthusiastically wield the kitchen knives frightens all the hospital staff, but they earned the right to do so because it ultimately resulted in the entire facility having an abundance of food. Every week the hospital orders one hundred kilos of potatoes from Polish farmers, which the Earthen Ones transform into dumplings lavishly drenched in melted butter.

Ready for Action!

That day, when I went to the forest, I wanted to become a tree myself. I wanted to rid myself of my deadwood—everything that had withered inside me. I wanted to shed all that was lifeless, everything that held me back, everything my spirit got snagged on, everything that was dragging me down."

After six months in the locked ward of the psychiatric hospital in Tworki, Anna Frenza has finally recovered! She's beginning to live her life—which is, in her case, of no minor significance, since for the past few months she has been someone else. Not simply impersonating someone else but truly embodying someone else. She was a firsthand witness to the dramatic events that took place in September 1628 in the ecclesiastical duchy of Neisse, when Suffragan Bishop Johann Balthasar Liesch von Hornau, who administered the duchy on behalf of Prince-Bishop Karl Ferdinand Vasa, incinerated women in a specially designed furnace—the first in Silesia built with the purpose of destroying living beings "created in the likeness of God." The victims were Mathilde Spalt, a professed believer in the Primeval Virgin, and all the remaining Earthen Ones who had miraculously survived an earlier massacre. The crime for which the women were tortured for many weeks and then burned to death, according to the leaders of the Catholic Church, was having instilled in other women the desire to abandon their homes and live in the forest, in defiance of traditional bourgeois values.

And although the justification for the suffragan bishop's verdict condemning the women to death was worded differently (he presented it as "Devil worship"), it seemed to many of the people assembled in the municipal court of Neisse that these women who had been nourishing the entire duchy with exquisite cheese and healing its residents with herbal remedies did not deserve such a fate.

The life path of Anna Frenza, who was accused of murdering her husband and acquitted by the supreme court after she was diagnosed with bipolar affective disorder, has led her through an agonizing ordeal. Accused and acquitted but confined to a psychiatric hospital indefinitely, only now does she seem to be returning to her original identity—the one that at least half the population of Poland would recognize from having seen her so many times on television and on the front pages of newspapers in the days immediately after the scandal.

Frenza has accomplished the same as the women who have become connected to her—the Earthen Ones, led by the congregation's founder, Helene Spalt, and her granddaughter, Mathilde. She's been leading women into the bushes surrounding the psychiatric hospital and teaching them how to enter a trance in which the Primeval Virgin will be revealed to them— a deity whose doctrines Frenza learned from Mathilde Spalt, with whom she spent over six months on the other side of the border between sanity and madness, learning from her all the wisdom that had been left behind by her grandmother Helene Spalt.

"Stumps, deadwood, withered branches—these aren't only in the forest, they're also inside me. I've started with the trees, but I wish, through this act, to come face-to-face with myself." At this point, Frenza pauses in her discourse and glances around, making a sweeping gesture with her hand to draw attention to her surroundings.

All pairs of eyes follow every move she makes in pious concentration. As if the pope himself were speaking to them. Except that they're not in the Vatican but in the Mazovia region of Poland. In the most heavily wooded section of the park surrounding the psychiatric hospital in Tworki. And instead of a papal bull, Frenza is wielding a powerful stick, which she'll use once again to instruct her companions on how to bang deadwood—an activity that will not only reduce their stress but will also, according to Frenza, allow them to establish contact with the Deity.

"With the Primeval Virgin," she says with deep solemnity, lowering her voice.

Hidden in the bushes during the break between music therapy and bullshit art sessions where they're forced to paint goddamn fake stained-glass windows on goddamn aquariums—which some goddamn pet store chain plans to buy in order to support Polish psychiatric institutions—they learn from Frenza how to dexterously wield sticks. They're just waiting for her signal to start banging.

In a wild frenzy, as if suddenly let off a chain, they run with the long wooden rods that they made for themselves from tree branches during their compulsory daily walks, disappearing briefly into the most secluded areas of the hospital grounds—into groves and thickets swarming with ticks and other vermin that are never visited by anyone. Adek helped the women whittle the sticks and branches they found and polish them with sandpaper, for he was fired up by their mysterious rituals. Cleft-sparking against the moss. Aligning their breath. Separating their souls from their bodies. Clenching and penetrating.

This young gay man, as gorgeous as Adonis, watches and learns from them, and later he'll present what he has seen at gatherings of the Polish branch of Wicca. Each of his fingers is bedecked with silver and gold rings that even Harry Potter would envy. Adek is the only male Earthen One, and the only Earthen One among the psychiatric hospital's staff. Unofficially, of course.

Frenza whistles for her pack.

"Turn around!" she shouts like the coach of the national soccer team. "We need to scour this forest until we find trees burdened with deadwood—just like in that other forest..."

"I'm ready!" Adek says, stepping forward with a long wooden rod in his hand.

"Like in what forest?" asks Aneta, the most aggressive of the ward's patients.

"The deadwood forest of the Earthen Ones," Pharaoh Adek replies impatiently.

"We carried long sticks for minor patches of deadwood," Frenza continues, "and rumblerods for the massive ones! Wham, bam, whack, and slam! If you haven't got a rumblerod, you can fuck right off!"

Those gathered around Frenza can't contain their excitement. Her speech is interrupted by cheers and thunderous applause. It's been a long time since anyone has fired up the patients as much as she has. They grab their rods again, and as soon as Frenza gives the signal with a nod of her head, they start running, tripping over each other and getting trampled. They rush at breakneck speed, and soon this motion causes them to lose connection with themselves and stop thinking, becoming nothing more than the swishing sound of the grass. Their breath becomes so rapid and shallow that they nearly start hyperventilating—a state in which consciousness begins to change, becoming diaphanous for any being who wishes to penetrate it. In psychiatry, this condition is usually classified as madness.

And when they start banging the trees beyond the Utrata River—a river that marks a clear boundary between normalcy and aberration—they're no longer merely the women whose names are recorded in the patient admission book and the hospital records. With every ounce of strength in their bodies, they hit the withered branches on these hybrid beings—the present-day trees in front of their eyes and the ones to which Frenza has led them. To which she has connected them. And when they emerge from the trance in which they bang the deadwood—as Frenza, during her therapy sessions with Dr. Charcot, calls the mystical practice that initiates the state of becoming possessed and penetrated by the original Earthen Ones—they fall to the ground, nearly passing out from exhaustion, having transcended themselves many times. And then they crouch over the moss on the ground and begin to rub their clefts against it, until they reach the wildest, most powerful orgasms of their lives, orgasms unlike any they've ever experienced with man or woman, with bunny- or penguin-shaped vibrator, and then—only then—are they truly happy. It's as if by abandoning their bodies and ridding themselves of the identities that hindered and constrained their true nature, by hungrily sucking up the moisture of subterranean currents with their lower lips, they've allowed themselves to recall their primordial state, the time when they were born of their mother—not only their biological one but also Mother Earth.

The ecstasy they experience while wallowing on the mossy forest floor like pigs in mud puddles is so intense that they dread returning to their former selves—the ones who cooked meals, washed dishes, scrubbed and ironed clothes, gave birth, and put on a brave face while dealing with all the crap of everyday life that was as boring as a slice of gouda or mortadella on white bread smeared with butter.

"Who the fuck needs all that?!" shouts Aniela Żarska during her mandatory weekly session with a psychiatrist who has become concerned about the growing tendency among the patients to embark on these voyages to the antipodes of lunacy.

"'Who needs that?' What do you mean?! After all, you wanted to leave this hospital as soon as possible and return home to your husband and daughter," the doctor reminds Aniela, who claimed before her treatment, when she was first committed to the psychiatric hospital in a state of delirium, that she had come from outer space.

"No, thank you," she says. "I'm quite happy here now."

Operation Holy Mountain

They escape from Tworki under the cover of night. There are as many women in the group as there were next to Mathilde as she floated down the river. Adek has checked the train schedule many times. They won't reach their destination until morning. They're carrying nothing with them but their long wooden rods, which they place politely on the luggage racks in their train compartment on the way to Warsaw.

They change trains in Warsaw, boarding one bound for the holy mountain in the south of Poland. They occupy two adjacent compartments, and after they settle into their seats, they break into song, belting out the medieval Catholic hymn "Bogurodzica" in a thunderous voice, then falling silent for the rest of the journey.

Finding seats next to each other wasn't difficult. Barefoot and carrying their long sticks, dressed in shabby, foul-smelling clothes, they created quite a peculiar impression and didn't exactly entice other passengers on the train to share their compartments.

In complete silence, which Frenza believes is the necessary state of concentration for carrying out their plan, they arrive in the town of Częstochowa. They get off the train and instantly blend into the crowd of pilgrims headed to the Jasna Góra Monastery, for they differ very little from them. There's the same level of frenzy in their eyes and the same determination to reach their destination. Even the large, heavy wooden rods they carry look similar to the typical sticks used by weary pilgrims. Nothing out of the ordinary. Like the bishop's staff held by Saint Nicholas.

They make their way slowly up the steep hill to the monastery at the top. They enter the shrine and stand before the painting of the Black Madonna. She gazes at them sadly through the darkness that surrounds her.

Frenza rubs the women's rods with the same ointment that Spalt and Kreppel used long ago in the forest glade. And then they start banging the deadwood.

They all agreed in advance that they wouldn't bang any of the pilgrims—only the priests. On their heads, their backs, their legs. They swing their rods and smash the men's knees so that they'll fall on their faces in front of the sacred painting. So blood will be shed. And so they'll suffer more than they ever have before.

After the first few rows of priests have been banged, Frenza rushes at the archbishop. She strikes him on the head with her rod so hard that he collapses on the altar and lies motionless, with no sign of life. Frenza strips off his chasuble, puts it on over her own clothes, then delivers a sermon on the Primeval Virgin to the worshippers, who are still kneeling on the floor, frozen with fear.

When she's done, she and her troops go outside into what should be fresh air but isn't because it's contaminated by Catholicism, which must be destroyed to save Mother Earth. She draws the air into her lungs ravenously. The Catholic pilgrims stare with gaping mouths as the women start searching for something on the concrete surrounding them on all sides.

Eventually they find some blades of grass growing here and there between the slabs of concrete, but no moss, because the forest that once grew in this spot was clear-cut so that the church and monastery could be built. The women begin to rub their clefts against the grass. And then—a miracle occurs. Whether it's because of their frenzied state or rather a result of the grace of the innocent, childlike maiden of the Jasna Góra Monastery—Our Lady of the Luminous Mountain—the blades of grass, moistened with the Earthen Ones' bodily fluids, seem to multiply, and suddenly, from between the concrete slabs, thousands of them grow and form a lush meadow right before everyone's eyes.

The women rub their clefts against the grass in a much deeper state of pious concentration than this so-called sacred place has ever seen. They slide their vulvas back and forth across the warm, sunbaked grass. And when they begin to emit high-pitched sounds, as if summoning yet another profound transformation, something happens that Frenza has been desiring most of all.

Suddenly, there She is—She has emerged from the painting. No longer dark, but luminous. Such an intense radiance emanates from Her, it's nearly blinding. Instead of sadness, there's now joy on her face. And the scar on her cheek is fading, as if it has healed.

The child in Her arms slowly transforms. It's no longer a boy, but a girl with a thin braid.

She sets the child down on the ground and approaches the Earthen Ones. She joins the circle. She takes off Her robes, revealing a body that's both young and old at once—still girlish but sagging and frail. Beautiful.

Frenza hands her own rod to Her and She first slides it between Her legs, as if baptizing it with Her holy moisture, and then—tossing it aside—begins rubbing Her cleft against the soft green ground.

It's then that they're able to see Her more clearly. The Primeval Virgin that Frenza has told them about. Replete with joy and life. She's me, and you. She's Kunegunde Kreppel, Helene Spalt, and her granddaughter, Mathilde. Your friend. Your sister, mother, and daughter. And your grandmother. She's all of us in our most sacred, beautiful, frenzied madness.

The Hexism Manifesto

1. With our claws firmly rooted in the ground, we proclaim through singing, howling, moaning, and shouting a new Hymn for the Creation of the World—a New Beginning.
2. Shaken by the tremor of an orgasm born of the womb, we proclaim that in the Beginning there was the *Cleft*—not God the Father but the Mother Goddess. Over time, strange growths protruded from this primordial Cleft. These new tissues were as abnormal as warts, moles, or scabs, with an extremely pathological etiology.
3. Loyal to the Sacred Cleft and, therefore, to the Ancient Tree Hollow, we hereby hiss in the ears of the hardheaded followers of the Old Order and the Herd of Christ that in the Beginning there was no Tree of Knowledge, but only the Tree of Life, the Tree of Tenderness. It was the only tree not struck by bright lightning bolts, later called "flaming swords" by the prophets of other religions. And it was the only tree that did not become overgrown by coarse dickery and cockitude. It was the best time in the history of humanity—a time when the Cleft, and not the musty but still brazenly erect rodkin, ruled the world. A time when women decided for themselves

what to put in their mouths, and they certainly weren't choosing a foul growth that needed to be eradicated like a tumor.
4. We call upon the women of the world to cease all practices aimed at keeping rodkins rigid. May they at last become soft and flaccid, thus yielding space for the revival of the Cleft, the moisture of which is the true Source of Life on Earth.
5. Instead of raising our hands to the smog-blackened sky, let's grab sticks, branches, and rumblerods and bang everything that is erect and dead. Political systems, social hierarchies, and "isms" in art! Let's bang everyone who believes that the only places for us are the maternity ward, church, and kitchen. Let's bang the patriotic epic poets—the Słowacki, Norwid, and Mickiewicz of every nation of the world—for imbuing us with docility, meekness, and weakness, rather than perceiving our creative power and dynamic strength. They preferred to pine for us and commit suicide after we rejected them, instead of respecting us for our fertility, creativity, intelligence, and resourcefulness. Let's tear to shreds all those who demand sacrifices from mothers while simultaneously funding monuments in honor of the Polish Mother. We, who have been treated like bitches and whores for centuries, are about to break free from our leash. We will burn to ashes the Fatherland, the symbol of which is the White Eagle. Never again will any dick-symbol bird represent our tribe. May the Scavenger Carrion-Eater become an emblem for the living dead to which WE—women—do not belong! We don't believe in the Father but in the eternally alive and life-giving Mother Earth—the Primeval Virgin, Cybele the Mother Goddess.
6. Let us crumble to pieces, unafraid of being absorbed by the dark Abyss, and then come together again. Let us be like cheese—milk that takes on a new form after being exposed

to heat, without changing its constituent parts in any way. May separation and unification be the basic principle guiding our lives. May we never be deceived by "NORMALITY" or the so-called complete personality. There is nothing more destructive for our freedom than the bourgeois norms supporting these two concepts, which are as dead and decaying as the quail carcasses in paintings by Flemish masters.

7. Let us elevate Milk, the most life-giving substance in the world, to the status of the Blood of Christ. Instead of shedding blood during wars and religious crusades, let us immerse ourselves in Sacred Oxytocin—the Love hormone produced during orgasm and breastfeeding. Bearing Life and Love, and not the fear-sowing Father—over and above everything!

8. Let us stop kneeling on the cold marble floors of churches and instead kneel on warm, moist moss and rub our naked bodies against it! Let us suck the mossy forest floor in through our clefts, receiving into ourselves the subterranean currents of the Earth, offering it our secret moisture in exchange. We shall offer it our fragrance as well, which contains not only the pheromonal aura of reproduction but also decomposition and decay, essential characteristics of all living beings—both plant and animal. Only through symbiosis with the Earth, only by forging an intimate relationship with Her, will we renew the Covenant made with Her at the dawn of humanity.

9. Let us take root in the forest! The forest is the great green vagina of the world. Our first home and also our last. In the event of a climate catastrophe, we will survive solely thanks to forests, for they will give us somewhere to hide from the heat, somewhere to quench our thirst. The harsh God of the Old Testament, in whom many of those who laugh at the climate crisis believe, frequently demonstrated a blasé indifference to natural disasters and cataclysms. Will this time be any dif-

ferent? We will survive if we protect the forests. They are the matrix of the world, the reverse of which is the land of the dead, feeding us with its decay. The oceanic waters flowing through the veins of the Earth. Life. Only within the womb can we feel as safe as this. There is no way to return to the womb, but the forest is accessible to all. May the head of one forester roll for every tree that is felled. Thousands of trees—thousands of heads. Millions upon millions.

10. Never, ever rid yourself of madness. It's impossible to win the battle against the stiff, rigid, tyrannical, and ubiquitous PHALLUS with your head. It's in your CLEFT that you'll find the necessary madness to win this battle. A madness that is unique, that is feared by the rigid patriarchy (the erect power of which is often artificially induced by Viagra). The VAGINA-WOMB-SKULL—the symbol of the transformative power of women and their inner, private religion exalting Tenderness, Fertility, and Love—will appear to you and guide you after you suspend your powers of reason, after you cease—even if only for a brief moment—to operate within the letter of the law. You must listen intently to yourself—in other words, not to your head, but to your wild, atavistic Cleft, whose pulse is aligned with Mother Earth's, and thus with the entire world's. Henceforth, your Cleft must be your best friend and adviser. Anything that stands between you and your Cleft must be eliminated immediately. Otherwise, it will be impossible for you to hear its whisper, and it is in this whisper that you will find all the guidance you need to live in harmony with the world.

Acknowledgments

I thank all women who, in their fight for equal rights and the wellbeing of our planet, are not afraid to use their madness as a political weapon. It's only through a close relationship with what exists in us at the antipodes of the Enlightenment's limp, flaccid "reason" that we can finally put an end to all that is Erect. By subverting the Erection in its symbolic, political, economic, and cultural forms, we will finally free ourselves from patriarchy and subjugation. This feat is impossible to achieve with our rational intellect. First of all, I would like to thank Annie Sprinkle and her wife, Beth Stephens, for immersing me in a completely new, much-needed vision of this world, in which Mother Earth becomes the Earth Lover, and feminism opens to water and the liquefaction of all that is stiff, ossified, and lifeless. While thanking Annie and Beth, I also want to pay tribute to two other queer people who change my life every day, and whose message connects me even more to the antipatriarchal and anticapitalist mycelium: Andrew Burt (@the_virgin_x) and Alok (@alokvmenon).

I also want to thank Anna Zajdel, Polish activist (witch) and close friend of mine, for what she said to me when I started writing *Hexes of the Deadwood Forest*: "Szpila, calamus has a flaccid rhizome, soft and wonderful. You don't need to masturbate with something hard . . ." I would like to thank all the activists in the world and ask them to join me in forming a mycelium against political Rodkins, for we—the activists—are the real witches now. And we will abandon and dismantle the Rodkingdom. I would also like to thank Daniel Zarewicz for his encouragement, friendship, and numerous consultations, and Piotr for his courage to be with me and derive pleasure from our life together. This book would not have been read by the English-speaking world if it were not for the extraordinary contribution of wonderful people dedicated to the *Hexes* cause: the translator Scotia Gilroy, who is very dedicated and emotionally involved in the ideas contained in the book; my agent in Poland, Piotr Wawrzeńczyk, who believed in me and the message that I carry in my works to the world; my American agents, Christopher Combemale and Szilvia Molnar; and the wonderful editor Naomi Gibbs, who decided to replant the original mycelium for the needs of the American market and cultivate it in a slightly different, more effective way.

My deepest gratitude goes to my daughters, who have allowed me to discover the true power of madness every day.

A NOTE ABOUT THE AUTHOR

Agnieszka Szpila is one of Poland's most critically acclaimed, bestselling, and transgressive writers. The Polish edition of *Hexes of the Deadwood Forest* was longlisted for the Nike Literary Award, the country's premier literary award, and translations will be published in at least nine countries around the world.

A NOTE ON THE TYPE

The text of this book was set in Electra, a typeface designed by W. A. Dwiggins (1880–1956). This face cannot be classified as either modern or old style. It is not based on any historical model, nor does it echo any particular period or style. It avoids the extreme contrasts between thick and thin elements that mark most modern faces, and it attempts to give a feeling of fluidity, power, and speed.

Typeset by Scribe
Philadelphia, Pennsylvania

Designed by Casey Hampton